LOVE ON THE LINE

LOVE ON THE LINE

C.W. FARNSWORTH

Entangled Publishing, LLC
644 Shrewsbury Commons Ave., STE 181
Shrewsbury, PA 17361
rights@entangledpublishing.com

Amara is an imprint of Entangled Publishing, LLC.

Visit our website at www.entangledpublishing.com.

Edited by Jovana Shirley
Cover illustration by LJ Anderson, Mayhem Cover Creations
Edge design by LJ Anderson, Mayhem Cover Creations
Stock art by photka/Gettyimages and Arkela/GettyImages, and kbeis/GettyImages
Interior design by Toni Kerr

ISBN 978-1-68281-659-2

Printed in the United States of America

First Edition May 2026

10 9 8 7 6 5 4 3 2 1

ALSO BY C.W. FARNSWORTH

KLUVBERG SERIES

First Flight, Final Fall
All The Wrong Plays
Love On The Line

RIVAL LOVE SERIES

Kiss Now, Lie Later
For Now, Not Forever

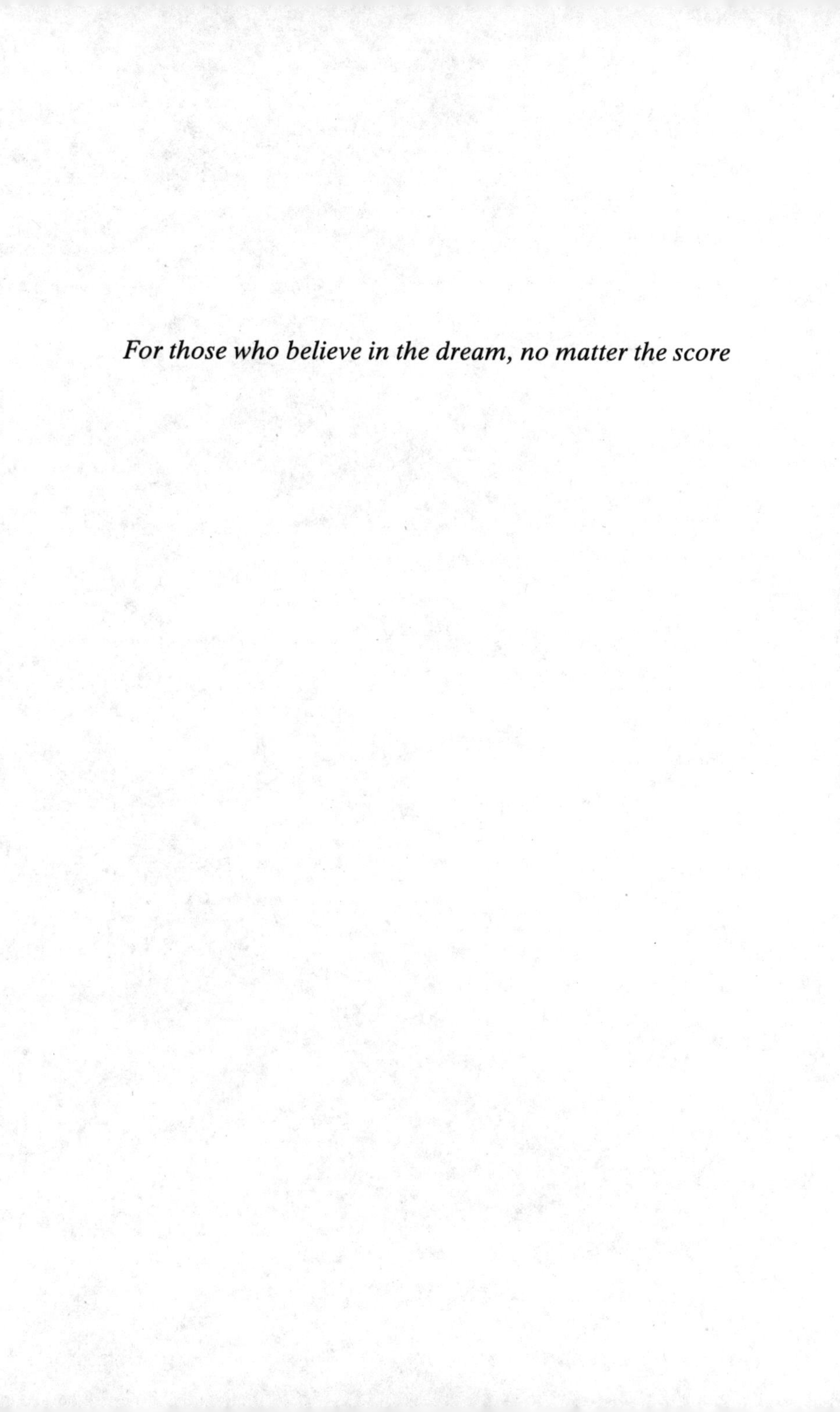

For those who believe in the dream, no matter the score

Content Warnings: *parental abandonment (past, off page), death of a parent (past, off page), dementia (parent), cancer (grandparent)*

Prologue

Otto

PARIS: SIX YEARS EARLIER

"Otto! Otto!"

"There he is!"

"Berger, over here!"

Beck glances at the clamoring crowd as we walk toward the exit. Shakes his head once. Twice when he sees my wide grin.

"Chin up, *Kaiser*," I say, nudging his ribs with my elbow. "I'm sure a few of them know who you are too."

A reluctant smile appears. I'm on a very short list of people who could tease Adler Beck about being irrelevant with a straight face and without getting decked, so I take full advantage whenever I can. I'd be joking around more if I wasn't partially preoccupied, busy soaking in the surreal realization that most of these people seem to be here to see me. The loudest ones at least because my name is the one I'm hearing shouted the most.

I traveled with Germany's football team to London for the last Olympics, but I didn't play. Gregor Nübel, the starting keeper for Ludlin—Kluvberg's main rival—was in goal for the entire tournament, a solid performance that culminated in a bronze medal for Germany.

Nübel is here, striding a few paces behind me and Beck. Four years later, our roles have reversed. I'm starting; he's backup.

In my home country, I've earned a reputation as the defensive wall behind Beck's aggressive attacks. He scores; I ensure our opponent doesn't. FC Kluvberg is currently known as the German club to beat. Our record against Ludlin has been perfect for the past two seasons, which I'm sure factored into my placement on the final roster.

Being the top German goalie isn't enough. I want more. This is my chance to be considered *the* best, no exceptions.

A young boy, around nine or ten, is pressed up against the temporary fencing that was set up, cordoning off the athlete arrivals from the general public. He doesn't move as we pass by, despite all the jostling happening around him. He stands firm, clutching a hand-drawn sign. My gaze drops, scanning it, and then I veer right, separating from my teammates.

I'm near enough to watch the boy's eyes widen as I approach the fence. To hear the creak of metal as the crowd realizes what's happening and presses closer before loud voices drown the protesting barrier out.

"Hi," I say to the boy. "I like your poster."

"T-t-thanks," he stutters.

I smile, attempting to put him at ease. "What's your name?"

His eyes widen. "P-Pierre."

"Want me to sign that for you, Pierre?" I ask, nodding to the poster he's gripping tight.

He nods eagerly, so I grab a marker offered from someone in the crowd, saying, "*Merci*," since we're in France. I scrawl my autograph in one corner of the paper poster, handing it back to Pierre with a grin. "There you go."

Pierre stares at my signature with an awed look on his face. I barely hear his thanks over the rising volume of the crowd, everyone trying to catch my attention next. We weren't told not to stop, but it wasn't expected that any players would. This isn't a presser or a planned appearance, just the last leg of our trip to Paris.

Several security guards have rushed over from other posts, trying to maintain order as I move along the line, shaking hands and signing more posters and posing for photos. Everyone seems to know who I am, even those not wearing or holding Deutschland memorabilia.

It's bizarre, being on this side of the barricade. I remember being the kid, praying his favorite player would stop. I'm not accustomed to being the one with the power to grant that wish. To that favorite player being me.

And as I reach the end of the line and continue after my teammates, I'm even more determined to be worthy of that worship. To be a gold medalist the next time I walk through this airport.

Chapter 1

Otto

Everything is gray. The clouds. The seat in front of me. The sweatpants I threw on early this morning, stained by a single drop of coffee that splashed mid-thigh.

My mood.

A few minutes later, wheels hit the tarmac with a jarring jolt. The collision of rubber and asphalt wakes the woman seated across the aisle from me. Probably would have woken me, too, if I hadn't been staring blankly out the window for the entirety of the eight-and-a-half-hour flight, adrift in a sea of self-pity as fathomless as the Atlantic below.

The impact of landing jostled my right arm, and my shoulder is protesting with a dull throb. An unnecessary reminder of how drastically my life changed in a handful of weeks. Of who I used to be.

I was midway through a winning season.

I was FC Kluvberg's starting goalkeeper.

I was a living legend—at least according to the collection of hardware displayed at my house outside the city.

And I was replaced.

I'm replaceable.

That reality stings worse than the healing incision from my shoulder surgery, even knowing I'm physically incapable of playing and my club had no choice *but* to bench me. Because I've built my career on being willing to do whatever it takes to win, and this isn't a setback that can be solved by training harder or by digging deeper. The opposite has been prescribed by the hordes of doctors who assessed me. Sleep. Rest. Inactivity.

Passengers are perking up in the surrounding seats as we taxi toward a gate, yawning and stretching, happy to havc nearly reached the end of a long flight.

Me? I roll my head right to look out the oval window and study Boston's airport. To *glower* at it, glaringly empty of the relief that normally accompanies safely arriving at a destination.

The sprawling structure is huge. Twice the size of the airport I flew out of. I've never been to Boston before, but I know it's a major American city. According to the online search I browsed while waiting to board, its population is estimated at six hundred fifty thousand people.

The odds of running into one would be infinitesimal—if I weren't here to help coach her club.

It's a matter of *when*, not *if*, I see Claire Caldwell during this long-term stay in the States. I know that, and I'm avoiding thinking about it because I don't *want* to think about it and because I've got enough weighing on my mind already.

The plane's intercom crackles to life after a brief screech of static, requesting all passengers remain seated until we reach the gate.

I'd prefer to stay in place until this aircraft returns to Germany.

I was on board with the suggestion that I leave Kluvberg for the remainder of the season. No keeper wants to sit on the sidelines, watching his team win or lose without him, helpless to assist. And while I don't mind fan attention—some would say I thrive around it—the months of recovery ahead are going to be frustrating enough without fielding questions, wondering how soon I'll be back on the field, every time I leave my house.

I was also on board with the suggestion I assistant coach on a temporary basis. I don't have much else to do for the foreseeable future, aside from regular physical therapy appointments, except feel sorry for myself.

By the time the part of the plan I was *not* on board with was revealed, backing out would have raised a lot of questions.

With a sigh, I power on my phone. The device buzzes with dozens of new messages.

I scroll through the flood of notifications, scanning them quickly. Most texts are from my teammates. Even Trent Banks, my backup, who should be focused on tomorrow's match, checked in.

Adler Beck, FC Kluvberg's captain—better known as *Kaiser* or Beck—messaged me the most. It's one of his unwritten responsibilities as the club's figurehead, and we're close. Close enough that Beck is worried about me for reasons unrelated to football. His wife, Saylor, who also plays football professionally, helped set up this arrangement with the Boston Siege. Her former college coach, Eliza Taylor, is the Siege head coach now.

I shut my phone off without replying to anyone. The clock on it already adjusted. It's five forty p.m. local time—nearly midnight in Kluvberg. I'm too tired and irritable to muster replies that will reassure anyone I'm handling this adjustment well, and the plane has reached the gate anyway.

My fingers drum against my thigh impatiently as I wait for the sealed door to open so that the five rows ahead of me can disembark.

German echoes around me in a flurry of clipped consonants. Likely the last time I'll hear my native tongue spoken for a while. My English is excellent, superior to my subpar Spanish or passable French. I'm unconcerned about a language barrier, but it's yet another reminder I'm far from home. I've traveled around the world with Germany's national team and with FC Kluvberg, attending tournaments and exhibition matches and international competitions. Those were much shorter trips than this one. More importantly, I was an active member of the roster.

My name pops up in a few of the surrounding conversations. I attempt to tune them out, fingers tapping faster as my impatience increases.

"Are you an actor?"

I glance toward the voice automatically. The question stands out: unexpected, spoken in English, and—based on the near proximity—aimed at me.

The speaker is young, appraising me with a curious frown wrinkling her forehead. She's seated diagonally across the aisle, staring straight this way.

"No," I answer since she does appear to be speaking to me.

"Are you sure?"

"Very."

I've appeared in a few advertisements, but no films. Unfortunately. I'd love to star in a spy thriller. But I could never risk getting injured in a stunt. At least tearing my labrum jumping off a roof would have been an entertaining story. Falling awkwardly after a failed save is simply a sad anecdote.

"So, you're not famous?" the stranger presses, still staring.

I'd guess she's around university age, in her late teens or early twenties.

"I play football," I tell her.

Meaning, in some settings, I'm *very* famous. And in others—like an American airport—I assumed slash hoped no one would give a shit I was here.

Her nose scrunches. "You mean soccer?"

"Yes," I respond wearily. "I mean soccer."

Wasting my dwindling energy on an argument about proper terminology—why wouldn't you call a sport played with your feet *foot*ball, especially when that's how the rest of the world refers to it?—feels pointless. I'd better get used to the American verbiage.

"Are you good?"

"*Yes*," another voice answers before I can. The emphatic reply came from the middle-aged man seated on the woman's other side.

She and I both look at him.

He flushes, fiddling with the strap of his seat belt. "Sorry to interrupt. I'm-I'm a huge Kluvberg fan. This guy"—he points at me—"is *incredible*. My favorite player."

The praise should make me feel good. Anyone commending my performance on the pitch typically ignites a warm glow of pride in my chest. I worked hard for success. I bled and sacrificed and fought for my shot to become one of the players I had grown up admiring. Having others acknowledge that is something special.

But this compliment cracks an icy frisson of panic in my chest, cleaving the cavity in two.

Never achieving a dream is a common fear.

Rarer and equally devastating? The realization that you reached your dream, yet your time living it might be over. I want to retire on my own terms, years from now, not because of a tear that necessitated surgery and *should* heal fine but *could* not.

"Thank you," I tell the fan, hoping he misses the raw emotion that roughens the edge of the words. My voice sounds like the uneven edge of a serrated blade.

He nods rapidly, expression reverent as he stares at me like I'm a holy apparition that might disappear at any second.

The fear in my chest expands. There are a lot of people invested in my recovery, and that's a heavy weight to carry. But no one is more invested in my recovery than I am. If I'm done, this guy will pick a new favorite player. Wagner will keep coaching. Beck will keep scoring. The team will move on without me if I can't resume at the same level as before surgery, and it's a terrifying realization. I have little clue who *I* am, separate from my identity as Kluvberg's keeper. All I have to offer, all I've ever been exemplary at, is a single skill a shredded muscle in my shoulder has rendered useless.

"What are you doing in Boston?" the girl chirps.

She's smiling, intrigued by her seatmate's admiration and oblivious to my inner tornado of turmoil.

"I can't play for a while," I say, shifting so she can see the sling cradling my right arm. "I'm here to help coach the Siege. Temporarily."

I hope it's temporary at least. I've never given much thought to what I'll do after I stop playing, but coaching probably would have been on the list. I enjoy helping out with clinics for younger players, watching others discover their passion for football.

She gasps. "The Siege?"

Her enthusiastic, surprised expression reminds me that, as

far as I know, neither my club nor Boston's team has announced my new role while I recover.

This reaction was unexpected. From what I've heard from Saylor and observed at international tournaments, football—soccer—isn't a huge deal in the States. Especially women's soccer.

"My family has season tickets for Siege games," the girl continues. "I grew up on the same street as Claire Caldwell. She used to babysit me."

I blink at the stranger, praying I misheard. That my ears are messed up from the air pressure and are playing tricks on me.

"She's a defender on the Siege—"

"I know who she is."

And I was already nervous about meeting the team in two days. Registering my body's reaction to hearing her name spoken aloud—quickened pulse, dry throat, uneven breaths—is accelerating my anxiety.

I'm just stressed about my shoulder, I tell myself.

It's a lie, or maybe it's not, but it's enough to refocus on the present. To register that the row ahead of me is standing, exiting, and I'm about to be able to do the same.

I aim a, "Nice to meet you," across the aisle as I straighten to my full height. My muscles protest, stiff from disuse. I went from a daily routine of sprints, push-ups, squats, lunges, and lifting weights to being told to limit all movement as much as possible to not disturb my shoulder.

I think the guy across the aisle snaps a photo as I walk by, but I don't glance back to confirm. And I definitely don't look at the girl Claire used to babysit. I didn't mention my name, but the man next to her certainly knows it. Is she texting Claire right now, telling her Otto Berger is on her flight?

Better question: Why do I care? Still?

Chapter 2

Claire

At first glance, Little Red Wagon Preschool is a well-maintained brick building. As I speed-walk past the playground, it feels like a judgment zone. A group of moms is clustered around one of the picnic tables, all of them dressed in down coats and cashmere hats.

I smile and wave as I hurry past, pretending not to notice the pursed lips as they survey the Siege windbreaker and track pants I'm wearing. The February wind is rapidly destroying what little remains of my messy ponytail, so my hair looks even less put together than my outfit.

Almost there. I yank the front door open so wide that I have to play tug-of-war with a gust of wind to get it shut again. The sudden blast of heat once I do makes my eyes water.

Tommy is the last kid left in the classroom, carefully stacking a pile of wooden blocks on the desk attached to his assigned seat.

I mouth a hasty, *Sorry*, to Mrs. Combs, who's seated at the front of the classroom, sorting papers.

Her nod is understanding, but I note the worry creased in her forehead and tightening the corners of her mouth. If I could assure her this would never happen again, I would.

I clap my hands together once. "Tommy boy!"

He glances over, excitement erasing the seriousness that was settled on his face. "Claire!"

Tommy abandons his blocks to hurtle toward me as fast as his four-year-old legs allow. I bend down and scoop him up, spinning him around. He shrieks with uninhibited glee, kicking his feet like he does during swim lessons.

My shoulders feel lighter as I listen to the happy sound.

"Can I go to work with you?" Tommy asks eagerly, tugging the drawstring of my teal windbreaker before I set him down.

"Not today," I reply. "I'm finished with training."

He frowns. "When?"

"Soon. The season is about to start, so we'll start playing games."

His whole face lights up at that last word. "And I can go?"

I ruffle his hair, the same cinnamon shade as mine. His is a little curly too. "You sure can."

His grin dims a little, like a cloud passing over the sun, as he blinks at me. "You *promise*?"

A lump expands in my esophagus. I have to clear my throat twice before I can answer. "Yeah. I promise. Go get your things and say goodbye to Mrs. Combs."

"Bye, Mrs. Combs!" Tommy calls, waving at his teacher as he rushes toward his decorated cubby.

"Bye, Tommy," she answers, standing from her desk and approaching. To me, she says gently but firmly, "Dismissal is at three p.m., Claire."

"I know. I'm so sorry." I shift my weight from foot to foot, jitters lending fresh energy to exhausted muscles. "I wasn't supposed to pick up today, and I wasn't able to check my phone during practice, and—" I swallow hard. "I'll do my best to make sure it doesn't happen again."

"Tommy's a wonderful boy, and I'm happy to help out. But I can't make a habit of staying late for one student."

"I understand. Thank you for staying with him."

"Ready!" Tommy announces, reappearing at my side with his coat and backpack on. His little hand slips inside of mine, squeezing tight.

I say goodbye to Mrs. Combs, and then we head outside.

The moms are still chatting. Their preschoolers are tackling each other in the six inches of snow that was dumped on Boston on Sunday evening, coating parts of the playground.

"Do you want to play for a bit?" I ask Tommy.

He shakes his head, walking faster and tugging me toward my car by our joined hands.

"Are you sure?"

He doesn't answer, just pulls harder.

What I know about kids is fairly superficial. Second-guessing during crucial moments has always been one of my biggest weaknesses as a player, and as far as I can tell, parenting involves plenty.

I'm not sure if I should ask Tommy why he doesn't want to play with the other kids or pretend that's entirely normal.

Before I can decide, he begins bombarding me with questions about soccer.

One thing I *have* learned about kids: they're curious. I'm not sure if Tommy inherited the athlete gene that skipped over every Caldwell except me or if he's realized it's the one topic I can talk endlessly about, but he's a never-ending source of sports inquiries. Of my few fans, he's by far the most enthusiastic.

Explaining the format of the upcoming season takes the whole drive home.

"How many games do we play in the regular season?"

"Twenty-six."

"Why?"

"Because that's how many the league decided on."

"Why?"

"Because they just did."

"But why?"

On and on and on. *Why* is Tommy's favorite word.

Cassidy calls as I'm pulling into the driveway. I ignore the buzzing, parking and grabbing my duffel and Tommy's backpack while he climbs out of his booster seat.

Salt crunches under my sneakers as we head up the brick walk that leads to the Tudor-style home my parents purchased as newlyweds. I still think of it as my *parents' house* in my head, even though my father hasn't lived here for years and I do—again.

I unlock the front door, hastily shutting it when the whiff of smoke in the air registers.

"Mom? Lydia?" I call out, attempting to squash the panic out of my voice. Aware of Tommy's footsteps following me down the narrow hallway, walls decorated with framed photographs of simpler times.

"In here!" Lydia's cheerful voice replies.

I relax in response to her tone as we round the doorway that leads into the kitchen.

Our next-door neighbor and my mom are seated at the table, a half-completed puzzle spread between them. Mom's typing;

Lydia's knitting.

"Hi, Lydia! Hi, Grandma!" Tommy says, waving at them.

"Hello, Tommy!" Lydia waves a needle back at him.

"I'm on deadline," Mom says. "No distractions."

I swallow hard, my smile threatening to slip. "Hungry, Tommy boy?" I ask, turning toward the sink to wash my hands.

"Ants on a log! Ants on a log!" he chants, struggling to pull himself up onto one of the stools that line the island.

"You got it," I say, staring at the soggy, charred remains of what I think was a grilled cheese for a few seconds before spinning toward the fridge to grab the peanut butter and celery.

"I had a client run late," Lydia tells me, coming to stand nearby as I search the cabinets for raisins. She drapes the red scarf she's working on over my left shoulder, judging the length. "I couldn't get over here until two, and she tried to make lunch…"

"Thank you so much for staying with her." I stab the peanut butter with a knife, trying to gather enough to spread.

"I just wish I could do more." Lydia frets, casting a quick glance at Mom's bent back.

She's oblivious, lost in a world of her own creation.

"You're already doing too much," I say, speaking one of my niggling worries.

Having Lydia come over a few times during the day used to be a solution. But it's becoming increasingly obvious that needs to change.

"Honey, I'm not doing half as much as you." This time, Lydia looks at Tommy, patiently waiting for his snack.

I set the plate in front of him. "Do you mind staying for a few more minutes? I need to make a quick phone call."

"Not at all," Lydia answers, ambling back toward the table with her knitting. "You're so tall. I need to add another foot to this scarf."

"Thanks, Lydia."

"Of course, honey."

I hustle upstairs, taking two steps at a time and ignoring my protesting calves.

My bedroom's a mess, but cleaning is going to have to wait until tomorrow. I kick a shin guard closer to one corner before sinking down in the chair at my desk, toeing the door closed with my left foot. While the outgoing call rings, I finally fix my ponytail.

"Why didn't you pick up earlier?" is how my older sister answers the phone.

When Cassidy can't reach me, she considers it a personal affront. Never mind that I'm the one with a job. With *two* jobs actually. At least through tonight.

I told Blake, the manager of Paul Rebeer's, that this would be my final shift. I can't juggle bartending during the season.

"I'd just gotten home," I tell Cassidy. "I had to check in with Lydia."

"You picked up Tommy?"

"Yeah, I did. Next time, more than an hour's notice would be nice."

Predictably, Cassidy bristles. "If you're not able to pick him up, just say that, Claire."

I pinch the bridge of my nose, releasing a long, frustrated exhale. I'm too tired to say anything that will spark an argument I don't have the energy to participate in. "It's not that. I was at practice. I wasn't checking my phone. Today was your day."

"They pushed the interview time. I'm a shitty mother for prioritizing employment?"

I twirl the end of my ponytail, surveying my messy room.

"I've never called you a shitty mother. And you know you're not one. I just had a long day. Tommy's fine. He's eating a snack in the kitchen."

Cassidy sighs. "I'm sorry. I had a long day too. Thank you… thank you for picking him up."

I wait a beat before tentatively asking, "How did the interview go?"

"Not great. They wanted a reference from my last job."

That seems…standard? But things are rarely typical with my sister. We're opposites in nearly every way.

"Okay?" I say carefully.

"Well, it wasn't *entirely* my decision to stop working there."

I knew—or at least, I suspected—when Cassidy showed up a month ago, saying she wanted to help take care of Mom and for Tommy to be around family as he got older, that there was more to the story than altruistic intentions. But I hoped I was wrong.

"What part wasn't your decision?"

"It was Drake's fault," she says defensively. "And mostly a misunderstanding."

I don't doubt Cassidy's most recent ex contributed to whatever got her fired. I liked Drake marginally more than her previous boyfriend—the winner who took off right after Tommy was born, never to be seen or pay child support again—but not by much.

I glance at the clock, deciding to table this discussion for later. "Are you almost home?"

"Why?"

"Because I have to leave for work in thirty minutes."

"What? I thought you were finished bartending."

"I am. After tonight."

Silence.

"It's on the calendar," I add, an edge creeping into my tone.

"I'm still downtown," Cassidy tells me. "With traffic, I probably won't be home for another hour."

"You're still downtown," I repeat. "Why?"

"I, uh, I met Josh for coffee after the interview."

My annoyance grows. The interview time changing is nothing Cassidy could control. But meeting her high school sweetheart for coffee? Entirely unnecessary.

She reads my silence correctly. "We were talking about job leads."

"Get home as soon as you can," I grit out, then end the call and toss my phone on the desk. It hits the wood with a clatter, knocking over my deodorant in the process.

One more thing to fix.

Chapter 3

Otto

Will answers on the third ring. For a few seconds, all I can hear is the rap music he likes to work out to blaring. The volume gets turned down, and then I hear his voice.

"Hey, man. Did you check out the burger place I told you about?"

He's breathing heavily. I definitely caught him in the gym.

"Yeah," I reply, glancing at the takeout container by my elbow. It's empty, aside from a smear of ketchup. "The food was really good. Thanks."

I tried to summon some excitement in my voice. The pause that follows tells me I didn't do a great job.

It took me two hours to reply to most of my messages this morning. It was easier to sound upbeat in texts, but Will's called me four times since I left Kluvberg. If I messaged him back, he'd probably just call again. Since I'm in his hometown, he seems determined to act as my virtual tour guide.

"Beck said he hasn't heard from you."

Great. They're talking about me instead of focusing on salvaging the remainder of Kluvberg's season. Banks is solid. They can—will—win without me.

I shove the burger container away, watching it sail along the marble counter and land in the sink. "I texted earlier, letting him know I landed. There's not much else to say." I glance around. "The apartment's fine. Small."

"Did you meet the team yet?"

"Tomorrow."

"That'll be good!"

I keep my contrary thoughts to myself.

I'm dreading tomorrow. Increasingly bothered by how easy it is to pinpoint the source of my unease.

I've interacted with plenty of celebrities. Models and actors and influencers. Political figures—presidents and prime ministers. I've played in matches attended by British and Spanish royalty. An introduction to a group of American soccer players shouldn't be a big deal.

Being around *her* shouldn't be a big deal. Yet my stomach feels like it's folding in on itself every time I picture it taking place.

"Juliette keeps texting," I say to fill the silence.

Will chuckles. "Poor you, receiving *get well soon* wishes from models."

I squeeze the foam ball in my fist. The physical therapist I met with yesterday recommended it as an exercise to maintain my grip strength.

"Weird timing, is all."

"What do you mean, weird timing? She obviously heard what

happened and is using it as a reason to reach out."

He's close, but not completely right.

Juliette's interested again because I'm injured. Because she thinks I might be done. Because football was the biggest obstacle in our relationship, and it's been temporarily—maybe permanently—cleared.

"Wagner enlisted every specialist in the States." I'm not even exaggerating our head coach's efforts. One of the doctors at yesterday's appointment flew in from Cleveland. "I don't need a nurse," I add.

"My guess is, she's offering more than medical care, Berger." I can hear the grin in Will's voice.

I roll my eyes. Toss the ball in the air, wincing when catching it causes a twinge in my shoulder. The adjustment from my in-season training regimen to walking and squeezing a chunk of foam hasn't been an easy one. But I've been warned how catastrophic any attempts to push my shoulder too soon could be. For a perfect recovery, I'd do absolutely anything.

I relax my fingers, allowing the ball to fall to the floor silently.

"She'll be in New York for a shoot next month. I agreed to meet her there for dinner. So, I guess we'll see."

"I don't know everything that went down with you guys, obviously. But if you ever want to talk about it, let me know. This could be an opportunity to figure things out."

I nod like Aster can see me. Then add, "Thanks," because he can't.

Will sounds nothing like the cocky troublemaker who swaggered onto Kluvberg in the midst of a media firestorm. He's seemed settled—content—lately, especially since he and Sophia got engaged.

I felt the opposite after I proposed to Juliette. Stifled, like the oxygen around me was being sucked away, slowly suffocating me.

Probably shouldn't mention that during our dinner. We broke up like it was a business decision, opting to focus on our individual careers. Juliette wanted an entertaining date who was available to attend the endless industry parties she sought out. And I wanted… I don't know what I wanted. To breathe easy again, I guess.

"I emailed you the flight details for April, by the way," Will tells me.

That catches my attention. "You're really coming?"

Before I left Kluvberg, Will told me he was hoping to make a trip to Boston for his brother's birthday. Since Kluvberg would still be in season then, I wasn't sure he'd be able to make it work.

"Yep, Wagner signed off since I'll only miss one practice. Sophia's coming too. We'll spend more time on a plane than in Boston, basically, but it's worth it to see Tripp. And you, of course."

Will and I chat for a few more minutes before he ends the call. It's past seven there, and he and Sophia are headed over to Beck and Saylor's for dinner.

If I were in Kluvberg, there's a fifty-fifty chance I would've gone too. Even odds because, as much as I enjoy spending time with my teammates and their significant others, hanging around two happy couples while you're single sort of sucks.

I abandon my spot at the kitchen counter and head for the couch. It takes about ten steps. The furnished apartment I'm staying in is about a hundredth of the space I'm accustomed to living in. It would probably bother me less if I had somewhere to go. People to see. I'm in an unfamiliar city filled with strangers, except for the one person I've met before, who's the same woman I'd voluntarily avoid.

Once I'm settled on the cushions, I open my laptop and search the Siege roster. It takes longer to type—to do everything—one-handed, but I manage.

The roster is sorted by jersey number, so she's in the second row.

I stare at her headshot, wishing she'd done something drastic to her appearance. Her bright smile and curly ponytail make it harder to convince myself it's been six years since I last saw her.

I navigate to Bookmarks next, clicking the first link.

"Why do you have a US women's soccer game saved on here?" Juliette asked once while borrowing my laptop.

"It's a good match," I replied, like I'd ever had the balls to watch it in its entirety and judge so for myself.

I battled against the urge to question why she was browsing through my Bookmarks in the first place. We weren't engaged yet. Weren't even living together.

"With *Americans* playing?" she responded, laughing.

Juliette's French accent always sounded sophisticated, even when she acted childish.

I didn't answer. If we'd been discussing the men's team, I'd have jumped on board with bashing them.

But I couldn't do that to Claire.

Not when I'd already done too much. And…not enough.

The video's a full recording. Coverage starts with commentators discussing the stars on both sides. Most of the conversation on the US team is centered around Saylor Scott, anticipating another stellar performance from Beck's now wife.

I zone out for the first half, my attention sharpening when players return after halftime. I mostly watch the ticking clock, hating each higher minute, knowing what's coming.

Then I hear it. "And what a moment for Claire Caldwell,

who's subbing in for Sierra Sanders. Caldwell, out of Boston—"

I slam the laptop shut. Lurch forward, resting my good elbow on my left knee and ignoring the way my shoulder protests the abrupt movement. The burger I ate for lunch is a leaden lump in my stomach.

Six years later, I *still* can't watch the end of that damn game.

And tomorrow, I'll have to see her.

Chapter 4

Claire

When I'm halfway across the parking lot, a "Hey," is grunted to my left.

I recognize the low grumble instantly.

My reply to Reyna Rodman isn't much more coherent.

Waking up early for a jog along the Charles sounded like a better idea when I set my alarm last night. I've never been a morning person, but another thing I've learned about kids since Tommy moved in: they don't like to sleep in. Or tiptoe around quietly.

The cold air and exercise woke me up fast, but I spent the subsequent drive to the Siege's practice facility wishing I'd slept in an extra hour instead. If we were starting with drills, like we normally do, I'd be fine. But first on today's agenda is a team meeting.

I chug half of my remaining coffee in one go. The bitter liquid burns my mouth. Cassidy bought groceries yesterday, part of her apology slash thank-you for my picking up Tommy the other day. Unfortunately, she forgot to buy soy milk. I avoid dairy—not as a personal preference, but because I'm lactose intolerant—so I was stuck with black. It tastes more caffeinated this way at least.

"Morning!" Savannah Robbe, a fellow defender, skips over to me and Reyna, who plays striker.

Savannah is younger, recently out of college, and grew up in Southern California. Cheerful. And currently sporting a sun-kissed glow since she spent the offseason in her home state.

Reyna and I, born and raised New Englanders, are pale and cranky.

We both manage greetings, bookended by yawns, which draw a knowing smile out of Savannah.

"New assistant coach is here!" she announces, her chipper tone undaunted by our low energy and the brisk wind.

Coach Willis announced her pregnancy at the end of last season. The team has known for months that someone else would be stepping into her assistant coach role for at least part of this season.

Selfishly, I'm irritated about a replacement. This season is going to be difficult enough. A change in staff is an unwelcome start. Temporary assistant coach for a women's team isn't a position many qualified candidates are scrambling to apply for.

"Know anything about her?" Reyna asks warily, likely thinking the same thing.

"Nothing," Savannah replies. "Except Coach Taylor said *he* was here."

Reyna and I exchange a quick, displeased glance.

"Great," I state flatly. "More men coaching women, in addition to all the men coaching men."

There are twenty teams in the women's league. Three have female head coaches. Coach Taylor is one of them. And she's the only one with an all-female support staff. Or, she *was* the only one with an all-female support staff.

Walking into the lobby of the Siege's brand-new facility improves my sour mood some.

I lost count of the number of times I've entered this building a long time ago. But it still feels special. It still hits me, every time, that I'm a professional athlete, playing for the city I grew up in. No matter how disappointing parts of my career have been, that's an accomplishment I can be proud of.

I resolve to enjoy it.

I default to defense off the field too. I'm always preparing to climb the next challenge rather than appreciating the flat section. Not that there's anything easy about competing at soccer's highest level, but it's simpler than the rest of my life has been lately.

Savannah and Reyna chat about a new television show as we walk down the hallway, passing a couple of administrative offices and the team nutrition area—a fancy term for cafeteria. The Siege is the second-newest expansion team in the league. Keeping with Boston's dominant sports dynasty, this facility was a multimillion-dollar project. It boasts an indoor field, two weight gyms, a playroom for children of players and staff, a sauna, plus our current destination—a video room that's essentially a mini movie theater. In addition to film sessions spent reviewing game footage, it's where our longer or more formal team meetings take place.

"Hey, Caldy!" Mallory calls out as she approaches from the opposite direction. She's holding two half-eaten granola bars, one in each hand.

I've learned that any attempts to dissuade my teammates

from shortening my last name are taken as an encouragement, so I just say, “Morning, Mallory.”

Her smile expands as she reaches us. She greets Savannah and Reyna, then falls in step next to me.

“Late night clubbing?” Mallory teases as a massive yawn overtakes my face.

If someone were handing out team superlatives, I’d win Most Likely to Bail on Going Out.

“Exactly,” I deadpan as we enter the video room.

At twenty-seven, I’m not the oldest or the most experienced player on the team. But my entire career, even as a rookie, I’ve been known as reliable and responsible. In elementary school, I organized the team snack schedule. In high school, my teammates would tell their parents they were sleeping over at my house, then sneak out to parties. I’ve been berated for being “too serious” before, but my teammates on the Siege seem to have accepted it. A few have told me they admire me for it, as if my predisposition to color inside life’s lines was a conscious choice. That sounds better than being afraid to take many risks.

We’re not the first players to arrive for the meeting, but there’s no sign of Coach Taylor or any other Siege staff yet.

I exchange small talk and smiles with a few other teammates before settling into a seat in the back row.

The wall facing the screen is covered with floor-to-ceiling posters. I’m featured on the largest one, located directly in the center. Sitting as close to it as possible means I won’t turn to talk to a teammate and accidentally lock eyes with a giant version of myself. I’m not sure why I was selected as the main feature, but I would have turned it down if I’d been consulted.

I’m one of two Massachusetts-born players on the team and the only one who grew up in a Boston suburb. Tasha is from

Sheffield. It's surreal, playing for my hometown team. But it means I'm never sure how much of the attention on me is assigned rather than earned. Whether the girls who attend games, wearing my jersey, chose it because I'm their favorite player or because I went to a neighboring high school and am the most obvious example of a path they'd like to take themselves.

"Seriously, you good?" Reyna asks after I yawn again, nudging my knee with hers.

She's on my left; Mallory and Savannah took seats to my right.

"I'm good," I promise, then drain the rest of my coffee to wash away the bitter taste of the partial lie.

This is, in my opinion, the worst part of being on a team. And of working with people you genuinely consider friends. All the typical boundaries between personal and professional are erased when you travel and sweat and commiserate with each other.

More players filter in. Tasha teases me for sitting in the back row, knowing exactly why I chose it, before taking the seat in front of mine.

My phone buzzes in my pocket, and I pull it out to squint at the screen. Probably Cassidy, asking me to pick up Tommy. She has another interview today. At least I'll be finished with practice with plenty of time to pick him up on schedule.

It's not my sister; it's my dad.

Heartbeats thunder in my ears as I stare at the preview line of his message.

Mark Caldwell: *We need to talk about …*

I bite the inside of my cheek, torn between curiosity and contempt as I wonder what he could possibly want to talk about.

My father and I have the dictionary definition of a strained relationship. In addition to the house, Mom got me in the divorce.

"Caldy," Mallory hisses, elbowing my ribs. "*Caldy.*"

I drop my phone in my lap and glance at her. "Huh? What?"

"He's here." The whisper is so low that I practically have to read her lips.

"Who? Oh." I glance toward the front of the theater, registering that she must mean the new assistant coach. There's no other *he* here.

I spot Coach Taylor first. She's busy unpacking a couple of thick binders onto the table beneath the screen. To her right, a blond man nods in response to what she's saying to him. He's unexpectedly tall—well over six feet—surprisingly young, and oddly…familiar.

His head turns to watch Grace and Maddie sneak into two remaining seats in the front row, revealing more than his profile, and realization dawns with rising urgency as I get my first clear glimpse of his face.

No.

I'm numb, no longer aware of the solid surface I'm sitting on. I'm floating somewhere above the three rows of seats, stuck in a state of utter disbelief. The surrounding room spins, then stands eerily and entirely still.

Nothing about the scene in front of me has changed.

No, no, no, no, no.

He looks different yet the same. Hair longer and a shade darker. Harder, expression serious instead of smiling, the edge of his jaw a straight angle, and his posture perfect. He takes up so much space; maybe that's why I can't seem to suck in enough air.

And the biggest change? He's not a photo on my phone screen or a face in my dreams.

Distantly, I register the prick of pain as my fingers curl into tight fists, nails creating crescents on my palms. No matter how rapidly I blink, he refuses to disappear.

"Do you know who that *is*?" Reyna says quietly.

She's not actually asking. It's a reverent, rhetorical question she already knows the answer to. Spoken in an admiring tone, echoed in the awed mutters around us.

Nothing was announced about who would be replacing Coach Willis. Most—I—assumed the replacement would be a former college coach or a recently retired player. Someone who would, at best, meld well with the team and, at worst, fill a spot on the sidelines.

A nonevent.

Not *him*.

Otto Berger is widely considered to be one of the best goaltenders to ever set foot on a field. Legendary to anyone with more than a superficial knowledge of the sport he calls football.

Everyone in this room already knows who he is.

What they don't know? He broke my heart.

Chapter 5

Claire

PARIS: SIX YEARS EARLIER

Impatient knocks bang on my door while I'm brushing my teeth. I still, spit, and pad over to the door. After a quick peek through the peephole, I flip the lock and let the hinges swing wide.

Three disappointed faces stare at me.

"Really, Caldwell?" Mackenzie asks, hand on one hip.

"What?" I reply weakly.

"You can't wear *that*"—Lucy's finger draws an imaginary circle around the oversized, holey Lincoln University T-shirt that falls almost to my knees—"out clubbing in *Paris*."

"Or, like, anywhere," Mackenzie adds, equally aghast.

"Oh." I squeeze the toothbrush handle tighter. "Well, I wasn't sure if..."

Their plan to party tonight was hatched during dinner.

I didn't know if, one, I was invited to join them and, two, if I should join them.

My mom jokes that I've been parenting her ever since I arrived on January 5—her exact due date. Others have put it less kindly—called me rigid or controlling or bland. But following rules landed me here. In France, as one of the youngest members of the national soccer team. By far the most excitement in my ordinary twenty-one years on this planet. And an opportunity with no rule book to follow. Less than 0.0013% of people alive are Olympians. It's not exactly a universal experience.

"We're not taking no for an answer," Gemma says, using my uncertainty as an opportunity to squeeze past me and enter my small room.

Lucy agrees with an emphatic nod. "We're a team; we stick together."

I doubt clubbing as a group is what our head coach meant when he expressed that sentiment earlier. I'm not really being offered a choice though, and a large part of me is relieved by it. If there was ever a time to get swept up in the current of spontaneity, the Paris Olympics are it.

"Where are the rest of your clothes?" Gemma asks, sifting through the contents of my suitcase. She drops a pair of athletic shorts atop a jean pair and aims an accusing look my way, like she already knows the answer.

"Uh, that's all I packed," I confirm.

Gemma snaps her fingers. "Mackenzie?"

"On it," Mackenzie replies, darting out of my room.

"Are you done with that?" Lucy asks, nodding at the dripping toothbrush I'm still holding in my right hand.

"Oh. Yeah."

"Good. I'll take that"—she plucks the toothbrush out of my

hand—"so Gemma can do your makeup."

By the time my makeover ends, my pores are invisible, and I'm wearing a dress I won't be able to sit down in. I barely recognize the reflection staring back at me. My usual idea of dressing up is mascara and lip balm.

"*Oh là là*!" Lucy declares, pretending to fan herself.

I roll my eyes at her dramatics, but I'm secretly pleased. I'm also tipsy on the intoxicating cocktail of inclusion. *Cool* inclusion, specifically. I've been on teams with plenty of "popular" girls over the years, and we rarely exchanged words outside of practice. *Responsible* and *fun* don't easily coexist, especially in the cliques of high school and college.

"Let's go!" Gemma declares, striding for the door. "I already ordered an Uber."

I double-check I have my phone, euros, and the badge needed to get back into the building, then follow my teammates down the hallway.

Forty-five minutes later, we're waved from our spot in line inside a dimly lit club.

It's sophisticated. The air is cool and scented with expensive perfume. The first men I spot are wearing slacks and button-downs. A woman, wearing a shimmering silk dress, brushes past us, pulling a cigarette out of a sleek purse as she steps outside.

Nothing is similar to Watering Hole—the off-campus bar I've only been to twice since my twenty-first birthday, famous for its cheap beer and temperamental jukebox that rotates through a small selection of '80s hits.

Gemma makes the executive decision to head to the bar for drinks. The rest of us trail behind her.

Lucy's eyes are as wide as mine as she glances around. She goes to UNC, if I'm remembering right. I doubt Chapel Hill's establishments boast the same chicness as Paris either. I'm not the only one out of their element here, but I think I'm the worst at pretending otherwise.

The rest of us look on as Gemma orders from the bartender in fluent French.

She smirks as she passes around the shots. "I looked up where the first Olympics I'd be eligible to play in were being held back in seventh grade. Language prep for London was unnecessary, obviously, so I learned some French."

Mackenzie and I exchange an impressed look before we suck down our shots. I grimace, fighting the urge to cough, as smooth, chilled liquor slides down my throat and sears my stomach.

"To winning gold!" Lucy cheers.

"We're supposed to toast *before* drinking," Mackenzie points out, setting her empty glass on the metal counter with a dull *clank*.

"And to not draw attention to who we are," I can't help but add.

We are still in college. There are countless professional athletes here who are *actually* famous, who sign autographs and score multimillion-dollar brand deals on a regular basis. As far as I know, we're not technically breaking any rules. We're allowed to leave the Village at night, and we didn't drink alcohol on the premises.

Cautious is my default setting though. Especially since I was named to the final roster, an elusive dream I'm terrified could dissipate into wisps of smoke at any second.

"We'll just have to do another round with a toast first," Gemma says, signaling to the bartender. "But Claire's right. We're undercover, ladies."

To my left, Mackenzie giggles.

I pass on the next shot, mindful of my low tolerance. Gemma wheedles the bartender into drinking it instead, waving the napkin he wrote his number on around like a sparkler as we migrate to the dance floor.

An hour later, the pulsing beat of the pop music isn't enough to keep me from yawning every other minute. Between jet lag and the excitement of visiting Europe for the first time, I'm running on a serious sleep deficit.

All the girls offer to leave with me, but I can tell they'd prefer to stay longer. So, I wave them off, saying I plan to call my boyfriend on the ride back and he'll keep me company. Which leads to ten minutes of questions about said semi-fictitious boyfriend, which I muddle through until a familiar song draws their attention back to the dance floor. After promising to text them once I'm safely back at the Village, I emerge outside alone.

It's cooler than it was earlier, but not by much. The night air smells like smoke from the cigarette butts littering the sidewalk. The ends of some still glow orange.

My nose wrinkles as I fish my phone out. For too long, I stare at the most recent message from Nolan, sent a few hours ago.

Nolan: *Stop being so childish.*

My thumb hovers, sorely tempted to swipe and delete it. To delete *everything*, the entire digital record of our relationship. I dated him to prove a point to myself, and the only lesson I learned is that's a terrible reason to enter a relationship.

I sigh and shut off the phone. I'll decide what to do about Nolan when I'm back in Boston. Right now, I have more important things to focus on.

Then I remember why I was on my phone to begin with and tap the screen again. This time, it doesn't wake up. It remains stubbornly black, the empty battery flashing a few seconds later.

Fucking Nolan. Even thousands of miles away, he's still managing to distract me. If not for his latest text, I'd have noticed the low battery and ordered a ride in time.

And fuck me for going out in a foreign city with a barely charged phone. I was ambushed about this outing, but still.

I glance at the long line of people waiting to enter the club, wondering how likely the bouncer is to recognize me and allow me to skip to the front. I decide to see if the man at the valet stand can help first.

"Excuse me?" I call out, stepping his way.

I have to repeat myself twice before he glances over, spitting out a steady stream of rushed French before resuming rifling through sets of car keys.

I stare at him blankly, struggling to decipher any of what he said. Unlike Gemma, I never expected to be at this Olympics. Hoped, sure, but never planned or prepared. I studied Portuguese in high school.

"Uh…auto?" I mime turning a steering wheel with my hands, then raise my thumb and pointer finger to pretend I'm making a phone call. "Taxi?" I tack on, hoping that's a recognizable word in any language.

More French flows from behind me. The valet's attention shifts past me, and he nods in response to whatever was said.

I sigh, shoulders slumping, resigning myself to the fate of standing in line a second time. Maybe my teammates will decide to leave soon, and I won't have to wait long, but the evening didn't seem to be trending that way. Gemma, at least, is waiting for the bartender to get off his shift.

"You need a ride?"

I spin toward the question like it's a life preserver. "Yes! I…"

My voice trails, the rest of what I was planning to say getting stuck somewhere in my throat when I see who spoke.

I stare.

He grins, amused by my muteness. Or maybe it's his typical reaction. There's an ease to the expression, like he smiles a lot.

The entire US team has a fascination with the German men's team, considering our captain is engaged to the captain of theirs. And the entire soccer world is aware of who Germany's goalkeeper is. Aside from Adler Beck—Saylor Scott's fiancé—he's the most recognizable player on the team.

In my opinion, goalie is the most challenging position on the field. One body guarding a net that's eight feet high and twenty-four feet long against lethal aim? It takes a rare combination of talent and bravery to even attempt to stand in the way of a kick. At any level, let alone the very top.

The guy in front of me is colloquially considered to be one of the best in the world at it. He'll be considered *the* best, if Germany wins the gold medal they're predicted to.

And he's looking at me with a familiarity that's disconcerting, like we're two old friends reuniting after a separation. Like he was out here, waiting for me, not the sleek sports car that another valet just pulled up.

His smile spreads wider as he holds out a hand. A dimple appears in the crevice of his left cheek.

Flutters appear in my stomach as I take it. Butterflies.

"I'm Otto."

Chapter 6

Otto

My first introductory session with the Boston Siege is mostly spent staring at a ten-foot-tall photo of number five mid-kick.

Directly in front of it, the actual Claire Caldwell refuses to make eye contact with me. She nods in response to something the woman next to her leaned close to whisper, she twirls the end of her ponytail, she sips from a water bottle. She listens intently as Eliza Taylor addresses her team.

One thing she doesn't do? Look at me.

Every other player stares. Some try to be surreptitious, but none succeed.

My presence is an anomaly, and there was no announcement ahead of time, if the sea of stunned faces when I walked in the room was any indication. I scrolled through the entire roster yesterday, but I couldn't have named a single player who was looking my way when I entered.

I'm so aware of Claire; it stuns me. I'm attempting to focus on Eliza talking, on paying attention and acting professional. And it's like there's a leaky faucet in the back of the room, a persistent *drip, drip, drip* that makes it impossible to direct my full concentration elsewhere.

It's a relief when Eliza dismisses her players from the media room for a brief break before today's training session begins. The tap turns off for a minute.

That was terrible.

"That went well," Eliza states once the entire team has left, hoisting two binders off the table.

I almost laugh at the irony. Turn it into a cough instead. "Seems like a great group."

Something a coach would say, right? Leon Wagner, Kluvberg's head coach, isn't the nurturing type. His attention means you're making mistakes while silence is a stamp of approval. He has a nonexistent tolerance for negligence and never coddles. I knew for certain how fucked my shoulder was when he showed up to the exam room as soon as that fateful match ended. Normally, he relies on trainers to relay injury updates.

"I had a feeling the team would be excited about you joining us." Eliza's tone is dry as she tucks the binders under one arm. "I decided it would be better to spring it on them rather than invite any speculation."

I nod. "I'm excited too."

I glance at the floor-to-ceiling poster of Claire one final time before walking out of the room. Her arms are raised in victory, a huge smile stretched across her face.

She looks happy. Euphoric even. I've existed around that vibrant version of Claire, and it's nothing like the woman who paid attention to everything except me.

I've been so consumed by how I'd be affected by this change that I failed to consider how my arrival might affect her. I'm selfish, accustomed to making decisions centered around myself. It also felt arrogant to assume my presence here would matter to Claire in any way.

As we walk toward the indoor field, Eliza points out a few additional areas we didn't pass on the walk to the media room. I nod along, asking a few questions about the impressive facility.

I liked Eliza as soon as we met in her office this morning. She's exactly as Saylor described—firm and fair. Someone I respect already. And I probably should have disclosed I had a past personal relationship with one of her players, no matter my first impression of her, but I feel extra guilty about failing to do so now.

Nothing about this arrangement is typical. I didn't apply or interview for the assistant coach position. No one expected me to peruse the Siege roster while I was recovering from surgery in a hospital bed. If I hadn't kept track of Claire's career and already known which club she currently played for, I wouldn't have known she was on the Siege until I landed in Boston.

I no longer can claim any ignorance, but I've still yet to mention it. I'm here, committed to working with the team. And what's there to say really? It's been six years.

Meg Jackson, the other assistant coach, meets us midway to the field. She shares Eliza's brisk attitude, her hair cropped short in a no-nonsense style. I get the distinct impression I'm being tested as she asks what coaching experience I have. Rattling off the long list of clinics I've participated in seems to mollify her. I name-drop Saylor, too, mentioning we've coached together, which seems to improve Meg's opinion of me even more.

Nicole Green, the head of goalkeeping, is the friendliest face I've met yet.

She gushes over my performance in the semifinals of the most recent World Cup, then begins offering Boston recommendations. I nod along, although Will has already sent me a year's worth of them.

"The path along the Charles is chilly this time of year," Nicole tells me. "But there's a beautiful view, and it's a lot less crowded than it'll be during the summer."

I nod. "Good to know. Thanks."

I don't mention I've already explored it. Or that it was the first place I went. Or why.

No one, not even blunt Eliza, has asked about my shoulder, despite the black sling. I wore a black T-shirt to make it less conspicuous, but my injury's obvious. My presence here makes it obvious. I should be on Kluvberg's practice field right now, preparing for Saturday's match.

Once we reach the field, Eliza runs through the plan for today's practice. I listen carefully, tensing each time another teal-clad player arrives and starts to stretch, only relaxing when I comprehend it's not her.

Claire is one of the last arrivals. I don't have any reference to if that's typical, but I'd guess not. She's not a morning person, but she prides herself on being punctual.

I track her in my peripheral vision, watching her smile at one teammate and shove another with a smirk. Her ponytail is higher than it was earlier, the strands barely brushing her shoulders.

She's gorgeous. And utterly unaware of it, which irritated me before and still does now.

But before, I wasn't one of her coaches, so I look away before she catches me staring.

I lean against one of the support beams, letting my good shoulder hold all my weight, observing closely as Eliza begins talking. She's running through the same schedule she already shared with me, so I allow my attention to drift. My eyes flick over the assembled players, attempting to better remember faces now that I'm seeing them in person.

A few make eye contact, glancing away quickly. Some miss my assessment, focused on their head coach. One—Savannah, I think—holds my gaze and winks.

Claire is angled as far left as physically possible. I stare hard at the *5* on the back of her practice jersey, my jaw tensed tight enough to ache, regretting taking Eliza up on her offer for me to only observe today. If I were the one running through today's practice plan, she wouldn't be able to ignore me. Or she couldn't without being more noticeable about it.

I'm used to attention being aimed at me. But I've never been more bothered by the lack of it until today. By her pretending we're not in the same place.

Or maybe she's not pretending. Maybe Claire is truly experiencing the indifference I'm striving hard for.

Considering I was too nervous about seeing her to eat breakfast this morning, that possibility doesn't make me feel any better.

Practice begins a couple of minutes later. The women run through a series of sprints, followed by reps of sit-ups and push-ups. Then split into position-specific drills.

I walk down to one end of the field with Nicole, introducing myself to the goalkeepers—Kristin McKinnon and Daniela Cascarino—before watching them work with Nicole. I offer a few suggestions, which are enthusiastically integrated, but mostly continue to observe. It's fucking weird, standing right next to a goal, knowing I'm currently incapable of blocking any of the kicks Nicole is aiming at it. She played in college—one local to the Boston area, she shared earlier—joining the Siege staff after the club's inception last year.

"Any improvements for me?" Nicole jokes as we head back toward midfield.

She's dragging a bag of footballs, which I offered to help with. She insisted she had it, staring at my shoulder, and I didn't offer again.

"Nope," I say lightly, tucking my left hand in one pocket.

"*Really*?" She lengthens the word, filled with disbelief. "I haven't played since college, which was…gosh, six years ago."

"Wouldn't have guessed," I lie. Not only would I suggest changes to her footwork, but I also figured she was in her early thirties, not younger than me.

We reach Eliza and Meg, who are passing out pinnies to players for the scrimmage that will end practice. I scan the field, a prick of disappointment appearing when I see Claire already has one on, then resume my same pose by a support post.

Play commences a minute later. A red player, whose name eludes me, sprints up the field, met by a yellow pinnie worn by the one Siege player I can immediately identify.

I lean forward involuntarily, watching them clash, studying the defender's movements like I'm trying to memorize them.

Claire triumphs over her opponent, stealing the ball and streaking up the field. She passes to another yellow player before she pivots around a red defender. The ball returns to Claire's foot a few seconds later—she's the only open player. She takes the shot without hesitating, a beautiful black-and-white bullet that blasts toward its intended target at an impressive trajectory.

I know it'll land long before Kristin lunges and misses,

fighting a smile as the back of the net bulges from the ball's impact.

To my left, Eliza shouts, "Nice work, Caldwell! Masters, get there faster next time."

Claire jogs back to position for the kickoff, a brief smile crossing her face as a teammate pretends to bow to her.

Just before she crosses the center circle, her gaze slides from the turf to me.

I'm not expecting the eye contact. By this point, I've convinced myself I was the visual equivalent of white noise to her. And I'm definitely not expecting the jolt that travels through my entire body like an invisible lightning strike.

I should smile, offer silent approval and friendliness, but my facial muscles are as frozen as my immobilized arm. It feels wrong to flash a grin like we're strangers. Even weirder to pretend we parted on good terms or that she's possibly pleased to see me.

So, for the few seconds our eye contact lasts, I just stare.

And realize why I've never been able to watch the ending of that match.

Chapter 7

Claire

In the five weeks since Cassidy moved back home, she's only been up before seven a handful of times. I'm not sure this—her sneaking in just after six—should count in the *responsible adult* category.

But that's mostly me being bitter that she inherited all the fun, carefree genes in the family. That I'm up early, obsessing over a guy I haven't seen in six years, while my sister is returning from a date. Based on her messy hair and swollen lips, she and Josh didn't spend all night discussing "job leads."

"*Jesus*, Claire," Cassidy huffs, doing a double take when she spots me slouched at the kitchen table.

"Morning," I say mildly, sipping more coffee.

Cassidy groans, grabbing a mug out of the cabinet before taking the chair opposite me and reaching for the pot I brewed an hour ago. She pours a full cup, swallows a hearty sip, and then slumps back in the chair. "Sorry for getting home so late."

"It's fine. I saw your text when I woke up. I take it the, uh, evening went well?"

"It was amazing," Cassidy gushes. "Incredibly romantic. Why did I ever break up with him?"

It's a rhetorical question, so I don't offer up the obvious answer.

Cassidy and Josh dated in high school while she was tethered to staying in Arlington. As soon as graduation rolled around and that string snapped, there was nothing that could or would keep Cassidy in town. She has the same wanderlust Mom has, except Cassidy takes it literally while Mom travels to fictional worlds.

"The timing wasn't right for you guys," I say reasonably. "And if you'd stayed together, then you wouldn't have Tommy now."

"That's what Josh said," Cassidy tells me.

Josh was always my favorite of Cassidy's boyfriends. He'd play soccer with me in the yard and always brought Mom flowers when he came over. I'm relieved, although unsurprised, to hear he still sounds like a more-than-decent guy. This is the happiest I've seen my sister in a while. And it would be good for Tommy, who's getting older and has a shortage of positive male role models, to have a guy around.

I'm impressed by—envious of—Josh's apparent ability to move past the feckless way Cassidy broke his heart.

Because you can think you've moved past someone, forgiven and forgotten, and have it blown to bits by reality.

I've known Otto Berger was in Boston for six days, been in the same building as him for hours, and I still have trouble looking at him. Since avoidance hasn't been helping, I've spent most of the past hour reading articles about Kluvberg's current season, including coverage of the dive that tore Otto's shoulder and necessitated surgery. There's a clip that I can't bring myself to watch, but I read every article recapping the moment, including the official statement FC Kluvberg released, stating their starting goaltender would be out for the remainder of the season. There was no mention anywhere that he'd be recovering in Boston.

The details don't help. I'm still dreading tomorrow's practice. The admiring giggles in the locker room. The extra energy required to not only avoid Otto, but also make it appear unintentional.

"Is Mom awake?" Cassidy asks, sipping more coffee.

I shake my head. "She was up late, working."

Cassidy sighs, turning her head to stare out the transom window that overlooks the fenced backyard. Patches of snow have melted, brown grass peeking through. Signs of spring's approach.

The squirrel feeder installed shortly after Cassidy left for college stands just outside the window. Mom was convinced one squirrel—I forget what she named it—returned every morning.

I wonder if Mom remembers the name. It bothers me that *I* can't. Like I'm letting down the one person who's always been there for me.

Dad left.

Cassidy left.

Mom stayed.

My phone screen lights up with an email notification. It's spam, a sale at a store I rarely shop at, but reminds me of the text—*We need to talk about your mother*—sitting unanswered.

"You told Dad?" I try to keep the accusation out of my tone—I really do—but some sneaks in anyway.

Cassidy's fingers tighten around the ceramic mug, answering for her, before she says defensively, "He asked how she was."

"Doesn't mean he deserves to know."

My sister sighs. "Look, I know you have your issues with him—"

I snort. Loudly. *Issues* don't even begin to cover the tattered state of my relationship with our father.

"But he's not a bad person," Cassidy continues.

"Debatable," I mutter.

Mark Caldwell does the bare minimum to ease his conscience, but never shows up when it's inconvenient.

"He's paying for Little Red Wagon," she tells me, confirming my assumption.

"Shelling out for private preschool doesn't make him a saint, Cassidy."

She taps her fingers on the mug, shaking her head. "And what has holding a grudge gotten you, Claire? He can afford to give Tommy things I can't. So what if it's out of guilt?"

"You can make whatever decisions you want for you and Tommy. I'm asking you to leave Mom out of it. And to not discuss me with him either."

"How else is he supposed to know what's happening? You won't talk to him."

Exactly, I think. *He won't.*

Cassidy sighs. "He was upset, Claire. Sad. He watched Granny Lou go through it."

"So did Mom," I snap.

"I know. I'm just saying… Dad wants to help."

I reach forward and open my laptop, closing out of all the tabs except one, spinning it so Cassidy can see the website displayed on-screen. "I don't need his help."

She leans forward to survey the Echo Glen website. Whistles under her breath. "Wow. I thought you were exaggerating."

"When do I ever exaggerate?"

"Good point." Cassidy stands, walking over to the microwave and setting the mug inside.

We both watch the two minutes count down.

"I remembered to buy your milk yesterday," Cassidy says, grabbing a carton of two percent out of the fridge and adding a splash to her now-steaming cup.

"I saw. Thanks."

She's avoiding the topic at hand, same as she's done ever since I told her Mom's diagnosis. Being the one always forced to lead the difficult conversations? Exhausting.

Finally, Cassidy returns to her seat, scrolling further down the site.

"I have to go sign some paperwork tomorrow afternoon," I say. "If you want to come with, you can see it in person."

"I have two interviews, but I'll see if I can—holy *shit*. This place costs *eight grand*? A *month*?"

I nod. "It's considered one of the best facilities on the East Coast. Mom and I discussed it; she wanted to join their waiting list as soon as possible, so that's what we did. It's rare for them to have an opening."

Cassidy leans back in her chair, propping her bare feet on a neighboring one. "Of course you planned ahead. So responsible."

Responsible isn't a dig. It's not a compliment either. Mostly an acknowledgment—of how different we are.

"I can't keep asking Lydia to come over. My season is about to start. I'll be traveling soon, and you..."

Cassidy lifts her left eyebrow. "And I what?"

"Are you staying...for good?"

Cassidy drops eye contact, blowing on her steaming mug. "I-I'm not sure yet." She slumps forward, cupping her chin in her palm. "I… It feels like I failed at leaving, and now I'm failing at being back too. I don't want to keep moving Tommy around. Now that he's old enough for school, that's not fair to him. I want him to know Mom, before…and Dad. They're his only grandparents. But I can't keep living here, rent-free, draining my savings. I'm an adult, living in my childhood home."

"So am I."

"It's different. You moved in to take care of Mom. And you're, like, a local celebrity. Everyone I run into asks about you."

I laugh. "I am *not* a local celebrity. And you and Tommy should stay. Once Mom moves… This house is way too big for one person."

"You're keeping the house?"

"You thought I was selling it?" I ask, confused.

Cassidy nods at my computer. "How else can Mom afford that?"

"She has savings."

"*Ninety-six thousand dollars a year* kind of savings?"

"And income from her royalties. I'm handling it."

"You mean, you're paying for part of it. Mom wouldn't want that."

"Mom didn't want a lot of things that are happening anyway. And…" I clear my throat. This is the first time I'm saying it aloud, and the words are harder to force out than I expected. "This is probably going to be my last season playing. Starting next winter, I should be making more—"

"Why?" Cassidy interrupts.

"Why what?"

"Why are you quitting?"

I bristle at the unflattering phrasing. "I'm *retiring*."

"Oh, please. You're twenty-seven."

"Sports have a very different timeline than—"

"Mommy!"

Tommy runs into the kitchen and barrels toward Cassidy, throwing his arms around her.

"Morning, my bug," she says, kissing the top of his curls. "How did you sleep?"

"Good. Aunt Claire made me waffles for breakfast. I ate them in my room while playing with dinosaurs!"

Tommy beams at me. I wink at him.

"That sounds awesome, bud," Cassidy says, setting him down. To me, she mouths, *Thank you.*

Tommy's cheerful chatter chases away the tension lingering in the kitchen.

But it'll be back.

Chapter 8

Otto

My office is clean, neat, and practically empty. Tucked in a corner at the end of a long hallway, on the back side of the facility, overlooking the outdoor practice field.

Despite the temporary nature of this arrangement, the engraved nameplate next to the door has my name on it. Seeing *Coach Berger* written in neat block letters is as strange as hearing it spoken aloud has been.

Today marks the start of my second week with the Siege, but it feels like it's been longer. Late June—my tentative return date—feels years into the future. I keep waking up in the middle of the night, squinting at strange surroundings and cursing the constriction of the sling I'm stuck with. Wearing it during the day is bad enough, but it's especially uncomfortable at night. The immobilization might be helping cartilage reattach to bone, but it's doing nothing for my REM cycle.

I yawn, tossing my jacket on one of the two chairs facing my desk. The office's furnishings are basic—desk, chairs, empty filing cabinet. Its former occupant cleared out any personal belongings, and I don't have any to move in. All I packed were clothes.

A large bulletin board hangs on the wall facing the window, copies of the season schedule and team roster neatly attached with matching pushpins. The season opener—against Chicago—is set to take place in two weeks.

I walk over to the window to stare outside. I have a perfect bird's-eye view of the field. The sky is gray and overcast. Snow covers the ground, pure white in some sections and stained gray in others. The turf field stands out like a tropical island dropped on an iceberg, a neat rectangle of brilliant green.

Sharp longing jabs at my ribs as I look at it, recalling the thousands of hours I've spent on a football field. I took being on the field for granted. Wouldn't change a minute of it, but I have a bad habit of not realizing how I feel about things until I lose them.

I knew I loved football. But I had no clue how gaping the hole of its absence would be.

Coaching isn't the same. So far, I've enjoyed it more than I expected to, but it's different from playing. You're watching someone drive a car rather than holding the wheel or pressing the gas yourself.

I might never play again. I've tried to stay positive, but it's a fear that resurfaces regularly, overshadowing any attempts at optimism. I spent Saturday walking the Freedom Trail and Sunday wandering through the galleries in the Museum of Fine Arts so I had something to report to Will and so I didn't sit in my apartment all weekend, wearing down all the *should*s and *likely*s the doctors used until I reached the worst-case scenario beneath what I hoped would happen.

I yank my eyes away from the field before my brain can spiral down that dark path now, swiping my empty water bottle off the desk and heading back into the hallway. Aside from my prescribed physical therapy, walking is the only form of exercise I'm cleared to participate in right now. I feel like a racehorse, pacing a small stall.

I stride around the corner, then come to an abrupt halt, nearly dropping the plastic bottle I'm carrying. The sole reason my grip prevails is the reflexes I've honed for two decades.

Claire Caldwell is standing at the water fountain, one hip casually propped against the metal ledge as she watches her thermos fill with water. She glances up, toward the sound of my approach, the relaxed expression on her face shuttering to blank as soon as our eyes connect.

She straightens immediately, shoulders tensing to a straight line.

I should say something. *Hi* at the very least. But my throat constricts, preventing air from entering or words from exiting as we stare at each other.

She's been avoiding me. Subtly, but it's no coincidence that she always goes to Meg when we pass out pinnies or footballs. That, no matter where I stand, she's on the opposite side of the circle. That, when I'm working with Kristin, she opts to practice with Daniela. And when I'm by Daniela's goal, she chooses Kristin.

I haven't made it harder for her. Haven't pulled her aside and forced this conversation.

I knew it was coming, that we couldn't coexist on the same team without talking for four months, yet I'm still foolishly unprepared for this interaction to actually take place. I had a whole speech planned for Melbourne, expecting she'd be at the most recent summer Olympics with the American team. And now that she's standing directly in front of me, I can't think of a single worthwhile word to say.

So, I keep staring. My gaze dips without permission, scanning the Siege apparel she's wearing. The joggers and fleece cover her completely. But I don't have to imagine what's beneath the fabric. I've explored every inch of Claire's body, and those memories are burned into my brain.

Splashing draws my attention to the water fountain. Her bottle is overflowing, water streaming down the sides. I watch it happen, and Claire follows my gaze. She swears under her breath, grabbing the bottle, and it fractures the silent stillness.

I clear my throat, the uncertain sound betraying my nerves. "Hey."

If Claire finds my first word to her to be pathetic or underwhelming—it's both—she doesn't let on. It's rare I'm unsure what to say, yet common around her.

"Hi."

Her voice clings to me like smoke. A throaty rasp so distinctive that I would recognize the sound anywhere.

"Do they know?" she continues.

I blink at her, confused by the question. "They? Know what?"

She huffs once, impatiently, like I'm being deliberately obtuse. "Coach Taylor and the rest of the staff. Do they know about..."

Oh. About *us*.

"No," I say swiftly. "I didn't think it—I didn't say anything."

Claire nods once, visibly relieved by my reply. "Good."

I swallow hard. "Sorry I didn't let you know I was coming.

I should have—I should have given you some warning. Things happened fast."

I don't add that, up until I stepped on the plane, I wasn't sure I would be coming. Or that she—that avoiding this exact moment—factored in that decision.

Claire caps her now-full water bottle, breaking eye contact as she twists the lid shut. "I didn't need a warning. It's been six years."

"I know how long it's been," I say, softer than I meant to.

Six words to sum up six years. Yet I couldn't count the number of times Claire has crossed my mind since Paris.

She tucks her water bottle between her thighs, tugging an elastic out of her hair and twisting it into a neat bun. I catch a glimpse of the scar on her right thumb before her hands fall back to her sides. She still uses the same shampoo; I can smell it.

I knew, when I lost Claire, that she mattered to me more than I'd realized. But I never expected that dull ache of regret to linger for this long.

"It's good to see you," spills out without me consciously choosing to say the sentiment.

Claire takes a deep breath. "Look, Otto—" She pauses and flushes. "I mean, Coach Berger."

"Otto's fine," I say, trying to ease her embarrassment. Still absorbing the shock wave of hearing her say my name again.

"*Coach Berger*," she emphasizes.

I fight a sudden smile. My first real one since the fall that landed me in an operating room.

"None of my teammates know about our…history either, and I'd like it to stay that way. We're… I mean, we're basically strangers anyway, right?"

Wrong. We don't feel like anything similar to strangers. But

I wasn't intending to treat her differently from any other player, which is what she's concerned with.

"I wasn't planning on advertising anything, Caldwell. If you haven't told them about us, they won't find out from me."

"Okay then," she says.

"Okay then," I echo.

Claire doesn't walk away, like I'm expecting her to. She's looking at my chest, specifically at the sling partially covering my Siege polo. "Are you—"

"Caldy! I thought we were meeting—oh. Hey, Coach Berger."

It takes me a second too long to drag my gaze away from Claire to look at the newcomer who interrupted whatever Claire was about to say.

Am I *what*?

Another few seconds pass before I'm able to sort through my tangled thoughts and come up with the correct name from the team roster. Mallory Wilson.

"Hello, Wilson."

Mallory smiles, elbowing a stoic Claire. "We were supposed to meet in the weight room five minutes ago."

"I was on my way there," Claire responds. "Just stopped to fill up my water bottle." She holds it up like proof. "Let's, uh, let's go."

" 'Kay!" Mallory flashes me a friendly smile, then follows after Claire, chattering away.

I stand motionless until they're out of sight. I should feel better now that our first interaction is out of the way.

I don't.

I remember why I walked up to a stranger outside a nightclub in Paris.

Chapter 9

Otto

PARIS: SIX YEARS EARLIER

"I know who you are," the brunette confesses after I introduce myself.

Her voice is unexpected. Low-pitched and husky. Sultry. So is the way she sucks her bottom lip into her mouth after dropping my hand.

"You do?" I reply, holding eye contact.

My ego's oversized enough to fill Sieg Stadium, according to Coach Wagner, but I'm not so conceited as to assume every American is up-to-date on the German football roster. I've gotten used to a certain level of recognition around Kluvberg, but notoriety in other countries, like the scene when we arrived at Charles de Gaulle, is new.

She nods once. "I do. I have a thing for goalies."

I grin.

The hue of her cheeks darkens to red, and I think it's unrelated to the summer heat radiating off the sidewalk.

"*Respect*," she adds hastily. "I have a respect thing for goalies. Not like an…other thing."

"Other thing?" I ask innocently. "Like a kink?"

A word I learned from the American dating show Beck claims to only watch so he can follow Saylor's rants about it. I watch it to support Beck being a good fiancé, of course.

"Right! I mean, right, as in, yes, that's what I did *not* mean. Not as in, yes, I have one." She mutters something else under her breath, too low for me to hear. "I played goalie for a single season because no one else wanted to do it. And it sucked when the opponents were seven-year-old girls who forgot which end to score in. I don't—I can't imagine what it must be like with higher stakes than that."

I grin. Again. Or still. I think I've been smiling ever since I saw her mimic driving a car. "You played football?"

"I play soccer," she replies, pride in her voice. "That's why I'm here."

And she's American. So, she's one of Saylor's teammates.

"This is your first Games?" I ask. My guess is, she's younger than me.

She nods. "I'm still in college. I'll be a senior at Lincoln University."

I've heard of it. One of the more prestigious American schools.

She taps her phone against her thigh, drawing my attention back to her dress. The dress itself, I couldn't care less about. But I'm very intrigued by all the smooth skin it exposes. She's tall, nearly to my shoulder in heels, the sculpted muscles of her thighs and calves on full display.

This isn't the first time I've checked a woman out without knowing her name. It's the first time not knowing it has bothered me though.

"Is it an American thing—to share your kinks instead of your name?"

She tilts her head, a rueful smile appearing. "It's Claire. Claire Caldwell."

"Claire Caldwell," I repeat, memorizing it.

"Yep." Claire sucks on her lip again.

I'd think she was being provocative on purpose, but she seems oblivious to her own appeal. Innocent almost, though not naive. Her eyes are alert as she tracks the people passing us in the street.

"Are you headed back to the Village?" I ask.

"Yeah." She glances at the unhelpful valet, who is waiting with my keys. "I came with some teammates who weren't ready to leave—"

"I'll give you a lift."

The offer is out before I decided to make it, and I'm almost as startled by it as Claire appears to be. Her green eyes widen—a vibrant color eerily similar to my favorite sight.

"Oh," she says. "Thank you. But I'll, um, I can figure it out."

"We're headed to the same place," I remind her, entertained by her hesitation.

Women usually pursue me. That was true before I signed my first contract with FC Kluvberg and has only become more common since I did. If I made a habit of offering rides, which I don't, I could accurately predict the response. And it's not *no.*

"I'll just..." Claire's voice trails.

"I can call Saylor?" I suggest, reaching for my phone.

Her "No!" is panicked. "I'm not sure we're supposed to be… out." She almost whispers the last word.

I've partied with Saylor Scott dozens of times. Captain or not, I doubt Beck's fiancée would discipline a teammate for having some fun. It's not like they have a match tomorrow.

But I relate to Claire's caution. I remember that teetering sensation of excitement and terror in London, eagerness to prove myself warring with the fear of fucking up if Nübel faltered and I was subbed in.

The valet calls out, asking if I'm ready to leave. There's a line forming behind the Maserati I rented for some sightseeing.

I ignore him, telling Claire, "I can call you a car if you want. But I would be happy to drive you back myself."

She studies me.

And I literally hold my breath, waiting for her decision. It's the same sensation as when I'm watching a kick fly my way. That suspension where the rest of the world is quiet and still. My surroundings blur, and it's just me and the incoming ball.

It's never happened anywhere else… Until now.

"Okay. Thanks, Otto."

A strange fizziness appears when she says my name. Like a bottle of champagne was popped inside my chest and is carbonating my bloodstream.

I don't know why I walked over here. I don't know why it mattered so much that she said *yes* to me. All I know is that I'm happy both happened.

I snag the keys from the rude valet, who's full of apologies now that he's assumed Claire is with me. Again, I ignore him, walking to the passenger side to open the door for her.

"Surprised you don't have a vanity plate," Claire comments, glancing at the trunk as she passes it.

"Is that an insult?"

"Just an observation," she replies, eyes sparkling with a mischievousness that's new.

"It's a rental," I admit, grabbing the door handle.

"So, you have one on your car at home?"

"You'll have to ride with me again to find that out."

Claire glances at the open door, a flash of surprise appearing. She wasn't expecting me to open the door for her, and it makes me very glad I did.

"What a gentleman."

Her breathing is rapid, like she's reacting to our close proximity.

"Not often," I admit.

She smiles before lowering herself to the seat slowly, careful to keep her knees close together. I plant my body directly in front of hers, blocking her from any passersby the same way I protect my goal.

Once she's settled, I shut the door and round the hood. I slip the valet a tip despite my lingering annoyance before climbing in the driver's seat.

I feel her eyes on me as we zoom down the street, and there's a flip in my stomach that's happened…never.

I'm weirdly nervous. Antsy. I clear my throat and fiddle with the volume knob of the stereo.

"I love this song," Claire comments.

I glance at the screen. "Dreams" is the name of the song playing.

"I mostly listen to older music," she continues. "Fleetwood Mac has some of my favorites. I only knew two of the songs they played in the club earlier."

"Did you have fun?" I ask, curious to know more about her

night. About her.

"Yeah," she answers, not sounding sure. "It was…different."

"Different from what?"

"I grew up outside Boston, in this small suburb where nothing that exciting ever happened. As you might have noticed, based on how I freaked out about you calling Saylor, I'm sort of a rule follower. I didn't go to parties in high school, and I don't go out much in college either. I bartend at a pub in the summers, but I don't go to places like that often. I don't party much. I play soccer."

There's a defensiveness to her tone, like she's expecting me to think less of her for it.

"Me too," I tell her.

When I glance over at a red light, Claire appears dubious. "You know where we met, right?"

"I never went inside the club," I say. "If I had gone in, we would have met earlier."

She scoffs, like she doesn't believe me.

And I want her to believe me, so I press the point. "You think I am lying, Boston?"

"You expect me to believe that you'd walk right up to me in a club and ask for my name?"

"I walked up to you outside a club and asked for your name. What is the difference?"

Claire doesn't reply right away. But then she says, "You were just being nice since I was obviously out of my element."

"I'm not nice." We're stopped at a red light, so I mimic her driving motion. "I was amused."

That's not quite the right word, but I'm not sure I'd be able to come up with it in German either. It was an instinct, to approach Claire, and I've learned to rely on mine.

I take a left, although I should've gone right, to prolong the drive with her.

"Why did you go out tonight if you do not normally?" I ask.

"My teammates wanted me to."

I frown. "And they let you leave alone?"

"No, they all offered to leave with me. I told them I was calling my boyfriend."

I don't get attached easily. Probably because so much of my life has been transitory. Football has been the one reliable constant. But I'm bothered Claire isn't single. It hits me like a letdown—a trip you were looking forward to taking getting canceled at the last minute.

"He did not answer?" I ask.

"He doesn't exist."

Just like that, my mood rebounds.

"Well, he *exists*. Just not as my boyfriend anymore."

"His loss," I say, taking another detour.

"You don't even know him."

"Yeah, but I have met you."

Her smile grows before she glances away, out the window. "He didn't get soccer. Said I was wasting my time."

"How many gold medals does he have?"

She laughs. "He's not an athlete."

"Do not take advice from anyone who does not share your goals, Claire."

I learned that lesson the hard way. My success boils down to one source—me. I never had anyone cheering me on, not until I reached the top.

She's silent. I think she's looking at me, but I keep my eyes on the street rather than check.

"Oh. *Wow*. There's the Eiffel Tower." Claire leans forward, and a vent blows her curls toward my side of the car. I can smell her shampoo—feminine, but not overly sweet. "You know where we're going, right? We didn't drive past it on the way to the club."

I wait until she glances over to smirk. "I know where we are going." We pass Paris's iconic landmark and reach another intersection. "Right—back at the Village in ten minutes. Left—will take a lot longer. Which way, Boston?"

She holds my gaze, and it's another hold-my-breath, incoming-shot moment.

"Left."

Chapter 10

Claire

"The Chain" blares in my ears. Cold wind blasts my cheeks. I tug the knit cap Lydia gifted me lower mid-stride, ensuring the wool covers the tops of my ears as I continue jogging alongside the Charles. It's early, barely March, and a Saturday. Only the hardcore are out this early, braving the elements.

And the avoiders.

Cassidy found a job; she's working at the same accounting firm Dad has been part of since before my sister was born. She swore that Dad had nothing to do with her hiring, that he'd merely mentioned an opening and she applied because nothing else was working out, but we both know that's bullshit. Not that Cassidy isn't qualified. She's one of the savviest people I've ever met. But Caldwell isn't that common of a last name.

Dad and Lindsey, his wife, were coming by the house at nine to take Cassidy and Tommy out to breakfast to celebrate. I know

Cassidy told me in the hopes I'd have an actual face-to-face conversation with my father. Instead, I set my alarm and snuck out earlier than she'd be awake. I don't have the energy to deal with that drama. I'm preoccupied with Mom's upcoming move to Echo Glen. With transitioning into a new season. With getting to know my nephew better. With Otto's low, "*It's good to see you*," which has been on repeat since our conversation on Monday.

I've said that to acquaintances who hadn't crossed my mind in years. But Otto didn't just say it. He said it like he meant it, like him being in Boston was a coincidence instead of a calamity.

It's been fucking with my head ever since, along with the fact that he didn't tell anyone about me. I figured he would have said something after seeing my name on the roster. Not the details, but an, *Oh, Caldwell? I've met her before, at the Paris Olympics*, would have made complete sense. Saying nothing seems more meaningful, somehow, but it's probably the wrong assumption. It's been six years. His eyes might have skimmed right over my name on the roster.

"I know how long it's been." He said that like he meant it too.

I run faster, harder, trying to drown out my thoughts with exertion even though today was supposed to be an easy jog. We have a preseason scrimmage tomorrow. The final score won't count in any official capacity, but it's an opportunity to set the tone for the coming season. To showcase what sort of opponents the Siege will be. We were so close last year, and I'm determined to end this year as champions.

My phone buzzes with an incoming call, interrupting my music, but I don't answer it. I'm certain it's Cassidy. She'll find the note I left on the kitchen counter soon enough.

"Everywhere" resumes, and I relax into the reassuring rhythm of *left, right, left, right, left, right.* Air rushes in and out of my lungs in steady streams. I'm moving too fast to see my breaths linger in the chilly air, but I know that they are. The car read twenty-eight degrees when I parked. Sunshine might have raised the temperature to thirty by now, but it's definitely below freezing. The gray clouds hovering overhead suggest more snow is coming soon.

I pass a woman walking a poodle, and then my eyes snag on a figure ahead. I squint, blink rapidly, do everything I can think of to morph the shape into someone else. Praying this is one of those instances where my subconscious is playing a trick on me, finding familiarity in strangers.

But it's him. I'm disturbed by how certain I am. I've avoided every opportunity to look at him, doing so only when absolutely necessary.

I blow past him, slow, pivot, and walk back the dozen feet to where Otto is leaning against the rail that separates the path from the bank of the frozen Charles.

There's no indication he noticed or recognized me. Even if he did, I could have claimed to have not noticed or recognized him.

But I have this fascination with Otto Berger. It runs deeper than his athletic talent. Than his perfect physique and rogue grin. Than anything superficial.

I convinced myself that interest had faded with time. That I occasionally checked Kluvberg scores out of habit, nothing else. But it'd been smothered, not extinguished, and Otto walking into the media room was a gust of oxygen, fanning flames back to life.

I exhale, vapor hovering before dissipating, as I stop beside him, gripping the railing with my gloves. "Hey."

"Hi." His voice sounds muted, somber, so unlike the adventurous, animated guy I remember. Blue eyes especially piercing against the pale, icy backdrop of a Boston winter.

This would be so much simpler if I'd only known Otto Berger for the two weeks he's been a Siege assistant coach. It could be a casual conversation, commiserating about how cold it is. Involving a little internal fangirling on my part—because he's even more famous than he was when we met. Otto's spent the past six years becoming better known and more successful. My career, by contrast, has, at best, plateaued and, more accurately, declined. I haven't earned a single cap since leaving Paris. He's won another World Cup.

He doesn't seem surprised to see me, which I assume means he did spot me running. But I can't tell for sure, and that bothers me.

"What do you think of Boston?" I ask.

"It is nice." He leaves it at that.

"I'm surprised you left Kluvberg," I admit.

He turns his entire body toward me, not just his head, resting a hip against the railing. It's oddly intimate and extremely distracting. Too reminiscent of how he'd focus on me, even when others—lots of others—were trying to capture his attention.

"Why?"

"I just…figured you'd want to recover at home?"

Otto doesn't reply right away, and it gives me too much time to look. I've run this route since I got my driver's license. The path is so familiar; I could navigate it blindfolded. And standing here, staring at him, is surreal. I returned from Paris and jogged along this path, praying no one would recognize me from the feature the *Globe* had run and holding back tears.

It's déjà vu and a dream—or nightmare—rolled into reality.

We're still just…looking at each other.

Otto never planned to be standing here either, if six years of silence were any indication, but only one of us chose this, and it sure wasn't me.

"This move made sense," he answers finally.

You'd think he was getting charged by the word to have this conversation with me. And forgot he was a multimillionaire.

"You're different," I blurt before I can think better of it.

"I cannot play," Otto replies, bitterness soaking each syllable.

When we met, I admired his focus on soccer. When we ended, I accepted it. When I saw he was engaged, I thought his priorities had finally shifted. If they did, his response revealed they'd moved back. I wasn't talking about his injured status; I was referring to the way he seemed to be a black-and-white version of his colorful self.

"You'll be back next season."

He sighs, the cloud of his breath hovering between us temporarily. He reaches to adjust his sling with his left hand, the strap making it impossible for his jacket to zip all the way up. The cold doesn't appear to be bothering him. He looks healthy—solid and capable.

"You *will*," I insist, his silence scaring me a little.

The smallest of smiles tugs at his mouth. "You a doctor now, Claire?"

There's nothing small about the reaction to him using my first name, paired with a glimpse of his former playful self.

"What did the doctors say?" I ask, forcing myself to remain in the present only.

Otto blows out another breath. "It was a bad tear. The surgery went as well as it could have. Nothing to do now but wait. I am stuck wearing this"—he adjusts the sling again—"for a couple of more days, and then physical therapy will start. After a few months, I will be cleared to start training again. Or not, and

I will… I don't know what."

"You're not a terrible coach," I tell him.

Kristin and Daniela have been singing his praises ever since Otto started working with them.

That earns me a short laugh. I hate—hate, hate, hate—how I almost smile in response.

"Thank you, Caldwell."

I also despise the brief burst of disappointment when he reverts to using my last name. But it's a needed reminder of our current roles. We're not old pals or friendly exes. We might be in the same place again, but it's temporary—again.

I straighten. "I should keep moving."

His eyes skim over the leggings and thermal top I'm wearing. The tight layers suddenly feel too flimsy. I fight the urge to cross my arms, erecting more of a shield between us.

"Today is your day off," Otto comments.

"I'm aware."

"You should be resting before the match."

I bristle at the imperiousness in his tone. "We're not at work, Coach Berger. I'll prepare for tomorrow however I want to."

Rather than appear offended, he smiles again, prompting another cardiac event in my chest. "You are the same."

I can't tell from his voice if that's a compliment or an insult.

And he must see it on my face because he adds, "Still stubborn, I mean."

There are very few people on this planet who would describe me as stubborn. But I can be, if it's related to something important or if I'm around someone I trust enough to stick around when I'm not shiny and accommodating.

"So are you," I tell him. "Which is how I know you *will* be back in goal next season."

Otto nods once, shoving away from the metal railing. I can't tell, from the slight movement, if he believes me. He opens his mouth, then closes it again. Rubs the back of his neck, and I want to close my eyes so I don't have to battle the urge to stare at the sliver of abs the motion reveals. I think I catch a glimpse of a boxers band and wonder if he wears the same brand. Wonder how different he truly is, beneath the depression about his injury.

"See you tomorrow," he finally tells me, starting in the opposite direction I was running in.

Does he live near here? Does he have a car in Boston? Was this his first time walking here, or has he come before?

I shove the questions deep down, close to the forbidden ones I'll never ask. Near, *Did you ever think about me?* and, *Do you have any regrets?* and, *Why didn't you marry her?*

Before I begin jogging again, I check the time on my phone. It's later than I expected; we talked for longer than I'd realized. Sure enough, I have a missed call from Cassidy, and I'll need to head home soon to check on Mom. Turning back now runs the high risk of running into Otto, so I resume my music and continue running the same way I was before.

Not because I don't want to see him again.

Because I do, and that's more dangerous than a swim in the frozen Charles would be right now.

Chapter 11

Otto

I stare at the final score, prominently displayed on the Jumbotron of the Siege's brand-new stadium. My first win as a coach. It was a preseason match, and there's a full season of games ahead. Matches that will matter for rankings and playoffs and a championship. Today's victory doesn't count, technically.

A smile tugs at the corners of my mouth anyway. Winning is an addictive sensation. No athlete ever thinks, *Okay, I've won enough*. Turns out, that's true for coaching too. I'm proud of the Siege, even though my role in their success is so different from what I'm accustomed to. Even though there's a full season ahead.

"Nach dem spiel ist vor dem spiel," is probably what Wagner would say.

After the game is before the game.

Every victory marks the start of preparing for another match. No goals or saves carry over to the next opponent. Getting to the top isn't nearly as difficult as remaining there, and there's a reason Wagner has kept Kluvberg dominant for the past decade.

I wasn't averse to the idea of coaching—not until Boston came up at least—but it seemed unnecessary. I'm discovering how necessary it was.

Since I arrived at the stadium, I focused on the Siege. On watching Cascarino manage a shutout and saying some choice words to the ref who'd given Rodman a yellow card in the first half. It got me out of my own head for the longest stretch since my injury had happened, a break that I desperately needed.

Most coaches would have told me to focus on nothing except recovery. But Wagner knew I needed an upcoming match to look forward to, even if I wasn't in goal for it. I feel a part of something again, like I'm connected to the Siege's success. Invested in the outcome of their season.

Not that I'll be here to see it. If all goes to plan, I'll be back in Kluvberg with a healthy shoulder by mid-summer.

"Nice work today, Otto," Eliza tells me, tucking a clipboard under one arm and offering me her hand to shake.

I do, aiming a brief smile her way. "You too."

Eliza smiles back. "I've got a good feeling about this season." She grabs the clipboard, glancing at the emptying stands. "The organization hasn't made an official statement about your role, but we might need to."

She's referring to the Kluvberg jerseys in the audience. My jersey, I'm assuming, although I didn't look long enough to tell for sure. I was focused on the match.

"Whatever you think is best," I tell her.

Eliza nods. "I'll check with the team publicist."

I nod back. As soon as Eliza walks away, Nicole approaches. "Your first win," she announces, beaming. "How does it feel?"

A child's shriek draws my attention left. Preseason games are free to attend, and there were a lot of families in the stands. Plenty of them have filtered from the stands down onto the turf field, congratulating players. It's been a long time since I witnessed a post-match celebration that was so casual. Barricades block any fan entry onto the pitch at Sieg Stadium for security reasons.

The screeching child—a young boy—is hustling after a rolling ball as fast as his short legs will allow. A Siege player chases after him, lifting the child and swinging him around. He laughs and wiggles. She kisses his cheek before setting him down.

All the air exits my lungs, like a football just collided with my chest.

It's Claire. Claire with a kid. Claire with a kid who looks just like her.

"Otto?"

I tear my gaze away, refocusing on Nicole. Shake my head. "Sorry. I was… It is strange, being on a different field, not playing. An adjustment."

Her expression softens with sympathy, prompting a burst of guilt. It's not a lie, but it's not the full truth either.

"Took me a while to adjust too," she tells me. "I had this fantasy of playing professionally. Getting to this level, but not actually playing…well—" Nicole laughs. "I know you can't relate to that part. You're Otto Berger."

She says my name the way a lot of people do. Like I'm a brand, not a person. And it's never bothered me before. But it bothers me now since that brand feels separate from me. That brand was a guy who never had to think about what he'd do aside from play football.

"I will get used to it," I say.

More shouting comes from the direction of the field, but I don't turn to look this time. My excitement about the team's first win has sapped away, like air leaving a leaky balloon. The stadium's celebratory, relaxed atmosphere suddenly seems stifling.

"See you tomorrow," I say, barely registering Nicole's nod before I continue along the sideline, avoiding eye contact with everyone I pass.

Claire's soccer career is public information. But her social media profiles are all set to private, and I never requested access. I didn't want to know what her life post-Paris looked like.

But now, I know. She had a kid. He looked young, but not that young. I'd guess four or five. Add nine months to that, and she didn't wait long to move on. He could almost be mine, but I know he's not. No matter what happened between us, Claire would have told me. I shared things with her I've never mentioned to anyone—like how growing up without a father affected me.

I already resolved to keep my distance after yesterday. Foolishly, it'd never occurred to me that Claire might still run on that path. Seeing her there was a shock, and I expected her to breeze by. Not to stop. Not to strike up a conversation. I knew—maybe from the moment a mention of the Siege cut through the post-injury haze I was in—that Claire still affected me. Being around her for two weeks should have shaken off any novelty. Instead, the opposite seems to be taking place. The more time I spend around her, the more I crave her presence. And I fell in love with her once, during one of the biggest moments of my career, when football should have held all my attention. Right now, I can't even touch a ball. It would be easier than falling—to dig up all those emotions again.

Calls of my name pull my attention to the stands. Two boys are standing on the closest seats, both wearing my jersey.

I hesitate for a second. I'm here as a coach, not a player, and interacting with spectators in the latter capacity sets a precedent I'm not sure I want to. If the Siege does release a press statement, odds are, more people will start showing up to games to see me.

Also, I'm in a shitty mood. The longer I linger, the more likely I am to see Claire's...boyfriend? Co-parent? She's never worn a ring. And that's a reunion I have no interest in witnessing. If he's not here, it'll just piss me off that she's ended up with someone who doesn't support her the way she deserves to be celebrated.

But the boys are bouncing with excitement, staring at me like they can't believe I exist in real life.

So, I veer in their direction, pasting a grin on my face. "Hey, guys! How is it going?"

One is too stunned to speak. The other starts talking a mile a minute—so fast that it takes me a few seconds to realize he's requesting I sign his jersey. I accept a marker from a middle-aged woman, who also offers a fervent, "Thank you so much. They're huge fans of yours," as her kids clamor about, spinning so I can scrawl my signature on their backs.

Once I have, a few more fans have appeared. I sign everything they hand me, pose for a few photos, and then hustle toward the exit.

My phone buzzes in my pocket as I stride through the gate toward the private parking lot. I pull it out, expecting it to be Beck or Will. Kluvberg played yesterday—a loss—so they're both off today.

It's Mila calling. She's been my grandfather's caretaker for the past few years. Despite having four children of her own to keep her busy (and that I only pay her to look after Opa) she checks on me regularly.

"*Hallo*, Mila," I answer.

"Otto! How are you, *liebling*?"

The warm endearment is nostalgic. So is hearing German.

"I'm better."

The past few times we've talked, I've pretended. My entire world was crumbling around me, my current life unrecognizable from my old one. But I am adjusting—and not just with the Siege. I bought an art print at the MFA to add to my apartment's spare furnishings. I walk along the Charles every morning. I buy my own groceries. It's different, but if not for the glaring absence of football, I wouldn't even say it's in a bad way.

I tell Mila about the win today. About the bookstore across the street from my new apartment. About Will and Sophia's upcoming visit.

I can sense Mila's excitement—her relief—as she prompts me for more details.

After she updates me on what her kids have been up to, we lapse into the awkward pause that predates every discussion about the reason these calls started.

"How is he?" I finally ask.

I don't have a bad relationship with my grandfather; I don't have *a* relationship with him. Opa was pleased—relieved, undoubtedly, to not have the burden of caring for a kid—when I was accepted to Kluvberg's academy at age nine. Up until he realized football was all I intended to do with my life. I was eighteen by then, no longer his ward. He couldn't do a damn thing to stop me from signing a contract. He tried, told me he'd never forgive me for abandoning the construction company he'd built from nothing; I signed the contract anyway, and we've barely spoken since.

He was wrong—I did have what it took.

He was right—his company folded a few years later without me stepping up to help run it.

I hired Mila when he started struggling to care for himself, and that's the only financial help he's ever accepted from me despite my attempts to do more. He refuses to cash checks, locks out housekeepers, and chases off landscapers. Mila, somehow, became the one person he tolerates assistance from.

And it takes me too long to realize she hasn't replied, swamped with the regret and resentment that accompanies any thought of my sole family member.

Mila sighs. "He's having surgery next week."

I fumble with the keys in my hand, pressing the lock button instead of the unlock one and nearly dropping the phone.

My grandfather is in his early eighties. His health was going to decline eventually. It already has—he hit a neighbor's fence, which was what prompted Mila's hiring. But that was cataracts, nothing serious.

Opa has always reminded me of a mule. Steadfast and sturdy.

I manage to open the car door and sink into the driver's seat. "Surgery for what?"

"He fell on the stairs and told no one." The sentence is rife with disapproval. "I took him to the doctor yesterday. He needs a new hip."

Fuck.

"I tried to have him call himself," Mila continues. "He didn't want to...bother you with it."

I'm sure Opa put it far less politely, but Mila has always been diplomatic about the disconnect between me and my grandfather. She's the one way our lives overlap, the single means of communication we have. A saint for tolerating our disfunction.

And I'm mad at her for telling me.

I haven't spoken to my grandfather since last summer. I spent a week in Tannfeld, handling all the repairs I'd hired workers for and that he'd chased off. He didn't call after the game that landed me in the hospital, let alone visit me there. I'm sure he's heard I'm sidelined for the remainder of the season. Mila would have mentioned it; so would have his neighbors. And still…nothing.

I blow out a long breath, staring at the row of cars in the parking lot. All stationary, and I feel stuck too.

I can't play. Can't fuel this conflict into anything productive. Can't use football as a barrier to block everything else out or as a scheduling excuse.

Mila stays silent, patiently letting me process.

"What day is the surgery?" I ask.

"Friday."

I could fly back Thursday. Stay a day. Return Saturday. I'd miss the Siege's first game next weekend, but it's a game I'm not playing in. Nothing I did on the sidelines today was anything Eliza, Meg, and Nicole couldn't cover for one match.

"He agreed to have a nurse stay with him after. We'll set up his bedroom in the living room. He'll love being closer to his books."

She knows Opa well. Better than I do.

"I know it's a difficult time for you right now. But I thought I should mention it."

"Thanks, Mila," I say.

I don't promise anything.

But we both know I would have told her I wasn't coming if I wasn't.

Chapter 12

Claire

"Too much space, Caldwell! Shadow her!"

The shout—the voice—is so unexpected that I nearly stumble, recovering my balance at the last possible second before pressing closer to Reyna, who's searching for a yellow pinnie to pass to.

Otto has worked with Daniela and Kristin individually. Post-practice, the Siege goalies have reported to curious teammates (while I eavesdropped) that he wasn't "chatty."

Which was weird. Because the Otto I know—knew—always had a lot to say. Well, *almost* always.

Maybe he's assuming a new persona as a coach. More likely, he's too preoccupied mourning the unexpected end of his own season and stressing about his recovery to bother with small talk.

I wish I didn't know that. I wish I'd kept running that morning along the Charles. His problems aren't my problems. He's one of my coaches. And, worst of all, he acts like our conversation never happened, essentially ignoring me ever since. He didn't even bother to congratulate me after Sunday's scrimmage. I contributed, in part, to Daniela's shutout, letting hardly anyone past, and no acknowledgment. He talked to Coach Taylor and Coach Green, signed a few dozen autographs, and left.

It's what I wanted. What I asked for. And it's pissing me off.

"Challenge Rodman, Caldwell!"

I grind my molars, fighting to stay focused and to not flip Otto off.

I was debating pressing closer to Reyna. Guarding someone is a delicate dance. Too close, and you risk fouling or allowing a fast pivot to leave you behind. Too far, and you allow them too much space and time to strategize a next move.

Unfortunately, Otto is correct. I'm not close enough, and the only reason Reyna hasn't passed is that my fellow defenders are marking better than I am.

I strike, catching the ball and sprinting ahead as soon as I feel it settle in the sweet spot of my foot. I boot it ahead to Mallory, and she dribbles up the field to attack Kristin's goal.

Jogging back to position, I glance at Otto. He should be tracking Mallory, but he's looking at me. Our eyes catch, and he nods.

A nod. That's all. No smile. No praise. But I don't need either. I'd rather he act like this, noting what I should have done all along. Acting as if excellence is what he expects from me.

And it hits me then—I like having him here.

I look away as soon as the thought strikes, worried he'll see it on my face. And refocus on the scrimmage, where my attention should have been all along.

Otto calls out more corrections as the scrimmage continues.

I was teasing, trying to lighten his mood, when I told him he wasn't a terrible coach. But I meant it. He's a really good one actually.

Some players make great coaches; some struggle with instructing others. The most talented players tend to make the worst coaches. They have a legacy to protect, they're accustomed to being the center of attention, and they're frustrated by players who can't perform at the same level they did. I placed Otto in that second category.

I was wrong, I decide, as he continues to call out feedback. By the time practice ends, he's commented on every single player on the field.

Otto—Coach Berger—didn't single me out again, and I try not to fixate on what it means that he focused on me first. I also attempt to ignore how this was one of the best practice performances I've had in a while.

I've always struggled with compartmentalizing. Some players suit up and are immediately in the zone. My brain has never worked that way.

Today, I was locked in. And it showed. After practice ends, Coach Taylor stops me to praise today's performance.

In the locker room, Mallory comments, "Caldy, you were on fire today," before tossing her sweaty jersey toward the hamper.

"Had an extra cup of coffee this morning," I say, busy digging through my bag for my phone.

I played the best soccer of my life in Paris. I wasn't reckless then, but I took more risks than I tend to take now. I've used being younger as an excuse for why my career hasn't improved from that point. Based on today, I should have given being in love with Otto more credit. He believed in me then, more than I believed in myself, and some of that faith appears to have survived the past six years. I want to be the player he sees, not the one who's mediocre more often than not.

"What brand of beans are you brewing these days?" Reyna wonders, making Tasha laugh.

I smile and shake my head, finally locating my cell at the bottom of my duffel. There are no new messages from Cassidy, so I don't need to rush to Little Red Wagon. Now that she's working full-time and my soccer schedule has gotten more hectic, Cassidy hired a babysitter to pick Tommy up and watch him until she gets home. I'm simply a backup.

I don't have anything from my sister, but I do have a missed call and a voicemail from Echo Glen. I raise the phone to my ear, gnawing nervously on my thumbnail.

"Do you think Coach Berger's going to be like that from now on?" Savannah asks, dropping dramatically on the bench.

Whatever Tasha replies has the whole locker room laughing, but I'm distracted by the voicemail. I drop my phone back in my bag and toss my cleats on top, hastily shoving my feet into my untied sneakers.

"What's wrong?" Reyna asks, noticing my haste.

"Nothing's wrong," I lie quickly. "I just forgot about an… appointment. See you guys tomorrow."

"You didn't even change!" Reyna calls after me.

I'm already out the door, mentally plotting the fastest route to Echo Glen.

…

The trip to Duxbury takes a full hour, thanks to afternoon traffic. There were closer—and cheaper—care facility options, but Mom's neurologist recommended Echo Glen most highly.

I silently pray, as I park and rush toward the automatic doors that lead inside the main building, that I didn't make a mistake.

Mom's primary nurse, Maggie, is waiting in the lobby. Her sympathetic expression makes me think I look as harried and stressed as I feel. "You didn't need to come all this way, honey."

"I don't mind." The words exit in a rush.

Maggie glances at my feet. I do too. My shoelaces are snarled and stained with mud, still untied. Her expression settles into the same kind concern Mrs. Combs would display when I picked up Tommy late.

"How is she?" I ask.

"She's fine. This is an adjustment period. There will be many more as her condition progresses. You asked me to keep you updated, so I was just letting you know she'd been asking about you."

I nod. "Thank you. She's in her apartment? I can go up and see her?"

"Of course. You remember the way to her room?"

"I do. Thanks."

Maggie reaches out and squeezes my arm. "There's the call button right by the front door if you need anything. I'll stop by in a half hour or so to check in. Book club is at four, if she feels like participating."

I thank Maggie, then continue down the hallway. There's an elevator, but Mom's room is only on the second floor. I opt for the stairs instead, pausing at the first step to knot my sneakers' dirty laces.

The carpet that runs the length of the hallway is a cheerful blue, the exact shade as the sky on a sunny day. Yellow walls are barely visible beneath the display of artwork created by residents. I toured five facilities before putting Mom's name down here.

It wasn't just the neurologist's recommendation. Echo Glen reminded me most of a home. Of a community, not a glorified hospital.

Mom's door is the last one, a corner unit. I suck in a deep breath, hating the apprehension that appears. This is my *mom*, the person who knows me better than anyone else. That version of her remains, always, even when she acts differently.

I knock before punching in the code that unlocks the door. Mom has a key to use herself, but each apartment has an auto-locking mechanism that can be deactivated by staff in case of an emergency. Or an unannounced visit. Since I can hear music playing inside the apartment, I doubt Mom can hear me knocking.

"Mom?" I call loudly, shutting the door behind me and toeing off my sneakers in the entryway.

No answer.

I continue walking, rounding the corner. The apartment's layout is simple. A living area connects to the dining room, then continues to a small kitchen. The bedroom and attached bathroom are across from it. It came partially furnished, the decoration a mix of generic and Mom's favorites we brought from the house.

I pause by the CD player to lower the volume of her favorite Tom Petty song.

"I'm working, Claire," Mom says, not glancing up.

"I see that," I reply, approaching the dining room table, which she has converted into an office.

Piles of papers cover every available inch of the wood—some printed text, some handwritten.

Mom's huddled at one end, jabbing her laptop keys with a voracity that has her loose curls bouncing in time with each tap.

She sighs when I press a kiss to the top of her head, reaching up to pat my hand with hers. “I guess I could take a quick break. Tea?”

“Tea sounds great,” I reply, lifting a couple of notebooks off a chair and setting them carefully on the floor.

Mom leaps up with an agility I’m envious of, bustling around her kitchen with brisk efficiency. I take a seat, wincing when one of the table legs connects with a bruise on my shin.

“I made you shamomalay,” Mom says, setting a steaming cup down in front of me.

My eyes sting as she purposefully mispronounces it, the same way I did when I was younger. “Thanks, Mom.”

Her nose wrinkles as she sits back down in front of her laptop. “You smell, Claire.”

I let out a watery laugh. “I know. Sorry. I came straight from practice.”

“Did you have fun?” Mom asks, lifting and lowering the tea bag in her mug.

The question she posed when she picked me up from my first summer camp and every time after. Never, *Did you score?* or, *Did you win?* A gift I especially appreciated when I called her on my way home from Paris, when it felt like I’d let everyone down. Mom never made me feel like I let her down.

I hope I still haven’t. Here, she’s surrounded by stability. By routines and activities and specialists and other things I couldn’t provide. Mom was adamant about this move when she first received her diagnosis. But planning ahead was different from it actually happening. From me having to make the decision.

“Claire?”

When I look up, she’s focused on me, not her tea or her laptop.

“I did,” I answer, recalling her question. “It was the best

practice I've had in a while actually."

Otto's presence during practice was a reminder of the player I'm capable of being. Soccer involves constantly shifting factors. Teammates, coaches, opponents, refs? Those can all change. But the only factor controlling how I play? Me.

"I don't know this place." Mom puts it out there, plain and matter-of-fact. Similar to how she shared the news about the divorce and that Cassidy was pregnant.

Except, this time, she's looking to me for answers instead of the other way around.

I swallow hard, attempting to dislodge the lump that's appeared. "I know. You just moved here. Cassidy and I thought it was someplace you'd like. You have a balcony to write outside on and—"

Mom interrupts with, "Cassidy is in Florida."

"Not anymore. She's back in Boston. She'll—we'll be here this weekend to visit you." I glance at the wall beside the opening that leads into the bedroom. "You know this place. Your painting is here."

It's a print, technically, purchased by my parents on their honeymoon. My father used to joke that Mom loved the piece of artwork more than him. Not very funny now, if you compare the current state of my parents' relationship to how I knew the print was the one item, aside from her laptop, that Mom would want to stay with her.

Mom follows my gaze.

"It used to be in your bedroom, above—"

"Above the dresser," Mom finishes.

"Exactly," I say, relieved. "It's here, with your clothes and your favorite books and the squirrel feeder."

Mom continues staring at the painting.

“It’s even more beautiful in person,” she tells me. “Make sure you go one day.”

“I will,” I promise, my throat thickening as soon as the two words slip out.

I’ve been to the Louvre. I’ve seen that painting in person.

Mom didn’t forget.

I never told her because I went with Otto. And because, after we ended, talking about the beginning or the middle hurt too much.

Chapter 13

Claire

PARIS: SIX YEARS EARLIER

A text from Otto was waiting as soon as my phone's black screen flickered to life, checking to make sure I'd made it back to my room okay. I replied—after screaming into my pillow for at least a minute about the fact that he'd texted. Since then, we've messaged constantly.

About soccer—football, as he relentlessly corrects.

But not only about the reason we're in Paris.

The group stage commences, officially kicking off the Olympic competition. Part of me expected that would be when our texts tapered off, when he started replying *I'm busy* or not responding. No matter how often my phone dings, my heartbeat quickens every time. If the message isn't from him, I'm disappointed. When it is, I soar.

I'm a cliché—crushing on the rich, hot, famous superstar, alongside what I'm sure is a healthy percentage of Germany's, if not the world's, population. I've never been adept at flirting. The few guys I've dated always pursued me. And I was always flattered but rarely invested. I was too focused on making it to this point. Now I'm here, and I've been counting down the final minutes of practice so I can check and see if Otto texted me.

My phone buzzes in my pocket as I walk down the hallway toward my room. My pulse flutters, heart hoping it's him, as I adjust the box under my arm—a care package from my mom—then round the corner. I nearly trip when I notice the tall figure leaning against the wall next to my door.

He's facing away, head down, yet I recognize the broad shoulders instantly.

"How did you get in here?" I hiss, casting a quick glance over my shoulder as I rush the remaining steps toward my room.

There are plenty of spaces in the Village where athletes from different countries can mingle. Residential housing is supposed to be segregated.

Otto turns, flashing me a smile that I feel everywhere. "Hi to you too. I pretended to be American."

His impression is impressive. There's no trace of the accent that clips some consonants.

"You still need a badge," I remind him, pulling mine out of my pocket to hastily unlock my room.

My teammates were downstairs, eating dinner, when I stopped by the post office, but that doesn't mean none of them are on this floor by now. I'm frazzled—thrilled—he's here, and I have no clue how to react to it. Again, I'm bad at flirting.

Otto motions for me to enter first, then follows. The door swings shut after us. My heart knocks against my ribs with the realization we're together. And alone.

We've texted practically nonstop. I glimpsed him in the cafeteria two days ago, and I watched most of Germany's match against Uzbekistan with Gemma and Mackenzie yesterday.

So, it's especially surreal, seeing Otto—the central focus of a game watched by millions—standing in my messy bedroom. I went yesterday out of curiosity. But I stayed out of necessity because it's so *obvious*, watching Otto in goal, that it is where he's meant to be. I had known he was a big deal before. Witnessing it firsthand was different, and I'm suddenly shy.

If Otto notices my uncertainty, he doesn't let on. He gives my room a quick once-over as he stands in its center.

"Nicer than yours?" I question as I collect some dirty laundry and toss it on the pile in the corner.

The space is smaller and sparser than the dorm I lived in freshman year, but it's fully functional. A twin bed, a side table, a desk, and a metal frame with hangers that serves as a closet are the only furniture. I lucked out with a single since most of my teammates are sharing.

"It is cleaner," Otto says, sprawling on my neatly tucked comforter like he's been in here a million times before. "Wirtz is messy. And he snores."

He's on my *bed*.

"So, you came here to get some sleep?"

Otto smirks, making my rapid heartbeat even more irregular. "Not exactly."

Is he here for sex? Does he want to have sex with me? I'm unprepared for that to take place. I would have showered and shaved and—

"These your family?"

I refocus on Otto, who's picked up the framed photo on the

small table beside my bed—the one personal item aside from the clothes, toiletries, and soccer gear scattered around the room.

"Yeah." I take a seat on the edge of the foam mattress, leaving a foot between us, glancing quickly at the photo even though I could describe it from memory.

It was taken at my eighth-grade graduation from Arlington Middle School. It's the final picture of my full family together. My dad dropped the divorce bomb a few days later.

"Are they here?"

I swallow hard before answering, "No."

Mom would be cheering me on in person, if she could. She's on tour for her latest book. Last I talked to Cassidy, she was "super busy," studying for her real estate exam and dating a chef named Marcus. It's entirely possible my dad doesn't know I'm in Paris. I sure didn't tell him.

Otto sets the photo back down, leaning back against the white plaster wall and crossing his ankles.

"What about you?" I ask. "Are your parents here?"

Our families are one of the few topics we haven't discussed. I haven't brought it up because I avoid talking about mine.

The pause before Otto says, "No," suggests he hasn't broached it for a similar reason. He hesitates, and I think that solitary syllable might be his only reply, but he continues a few seconds later. "My mom had me young. I have never met my dad. My mom died a long time ago. I lived with my grandfather until I was nine, and then I started training at Kluvberg's Academy."

I stare at him, startled and unsettled by the matter-of-fact depiction of what sounded like an awfully bleak childhood. "I'm so sorry about your mom," I say. "I-I didn't…know."

That second sentence felt necessary to add because people are invasive enough with celebrities. I'm guessing parts of his background are public information. I want to know Otto based on what he chooses to share with me, nothing else.

He nods. "I used to make up stories. I would tell people my dad was in the military or my mom was a spy. Sometimes, I would say they were happily married and on a trip. I never shared the truth with my teammates. Still avoid the question in interviews. It is in the past, and I am focused on the future."

I frown. "You get asked about your personal life in soc—football interviews?"

He smiles when I correct myself. "Yes. Often."

"I guess that makes me glad no one has ever wanted to interview me."

"They will," Otto says confidently.

Warmth unfurls in my chest. There are plenty of people who have encouraged me over the years. Mom…teammates…coaches…friends…boyfriends, until they lost patience, have all offered support. But that's different from belief. From certainty. Otto makes it sound inevitable that I'll matter enough in this sport that someone will care what I have to say. That faith would mean something coming from anyone. It means the most, coming from him.

"I don't talk to my dad," I confess. "He divorced my mom and married the woman he'd been cheating on her with a few months later. My sister, Cassidy, went to their wedding, but I refused to. Even my mom tried to get me to go, saying I'd regret it later."

"Do you regret not going?"

"No. But I do…I do miss my dad. When I was younger, we were really close. I wanted to be a zookeeper—"

He smiles. "A zookeeper?"

"Shut up. I was six." I knock my knee against his rock-hard

thigh and sort of...leave my leg leaning there. "My dad grew up in Detroit. Every summer, we'd go visit my grandparents for a week. When I was in my zookeeper phase, he would bring me to the Detroit Zoo every single day. I got a token from this souvenir machine, and I still carry it around with me everywhere. I've never played a game without it in my pocket." I pull it out now, dropping the coin on the comforter between us.

Otto picks it up, peering at the impression stamped on the surface, shiny from years of being transferred around. My stomach flips when I see the flat piece of metal dwarfed by his huge palm. He might as well be holding a chunk of my heart—that's how exposed I feel. Even my mom doesn't know I still carry that around.

I laugh awkwardly. "Please tell me you have a good-luck charm so I feel less weird about it."

Otto carefully sets the coin next to the framed photo. "No good-luck charm. But not because I think it is weird. Nothing I care about enough to carry around."

He hasn't moved his leg away. Neither have I. An electric current is pulsing from that point of contact, wreaking havoc on my nervous system.

I like my body. I can run ten miles without stopping, and I always beat every boy in gym class during sit-up contests. But my body isn't the svelte sort of fit-but-not-too-muscular model frame most guys seem to fantasize about. I beat one of Nolan's buddies in a drunken arm-wrestling match, and the next morning, Nolan suggested I should lay off lifting for a while. I broke up with him two days later, but I hate how that comment has stuck in my head for so much longer.

Now, I'm wondering if Otto likes my body. If he'll care that I'm wearing a spandex sports bra or about the scrape on my knee from a tackle earlier that's raw and red.

There was a moment, before I climbed out of his car, when I thought Otto might kiss me. He didn't. He hasn't, and it's feeding all my insecurities, which were already multiplied by the fact that he's not only a hot guy, but he's also an international soccer star who must attract attention anywhere he goes.

And I'm…me.

I fiddle with the flap of the box from Mom, searching for something witty to say. Swear when my thumb catches on the rough edge and cardboard scrapes a slice of skin away. Blood wells immediately, trickling down to my palm, and I curse again.

"Here." Otto's grabbed a handful of tissues, pressing them against the cut.

"Thanks," I say, suppressing a wince. I'm annoyed at myself, more than in pain, for ruining the moment.

I climb off my bed, hustling into the attached bathroom to wash my hand. The cut is shallow, but it'll scab. Possibly scar. I hunt through my toiletry kit for a couple of Band-Aids while Otto hovers in the doorway, repeatedly asking if he can do anything.

"All good," I state, flashing him my bandaged thumb.

He catches my hand in his, which I'm not expecting, peering at my thumb. "Are you sure?"

"I'm sure." My voice is breathy, and I think he hears it.

He's so close. I could—

Someone pounds on my door, followed by, "Claire!"

Mackenzie's voice.

My stomach drops. *Shit.*

I glance at the window, and Otto laughs.

"No fucking—"

I slap a hand over his mouth, feeling his smile press against my palm. Shivers race down my spine in response.

"Don't say anything," I whisper, reaching for the hem of my shirt.

He stays silent after my hand drops. But I think it has more to do with surprise than the instruction as I slide the straps of my sports bra off my shoulders next. His Adam's apple bobs once, and heat streaks through me.

"Claire!"

"One sec!" I call back.

I reach for the towel hanging on the back of the door and wrap it around my torso, taking the second smaller one and covering my hair with it.

I take a deep breath, then open the door a crack.

"Hey—" Mackenzie pulls up short, mid-step, when she realizes I'm not opening the door any wider.

"Hey. I just got out of the shower," I lie. "What's up?"

"We're watching a movie in Lucy's room. You in?"

"Uh...maybe." My grip tightens on the door handle. "I've got to get dressed, and then I was going to call my mom."

Mackenzie nods. "Cool. Stop by if you feel like it."

"Okay. Thanks." I close the door, then release a relieved exhale.

I glance at Otto, who's leaning casually against the wall between the door and my bed, a wide smirk on his face.

I hang up the towels and fix my bra straps. "If Mackenzie had found out you were in here, the entire Village would have known by tomorrow."

He nods. "I should leave before it gets late. Beck wants to meet. I just wanted to wish you good luck before your match tomorrow."

"Oh. Thanks. You coming?"

His second nod floors me. That was a joke.

I laugh nervously. “No, you’re not.”

He grins. “Yes, I am. Beck changed our training time so he could support Saylor. I want to see you play.”

“I won’t play. I’m not a starter.”

“So? That does not mean you will not play.”

“You *really* don’t have to come.”

“Do you not want me to?” Otto looks uncertain all of a sudden, and it occurs to me that maybe he’s not as sure as he seems about everything.

I step closer, shrinking the distance between us down to inches. His gaze dips to my cleavage, and I get an answer to one question. He doesn’t care about my sports bra. His eyes are heated, hungry, as they scan my exposed skin.

“I want you to,” I whisper.

And then I rise up on my tiptoes and kiss him.

Chapter 14

Otto

Much sooner than I expected to be, I'm back in Germany. Beck insisted on picking me up from the airport, and he's driving a black SUV that became his default ride once his daughter was born.

"You didn't need to do this," I tell him, watching Kluvberg's familiar scenery fly by outside. It's nice to look out the window and know exactly where I am.

Eliza didn't hesitate to tell me to take all the time I needed after I explained the situation, even though this trip meant I'd be missing the first game of the season. So, with no excuse not to, I booked the flight home.

Beck scoffs at my comment, not bothering to reply. "You look good," he says instead.

The sling is gone. It's a massive improvement, not wearing a physical reminder of my injury, but it doesn't change the fact that my shoulder is still stiff and sore.

"I always look good, *Kaiser*."

I grin when he includes *großspurig* in his response.

He's smiling, too, obviously relieved I'm in a better mood than the last time we talked. "Boston not as bad as you thought?"

"It wasn't the city I wanted to avoid."

I *feel* his surprise. It fills the practical car.

When we don't discuss football, we talk about Beck's life. Saylor and Gigi. Sometimes Sophia and whether Aster is worthy of her. We don't discuss my life.

At least Beck attempts to mask his shock as he cautiously asks, "What do you mean?"

I don't answer right away.

I've never discussed Claire with anyone. I don't know where to start. How much to say. Six years later, the past still feels too raw to talk about. The present—how often I catch myself staring at her without ever choosing to—scares me as much, maybe more, than my torn shoulder. She's a player; I'm currently her coach. She lives in Boston; I live here. She's moved on; I thought I had. Maybe mentioning some of it aloud will relieve some of the pressure in my chest.

"Remember the Paris Olympics?" I ask him.

Beck grins. "Of course."

That tournament means something different to every other German player who was on the roster.

I glance out the window. We're outside the city limits, looming mountains visible ahead. I'm staying at my house tonight instead of my flat near Sieg Stadium since it's closer to Tannfeld. I told Mila I would drive Opa to his surgery, so I have to be there first thing in the morning.

"I met someone there. Didn't see her for six years. She plays for the Siege now."

"She's *American*?"

"So is Saylor."

Beck scoffs. "I'm aware of my wife's nationality, Berger."

I resume staring out the window.

"What happened?"

"It didn't work out," I say dully.

"I put that much together since you've never mentioned this woman before. Just like you hadn't told me Juliette was moving in with you, and then she was there when I came by after practice. This happened six years ago, and you're bringing it up now. Why?"

"I was just… I was nervous about seeing her again." The longer we discuss Claire, the more likely I am to say something stupid. "I'm flying back through New York and getting dinner with Juliette."

I expect Beck to focus on that revelation, especially since he just brought my ex-fiancée up. Instead, he asks incredulously, "You were *nervous* about seeing her again?"

Something stupid…like that.

I'm energetic, not anxious, before matches. I'm usually volunteered for extra press interviews because I don't clam up like some of the guys do. Confidence is never something I've lacked. So, yeah, I guess this is the first time I've admitted to being nervous about anything.

"Did you hear me, about Juliette?"

"I heard you." A pause. "You nervous about seeing her?"

I scowl. If Beck wasn't driving, I'd shove him. "Fuck off."

"Was she nervous about seeing you?" His voice has lost its teasing edge. He's serious.

"Stunned, I think. I hadn't told her I was coming."

"Had you guys talked since Paris?"

"Not a word."

"Were you—"

"Can we stop talking about it? Please?"

"Sure. It's not like you ever hung a banner that said *Saylor Scott's Inspiration* for the entire fucking club to see. I'll respect your privacy."

I roll my eyes. "Well, it all worked out for you, didn't it?"

I'm taken aback by the note of bitterness in my voice, and I think Beck hears it too.

"It didn't all just work out, Berger. It took a lot of work to get there, to figure things out. But I love her, so I fought for us."

"I didn't fight," I admit. "That's why it didn't work out. And I'm reminded of that every time I think about her and every time I look at her now, and that fucking pisses me off."

"Does she know that?"

I shake my head. "She's moved on. She—there's no point."

A pause.

"You're meeting with Wagner while you're back?"

"Yeah."

"If you mention you'd recover better here, he'd—"

"No." I startle myself with the swiftness and surety of my reply.

If we'd had this conversation before I left for Boston, I might have given a different answer. But I knew then that I didn't have to go. If I'm being entirely honest, part of me *wanted* to see Claire again, as much as I was dreading it. And now that I have, I feel compelled to stay in Boston for as long as I committed to.

"I've got a routine there," I add. "I like the doctors. And once I'm cleared for some activity, the Siege facilities will be perfect to work out in. They're private and brand-new."

"All right," Beck says. "It's your decision, Berger."

I appreciate him choosing not to mention that those are flimsy excuses.

Or pointing out that dinner with Juliette didn't make the list of reasons to return.

• • •

The following morning, I climb behind the wheel of my newest Audi and drive to Tannfeld. Driving, like just about everything, is a lot easier without the sling. Not that I let it stop me. The only times I hired a professional driver since my injury were returning from the hospital and going to the airport last month.

It's not just the lack of a sling. The country roads are wide open, and I allow the speedometer to drift higher than the speed limit. The hit of adrenaline improves my mood…up until I park in my grandfather's driveway.

I'm expecting the surprised scowl that spreads across Opa's wrinkled face when he opens the door.

"What are you doing here, boy?"

He looks thinner than he did last summer. Paler, too, although that's typical this time of year. Leaning heavily on a cane, unsteady on his own feet.

Last visit ended with a slammed door, so I squeeze through the doorway before he has a chance to repeat that trick. "*Hallo*, Opa."

He repeats the same question while I give the first floor a cursory sweep. It's cluttered, but not a complete mess. His recliner's in its usual spot. Stacks of books surround it, too many to fit on the stuffed shelves.

I've had fans scream and sob when they catch sight of me. My own flesh and blood can't manage to wipe the annoyance I flew four thousand miles to be here off his face.

"I'm here to drive you to the hospital," I answer curtly. "Are you ready?"

"Mila is driving me."

I pinch the bridge of my nose, cursing the headache building at the base of my skull. I think I'm just hungover from the beers I had after Beck dropped me off last night, plus jet lag, but it might be a migraine. The specialist I went to a few years ago gave me a list of potential triggers that I've half-heartedly avoided. I might have to make a better attempt.

"Do you have any painkillers?" I ask, continuing into the kitchen.

Scuffing and tapping tells me my grandfather is following me.

"I have a head—" I pull up short, staring at the open bottle of Korn on the counter.

I thought Opa's clumsiness was due to his bum hip. Another equally plausible explanation is, he's drunk, just like he normally is.

I don't remember if he drank before my mom died, but he sure did after. And it's a destructive hobby he's stuck with ever since. I don't know where—or how—he gets his supply since it's the one aspect of his life I've never facilitated, but the cabinet's always full. I dumped every bottle in the house one summer in my teens. The next time I returned from the academy, it was full again.

"Are you fucking serious?" I ask, glancing at his stony expression. "You're supposed to have surgery today."

"I'll drink whenever I damn want." Opa limps over to the faucet, adding some water to a half-full glass of suspicious contents.

"Is that how this happened? Were you drinking when you fell down the stairs?" I huff a frustrated sigh, then head into the half bath located off the kitchen.

Once I've located and swallowed a couple of pills, I return to the kitchen.

It's empty.

I groan, aiming a murderous glare at the liquor cabinet as I pass it by.

Opa is in the living room, reclined in his favorite armchair with today's paper. He reads it cover to cover every single day. Although, based on his blank look whenever I talk about teammates, he skips the football articles.

"Time to go," I tell him.

I'm not sure they'll even be able to operate on him in this state, but we'll find out.

"Mila is driving me."

I sigh. "No, she's not. Mila called me, told me about the surgery, and knows I'm here to drive you to it."

The revelation seems to upset him more than my presence.

Most of the time, I'm relieved that Mila's role allows me to carry on with limited interaction with my grandfather. Other times, like now, I realize it's widened the gulf between us. We communicate with each other almost exclusively through her. We didn't always have that shortcut, and it meant we spoke directly. Not often, but more than we do at present.

"Do you need me to help you get to the car?" I ask, knowing it'll get him moving.

The only thing Opa loves more than alcohol and arguing is proving people wrong.

Sure enough, he lumbers to his feet a few seconds later. More agilely than I was expecting. He reaches for the glass on the table, but I'm faster, swiping it away.

Opa glares. "A man should get to spend his last day how he wants to."

He's scared.

The realization hits me with the subtlety of a sledgehammer, coming from someone whose default settings are grumpy and grumpier. Who would deny being scared until the day he is dead.

"It's not your last day. I had surgery at the same hospital and survived." I open the front door, nodding for him to walk out first. "You'll be fine."

I use the hidden key to lock the front door while Opa watches like he's expecting me to mess up the simple task. I should have parked closer to the door, but I was attempting to maintain the element of surprise.

Offering to move the car will only irritate him more, so I walk behind him instead, ready to assist if necessary. He grumbles the entire walk, about the overcast weather and the neighbors' yapping dog and the ridiculous car I drive. My sympathy well is dry by the time he's inside. Steps dragging, I walk around the rear, delaying the drive that's to come.

I say nothing as I click on my seat belt and start the engine. We coexist mostly peacefully in silence.

"They must be making a real fuss over your recovery."

I glance at Opa, taken aback. He has some sense of my success—he knows I can afford to hire him help, and he's seen his neighbors ask for my autograph—but he's never directly acknowledged any of what I've accomplished. Probably because doing so would imply my decision to pursue football wasn't the massive mistake he made it out to be.

He's never apologized.

I've never offered any forgiveness.

We're frozen around each other, stuck at the same impasse.

Yet I think that was his own stubborn way of asking if I was okay.

"They are. There's a whole team of specialists working with me. The doctors expect I'll make a full recovery, be back in goal this summer."

He grunts. "Football won't last forever, boy."

Neither of us says anything else for the remainder of the drive.

Chapter 15

Claire

Chicago—an opponent we should have easily beaten—wins by two goals in our first game. At least I didn't have much time to get attached to the possibility of an undefeated season. It's gone, just like that, morale dissipating with it.

Otto—Coach Berger—missed the game.

"He had to return to Germany for a family emergency," was the explanation Coach Taylor provided us before the match.

Which sparked intrigue and concern among the entire team because the novelty of our new coach hadn't worn off yet.

But no one on the team, aside from me, knows that Otto doesn't have any family. None that he's close to at least, unless things have changed drastically.

Maybe they have. I mean, it's been six years. My life isn't identical to how it looked when we met.

I stare at the exterior of my parents' house, tired and

annoyed. Maybe we should sell it. Mom has settled well at Echo Glen. And she's not going to get any better, only worse. Chances are, Cassidy will end up moving too. Before she called to tell me she was coming home, she'd never expressed any intention of living in Boston long-term.

And I… I could start over, sort of. Selling would make money a non-issue for a while. Allow me to play without worrying how to stretch my salary.

I sigh. I'm not sure I can let this house go. I can't let the silly Detroit Zoo token go; it was in my pocket during our loss earlier. I keep paying more to fix this car than it's worth, because Mom went with me to pick it out. I can't stop thinking about Otto, my memories a muddled mess of moments from Paris and "*It's good to see you*," and "*I know how long it's been*."

I shouldn't be worrying about what might have been urgent enough for him to rush home. I could ask; I still have Otto's number saved in my phone, assuming he hasn't changed it—which is a big if, based on his level of fame.

But I can't call him. I don't even know why I would want to.

I bang my skull against the headrest once, then climb out of the sedan and start up the front walk. My hand slides into my pocket, thumb rubbing against the grooved side of the coin. It hardly weighs anything, but it's a comforting heaviness anyway.

"Claire! Claire!"

I glance left, spotting Lydia shuffling this way.

"How did the game go?" she asks eagerly.

She brought Tommy to our preseason game last weekend since Cassidy had a training seminar for work and came to some matches with Mom last season.

I force a smile. "We lost."

Lydia's face falls. "Oh, I'm sorry, honey."

I shrug. “It happens. Can’t win them all.”

Win Some, Lose Most could be the title of my autobiography.

“Maybe this can be a good-luck charm.” Lydia holds out the maroon scarf she’s carrying. “I finally finished it. Matches your hat.”

“Thank you so much.”

I give her a tight hug, and she pats me on the back.

“Let me know the next time you head down to visit your mom. I knit her some socks.”

“I will.”

Lydia gives me a sympathetic smile, which makes me think I’m not doing a great job of hiding my disappointment about the loss, and then heads back into her house.

I continue inside, calling out, “Cassidy? Tommy?”

A cheerful, “In here,” comes from the living room.

I hang up my coat and the scarf from Lydia in the front closet, then continue down the hallway and into the living room.

Cassidy’s curled up on the couch, nursing a glass of wine and flipping through a paperback.

“One of Mom’s?” I ask.

“Mmhmm.” She reaches for her glass, swallowing a healthy sip. “I’m, like, ten books behind.”

I smile as I sit on the rug. Mom’s written over thirty mystery novels, churning out one a year ever since she started writing during her maternity leave with Cassidy. By the time I arrived, it was her full-time career.

“Let me guess. You’ve read them all.”

“It’s not a competition, Cass.”

On the days Mom’s recollection of reality blurs, she retreats into her fictional worlds. I tried to reach her there.

I crane my neck to see the cover. “Who do you think did it?”

"The brother seems suspicious to me. Why was he wet when—don't make that face!"

"What face?"

"That face. It's not the brother?"

I lie flat on my back, lifting a leg to stretch my hamstring. "I said nothing."

"I was sure it was the brother," Cassidy mutters.

I drape an arm over my eyes, hiding my smile with the sleeve. It is the brother.

"Where's Tommy?"

"Dad and Lindsey took him to the park."

"Fun."

Cassidy sighs. "Lindsey offered to plan his birthday party."

Our stepmother has her own event planning business. By reputation, it's considered very successful, one of the more coveted companies in Boston. But I've never attended a party they've thrown, including Lindsey's wedding to my father, so I really couldn't judge for myself.

"He's turning five," I say flatly. "Is it going to be black tie?"

"Actually, she's on board with the dinosaur theme. And she agreed it would be nice to have it here."

I scowl into my fleece. Obviously, I was planning to attend my nephew's birthday party regardless. But if it's hosted here, my dad and Lindsey will be inescapable. I've managed to avoid them every time they stop by, sometimes purposeful and sometimes happy coincidence, but that can't last forever.

"Dad said he's texted you a few times…and no response."

I sit up, reaching for the open wine bottle on the coffee table and taking a swig straight from the bottle.

Cassidy's lips purse as she watches me. This is a rare reversal of our usual roles.

"I thought we talked about you not discussing me with Dad."

"I was just passing along the message," she says tersely.

"Thanks," I reply sarcastically. "Much appreciated."

I take another sip from the bottle, and my sister studies me. I don't appreciate her expression—a mixture of exasperation and concern. She's my older sister, but most people would guess the opposite.

"I'm sorry about the game earlier."

"Thanks," I mutter, shifting position so I can stretch my other hamstring. No sarcasm this time. "And thanks for coming."

I'm upset about the loss. I didn't play well, letting too many attackers approach Daniela. Letting my teammates down has happened before. But today was the first time Cassidy had seen me play since high school. Tommy's been talking about going to the game nonstop since Lydia brought him to the scrimmage last weekend. It feels like I disappointed them, too, even though Cassidy couldn't care less about soccer and Tommy probably won't remember it in a week.

"It wasn't what I expected."

I glance up. "What do you mean?"

"That stadium is huge. And I swear, half the people there were wearing your jersey. Tommy told every number five that he saw that you're his aunt. You *are* a celebrity."

I laugh. "Hardly."

"I sent Josh some photos. He wants to come to a game."

"Is he still in San Diego?"

"Yep." Cassidy checks her phone, smiling at the screen before firing off a quick reply. To Josh, I'm guessing.

"The conference going well?"

Josh does something in medical sales, but I'm fuzzy on the details. I think Cassidy is, too, based on her explanation of his job. But it seems like he's been very successful at it.

"I think so. He's at a lunch with some colleagues now."

"And clearly paying *very* close attention," I comment as her phone buzzes with another new message.

"Well, duh, he'd rather sext me."

"Ew. Can you do that somewhere else?"

"I was in here first. Don't be a prude, Clairey."

I lie back down on the floor with a sigh.

"What about you?"

"What about me?"

"Are you seeing anyone?"

I aim an incredulous look at her. "We've been living together for almost two months, and you think I have a secret boyfriend?"

"Well, I don't know. We haven't talked about it. You mentioned that lawyer, like, once over a year ago and no one since."

"I'm not seeing anyone."

"Why did you and"—a pause as she searches for his name—"Simon break up?"

"I ended things with *Steve* because I didn't have time for a relationship. I'd just signed with the Siege, and things with Mom were…progressing. It wasn't working."

More silence before Cassidy says, "I'm sorry I wasn't here."

"I wasn't trying to make you feel guilty. That's just… That's how things were then."

"Would you get back together with Steve now?"

I don't have to think about it. "No. The only guy I'd ever—" I stop talking abruptly. I blame the wine. In season, I rarely drink. My alcohol tolerance is practically nonexistent.

"Who?" Cassidy asks eagerly. "Nolan?"

My incredulous laugh won't stay contained. "God, no."

I haven't spoken to—much less thought about—Nolan since that phone call in Paris.

The flash of hurt that crosses Cassidy's face is brief, but not so short that I miss it entirely.

The end of my college years overlapped with the start of Cassidy's post-grad life. We spoke infrequently and rarely about anything meaningful. I never shared many details about my breakup with Nolan, and I realize Cassidy assumed that meant I was too heartbroken to discuss it.

"I've been over Nolan for a long time," I explain.

"Then who—"

The doorbell interrupts Cassidy's question.

I roll on my stomach, then stand. "I'll get it."

"It's probably Dad," Cassidy warns once I'm already a few steps from the doorway.

I swallow hard, nod, then continue walking. I can't put this off forever.

As soon as the door is open, a blur of teal collides with me. "Claire!"

"Tommy boy!" I hoist him up in the air, planting a kiss on his cheek. "Did you have fun at the park?"

He nods. "Grandpa played goalie so I could practice my penaty shots."

"Penalty," I correct gently as I set him down. "And good. You'll have to show me later."

I take another deep breath, then shift my attention to the figure hovering on the front porch.

Cassidy and I both look more like Mom, but I can see traces of my appearance in my father. Our eyes are the same green, and I inherited the cinnamon shade of his hair, although it's curly, like Mom's. But the rest of him is unrecognizable from the man who used to block my shots in the nearby park.

"Hi, Dad."

"Hello, Claire." He flashes an uncertain smile at me.

Tommy tugs on the hem of my fleece. "Can you make me ants on a log?"

"Of course. One sec."

I'm eager to end this interaction with my father as quickly as possible, but not so cold as to immediately slam the door in his face.

"Okay." Tommy wanders deeper into the house, leaving us semi-alone.

I can hear Cassidy talking in the living room. Lindsey is sitting in the passenger side of the silver Lexus running along the curb. It must be uncomfortable for her, visiting my mother's house. She and Dad never had a reason to come over here before Cassidy and Tommy moved in.

"Tommy is quite the soccer fan," Dad comments. "That's all he wanted to do at the park."

I nod, fighting the urge to fidget. "I'm glad you guys had a nice time."

"He's a great kid."

"He is," I agree.

Dad exhales. "I was hoping we could—"

"Hey, Dad!" Cassidy appears beside me, her wide smile genuine and bright. "Thanks so much for taking him to the park."

Dad's expression is open and happy, nothing like when he was looking at me. It's my own fault that I have essentially no relationship with my father. I've pushed him away at every opportunity.

But there's a stab of envy as I watch them chat easily about Tommy's party and make plans to eat lunch together this coming week.

"I should make Tommy's snack," I say after they've sorted their plans. "Bye, Dad."

The transformation in his face is immediate as he glances at me. Tentative. "Bye, Claire. If there's a good time to talk, I'd really like to."

Talk about Mom, he means. Maybe Cassidy's stopped passing information along, like I asked. Maybe he wants to know details she doesn't. I was the one at doctor's appointments and meetings with lawyers.

I nod. "I'll text you."

I probably won't, and we both know it. But he doesn't call me out on it. Our conversations are as awkward for him as they are for me.

I spin in my socks and hustle down the hallway after a giggling Tommy, shouting, "Ant attack!"

As I slip and slide along the varnished floorboards, I wonder if my dad recalls doing the same thing with me.

Chapter 16

Otto

Juliette looks the same as the last time I saw her—watching from a window as she climbed into the back seat of a chauffeured car while the driver loaded her luggage. I spot her instantly, willowy and blonde, as soon as I step inside the upscale restaurant she suggested we eat at.

I've contemplated canceling this dinner more than once the past few weeks. I even wound up with a good excuse, thanks to my last-minute return to Kluvberg. But the scheduled flights ended up aligning perfectly for me to fly back to the States via New York, then take a train back to Boston early tomorrow morning. If I'd flown into Logan directly, I would have missed tomorrow morning's practice.

Maybe I took the seamless logistics as a sign that this night was meant to happen.

Mostly, I'm looking for a distraction from the woman who

occupied my thoughts while I sat in a waiting room for two hours. After a surgeon informed me Opa's procedure had gone smoothly and I could see him soon. As I dumped all the liquor in his cabinet down the kitchen sink. On the drive to the airport.

I can't stop thinking about Claire, and I need to.

"Otto!" Juliette trills my name, rising from her chair with swan-like elegance as the maître d' leads me over to a corner table situated right by the windows.

This is not a restaurant I would have chosen. I might have the money necessary to eat at a place like this, but I'm a boy from Tannfeld beneath it all. I can already tell, walking past some tables that have already received their food, that I'll have to order room service oncc I'm back at the hotel. Most of the portions are smaller than my fist.

"Juliette," I greet, brushing my mouth against each cheek in the expected greeting.

The fragrance she's wearing fits this setting. Floral and bubbly, like orchids and champagne.

"New perfume?"

She steps away, lips pursing as she reaches for the flute of sparkling wine set next to her plate. "No."

I force a smile. "It's nice."

Juliette never appreciated my abject lack of interest in fashion or beauty when we were together, and that doesn't appear to have changed since we broke up.

I take the chair across from her, accepting a menu from the maître d'. I make eye contact with a woman seated one table over, and she quickly stops staring. I can still feel other eyes on us.

They likely recognize Juliette, not me. I'm a German goalkeeper who's not even an active player at the moment. She's plastered on billboards across the city. I passed two on the drive from the airport to the hotel.

"It's so wonderful to see you." She smiles, and it's poised, like everything else about her.

I thought living with Juliette—planning to marry her—might reveal another side. That escalating the seriousness of our relationship would lead to moments between us that were more messy or vulnerable. Real.

But we never moved past the stage of playing parts. Even our breakup was amicable. I went to practice the following morning; she flew to Milan for a fitting.

"You too," I tell her. "You look beautiful."

She always does, even if it's an icy, reserved sort of ethereal. Attraction was never an issue between us, but intimacy sure was.

Juliette preens with pleasure at the compliment.

"You're in New York for a shoot?" I reiterate what she already told me, trying to spark some neutral conversation.

I'm not sure what I want out of this evening. We've barely spoken since we broke up, but it doesn't feel like there's a lack of closure.

I'm not sure what Juliette's expecting. Even after a relationship that lasted a year and a half, I have a hard time reading her intentions.

"Yes," she confirms, tapping her manicured fingers on the leather-bound menu. "For Chanel."

"Congratulations," I say, knowing that's a collaboration she coveted for a while.

The *crème de la crème*, she always called it.

"Thank you." Her fingernails tap the side of the champagne flute now. "I was sorry to hear about your season."

"Were you?" I ask wryly.

Juliette was never a football fan. I appreciated our diverse interests at first, liked that she didn't give a shit what I did for a living. We met toward the end of a brutal season, when the spotlight was bright and expectations were high. Being around Juliette was an oasis from the attention and speculation and pressure.

But she also didn't like being isolated at my house outside the city. Didn't like attending football-related events with me either.

Diverse interests started to feel a lot more like a lack of support. Like disdain of the sport I'd dedicated most of my life to.

"I was sorry you got hurt," she clarifies, which is sincere.

I nod. "Thanks."

No matter what she says, Juliette endorsed anything that drew my attention away from football. An injury serious enough to make me sit out the remainder of a season? If that had happened when we were engaged, there might have been a wedding.

Even if we had gotten married, we wouldn't still be together now. I'm certain of that, suddenly.

I wasn't nervous to see her. I didn't plan out what I was going to say tonight on the eight-hour flight to New York. I watched the Siege lose to Chicago and then game footage of Atlanta—the team's next opponent.

I know what it's like to see an ex and realize old feelings are still there.

This? This isn't what it's like.

Juliette calls my name, and my attention jerks back to her. There's a new tightness in the corners of her smile that tells me that wasn't the first time she tried to get my attention.

"Sorry," I say, reaching for my water glass. "Long flight."

She nods, accepting the excuse, but that's exactly what it is. I used to blame football—I was tired from practice, or I was focused on an upcoming match.

Football was only one of the issues in our relationship, and that's especially obvious now that it's a non-factor.

She tilts her head. "Why did you fly back to Kluvberg?"

"Meetings." The lie exits easily before I can even consider telling the truth.

Juliette knows I have a strained relationship with my grandfather. She never met Opa. Never asked to and I never suggested it. If our engagement had ended with a wedding rather than a mutual return to work, I have no idea if my grandfather would have shown up to the ceremony. Juliette used to say he wasn't my responsibility, that Opa was fully capable of making his own choices. Which is true, but I'm certainly not blameless in our estrangement. He was there for me when no one else was, and then I walked away at the first opportunity.

But I don't want to discuss any of that with Juliette, and she's not interested enough in my job to ask for details about work meetings.

"How long are you in New York for?" I question, turning the conversation back to her.

And as Juliette starts talking about the various campaigns she's working on, something occurs to me that I probably should have realized a lot sooner.

When we met, I didn't like that Juliette had no interest in football.

I liked that she didn't remind me of Claire.

Chapter 17

Claire

PARIS: SIX YEARS EAR*LIER*

"C*'est mag*nifique," I comment as we pass a fountain, headed toward the glass pyramid that's far more impressive in person than in photographs.

To my left, Otto *grins. "Tr*es bien."

He's been teaching me some basic French phrases. We started *with, "Tu peux m'appeler* un taxi?"—Can you call me a taxi?—so I don't get stranded again. I also bought a portable phone charger, just in case.

"I can't believe this place exists," I say, switching to English because I have no clue how to say it in French. "Just right here, in the middle of the city. It's like stepping back in time. Is this what Kluvberg is like?"

"Parts of it," Otto replies. "There is a big art museum o*pposite*

*Dom St. L*iobarda, on the other side of the canal." He grabs my hand, tugging me to the left of the glass pyramid. "Entrance is this way."

My entire body buzzes from the sensation of his palm pressed against mine.

"That's the German goalie," someone whispers in English, walking past us.

I glance at Otto. If he heard the comment, he doesn't react to it.

I'm accustomed to soccer being overlooked. Lincoln has a reputation for being a pipeline for professional athletes, but the powerhouse football team steals most of the interest on campus. No one has ever recognized me or looked starstruck.

Forty million.

That's how many results come up if you *search Otto* Berger. I did, once, curious about his age—twenty-three—then quickly shut off my phone like I had been caught doing something forbidden.

He's twenty-three, and his name has forty million results.

I saw a m*an wh*o might have been Matt Damon at a restaurant in Cambridge once. That's the extent of my celebrity exposure up until now.

We reach the main entrance, flanked by twin columns. A group of tourists slows as they walk by, headed in the opposite direction, all staring at Otto.

Again, he appears oblivious to the attention. Or very used to it. In Germany, he must get recognized everywhere.

Rep*eating c'est mag*nifique feels redundant—and I don't know any other impressed French praises—but the entrance to the Louvre is as dazzling as the exterior.

Boston is full of historical buildings. But history is relative.

When you're walking into a palace that was built in the thirteenth century, events of the 1700s sound comparatively recent.

The Louvre is a work of art, housing works of art.

We wander through gallery after gallery, filled with priceless paintings and sculptures. Between rooms, I peer at the map provided by the woman at the admission desk, trying to navigate through the numbered maze.

When I mentioned to Otto I wanted to visit the Louvre to see a specific painting, him offering to accompany me never occurred to me. Him actually coming seemed improbable. But here he is, reading placards and pointing out signs so I can orient us on the map.

Finally, we reach the right room.

I st*are at Les Murmures de* l'Aube, struck by the strange, surreal sensation of familiarity amid foreign. I'm far from an art aficionado, but I would recognize this particular painting anywhere. A framed print of it has hung in my parents'—now my mom's—bedroom since before I was born. The English translat*ion is The Whispers of the Dawn*, according to Otto. For someone who claims his French isn't that great, he seems awfully close to fluent.

I peer as close as I dare to, under the watchful gaze of the docent stationed in the doorway, afraid to accidentally activate a sensor and set off the alarm.

Les Murmures de l'Aube is simple, comparatively, to some of the other works we've walked past today. A woman in a pale blue dress stands, barefoot, at the edge of a mist-covered lake. Her face isn't visible, gaze fixed on the horizon, where a church spire is barely noticeable through clumps of fog that veil a flock of birds in flight. The palette is muted, the brushstrokes precise. It has the haziness of a memory, the scene salient yet half remembered. I asked my mom once what the woman was waiting for, and her answer stuck with me.

"Maybe she's not waiting for anyone. Maybe she's simply standing in the stillness."

"Are you named after her?" Otto asks. He's looking at the card that lists the name of the painting and the artist—Claire Marquant.

I nod.

"Did she paint anything else?"

"Nope. Just this." I stare for a few more seconds, then step back. "Okay. I'm ready to go."

"Are you sure?"

"I'm sure."

I'm also starving, a fact that becomes obvious when my stomach gurgles in the next gallery. We practiced for two hours this morning, and then I scarfed down a quick lunch before meeting Otto.

Otto hears it, smirking as he suggests, "Dinner?"

"Dinner sounds good," I say, secretly thrilled that he's suggesting we extend our outing.

I'm not sure it's that secret at all actually. I think anyone who looks at us would be able to tell that I'm giddy around him.

We wind up eating at a hole-in-the-wall Greek restaurant Otto claimed was excellent—he was right. Then we stop for gelato—sorbet for me—and walk along a lit street that runs parallel to the Seine with our dessert.

Twinkling lights illuminate the bridges. Lush leaves sway overhead, dancing in the warm breeze.

It reminds me a little of the path along the Charles River, where I like to run. I tell Otto about it, and he asks me more questions about Boston.

We finish eating but continue walking. There's something magical about being in Paris, but it's infinitely more special to be exploring the city with him. We could be anywhere, and my stomach would still be filled with bubbles and butterflies.

An older man is playing the violin right next to one of the pedestrian bridges that crosses the Seine.

"Want to dance?" Otto asks as we approach the music.

I glance at him, startled. "What?"

He doesn't ask again. He grabs my hand, pulling me closer to the musician. Other people are dancing—a few older couples and a little girl with her parents—but that doesn't alleviate my self-consciousness as Otto spins me and then pulls me into his chest.

I tip my head back so I can see his face. "I'm not a great dancer."

"You are good at other things."

I smile. "Like French?"

He grimaces a little. "Like keeping Hanna Bjorn from scoring."

I was happy when we beat Sweden, but that's nothing compared to how I feel, hearing Otto compliment my playing. I got subbed in during the second half, and I think there's a decent chance I performed well enough to make it on the field again.

I played in an Olympic match.

And if I can do that, I can be bold enough to ask, "What about kissing? Am I any good at that?"

His eyes flare with heat, fingers flexing around mine. I thought our kiss was good—life-altering really—but it didn't progress any further before Beck called him and Otto snuck out of my room. And he hasn't initiated one since. He's the only hot, famous athlete I know, but I've met plenty of guys. Not a single one has advocated for taking it slow.

"You know you are," he says huskily.

"Then why haven't you kissed me?" I practically whisper the question. If we weren't pressed so close together, I doubt he'd have heard it.

"Because..." His eyes close briefly. "Because I am trying to—I have never done this before."

"Dance?" I quip. "It was your idea."

One corner of his mouth lifts. "I am not sure how to say this."

"Try."

"This is different. With women, I usually just..." He clears his throat. "When I kiss you, I know I am not going to be able to stop. And I want to kiss you—kiss you everywhere. But I want this to be more than that too. It is different with you, Claire."

Maybe it's a line. Maybe this is his big move—acting like I'm the one who's different from the many who came before.

But I believe him.

"It's different for me too," I say, and a full smile breaks across his face. "And I'd really like you to kiss me, if you can control yourself in public. I don't know what France's public indecency laws are—"

His mouth covers mine, and I forget what else I was planning to say.

• • •

My phone buzzes while I'm snuggled up against Otto in the back seat of a taxi, headed back to the Village. I sigh when I see Nolan's name on the screen, quickly turning it over.

"Your ex?" Otto asks in my ear.

"Yep."

"Answer it."

I glance at him—surprised and...hurt. He wants me to talk

to my ex? If the roles were reversed, I'd be thrilled to see him ignore the call.

"I don't want to talk to him."

"You said he keeps calling. Tell him to stop."

"I have," I grumble, but I grab my phone and hit the green button.

I did tell Nolan not to contact me before leaving campus. But not since, and he obviously needs a refresher. My conflict-avoiding self hasn't wanted to deal with it.

I answer the call with a curt, "Hello?"

A long pause stretches before Nolan says my name in a startled tone that tells me he wasn't expecting me to answer any more than I was planning to.

He clears his throat twice before saying, "Hi."

"Why are you calling?" I'm proud of how assertive I sound.

"I, uh, I just..."

I nearly smile, listening to Nolan fumble for an excuse. We didn't part on ambiguous terms. I was very clear our relationship was over, and the extent of our communication since has been me ignoring his attempts to talk to me. He hasn't had to justify the pestering since.

"I'm in the middle of something," I say impatiently. "What is it?"

"Why'd you answer if you were busy?" Nolan shoots back, finally locating his usual petulance.

"Because I'm sick of you calling and texting! We broke up, Nolan. We're done. Over. Finished. What else do you want to talk about?"

"You don't really mean it," he says, sounding very much like a child who had a toy taken away. A distracted toy that never gave him the attention he wanted. Until now, when my limited attention is apparently better than none.

"I do mean it. I…" I plan to add more, but the warm pressure of Otto's palm landing on my bare knee steals the rest of the sentence.

My eyes fly to Otto. He's already watching me, one cheek creased with a dimple.

I feel my pulse everywhere. My fingertips. My knees. Between my thighs.

I try again. "I told you before I left campus that we were over."

Otto's thumb moves, rubbing tiny circles. It's innocent. I've never ever thought of my knee as a sexy spot. But I'm already so wet that I can feel my underwear clinging.

Nolan's talking again, but I'm not listening to a word. It sounds garbled, like I'm underwater and he's above the surface.

Otto's hand is sliding higher up my thigh. Slowly, so slow that I want to grab his hand and yank it higher. I feel dizzy, sucking in an unsteady breath.

Okay? Otto mouths, watching my expression carefully.

I nod rapidly, and he grins.

"*Claire*!" Nolan's annoying voice cuts through the blissful haze.

Otto's palm is halfway up my thigh now.

Our cab driver is oblivious to anything happening in the back seat, awash in shadows, talking in rapid French on the phone. The radio is on, playing a pop song with foreign lyrics. Horns honk around us.

I spend a lot of time recalling the past. Worrying about the future. Right now, I'm entirely consumed by the present.

His hand is under the hem of my dress, pulling it an inch higher and revealing the paler skin usually covered by my soccer shorts. I track its progress like it's the most fascinating sight I've ever seen. I better understand what Otto said earlier, about not being able to stop. I don't care about anything except him continuing to touch me.

"I don't want to talk to you, Nolan. Keep calling, I'll block your number."

I hang up the phone without waiting for a response. Roll my head to look at Otto.

We stare at each other.

His hand is still. About three inches from where I really want him to touch me.

"Can we go somewhere else?" I whisper. "Somewhere we won't have to stop?"

Otto holds my gaze. "Are you sure?"

"I'm sure."

I've never been so sure. Never wanted anyone more.

He smiles, then leans forward and says something to the driver in French.

Chapter 18

Claire

The photos show up the same morning Otto is supposed to return. And they're brought up in the locker room five minutes after I arrive.

"How is New York on the way back from Germany?" Savann*ah* laughs before passing her phone to Reyna.

"It's not," Reyna states, grinning. "Good for Coach Berger. She looks like a model."

"She is a model," Savannah says, grabbing the phone next. "Juliette Dubois. She's the face of, like, everything. Hey, Cascarino!"

Daniela wanders over with a half-eaten apple in one hand. "What's up?"

"Coach ever mention his hot, famous girlfriend to you?" Savannah flashes the screen at Daniela.

She and Kristin are considered the resident Otto experts

since the two goalies are the only ones who have worked with Otto individually.

Daniela shakes her head. "Nope. He pretty much sticks to talking about footwork or catching versus parrying. No gossip."

"What gossip?" Mallory asks, approaching her locker, two down from mine. She drops her bag on the bench and eyes us all speculatively.

"Coach's hot-date detour."

I keep my eyes on the laces of my cleats as I knot them, relieved no one's asking for my input. I'm never up-to-date on pop culture, so my teammates are used to my lack of participation in conversations like these.

I saw the photos first thing this morning, posted on an Otto Berger fan account that popped up on my feed because I stupidly used to follow the page, up until it announced his engagement. He was wearing a suit, she was in a glamorous dress, and they were exiting a fancy-looking restaurant in Manhattan. The caption speculated their engagement must be back on.

I spent most of the weekend worrying what could b*e urg*ent enough for Otto to fly back to Kluvberg and miss our first game, and what was he doing? Wining and dining his former fiancée.

Prick, I think vehemently, conveniently forgetting he has every right to go anywhere and do whatever he wants.

But it feels spectacularly unfair—that he's allowed to do that and then come back. The day I saw his engagement announcement, I didn't have to face him in practice a few hours later. Or listen to my teammates theorize about their relationship. Or know he skipped out on his job to see her.

Maybe he's not even back. Maybe he overslept in some swanky hotel with silk sheets. Maybe he's returning to Kluvberg for good and giving up the assistant coach position he's clearly not committed to.

The worst part of this shitty morning? The possibility of Otto leaving—of never seeing him again—isn't accompanied by relief. My stomach lurches with the same scary sensation as missing a step on stairs, that terrifying moment of slipping from gravity's grasp. The aftermath is a pit of nausea in the bottom of my stomach.

"You see these, Claire?" Savannah asks me, aiming the dreaded phone my way with a cheeky smile.

My least favorite shot is on the screen. Otto is shielding Juliette from the cameras, one arm raised in an ineffective attempt to block the shot and the other curved protectively around her waist, guiding her toward a waiting car.

They look good together. Regal and *rich, like European royalty.*

I make a noncommittal sound that could be interpreted in the affirmative or negative—but hopefully not as I spent twenty minutes staring at them this morning—and quickly stand. "See you guys out there."

My eagerness to leave the locker room backfires when the practice field comes into view.

Otto did return from New York. He must have left at dawn to make it back to Boston this early—unless he chartered a private jet or something—but he looks well rested.

Guess the date didn't go as well as it looked in the photos. That, or he doesn't last as long in bed as he used to.

I deliberate doubling back, pretending to have forgotten something in the locker room or dumping and refilling my water bottle, but I square my shoulders instead.

Otto is talking to Coach Taylor, but his eyes flicker toward me as I approach the sideline. I quickly avert my gaze, dropping my water bottle by one of the benches.

"Good weekend, Caldwell?" Nicole's approaching, carrying a stack of cones.

"It was fine," I reply. "You?"

"Not bad. I saw this great band at Paradise Rock on Saturday night."

I nod and smile. Nicole's the head of goalkeeping, so I don't interact with her as much as Coach Taylor or Coach Jackson. She's younger than them, close to my age, and has always felt like less of an authority figure.

Nicole walks on the field to set up the cones. I start to warm up on my own, jogging in place with high knees for a couple of minutes, then running through a series of leg swings and forward lunges. The entire time, I keep my gaze locked on the white line between my cleats, counting the number of reps in my head.

I've just settled on the turf for some sit-ups when a pair of sneakers too large to belong to anyone else approaches.

Otto announces his presence by saying, "Rough start to the season."

I consider standing, decide that's an unnecessary gesture of respect for someone who skips games to get laid, and lift a hand to shade my eyes from the sun.

It poured all day yesterday. Of course today would be sunny, the sky overhead clear and blue, like Boston is celebrating his return.

I glance at Coach Taylor, bent over a clipboard with Coach Jackson. Neither is paying any attention to us. It's perfectly normal for a player to talk to a coach prior to practice.

But everything about talking to Otto feels charged and forbidden, beginning with my response to his comment about our loss to Chicago.

I adjust my shin guard, then pull up my sock. "You found time to look up the score? Nice coaching."

The words alone are bad enough. But the bitter bite to them is much more damning. I sound mad—I am mad—and I didn't want him to know that. Whether or not he's standing on the sidelines for a Siege game shouldn't make any difference to me. Losing shouldn't have felt worse without him there.

Seconds stretch like hours as I wait for his response. I'm out of line—so far past the bounds that I can't see the perimeter. If it were possible to shove the words back in my mouth, I would.

Otto's still said nothing.

I gather the courage to glance up. He wipes the smile away quickly once I do, but not fast enough.

My eyes narrow. He thinks this is funny?

Otto crouches down a second later, and I fight the urge to scooch back. He's a couple of feet away and too close. Way too close.

"You allowed too much space on the wide plays," he tells me. "Close them down earlier to prevent crosses from coming in."

Fine, he watched the game. Not the same as showing up.

"Will do," I say cooly.

Don't mention New York. Don't mention New York. Don't mention—

"How was New York?"

This time, I manage to keep my tone reserved and polite, but the question itself is bad enough. At minimum, I'm admitting I saw the photos. And people don't normally ask questions they don't care about the answers to.

He holds my gaze. I really want to look away, to yank at the turf or adjust my shin guard again or do anything that's not this searing eye contact, but I can't.

I wait for the clipped, *None of your business*. I'm practically asking to be benched for insubordination. *Me*, who'd never even called a coach by a first name until Otto arrived.

"Not my favorite city, Boston."

I go completely still. I feel like I was just slapped, the surprise hindered by numb shock.

I don't like nicknames. Hate being called Caldy by teammates or Clairey by Cassidy. But I never once protested Otto calling me Boston. I never asked him to stop, but he did anyway.

"Caldwell!"

I startle, my eyes darting from Otto to Coach Green. She's standing by the line of cones, staring this way with a puzzled smile on her face.

"Yeah?" I call back, standing quickly.

Out of the corner of my eye, I watch Otto stand too.

"Could you help me with another line of these?" Nicole asks. "I want to make sure they're straight."

"Of course." I jog onto the field.

I don't look back to see if Otto is staring after me.

But I'm pretty sure he is.

Chapter 19

Otto

"What do you think of Caldwell?"

My grip tightens on the plastic arm of the chair. I wish I had my foam ball to squeeze. "What do you mean?" I ask Eliza.

When she asked me to stop by her office after practice, I figured it was about the photos from last night. If Claire saw them, the entire team must have, and I was right.

Practice was filled with whispers and smirks from the Siege players, and I was a fool not to assume the paparazzi I'm fairly certain Juliette's publicist tipped off would waste no time in plastering the snaps of us all over the place. A model and a professional athlete being spotted together is hardly a rare occurrence, but the public appetite for it remains.

Eliza hasn't brought the photos up. She asked about my grandfather's health and updated me on her practice plan for the week.

And now, we're discussing Claire.

I'd rather explain why I was photographed with my ex-fiancée last night. I'm still shaken from my slipup earlier. I didn't mean to call her Boston; it just came out. And it might have been fine if Claire hadn't frozen as soon as I said it. Her stricken face haunted me for the rest of practice, along with all the wrong assumptions she'd made about my absence. She had a child with someone else. Why does she care who I eat dinner with?

Eliza leans back in her swivel chair, tapping a pen against her desk. "You watched the game against Chicago?"

I nod. "I did."

She sighs heavily. "That should have been a win for us. It wasn't just Caldwell; the entire team underperformed. I thought we had the momentum, coming off such a great preseason."

"One game won't ruin the whole season."

"You're right. But it's a bad start. And Caldwell was sloppy during practice earlier."

I'm seized with a sudden burst of panic. I distracted her today. And I can deal with a lot, but I can't deal with negatively impacting Claire's career.

"She is one of the top defenders in the league," I say. "Her blocks and interceptions are—"

Eliza interrupts, "I'm aware of her stats, Otto."

"Right. Of course." I bounce my knee, then shift in the chair, worried I said too much. That my defensiveness revealed too much.

"Every player has off days," Eliza continues. "The problem with Caldwell's, they affect the entire team. She has a captain spot in every way except seniority. She's who the rest of the team looks up to."

Pride flares as Eliza mentions what I already recognized

from observing the team.

"Her concentration against Chicago was nowhere to be found," Eliza continues. "I had Caldwell talk to a sports psychologist last season, and it didn't seem to help. I was wondering if you'd be willing to do a few individual sessions with her. I think it would be good for her to work with someone unfamiliar. You can offer some new insight."

This.

This, right here, is why I should have been honest from the start. I'm the last person Claire would want individual sessions with, and I'm the furthest thing from unfamiliar. Even ignoring our personal past, I can guarantee I'm better versed in Claire's career than Eliza is. I know the final scores from her last year at Lincoln. What round she was selected in the draft. The standings from her time playing for Denver.

And I can't come clean to Eliza now because I assured Claire I wouldn't say anything.

I clear my throat before answering, "Of course. I am happy to help out however I can."

"Great." Eliza smiles, dropping the pen on her desk. "Nicole has really appreciated your help. McKinnon and Cascarino have been noticeably improving, and you deserve a piece of that credit. We're happy to have you back."

"Happy to be back." I clear my throat. "And about the photos. It was dinner with an old friend—"

Eliza reaches for one of the binders on her desk, waving my explanation away. "You were taking personal time, Otto. How you spent it is your business."

I nod, relieved by her response. Wagner would have had a lot more to say about it. When I met with him, he grilled me on my schedule and how I need to remain focused on recovery.

"It will not happen again," I say.

"Every publication that posted those photos mentioned your current role with this team. Management is thrilled. It's the most publicity the Siege has received since the club's inception. Ticket sales have skyrocketed since this morning."

"Oh. Okay. Well, that is…good."

For the team, maybe. For me, not really. Half the point of coming here was anonymity.

Eliza flips a binder open, effectively dismissing me. "Let me know how it goes with Caldwell."

I stand. "Will do."

Once outside Eliza's office, I continue down the hallway. It dead-ends at one of the doors that leads down to the practice field. I step back out into the sunshine, sucking in deep breaths and releasing long exhales as I follow the short path that leads to the turf.

Eliza's parting comment suggests I'm supposed to approach Claire about working with her individually, and I have no clue how to do that. Treating her the same as any other player isn't getting any easier, and if it's affecting her career… I should probably ask if she wants me to leave and respect the *yes* that's sure to follow. Return to Kluvberg. Get my groceries delivered and run through my rehab exercises in the private gym.

I reach the edge of the field, tucking my hands in my pockets as I survey the turf.

"Hi!"

I spin in place, staring at the young boy standing a dozen feet away. His smile is tentative but friendly, eyes wide as he stares at me and at the field.

They're brown. Not green, like Claire's. But other similarities—the hair and the nose—are unmistakable.

"Hi." I smile back. "Are you here to visit your mom?"

"She's at work." The boy's attention wanders back to the field. I recognize the wistful expression on his face.

"You like fo—" I sigh. "Soccer?"

"Yeah." His voice is quiet, but the excitement is impossible to miss.

"Do you want to play?"

"Really?"

"Yes." I walk over to the equipment shed, using my key to unlock the door and grabbing a ball and a stack of cones out. "What is your name?"

"Tommy Caldwell."

I can't decide if I'm glad or mad that he has her last name. Does that mean his dad isn't in the picture?

"My name is Otto," I say, shoving all thoughts of his connection to Claire far away.

Tommy nods, more focused on the ball than on making conversation.

I smile, setting up the cones. I've assisted with some clinics in Kluvberg, but those children were older. Most of them had already reached the point of taking football seriously. It's been a long time—probably since I was the same age as Tommy—that playing football had no purpose. But that's exactly how it feels, kicking the ball toward Claire's kid and telling him to try to knock over the cones.

Tommy hits three out of five, the smile on his face beaming brighter than the bright sun overhead when I congratulate him on his accuracy.

"This time, try—"

"TOMMY!"

We both glance toward the loud shout, watching Claire sprint this way. She's in jeans but still wearing her practice jersey, her hair free from its usual ponytail and streaming behind her.

She doesn't stop running until she's a few feet away, casting a quick, uncertain glance at me before bending down to Tommy's level. "What are you doing down here? You were supposed to stay with Lydia until I came out to get you. We've been looking everywhere."

"Sorry, Claire," Tommy says sheepishly, looking down and rolling the ball under his foot.

A frown creases my forehead. Why doesn't he call her Mom?

Claire exhales, breathing heavily. With panic more than exertion, I think. "You can't wander around alone. Someone needs to *always* be with you, understood?"

Tommy looks at me. "I was with Otto."

I smile at him. His immediate acceptance of me is cute.

"Otto is a coach," Claire says. "He isn't here to look after you, like Lydia is or like I am. One of us always needs to be with you."

Tommy nods, looking crestfallen.

"I did not mind," I say, like an idiot.

Claire shoots me an exasperated look. I think she's more annoyed with me than Tommy now. "Come on," she tells him brusquely.

Tommy doesn't move. "I want to keep playing with Otto."

"He's busy."

This time, I'm smart enough to keep my mouth shut.

But when Tommy asks, "Doing what?" I have to work to keep the grin off my face.

Claire glances at me, frustration evident in her expression.

I shrug my good shoulder. "I do not mind playing more."

If we'd first met a few weeks ago, I'd understand her reluctance to leave her kid with me. But we didn't.

She holds my gaze for a few seconds, and it's a hold-my-breath moment I haven't experienced in six years. Waiting… Hoping she'll choose to trust me.

"Okay," Claire finally says, and I exhale. She glances at Tommy. "I need to let Lydia know I found you. I'm going to finish changing, and then I'll be back down here to get you. You listen to Otto, and you stay with him, okay?"

Tommy nods somberly. "Okay."

Claire looks to me, mouthing a quick, *Thanks*, before she turns and jogs back toward the building.

"You really think I'm good at soccer?" Tommy asks me, walking over to the abandoned ball.

"I do," I confirm. "Your mom is one of the best players I know."

His nose scrunches up in confusion. "Huh?"

"Claire? Your mom?"

"She's my aunt," Tommy says, as if it's common knowledge.

Maybe it is; I didn't know.

And it should really make no difference. It doesn't mean she's single. Doesn't mean she's thought of me once in the past six years.

But it does mean a wide smile stretches my face as I set up the cones again.

Chapter 20

Claire

Driving home from our weekly visit to Mom, Cassidy casually says, "You're still free tonight, right?"

I glance in the rearview mirror at Tommy, who's happily coloring in a picture book. Rather than scribble inside the lines, Tommy appears to be drawing soccer balls. Since he played with Otto, Tommy's interest in soccer has grown even more.

It was a collision of worlds I was wholly unprepared for. It was one thing for Otto to invade work. Soccer has reminded me of him plenty of times. But my nephew asking me to set up the cones "like Otto did"? That was an unwelcome adjustment. Nearly as hard as watching Otto patiently play with my nephew was. Does he want kids? The closest we came to discussing the topic was a responsible conversation on preventing pregnancy.

"Claire?" Cassidy prompts, and I realize I zoned out.

"Sorry," I say, eyes returning to the road. "Tonight. Yeah.

I'm free."

Cassidy's Saturday nights with Josh have become a standing date at this point.

Yesterday's game was away, against New Jersey, and a much-needed win, so I have tonight and tomorrow off. Icing the ankle I tweaked during a tackle while watching cartoons and eating mac and cheese is my plan for the evening.

None of my childhood friends live in Boston. We'll get together around the holidays when they come back to visit family, but that's it. I needed to be home with Mom, so I turned down most invitations from my Siege teammates, until they stopped coming. Now that Mom's at Echo Glen, I could go out more, but I haven't.

"Great," Cassidy replies brightly. "I asked Lydia to watch Tommy."

"Wait. What?" I glance at her. "Why did you do that? I told you I'd watch him."

"Josh has a college friend visiting this weekend."

It takes me a second, and then the pieces click together.

I groan, "No."

"And we thought it'd be fun to—"

"No," I repeat more forcefully.

My sister continues like I said nothing, "He's nice, and you could use a fun night out. All I've seen you do is work, exercise, and sleep. And worry about Mom. You're coming out with us."

"I hate double dates."

"When have you ever been on one?"

Never, but an outing with my sister, her high school sweetheart, and a guy I've never met before sounds like a bad attempt.

Not that I doubt Josh has decent taste in friends. And

Cassidy and I have been getting along surprisingly well, settling into a new routine centered around taking care of Tommy and visiting Mom. But I'm very much not in the first-date headspace. I'll spend the evening comparing myself to Cassidy, who's always been effortlessly popular with guys. Who knew what to say and what to wear while I never did.

Also, I had a dream about Paris last night. I woke up disoriented, wondering why the Eiffel Tower wasn't in view past my curtains. And wet.

Warmth creeps across my skin as I recall it.

Steve and I broke up over a year ago. I'm not going to hook up with Josh's friend, but I should at least consider dating again.

"It'll be fun, Clairey. A chance for you to catch up with Josh. And we live together, but I hardly see you."

I sigh, knowing I'll agree. Maybe this will be a good transition into dating. Maybe I'll really like the guy. At minimum, it'll make my sister happy.

"I'll go on one condition," I say.

Cassidy sighs. "What?"

"That you pick out an outfit for me. I never know what to wear on first dates."

My sister's laugh is startled. Pleased. "Deal."

...

We meet Josh and his friend outside a new seafood restaurant that recently opened in Seaport. Walker—I don't know his last name—and I smile politely at each other while Josh and Cassidy share a lengthy hello kiss.

"Nice to meet you, Claire," Walker says, holding a hand out.

I shake it, relieved he seems friendly and normal. "Nice to

meet you too. Welcome to Boston."

He smiles. "Thanks."

Walker is a couple of inches taller than me—five-ten or five-eleven. Clean-shaven and wearing a button-down without a single wrinkle in the fabric. He absolutely does not look the type to offer a stranger a ride outside a Paris nightclub or to have a glitzy dinner with a model in Manhattan. The tops of his ears turn red after he looks at my chest—cleavage displayed in a low-cut black top borrowed from Cassidy—which I find endearing.

"It's so good to see you, Claire," Josh greets, giving me a warm hug.

"You too," I reply, smiling when we separate and he immediately reaches for Cassidy's hand again.

Walker works in medical sales, same as Josh. Talking about their respective jobs and the recent conference in San Diego fills the lags in conversation between us being seated and ordering drinks and appetizers.

I'm bored by the topic, but nod along at what I think are the appropriate parts between bites of focaccia dunked in olive oil.

Cassidy mostly beams at Josh.

Her lovestruck expression is a little nauseating to witness, but it's also nice to see my sister look so happy. I'm not sure how serious she and Josh are, if it's just a rekindled flame or a new progression, but after witnessing this, I'm leaning toward the latter. Josh hasn't been introduced to Tommy yet, which is why we met the guys here, but he's looking at Cassidy the same way he did in high school.

The waiter delivers our entrées, which all look and smell amazing. I'm relaxing in my seat, picking up my fork and thinking how tonight is going better than I expected, when I see him.

I recognize Will Aster first because he was—is—rather

infamous in the soccer world. He's from Dorchester originally, which is why his career in Seattle was sometimes covered by local papers. Will no longer plays for Seattle. He plays for FC Kluvberg—a detail that stuck in my head only because of who I associate with that club.

I start searching as soon as I spot Will, my brain already connecting the dots. A beautiful blonde woman is holding hands with Will. A man in a wheelchair, who closely resembles Will, is with them. Behind the three of them is Otto. He's nodding in response to something the hostess is saying. She's leaning over the stand, as close as possible to him, and I frown right as Otto looks this way.

A low buzz hums in my ears, drowning out all the sounds surrounding me, as we look at each other. My appetite vanishes, my stomach more preoccupied with an acrobatic routine than eating. It's the first day he showed up at the Siege facility all over again. His presence at practice and games is one thing. He wasn't supposed to be here.

I look away first, reaching for my full wine glass and swallowing half in one sip. Josh ordered a bottle, and I wasn't planning on drinking any. But I need something to do with my hands. Some distraction from—

"Hello, Claire."

I glance up into Otto's smooth expression. "Hi, Coach Berger."

There's a chuckle from Will—who's behind Otto—that he quickly covers with a cough. It's enough to tell me he's familiar with the Otto I remember meeting, the guy who would have also laughed about being addressed as an authority figure.

The hostess is past our table, holding a stack of menus. Will, the woman, and the man in the wheelchair are all following Otto. He's holding them up, deliberately stopping to talk to me, and everyone at my table is glancing curiously between us.

My cheeks feel like they're radiating heat, and I hope it's not obvious.

This is another collision, with my sister, with the guy I'm on a date with, and all I can think about is last night's dream.

His eyes flick down from my face, so quick that I nearly miss it. His expression doesn't change. I feel like I was just lit on fire. My boobs are nothing special, perky but small, and he's seen them before. But this is the first time I've worn something other than athletic attire around him, and he looked.

"You're one of Claire's coaches?" Cassidy asks, surprise and appreciation evident in her voice.

As separate as I'd like to keep the past and present, it's strange to realize my sister has never met Otto.

"I am. Otto Berger." He reaches out a hand to shake my sister's hand. "You must be Cassidy."

I go completely still. I mentioned my sister's name to him *once*. Years ago. There's no way he remembered that, right?

"I met Tommy the other day, after Siege practice," Otto continues. "Good kid."

"Yeah, I like him," Cassidy says affectionately. She glances at me. "He loves going to visit Claire."

Everyone's looking at me. I force a smile, reaching for my wine glass again.

"When did you start coaching?" Cassidy asks Otto. "You weren't at the first game."

"I am subbing in for part of the season," he replies. "I missed the match against Chicago because of… I had a family matter."

I suppress a snort. The photos of him with Juliette Dubois last weekend were posted all over the place, and that's still the story he's sticking with?

"Enjoy the rest of your dinner," Otto continues. "See you tomorrow at ten, Caldwell."

My head snaps toward him, no longer feigning nonchalance. For a second, I think I've lost my mind, but today is definitely Saturday. Tomorrow, Sunday, is a day off.

Otto's already walking away, continuing after the hostess. The rest of his party follows, headed toward another four-person table closer to the wall of windows that overlooks the water. A waiter is whisking one chair away to accommodate the wheelchair.

I stand, the legs of my chair scraping the mosaic tiled floor that ties in with the restaurant's Mediterranean theme. "I'll be right back," is the only explanation I offer before hurrying after the group.

"Ot—" I catch myself just in time. "Coach Berger, can I talk to you for a minute?"

I'm not sure how he hears me over the overlapping conversations and the music playing, but Otto pauses, saying something to Will before turning and walking back this way.

We meet beside a row of ropes that hang from the ceiling and tie to the floor, serving as a nautical divider between the bar section and the rest of the restaurant.

He tucks his hands in the pockets of his slacks, the rolled-up sleeves of his button-down showing off the raised veins and defined muscles of his forearms. I'm not sure what limitations are still on one shoulder, but his right arm looks no different from his left.

I swallow hard, mouth dry. "I just wanted to clarify, we don't have practice tomorrow?" I'm certain of that, but it comes out like a question.

"The team is not training tomorrow. We are."

"We?"

"You and me."

I shake my head, dislodging some of the strands Cassidy carefully styled earlier. "You're—I don't know what you're talking about."

Otto untucks one hand, and there's a moment when I think he might reach out to brush the hair out of my face. Instead, he runs his thumb along the line of his jaw.

My exhale is dizzying. I'm a little disappointed, which is ridiculous.

"Coach Taylor asked me to do an individual session with you," he tells me.

"Why?" I demand, refocusing on the topic at hand.

"You allowed six turnovers against Chicago."

"I allowed *none* yesterday."

"She asked me to work with you, Caldwell. I am doing my job. Would you rather tell Eliza why you do not want to train with me?"

No, I really wouldn't. Everyone on the Siege—players, staff, Coach Taylor—adores Otto. Media coverage has increased this season. Same with ticket sales. No way am I complaining to my head coach that I can't take criticism from my ex, and Otto knows it.

"You're a goalie," I state. "Not a defender."

"Eliza knows that." A pause. "A few people have also called me one of the best footballers in the world."

Lots of people have called him that. Including me. Still, his arrogance is irritating. Enticing too. Confidence is contagious.

I take a deep breath. Unfortunately, it smells like him. "Does it have to be tomorrow?"

"Do you have a conflict?" The question sounds like a

challenge. His gaze flicks to a spot behind me. To the table I left, maybe.

"It's late notice. What if we hadn't run into each other tonight?"

"We did," he counters. "Is ten too early?"

Another challenge.

I cross my arms. His eyes dip a second time, and I'm awash with heat all over again.

"I—that's—ten is fine."

I'm flustered and frazzled and it's entirely his fault. Or mine, for allowing him to have such an effect on me. Problem is, that effect has never felt like a choice.

"See you then." Otto turns and strides toward his table, leaving me staring after him.

Confused.

Annoyed.

And…excited.

Chapter 21

Otto

PARIS: SIX YEARS EARLIER

I can't stop kissing her.

We stumble into one of Hôtel de Lumière's suites, nearly upending the vase filled with fresh flowers set on a side table. Distantly, I hear the door click shut, distracted by Claire's hands sliding down my chest and slipping under my shirt. We're stepping out of our shoes, colliding with a wall. I've never been this hard, the ache almost intolerable. I could come from this, her needy whimpers and eager lips and how she grinds against my hand when it slips between her thighs. Her lacy underwear is soaked.

My name is a frustrated exhale when my mouth moves to her neck, her head pressing against the wall right next to a framed painting that could be in the museum we visited earlier.

I swipe my tongue over her pulse point, then sink to my knees.

"Why—what are you doing?" Claire asks, confusion creeping into her voice.

Enough to tell me she hasn't done this before, and that's accompanied by a burst of satisfaction.

"Is this okay?"

She bites her bottom lip. "Yes. But you don't…have to."

"I want to. You are wet."

"I know," she says, a trace of embarrassment in her tone.

I hitch her knee over my shoulder. Trail my fingers up along her inner thigh, until my hand is just below the crease of her hip. "You could be wetter."

Claire swears softly as I hook her underwear, pulling it aside and exposing her pink pussy. I swipe her seam with my tongue, then suck on her clit.

Her "fuck" is louder this time, startled and amazed. I apply more suction, then trail my tongue lower to prod at her opening.

Her hands are in my hair now, her hips tilted and legs wide open. Silently asking for more. Begging aloud, too, my name a constant refrain as she comes against my mouth. I kiss my way back down her thigh, smearing her arousal everywhere. It's all I can smell or taste. I slip her leg off my shoulder and stand, smirking at the expression on her face. Dazed green eyes and parted pink lips.

I kiss her again, the bulge of my erection pressing against her stomach. She shoves against my chest, and I step back, thinking she needs a moment. To use the bathroom or to explore the room. This is one of Paris's poshest hotels, the Eiffel Tower visible through the windows.

Instead, she's unbuttoning and unzipping and tugging until my chinos drop and my cock bobs free. Her quick, surprised inhale at first glimpse is almost as good for my ego as how fast she came for me.

I grunt as she grips me, fists clenching as I fight the urge to fuck her hand. Had I known she was going to suggest this detour after our date, I would have jerked off earlier to take the edge off. You don't become a professional athlete by accident though. Discipline is something I have in excess.

Claire's staring as she slowly strokes my dick, tracing the vein that runs its length and then circling the flared tip with her thumb.

I groan, and her eyes lift to meet mine.

"Kinda thought about this all day," she tells me.

"Sex?" I rasp.

Her teeth dig into her lower lip, leaving white impressions behind. "Sex with you."

"If you had mentioned that earlier, we never would have made it to the museum."

She laughs, then kisses me, the collision of our mouths needy and desperate. I tug the strap of her dress down, low enough to reach the clasp of her bra. It droops enough for me to palm her breast, circling the point of her nipple with my thumb.

Claire sucks on my bottom lip, biting gently as her hips rock against mine. We're still against the wall, only a few feet inside the massive hotel suite. Both partially undressed.

Her hand finds my dick again, guiding it between her legs.

We're both breathing heavily, trying to pull in as much air as possible between kisses.

"Claire—"

"Please. I need—I need you to fuck me."

"There is a bed in here," I remind her. "We could have done this"—I palm the wall beside her head—"in your tiny, messy room."

"You're the one who left."

I smile. "I was trying to be a gentleman."

"Well, I don't want you to be a gentleman. I want you to fuck me against the wall because you want me too much to make it all the way to the bed."

I groan, then reach for my pants on the carpet. "Turn around. Hold on to something."

She listens, tugging the other strap of her dress down and tossing her bra away. Her boobs bounce as she bends over the wooden table we almost knocked over when we entered, gripping the ornately carved edge.

I find the condom in my pocket, tearing the wrapper open with my teeth and rolling the latex over my throbbing cock. I push her dress up around her waist and pull her underwear down. My left hand lands on her thigh again, for no reason except I want to touch her, while my right lines my cock up with her cunt, displayed at the perfect height. I feel from the first inch how tight she is. How slippery and slick. I push deeper, feeling her pussy spread to accommodate me. Watching as she takes more and more, moaning the entire time.

I admire how it looks for a few seconds, and then the need to move—to pump—becomes unbearable. I set a brutal pace, deep, steady strokes that she contracts around. My fingers find her swollen clit, tapping in time with my thrusts.

It's quick and dirty and perfect. She comes once, and my entire body is screaming to do the same. I fuck her through her release, her gasps and sobs transitioning into moans again.

The vase of flowers topples, and I don't even notice where it lands.

When Claire convulses for a second time, I let go too. Heat flares as my hips jerk, cum pouring into the condom.

She speaks first, the syllables staccato between rapid breaths.

"*C'est magnifique.*"

I laugh, pulling out of her. There's a box of tissues on the table that didn't fall with the flowers, and I grab two to wrap around the condom, tossing it in the trash can.

Claire turns to face me. Her dress has dropped now that she's standing, and she's entirely naked. My eyes trail over all the exposed skin, lingering on her chest. The skin is pale compared to her tanned arms and stomach from training outdoors. A reminder I get to see her like this. No one else.

"You are so beautiful," I tell her, the rest of my English vocabulary falling spectacularly short.

Sex isn't usually a conversation. It's a physical act, a release that helps me perform at my peak. Sure, it's fun, but it serves a purpose. It's an outlet, same as eating well or running.

That's not what just happened.

Claire tucks her bottom lip in between her teeth, a shy smile pulling up the corners of her mouth. She walks closer, shoving her hands under my shirt again. Her palms splay over my abs. "Is this a really good dream I'm about to wake up from?"

"If you are, I am having it too."

She smiles, sliding her hands up and pulling my shirt higher. "Take this off."

I do, adding my shirt to the pile of clothes on the floor. Her fingers travel from my biceps to my shoulder, then down the center of my chest, brushing the lines of muscle between my hips. My cock jumps.

"Can we do that again?"

"We can do it as many times as you want."

"Well, I have a training session in the morning, so I need to be able to walk."

I grin. "No promises, Boston."

Chapter 22

Otto

She's early.

"You are early," I state, approaching the metal bench Claire is slouched on.

It's quarter to ten, and I was expecting to have more time to prepare. Working with goalies or making general observations was one thing. But I'm not a real coach, and I'm not sure what magical purpose Eliza thinks this session will serve. Fifteen minutes wasn't a ton of time to figure it out, but it was something.

"Ten isn't that early," Claire replies cooly, reaching for the thermos next to her thigh. She's wearing shorts today, which is not as bad for my concentration as the revealing top she had on last night, but is not great for it either.

"You used to think so." I pull keys out of my pocket, unlocking the equipment shed and grabbing a single ball out of the mesh bag.

When I turn back around, Claire is staring at me. There's a crease in her forehead that smooths when we make eye contact. She asked me not to tell anyone about our past; she didn't say not to mention it when we were alone. I've been hyperaware of how I act around her. If I'm looking too long, standing too close, commenting too much. She becomes a spot of brilliance amid a whole lot of gray, and pretending otherwise is exhausting.

I drop the ball to the ground, flicking the black-and-white sphere up with my foot and bouncing it on my knee a few times.

Claire doesn't appear impressed by the trick. Her expression doesn't change as she says, "Tommy doesn't think so. Most days, he's up around seven."

"He lives with you?" I ask casually. At least, I hope it's casual.

"He and Cassidy are staying with me for now, yeah."

I want to ask more questions, but it's none of my business.

"I thought he was yours. Your kid." I kick the ball toward the field, avoiding her gaze after the impulsive confession slips out.

"A lot of people do. We look more alike than he and Cassidy do. We both got my dad's nose."

I glance at hers with an exaggerated wince. "Poor kid."

She fights it, but the corners of her mouth quirk. "Is this part of your coaching strategy? Insulting my appearance?"

My eyes skim up the length of her exposed legs. "There is nothing to insult, Caldwell."

True. Stupid to say aloud.

I start after the ball before I can gauge her reaction, stopping just outside the center circle. Restlessness hums along my skin. I'm full of unspent energy, with annoyance about her date last night, with impatience about my injury, with frustration about everything I didn't say then, which would be wildly unprofessional to say now.

Claire follows me onto the field. I pass the ball to her, and she traps it automatically, her expression unreadable as we face off.

"First to ten," I tell her.

"You can't play," she states.

"Avoid my right shoulder, and I will be fine."

There's concern on Claire's face. Worry for me, I realize, which burns in a potent mixture of pain and pleasure.

"I am cleared to ease into noncontact training, like running," I add.

"Pretty sure that means jogging on a treadmill, not scrimmaging."

"I am fine, Caldwell. Do you really think I would do anything to risk my football career?"

She knows what football means to me. I don't think through why—how else those words could be interpreted—until her expression smooths to emotionless. I wish I could shove those words back in my mouth. But they're out, hovering in the air between us.

"No," she replies, her smile tight. "I know you wouldn't."

I clear my throat, fighting to keep my composure. A football field is normally the one place I can think, where the rest of the world fades away. All I can see is her.

"I will imitate how Sears played last match. Keep your eyes on the ball, not on me, when I gain possession."

Claire nods, her smile tight-lipped. "*If* you gain possession," she says, then dribbles forward.

It's been months since I played.

It's been at least a decade since I played in such an informal setting—a ball and an empty field and a solitary opponent.

Muscle memory kicks in immediately. I shadow Claire, mirroring her movements based on a combination of subtle cues and what I've observed about her playing style.

It's a dance. A balance of predicting her plan and altering my own, searching for an opening to steal.

A sense of peace—of relief—washes over me. For the first time since searing pain shot through my shoulder, I'm not bitter or afraid. I wouldn't be here, wouldn't be feet from a woman who's haunted me more than I realized, if my injury hadn't happened.

I missed football. This version of it—no cameras or screaming fans or expectations.

I missed her. The stranger who caught my attention the second I saw her and the determined athlete challenging me now.

I'm close enough to my end to attempt a shot. I aim, sooner than I should, wanting to test myself.

To my left, Claire lunges to block it. She barely misses the ball. She makes contact with me, ass grazing my crotch. It's brief, a brush I wouldn't think twice about with anyone else. But it's her, so I freeze. Unexpectedly, so does Claire.

We're completely still, watching the net flex and flatten as my kick hits the goal.

"One–nothing," Claire says, stepping away and jogging after it.

While her back is turned, I drag a palm down my face. I'm almost thirty, for fuck's sake, not a teenager. I should not be getting hard from that.

We restart from the center, Claire taking possession. We're inside my defensive zone, but she can't find a clear shot past me. I'm as close as I can be without fouling. Or accidentally touching her again. I'm also taller and broader than the women she's accustomed to playing against.

She shuffles left, trying to find an opening.

I anticipate correctly, blocking her angle.

Her eyes narrow as she spins, attempting a breakaway. I lunge, knocking the ball into the sweet spot on my foot before pivoting and heading in the opposite direction.

Claire catches up just past the center line. I can hear her heavy breathing, sense her frustration about the steal, as she shifts to guard me.

I can blame her being faster on my extra bulk, but she's also in better shape than I am right now. For weeks, the extent of my training has been limited to various strengthening exercises for my shoulder, back, and arm muscles. Playing one-on-one wasn't part of my routine prior to my shoulder injury either.

Claire's a defender. She's poised in her natural position, whereas I'm a long way from the goal.

I feint left, but she watches the ball like I told her to. She doesn't take the bait. Instead, she edges forward, forcing me back, and I smile.

"Perfect, Caldwell."

I catch the surprise as it flashes across her face. She was expecting criticism, not praise.

She scores next.

I pull ahead again less than a minute later.

We volley like that, matching each other steal for steal, breakaway for breakaway, rebound for rebound.

Goal for goal.

I don't think she's going easy on me, and I'm sure as hell not going easy on her.

We agree on a water break right after she scores her fifth goal into the empty net, evening the score yet again. I'm breathing hard, soaked with sweat and swimming with adrenaline. I lift my shirt to wipe my face, salty perspiration stinging my eyes. I need a haircut.

When I drop my shirt, Claire quickly averts her eyes. Meaning she was looking, and it makes me feel a little less guilty about repeatedly checking out her tits last night.

I unzip my equipment bag, pulling out my phone and setting it on the bench as I search the contents for my water bottle. I pull out a towel, too, using it to wipe my face before I swallow a large sip of water.

"I wouldn't mind practicing some passing," Claire says, capping her water bottle. "Sometimes, linking up, I'm sloppy on the counterattack. That's what happened with most of the turnovers."

I nod. "Change up your passes more. Accuracy matters as much as timing does. And keeping your weight over the ball will—"

My phone begins vibrating on the bench. The metal makes the vibrations louder.

Claire glances toward the sound, then quickly away.

I reach for my phone, the screen flashing the caller's name, then toss it in my bag.

"Keeping your weight over the ball will help avoid lifting it," I say, ignoring the interruption.

She nods, setting her bottle down. "Great. You ready?"

I don't reply right away. The sudden tension pulls tighter, like we each tugged at the end of a thread.

"Mila is my grandfather's caretaker. He had hip surgery recently. That was the family emergency I flew back to Kluvberg for. He and I do not talk much. She calls to tell me how he is doing."

I zip my bag, shoving it under the bench.

"How is your grandfather doing?"

"He is the same, with better mobility." I hear the harsh edge to my voice, so I'm sure she does too.

"It's his loss," she tells me, understanding what *same* means.

I stand. "You have never met him."

"Yeah, but I've met you."

I know, based on her smile—half sympathetic, half bittersweet—that she's recalling the same conversation I am. Since she's the one who brought up our past, this time, it feels fair to comment on something I wanted to say earlier.

"You and Cassidy must be getting along, if she is staying with you."

"Yeah, we are." She reaches up, yanking the elastic out of her hair and redoing her ponytail. Not really looking at me, but not avoiding either. "My dad's been coming around more, to see her and to spend time with Tommy. That's been the hardest part of Cassidy moving back. I feel like an interloper in my own family. I'm the grudge-holder who hasn't gotten over the past, and it… sucks." She shakes her head. "I'll get over it."

"You mean, forgive him?"

"If I knew how to forgive him, I would have done it a long time ago."

"You know how to forgive him, Claire. You are just not sure you want to."

"I guess," she says softly.

"How is your mom dealing with it?"

Claire blinks rapidly. "What?"

"Your dad being around more. Is your mom…okay with it?"

"Oh. Fine." She's closed off all of a sudden, and I'm not sure why. What I said wrong. "Ready?"

She's already walking away, not waiting for a reply.

I blow out a breath, then follow.

Chapter 23

Claire

We walk in silence. I'm sweaty, exhausted, and jubilant.

I wondered, when I saw him play in person for the first time, what it would be like to be on a field with Otto Berger. What it would be like to witness that intensity up close, without the barrier of a screen or the distraction of a screaming crowd. I wish I could say the experience was a disappointment.

We reach the top of the path, passing a door that leads inside the practice facility. I wasn't sure if Otto might be headed inside, but he continues toward the parking lot with me. Meaning he really did show up just to practice with me, and I can't decide how to feel about that. Coach Taylor asked him to work with me, which is embarrassing and also means this wasn't his idea. But he never acted like it was an imposition. I caught him smiling a few times while we were playing, and my emotions are mixed about that too. I like being part of his recovery, but I won't be—

soon. He'll leave, and I'll stay, and all I'll be left with are more memories.

The silence between us isn't uncomfortable, but it's charged. I've hardly said anything to Otto since he asked about my mom, and I know I need to.

"That was..." *Fun. Exhilarating. Special.* Coming up with the right adjective takes a few seconds. "Helpful," is what I settle on. Also true, but not nearly as revealing.

"Good," Otto says.

I risk a glance at him, eyes lingering where his damp shirt clings to his torso. This would be easier if I wasn't so attracted to him, if he hadn't told me about his grandfather's surgery and made me feel like even more of a jerk for my reaction to his New York trip. He was engaged to Juliette. She must know about his strained relationship with his grandfather. He probably had dinner with her to discuss it. Juliette hopefully made him feel better, and I'm a terrible person for resenting that.

"Are you and Will close?"

I wasn't planning to bring up last night, but I'm curious to know more about his current life.

"You know Aster?" He sounds perplexed, like it didn't occur to him that I might have recognized who he was with at the restaurant.

"We've never met," I reply. "I just know who he is. He grew up in Dorchester. There was a lot of coverage of his, uh, what happened in Seattle. I saw he got traded to Kluvberg."

"He is a friend," Otto tells me. "I should have introduced you."

"I wasn't—I didn't mean it like that," I say awkwardly. "I was just curious about your... He came to visit you?"

"And his brother. It was Tripp's birthday."

"Who was the woman?"

"Will's fiancée. Sophia Beck."

"Beck as in…"

"Beck's sister, yeah." Otto chuckles, running a hand through his hair and mussing the windblown strands even more. "That got a little…messy. But it all worked out. Will proposed before I left Kluvberg."

I smile. "And Saylor and Beck had a kid?"

I know they did; I follow Saylor on social media. But I'd rather hear it from him.

Otto nods. "A daughter, Gigi. She is cute. Probably a future footballer."

"Good genes."

He laughs again. "Exactly." Then glances at me, amusement fading. "You keep in touch with her? Saylor?"

I shake my head. "She was always nice, but we didn't spend much time together. And we haven't played together since… It's, uh, been a while." Nervously, I tuck a piece of hair behind one ear.

We're treading dangerously close to the topic of Paris. And maybe that would be a healthy conversation to have, to clear away the cobwebs of the past rather than continue to ignore their clutter.

But it will hurt. I feel a phantom spasm of it, threatening to tear my chest apart, and flinch away from the pain. I can't change what happened; neither can he. What difference will discussing it make?

We've reached the edge of the parking lot.

Otto swallows.

I brace myself, studying the bob of his Adam's apple.

"I thought you would be in Melbourne," he states.

This is another prime opportunity to tell him about Mom. I want to—with an intensity that startles me. I'm battling between safety and impulsivity, and there's a very real possibility I'll choose to be rash. To just tell him so there's one less thing unsaid between us.

"Otto!"

We both turn toward the sound of his name, watching Nicole walk toward us. She's wearing her typical friendly smile, but her forehead creases with uncertainty as she glances at me.

I take a reflexive step back, even though we're not standing that close to each other.

"Hello, Nicole." Otto's tone is even and polite, no trace that our conversation affected him at all.

I run my tongue along the backs of my teeth, striving for that same indifference.

"Wasn't expecting to see you here," she says, reaching us. "Hi, Caldwell."

"Hey, Coach Green," I respond, tightening my grip on the water bottle. Remembering I'm sweaty and red-faced while she's wearing a cute sweater and jeans.

I probably would care about the contrast between our appearances less if Nicole wasn't eyeing Otto the same way I've seen a lot of women stare at him. She's not one of his players. I know nothing about her personal life, but based on the admiration on her face and lack of ring on her finger, she's single.

"You're dedicated, here on your day off." It could apply to either of us, but she's looking at me.

Otto replies before I can, "We ran a few drills. Eliza had suggested it."

We did more than run a few drills. We've been here for nearly three hours.

Nicole nods, the smile still fixed on her face. "We're all lucky to have your expertise."

"I do not know about that. I am just a keeper."

A snort escapes before I can stop it. He's teasing me, for using his position as an argument last night. There's no sign of arrogance now, just false modesty.

Nicole glances at me, her forehead wrinkling again.

I cough, then sip some water. "Allergies."

I don't dare look at Otto, but Nicole does. "I stopped by to grab something from my office, but I forgot my key card. Do you mind letting me in?"

"Of course not," he responds, pulling his out of his pocket.

"Thank you so much," Nicole gushes. "I really appreciate it."

He's swiping a card, not giving you a kidney, I think.

The venom behind it surprises me; I've never had any issue with Nicole before. All the elation has drained away, leaving emptiness behind. I remembered what it was like to have fun with Otto. And this is a reminder of the opposite. Intensity isn't specific to happiness.

The highs were higher around Otto. The lows were lower too.

"I'll see you guys tomorrow," I say abruptly, turning toward my sedan without waiting for any response. Purposefully lumping them together when I should have thanked Otto individually. Problem is, I'm scared of what else I might say.

Once I'm safely inside my car, I release a long exhale. Against my better judgment, I glance in the rearview mirror, watching them walk and talk and smile as they approach the main entrance.

I blast "Silver Springs" on repeat during the drive home, and I'm still in a shitty mood when I park in the driveway. I'm too tired from playing with Otto to go for a run, my usual mood booster, so I head to the garage to tackle a task I've been putting off.

I'm crouched, stabbing the damp dirt of the front flower beds, when I hear the door hinges squeak.

"Do you need help?" Cassidy asks, taking a seat on the front steps.

She's wearing a fleece jacket that she zips up almost to her chin. It doesn't feel as warm as it did when I was exercising earlier, but it's still the nicest day we've had this year.

I swipe the sweat off my forehead with the back of my arm. "I've got it."

My sister glances at the small shovel I'm holding. "You hate gardening, Claire."

"No, I don't."

I do hate gardening.

I hate kneeling on the ground. I hate how dirt collects under your fingernails. I hate the bugs. And I especially hate how repetitive it is—how new weeds grow and new mulch has to be spread and new seeds planted.

But Mom loved gardening. *Loves*, I quickly correct, although it's no longer the constant it once was.

During our latest visit to Echo Glen, several of her indoor plants had browning leaves.

Every spring, she'd plant dahlias in the yard, digging up the tubers for the winter and transplanting them back into the flower beds each spring, so I'm doing the same.

Last year, Mom and I did this together.

A lot can change in a year. A year ago, I never thought I'd see Otto Berger again. Never thought I'd have to witness another woman flirt with him.

I can't even blame Nicole. She has no idea what Otto means—

meant—to me.

Cassidy cups her chin, watching me smooth dirt. "Tommy and I are riding bikes to the park. Want to come?"

I shake my head. "No thanks. I just want to finish this and take a shower."

"Okay. Also…Josh wants to make dinner tonight."

I nod. "I'm free to watch Tommy."

"Actually, I was thinking I'd bring him with me to Josh's. Unless…you think that's a bad idea?"

"I don't think it's a bad idea," I say, touched she's bothering to ask my opinion. "Tommy will love Josh."

I struggled to pay attention after talking to Otto last night, but it was impossible not to notice how happy Cassidy and Josh were the entire evening. If they don't last this time, I'll lose what little faith in love I've managed to retain through my parents' divorce and my own unhappy endings.

Cassidy smiles. That was obviously the answer she was hoping to hear.

Yet my sister still lingers on the steps, which is surprising, until she says, "Walker asked Josh for your number."

I haven't thought about Walker since saying goodbye to him last night, which bodes poorly for a romantic relationship. As does the fact that he lives in Hoboken and works in a Manhattan high-rise. If I wanted a long-distance relationship, I'd date… someone else.

But Otto isn't an option. He's my coach and my ex, and he might be reconciling with his former fiancée. He proposed to someone else. Whatever reason their relationship ended, they intended to get married. Solid, irrefutable evidence he's moved on.

And I haven't. I've tried to, but I haven't fallen in love since him. I've told myself it will happen, half-heartedly believing it—because I haven't needed to believe it. I've avoided thinking about Otto, just like I've avoided seeing my dad—because it's easier.

"Claire?" Cassidy prompts.

I forgot she was here. Maybe Mom was right; gardening is therapeutic.

I glance up. "Give it to him."

Cassidy tilts her head, studying me rather than celebrating her matchmaking skills, like I thought she would. "You sure? You didn't seem that…into him."

"I liked him," I insist, which is true.

She nods slowly. "Okay. I'll give Josh the go-ahead."

"Cool," I say, grabbing another tuber.

Still, Cassidy lingers. "How was practice?"

My sister has never, not once, asked me that.

"Fine," I answer.

"Really? You seem sort of…upset."

"Just tired."

"I'd ask if it was for any fun reason, but you came home with me last night, not your date."

I manage a small smile.

"I looked him up."

"Walker?" I ask, confused.

"Otto Berger."

I glance up, heart pounding. "What—why would you do that?"

"I was curious."

"Josh doesn't mind that you research other men?"

Cassidy rolls her eyes, then leans forward. "Why does Mom have a book with a killer named Otto Serger?"

I play dumb. "What?"

"Don't bullshit me, Claire. You've read all her books. You never noticed one of her villains had almost the exact same name as your coach?"

I rub my thumb along the shovel's wooden handle, debating what to say. Debating how much to say.

I told Mom including the name was a bad idea, but she insisted it was harmless. She was intent on trying to cheer me up.

"It wasn't just the book," Cassidy continues. "There was this…vibe between you guys. You acted differently after he arrived."

"We met in Paris," I say.

Aside from basic details, I've never discussed boys—men, at this stage of our lives—with my sister. There wasn't much to say on my end when we were younger. Cassidy was the popular, fun, outgoing Caldwell sister while I was the serious, socially awkward tomboy in grass-stained clothes.

"Sounds romantic."

"It was."

"What happened, Clairey?"

I turn the shovel over, blinking rapidly because I'm suddenly, embarrassingly on the brink of tears.

"Are we still going to the park, Mommy?" Tommy appears, and I steal a quick sniff while the commotion of the door opening and closing covers the sound.

"We sure are," Cassidy replies. "Go put your shoes on, and I'll be right in. I just need to talk to Aunt Claire for another minute."

"Okay," Tommy says happily, heading back inside.

Cassidy says nothing, waiting for me to reply.

"It was the Olympics," I tell her. "He went home. I went home. If I hadn't gotten so wrapped up in…everything, I would have seen it coming a mile away. And it was a long time ago. It's ridiculous I'm even… It's just weird, seeing him again. Hard—harder than I thought it would be."

"So, you still have feelings for him?"

"It doesn't matter, Cassidy."

"Well"—she stands—"I'd be curious to know the answer. And based on how Otto looked at you last night, it would matter to him."

My sister heads inside to help get Tommy ready for the park, leaving me sitting in mud, more confused than ever.

Chapter 24

Otto

I grab the bottle of water and pack of gum off the register counter, tugging the brim of my Red Sox ball cap lower when a guy passing slows to stare at me. He doesn't call out, and I don't hang around to see if he recognized me. I stride down the corridor toward Gate 19, tucking the pack of spearmint in my pocket.

The Siege is collected in the section of seats closest to the window that overlooks the parked plane being prepared for our trip to Los Angeles. According to the display behind the desk, we're boarding in twenty-five minutes.

Most players are on their phones. A few glance up and smile, registering my return.

I walk over to where Eliza, Meg, and Nicole are huddled. I assume they're talking strategy, until I get close enough to hear Meg complaining about her mother-in-law. They all glance up as I approach.

“Here you go.” I hand Nicole the pack of gum she requested.

“Thanks, Otto,” she tells me, smiling as she takes it.

I don’t miss the amused look that passes between Meg and Eliza. Nicole is friendly with everyone, but she’s especially friendly with me.

We’re often thrown together during practice, working with the Siege goalies. We’re roughly the same age. And Nicole told me about a bad date she went on last weekend, so I know she’s single.

I sort of assumed a coach-coach fling would be frowned upon, but no one seems to be frowning about it. I don’t know if there are any official rules prohibiting one. I don’t care if there are any official rules prohibiting one because I can’t see past Claire, who is absolutely off-limits.

My phone rings with an incoming call.

“Take it,” Eliza tells me. “We’re just gossiping.”

I smile, nod, and pick up. It’s Beck, headed to practice. I wander over to the windows, listening to his update on the team. Kluvberg has lost two of their past three matches. They’re playing poorly overall, and a small part of me is relieved by it, thinking I’m not entirely replaceable. The rest of me, invested in the club’s success and not my own issues, hates hearing it.

Beck and I would sometimes travel to training together since my flat in Kluvberg is close to his and Saylor’s place and so he could appreciate my new cars after he defaulted to his boring SUV. Listening to him talk is a poor imitation of those trips, but closing my eyes, I can almost picture him in the passenger seat, rolling his eyes as I boasted about horsepower.

It feels like another lifetime. Like a former reality I’m already detached from. It makes me uneasy. Has part of me already given up on returning? Playing with Claire didn’t give me a damn clue about my former abilities. I won't know for months if my shoulder will fully recover, my future in flux until I receive that final verdict.

I hang up with Beck once he arrives at the facility, glancing out the windows at the workers loading luggage and really tracking her return in my peripheral vision.

A man bumps into her, not looking before he turns around from dumping something in the trash can. He says something—presumably an apology—and Claire smiles and nods in response before continuing in this direction. His eyes linger on her ass as she walks away, and my jaw clenches.

Somehow, Claire still seems oblivious to her own appeal. Unaware of the fact that she's the most beautiful woman in any space.

She walks over to an empty section of seats, sinking down into one and pulling a pair of headphones out of her backpack. She reaches into her pocket, but pulls nothing out. Checking on her Detroit Zoo coin, I'm guessing, sure she still carries it with her.

She's not inviting company, yet I walk in that direction anyway.

We've barely spoken since we practiced together on Sunday. The timing of Nicole's interruption was terrible. Had I known another coach was about to appear, I wouldn't have brought up Melbourne. But I did, and it's hovered between us ever since.

Claire glances up as I approach, slipping the headphones off.

I sit, leaving an open chair between us.

"Mila?" she questions, nodding toward the phone in my hand.

I smile. "Beck. He was on his way to practice. Just checking in." I pick up her headphones, guessing, "Fleetwood Mac?" even before I hear "Go Your Own Way" playing through them.

It's bittersweet, discovering more similarities that exist between this Claire and the younger version I met years ago. A collision of relief and regret.

"Nice hat."

I set her headphones down and tug the brim again. "Thanks. I went to a game with Tripp."

"Did they win?"

"No. And I had no clue what was going on. I think Tripp invited me, thinking I would be able to explain the rules to him."

"Not a lot of baseball fans in Germany, huh?"

"Not so much." I glance down, rolling the water bottle in my palm. "What is wrong?"

"Nothing's—"

I look over. "Claire."

She plays with a string of her teal hoodie. "It's not about football."

It's the first time I've heard someone refer to our shared sport by its proper name since I arrived, and I appreciate her using it for my benefit. "When have we only talked about football?"

Claire exhales, tugging harder on the string. "When you asked about my mom…I lied. She's not fine. She's sick—she's been sick. That's why Cassidy moved back. Why—part of why—I wasn't in Melbourne. I'm not trying to use it as an excuse. I-I don't have what it takes anyway."

I lean forward, resting my elbows on my knees. It takes me a minute to absorb and sort through everything she just said and reply, "I am so sorry about your mom. Is there anything I can do?"

"No." Claire glances away, out the window. "It's dementia. There's nothing anyone can do. But thank you for asking."

I process that, then recall what else she said. "You have what it takes, Claire."

"Don't lie to—"

"I have never lied to you."

"Then don't pretend I would have made the national team. Not after what happened in Paris."

I shake my head. "You are going to let one loss define your entire career, Claire?"

"That one loss *does* define my career."

"Because you are letting it."

She leans closer, glaring at me. "You don't get it, Otto. You *win*, under pressure. I…choke. I'm not cut out for big moments."

"You think I—"

"Caldy! Last bathroom call. You in?"

Claire glances at the group of her teammates, paused along the section of seats we're sitting in.

One—Savannah Robbe—smiles at me. "Are you a Sox fan, Coach Berger?"

"I prefer football," I state, leaning back.

"Oh, so you're a Patriots fan?"

Reyna Rodman laughs. "They play with their hands, Sav."

Robbe winks at me. "Just helping Coach adapt to local culture."

Claire stands. "Only five minutes until boarding. Let's go."

I relax in my chair as the women walk away. I don't have a chance to talk to Claire again before we board.

But we wind up beating LA, 0–4, in large part because of Claire, which hopefully reinforced some of what I said.

Chapter 25

Claire

Savannah leads us to a tiki bar down the block from our hotel. Fake bamboo and wooden carvings decorate the walls as we head for an open table.

"I'm in the mood *for a mai tai," Reyna announces.*

"Mango mojito? Yes, please," Tasha declares.

*I open one of the sticky menus. The last tim*e I was in a bar was my final shift at Paul Rebeer's. The last time I went out for drinks with my teammates was...Daniela's birthday last year, I think?

LA was ranked first in the league, and we kicked their asses earlier, winning by four goals. Daniela had a shutout. I got my first assist of the season.

So, when Savannah slyly suggested going out tonight, I shocked everyone by being the first to agree.

A waitress comes by to take our orders a few minutes later. I scan the four-page menu, settling on a margarita.

"To Caldy!" Tasha cheers, lifting her glass.

"It was a team effort," I insist, thanking the waitress when she sets my drink down next.

"A team you fucking carried," Reyna says. "Stop being modest and keep doing whatever you did to prepare for today."

For the first time since the final whistle was blown, my smile wavers.

Sure, I'll confide in our assistant coach, who also happens to be my ex, about my personal problems more often. Great idea.

Part of me still can't believe I told Otto about Mom. It's a level of trust I hadn't realized we still shared. He might have broken my heart, but he was honest while he did it. I didn't just tell him because he asked. I told him because I wanted to. And I certainly didn't tell him because he was one of my coaches.

I lift my margarita, shoving thoughts of Otto far away. "To Boston Siege supremacy!"

"Hell yeah," and "Let's fucking go," echo around as glasses clink.

I suck down a healthy sip of my cocktail, a delicious combination of sweet, sour, and smoky. I relax on my stool, taking occasional sips, as I listen to my teammates laugh and bicker. Warmed by the alcohol and the feeling of community.

Savannah is complaining about shin splints. Mallory is browsing for gifts for her sister's upcoming birthday. Grace Masters is watching the Bruins' playoff game on her phone.

Reyna leans closer to me and asks, "What were you and Coach Berger talking about?"

I cough on nothing. "What?"

"Before we boarded, you guys were talking. It looked intense."

"Oh. That. We were..." It should have occurred to me that my teammates might be curious enough to ask. Anything Otto does seems to incite some level of interest. But it didn't, and I'm unprepared to answer. "I barely remember. Today's game mostly?"

"What are you guys whispering about?" Grace asks.

"Nothing," I reply.

At the same time, Reyna says, "Coach Berger."

And, of course, everyone's attention is on us now.

"What about Coach Berger?" Savannah questions.

"I was curious what they were talking about earlier," Reyna comments, taking a sip of her peach-colored drink.

"And?" Savannah prompts, her eyes on me.

I shrug a shoulder. "Small talk." I sip some margarita, hoping it'll improve my acting skills. "He mentioned going to a Sox game. Asked if I was ready for today's match."

"Do you think he and Coach Green went to the game together?" Grace wonders.

She's not asking me, so I don't reply, even though I know the answer. The sooner we move on to another topic, the better.

But everyone else seems happy to speculate.

"I don't think they've gone out," Mallory says. "Not getting that vibe when they're together."

"You're not?" Savannah responds. "I think Coach Green is into him."

Reyna chimes in with, "According to Daniela, she definitely is. Coach Green asks his opinion on everything concerning her and Kristin."

I polish off the rest of my margarita. "We're failing the Bechdel test."

"The what?" Savannah asks.

"It's when women only have conversations about men," Reyna explains.

Savannah laughs. "We're not talking about men, Caldy. We're talking about our soccer-god assistant coach. You're single. If Coach Berger made a move, you'd turn him down?"

Our waitress chooses this moment to return, asking if anyone needs a second round, earning my eternal gratitude.

Obviously, I would have answered yes. And everyone would have believed me because I'm a responsible rule follower. But yes would have been a lie.

In addition to being a liar, I'm also a hypocrite. Because the group moves on to discussing other subjects after the waitress leaves, but I'm still thinking about a boy.

. . .

"I love you, Caldy," Savannah announces loudly, throwing her arms around my neck. Nearly toppling me.

I steady myself by grabbing the railing, then pat her back with my other hand. "Love you too, Sav. Drink some water before bed, okay?"

"Mmhmm. Yep. Water. Great idea." Savannah releases me and hustles after Mallory, Reyna, and Tasha, who are waiting in the hallway. She leaps on Tasha's back right as the elevator doors slide shut.

I laugh, then yawn. The doors open again on my floor, and I head down the carpeted hallway. I'm not sure what time it is, but it's late. The hallway is quiet and empty.

My steps slow as I near the door I saw Otto enter earlier.

Bad idea, my brain blares in warning. *Keep walking.*

I do keep walking, but only until I reach his door. There, I end up stopping. Knocking. It's like I'm in a fugue state. I know I shouldn't be doing this—I can't believe that I'm doing this—yet my knuckles are tapping wood.

A flash of panic strikes like a lightning bolt, splitting the surreal, but I don't have time to bolt before the door swings open.

Oh.

Oh *no.*

For a split second, I truly consider running, like this was a childish prank. But I'm frozen, staring.

"You couldn't put some clothes on before answering the door?"

Otto leans a shoulder against the doorway, his eyes doing a slow sweep of my body. It's like the time he glanced at my boobs, but a thousand times worse. We're alone, a bed is nearby, and I downed two celebratory margaritas.

"I did."

Did—oh. Right. He slept—sleeps—naked.

I try to swallow, but my throat is too dry for the action to accomplish much of anything.

I look at him, and he looks back at me, and I wonder what he'd do if I kept walking—right into his room. Would he tell me to leave? Say it was inappropriate? Touch me?

I have more on the line. His time here is temporary. This is my team. My career. My reputation.

He had six years to reach out, and he never did. I'm mad about that. Madder that I want to walk into his hotel room anyway.

"Claire?" His voice is soft.

I shake my head. "Sorry, I—"

"Do not apologize. Not to me."

"I just—" I swipe my dry lips with my tongue, and Otto tracks the motion.

I recognize the expression on his face, and my muscles quiver with the effort of staying rooted in place. I want to be closer. This isn't near enough. I want him on me. *In* me. He ruined sex for me, setting a standard no one else has managed to reach.

I could sneak out early.

No one would know, except us.

I didn't *know* it was the last time, our final—

The memory hits with a tangible impact. I step back, away from it, the pain as visceral as it was then. I'm incapable of casual sex with Otto. I learned that lesson already. Won the heartbreak trophy and left Paris without a gold medal.

Nothing's changed since then. He's headed back to Germany—again. That's always been the case—will always be the case—so I resent how often I've had to remind myself of it.

"I, uh, I just wanted to say thank you. For listening, at the airport. I didn't have a chance to..." There's nowhere safe to look. Not his eyes or his mouth or his abs or the defined V that points at the shorts that are all he bothered to pull on before opening the door. I keep getting distracted, words harder to hold on to than cupped water as I focus on the carpeted floor.

"You are drunk." He sounds amused.

When I glance up, he looks it too. One corner of his mouth has curved up, that damn dimple creasing his cheek.

"I had a couple of drinks," I concede. "We were...celebrating."

"Good."

"You're my coach. You're supposed to tell me to stay focused, not chug margaritas."

His smile grows. "You do not need anyone to tell you to stay focused, Claire."

I sigh. "You sound like my sister."

"Ouch."

I forgot he knows my relationship with my sister is complicated.

"Cassidy and I could be best friends now," I say defensively.

"Are you?"

"We're…better," I say. "We double date now."

"I noticed." His tone is dark, mouth smoothed to a straight line.

"Oh, right. You were there. I…forgot."

I'm not great about achieving casual on a good day. Late and tipsy on tequila? Not even close.

"You forgot." It's a statement, not a question. "That is a surprise, considering you left your date to chase after me."

I scowl at him, crossing my arms. "Only because—what are you doing?"

Otto steps into the hallway, shutting his door behind him. He pries the paper envelope containing my room key from my palm, glances at the number written on it, and heads left.

I hurry after him, hissing, "I don't need an escort."

"Well, you have one."

He slows his pace, allowing me to catch up with him. My door is only three down from his. We reach it quickly, Otto swiping the card and turning the handle. He enters first. Annoyance and anticipation kick my heart rate into higher gear as I follow.

"I *really* don't need—"

"Drink this." He shoves a water bottle into my hand, then heads into the bathroom.

I'm tired and tipsy enough to care less than I otherwise would, but I distinctly remember leaving a mess of makeup and toiletries on the countertop. I close my eyes and chug water, wishing I'd wake up and realize this was all a dream. That I walked straight back to my room after stepping off the elevator.

Otto returns with an elastic and my toothbrush, a neat line of toothpaste already on the bristles.

I set down the water bottle and take the elastic, the fluttering in my chest as I tie my hair back impossible to ignore. I'm not used to being taken care of. I'm always the one taking care.

"Won't your girlfriend care that you're in my room?"

I should be more concerned with other people—particularly one of my teammates or Coach Taylor—but I'm not.

"I do not have a girlfriend."

"Fuck buddy then." I deliberately use the crassest phrase I can think of as I take the toothbrush from him.

"Do not have one of those either."

"I saw the photos," I remind him.

"Of me *fucking* her?"

I flinch before sticking the toothbrush in my mouth and walking into the bathroom.

He follows, leaning a shoulder against the doorway again. Still shirtless. Still staring at me.

I brush, spit, and turn on the tap. "This is unprofessional, Coach Berger."

"So was showing up at my door, Caldwell."

"I'm a hypocrite. Is that what you want to hear?"

"I want to know why you care about Juliette."

It stings, hearing him say her name. Salt in a wound that's staying stubbornly open.

I glance at the scars on his right shoulder. They're small. Neat. Healed. Proof he'll be gone soon.

"I don't care," I say, heading back into the room and over to my suitcase. I dig through it, looking for a shirt to wear to bed.

Behind me, I hear a sigh. "I have never lied to you, Claire. But I have never been able to tell when—if—you are lying to me.

If you meant it when you told me to not come to that game or to—"

"You should go." I spin to face him, panic spreading through me at the mention of Paris. "Please go."

His eyes drop from my face, to the fabric I'm holding. I watch the emotions play across his face—surprise, realization, resignation. "Well, you lied about something."

Otto heads for the door, leaving me holding the black *Deutschland* shirt.

Chapter 26

Otto

PARIS: SIX YEARS EARLIER

"No." I reach for Claire, pulling her back onto my chest. "Not yet."

"We have a team meeting," she tells me. "I have to shower."

But she doesn't move. She tilts her head, pressing a kiss against my jaw.

My hold on her tightens. It's fucking uncomfortable, lying on the floor amid the mess that's her room. But there wasn't enough room for her to sit on my face on her tiny bed, and that's one of my favorite ways to watch Claire flip from quiet and serious to loud and needy. And I was too impatient to suggest moving after she came, so we had sex between one of her cleats and the pile of laundry she pushed to one side.

"I should shower too," I say suggestively.

She laughs, fingers tracing lazy circles on my chest. "You won't fit."

"That is what you said before. And yet..."

My hand moves between her thighs.

"*Otto*."

If she's trying to deter me, she's doing it the wrong way. I'm already calculating, deliberating if I should pull her on my lap or if I should—

My phone buzzes. I ignore it, covering Claire's mouth and exploring it with my tongue. I know exactly how she likes to be kissed, what will make her moan and beg and seek more friction, which is exactly what she's doing now.

My mouth moves down her neck, headed for her breasts, when she repeats my name. This time, she sounds serious.

"You're getting another call."

I groan, rolling on my back and reaching for the vibrating device. I swear when I see it's Beck calling.

I told him—fuck, I can't remember what I told him. The call goes to voicemail, and I curse again when I see the time. "I have to go."

I twist to give Claire a last lingering kiss, then sit up, sorting through the mess of clothes on the floor. "Have you seen my shirt?"

"No." She's standing, grabbing a towel and wrapping it around her.

I pull on my pants, locate my hoodie, then resume looking for my shirt.

"Who was calling?"

"Beck," I reply, tossing my favorite bra—black lace—toward the laundry pile.

"Is he upset you're with me?"

"What?" I glance at her, frowning. "He does not know I am with you."

"You're still lying to him?"

"Well…yes."

I give up on my shirt, standing and yanking my hoodie on.

We're one match away from a gold medal. If I tell Beck I've been sneaking off to have sex every chance I get, he'll lecture me about prioritizing getting laid over winning. And I don't need a lecture. I know what I can handle. Claire's been good for my concentration. I haven't gone out partying once since the night we met. I sleep, practice, and spend time with her.

When I finally do tell Beck, he'll probably say *I told you so*. He maintains his relationship with Saylor has helped his performance, which I privately considered unlikely.

"So, you haven't told anyone about us?" Claire asks.

"Uh…no." It's the honest answer, but I'm suddenly not sure it's the right one.

My closest friends are here in Paris, on the team with me. My teammates who aren't here are busy enjoying their summers before preseason starts. My parents are gone, and I can't have a civil conversation with Opa about the weather, let alone a woman. My publicist will say being single is part of my brand or some shit like that.

Who would I tell?

"Do you…normally?"

I still, unease trickling through me. Claire has never asked about other women. We had the exclusive conversation before we stopped using condoms, so she knows I'm not sleeping with anyone else. And I assumed she had some sense of my reputation, that photos of me exiting clubs with a woman—sometimes with women—get posted online and are speculated about by the press.

I don't share those sorts of details, so there's never been anything to tell my friends or teammates.

If she's not aware of my reputation, I'm not sure how to phrase that in any way that won't lower Claire's opinion of me.

"I do not normally do any of this."

Also true. But once again, I feel like I've said something wrong. Neither of us has moved, but it suddenly feels like there's more space between us.

I rub the back of my neck. "I just meant…" My voice trails.

I'm not entirely sure what I'm trying to say.

"I know what you meant."

My forehead furrows. If I don't know, how does she?

"It is not… We are private. Not anyone's business."

If I went public with a relationship, there would be media attention. Team attention. It took six months after Beck started dating Saylor for the guys to stop making whipping sounds when he walked into the locker room.

"You mean, this is just sex to you."

I scrub a palm across my face.

I'm fucking this up. I knew I would.

"Of course not, Claire."

She says nothing.

"We are not having sex right now," I point out.

She rolls her eyes.

Yeah, that was a bad response.

I'm unprepared for this conversation. I've never had this conversation with a woman—because every other time, it has just been sex. I let myself get caught up in the thrill of sneaking around and the excitement of making it to the final, and there hasn't been space for anything else.

"Have you told anyone about us?"

"No," she answers.

"Okay. Why is that any different?"

She huffs. "You know why."

My face must convey what I'm thinking—I don't—because she continues.

"Because you're hot and rich and famous, and anyone I tell about us is going to ask how big your dick is and then tell me not to get attached because you'll be photographed at a club with a girl on your lap next week."

Okay, so she is aware of my reputation.

I swallow hard. "I cannot change the past. That was all before I met you."

"I'm not asking you to change anything, Otto. I'm just…" She glances down, dropping eye contact before looking up again. "You're going home. I'm going home. It is what it is. Maybe I'll… Maybe I'll see you at the next Olympics."

"The next Olympics?" I gape at her, dumbfounded. "In four years? Sounds like this was just sex to *you*."

Claire glares. "What did you think was going to happen with us?"

Truthfully, I haven't given it any thought. I've been focused on each day. Each match. Each win. Claire came out of nowhere. And I've avoided thinking past the closing ceremonies because she's right—there's no simple solution.

She has a year of university left. I'm under contract with Kluvberg. Even if I wasn't, I can't imagine playing anywhere else.

"You could play in Germany after you graduate?"

That's what Saylor did. It's worked for her and Beck.

"Perfect." Claire's voice is thick with sarcasm. "Why don't I leave behind everything I know—my dream of playing professionally for my own country—to move to Germany in a year? Why didn't I think of that?"

I scowl, shoving my hands into my pockets. "What is your solution that has us in the same place? *I* play in the States?"

I chuckle at the impossibility, the sound trailing awkwardly while she stays silent.

That was the wrong thing to say. Again.

"There aren't any solutions," she says. "That's why neither of us has brought it up before now."

Her eyes are shiny, and the realization of why hits harder than any kick that's ever collided with my chest.

I step closer. "Claire."

She shakes her head. "Obviously, this isn't going to last longer than the Olympics. We both know it."

Do we? Do I?

I've treated us like an active match, focused on the guaranteed time rather than considering added minutes or overtime. The outcome.

Football is all I have. FC Kluvberg has been my family, my focus, my purpose for as long as I can remember. Nothing's escaped sacrifice in my pursuit of the singular goal of cementing my place as one of the top goalkeepers of all time.

I'm twenty-three. I'm playing the best football of my life. The best years of my career still lie ahead.

Claire musters a smile. Too tight and too tiny to be her real one. "This was fun, okay? We're good."

I scoff, miffed and—fuck—hurt by the easy dismissal.

She's ending this. Cutting herself out of my life, and I can already feel the hole of her absence. The size of it stuns me.

"I do not want this to be over," I tell her, finally managing to say something right in this conversation.

I don't have any answers, but I do know that much.

"You're looking for a relationship?" Claire arches an incredulous eyebrow.

"I…"

I don't know, is the honest answer. Which is light-years from the emphatic *no* I would have given before I met her, but not the *yes* she wants to hear.

I laughed at Beck's trips to visit Saylor when she was still at university. I'm accustomed to doing what I want, when I want, unless it's a directive from a coach. Would I remember to call her after an exhausting match? Could I commit to flying nine hours to see her on any sort of regular basis?

I don't know, and she reads it on my face.

"I want you," I say, which is the truth.

I want Claire.

I also want her to win. I want her to have the career she's dreamed about, the one she's worked so hard for.

And I don't want to lie. Don't want to promise she can have both when I can't guarantee anything.

"Good luck on Saturday."

I nod, then swallow hard. "I will be at tomorrow's match."

There's still time. Time to think, to plan, to fix.

Claire shakes her head. "Don't come."

I frown. "Why not?"

"You should be focused on your final. And I… If I know you're there—just…please. Don't come." She heads for the bathroom.

"Claire."

She slows. Not a full stop, but a stutter.

I try and fail to put the past few weeks into words. It's bizarre—to realize I met her a month ago. Now, if I had to pick a person to get everything they wanted, I'd pick her.

So, I tell her that. "I hope you get everything you want."

"You too, Otto." She fumbles with the door handle for a second, adding a "Bye" and shutting the bathroom door without glancing back.

I blow out a long breath, staring at the closed door. I don't want to leave, but I can't stay. There's nothing else to say—at least not right now—and I'm running dangerously close to being late for a team meeting.

I glance around her room one final time—maybe for *the* final time—and then head into the hallway. I'm careful to close the door quietly behind me, listening to it lock before starting toward the nearest exit.

I'm almost to the stairwell when I hear, "Otto?"

I turn. Saylor is walking this way with another woman dressed in Team USA apparel. She tilts her head, studying me quizzically.

"Hey." I swallow hard, shoving all the emotion deep down and managing a smile.

"What are you—" Saylor glances behind me. "What are you doing in here?"

"I was looking for you."

"Me?" Her curious expression turns concerned. "Is Beck—"

"He is fine," I assure her. "Just wanted to wish you luck tomorrow."

"Oh. Thanks." She walks closer, rising up on her tiptoes and giving me a quick hug. When she steps back, she looks worried again. "You sure you're good?"

"I am great." I flash her a grin, relieved when it comes easier. "See you later."

I spin and keep walking. As soon as I'm alone, my smile disappears.

Chapter 27

Claire

Sweat trickles down the back of my neck as I hustle toward the parking lot at the fastest speed I can deem a "reasonable" pace.

Otto knows I'm avoiding him. I know I'm avoiding him. We both know why.

Coach Taylor does not know I'm avoiding Otto. Or why.

And if admitting to my head coach that I had a summer fling with our new assistant coach six years ago would be embarrassing, telling her that I got drunk and showed up at his hotel room door last weekend was absolutely not an option. When Coach Taylor stopped me after practice on Monday to highlight how well I played against LA and to ask if working with Otto was helpful, I nodded.

So, here we are again.

I've avoided looking at him ever since I met the team in the lobby, hungover. I've been waiting for him to bring that night up. At the very least to ask for his shirt back.

But he hasn't. He left when I asked him to, and he hasn't treated me differently from any other Siege player since, and it's exactly what I wanted and also driving me insane.

"I liked the clearing crosses drill," I finally say. "We should run it with Kate and Amanda."

Otto nods. "I will mention it to Eliza."

We continue walking. Our cars are the only two parked in the lot—my old sedan and his shiny SUV. The team lifted this morning, but we technically had this afternoon off.

"Nice day," I comment.

It officially feels like spring. It's a perfect day really, sunny and warm and bright.

He hums an agreement, and that's my final straw.

"Are you mad at me?"

"Of course not. Why would I be mad at you?"

If he were anyone else, if we were discussing anything except us, I'd commend him for how neatly he turned the tables on me.

"Because of LA."

"What about LA?"

I chew on the inside of my cheek. "You know what."

"If you want to talk about LA, tell me what part you want to talk about."

"I-I shouldn't have shown up at your hotel room."

"You should not have," he agrees.

"S-sorry," I stutter, taken aback by that response.

"You do not want me to treat you differently from any other player, right?"

"Right."

"Then we should stop these sessions. If you need extra

assistance, work with Meg."

"I didn't ask for your help," I snap. "Coach Taylor asked—"

"I will talk to Eliza."

"And tell her…"

Otto scoffs. He might have claimed not to be mad, but he looks pissed. "Do not worry. I will not mention Paris. What is there to say about it?"

Nothing.

There's nothing to say about Paris. We didn't part on confusing terms. We ended it. We said goodbye. And six years later, I still can't find any closure where Otto Berger is concerned. Worse, since he showed up, any finality I felt continues to slip away. I'm more confused every moment we spend together.

"See you tomorrow," he says, veering toward his car before I can summon any sort of response.

I watch him walk away, the set of his shoulders strong and imperious.

It seems impossible that I could offer Otto Berger anything he doesn't already have. It's been well established that our lives were—are—incompatible. I know it. He knows it. So, why is he acting like I let him down in some way by saying so?

I trudge toward my own car, my mood sour despite the sunny weather. Standing around, wondering, isn't an option. I have to pick up Tommy from preschool, and then I was planning to drive to Echo Glen to visit Mom. There are sprawling gardens surrounding the care facility we can walk through. The dahlias in the yard are beginning to bloom, and I snapped a photo before leaving the house this morning to show Mom.

I climb into the sedan, turn the key, and…nothing. I repeat the motion, thinking it was a fluke. Still, silence.

"Fuck," I mumble, resting my forehead against the steering

wheel and blowing a long breath that releases every bit of air from my lungs.

I pop my door open, walk to the front of the car, and lift the hood. Everything looks normal, not that I'd know if it didn't.

I pull my phone out of my pocket, deliberating whether to call Lydia to ask if she can get Tommy or abandon my car here and order an Uber to get to Little Red Wagon.

"It didn't start?"

My stomach sinks all the way to the asphalt.

Of course Otto didn't drive off without a backward glance. Of course he's here, witnessing another humiliating moment.

"No."

He stops beside me, bare arm brushing mine as he leans over the engine. The brief, innocent touch burns. I stare at the spot, surprised there's no visible scorch mark on my skin.

"Have you had problems before?"

"No. I mean, yes, it's an old car. I've had to bring it in for repairs before. But nothing recent. It's never not started before, just made weird sounds."

He says nothing, appraising the mess of gears and wires and tubes with the easy nonchalance of someone who knows exactly what they're doing. I'm not sure if he does or doesn't. As far as I know, his vehicular knowledge only extends to the fast, expensive variety. My ancient sedan is neither.

I gnaw on my thumbnail nervously, waiting for him to say something.

"You need a tow truck," Otto tells me a couple of minutes later.

My heart sinks. "Oh."

A tow truck means a serious issue. And likely an expensive one.

"I think it is the timing belt. You will need a new one."

"Are they exp—will a new timing belt cost a lot?"

Otto studies me. He must be aware of the massive discrepancies in our salaries, but I feel like I revealed too much, asking that.

"It should not be that much," he answers. "For the part and labor"—he thinks—"less than a thousand?"

I exhale. That's not great. Not terrible.

"Okay. Thanks."

"You might want to consider... Other parts of the engine have problems too. Replacing the car would make the most sense."

"Yeah. Thanks."

I'm not sure I can afford to buy a new car right now. I haven't seen Mom's royalties for this quarter yet. I haven't decided if I'll retire after this season—or what I'll do with my business degree if I stop playing. Dipping into the safety net of my savings doesn't seem like the savviest financial move.

Otto pulls out his phone, types something, and then raises it to his ear. I don't comprehend why until he relays the address of the Siege's practice facility and starts talking about timing belts.

In relationships, in friendships, with family, I'm almost always the one to take charge. It's unsettling, though not in an unpleasant way, to watch someone else manage everything. To fix a problem before I can.

Otto hangs up a few minutes later. "The truck will be here soon."

"Thank you," I say sincerely.

He nods, walking back toward his SUV.

I send a flurry of panicked texts to Cassidy, letting her know what's going on. I even call my dad's office directly—something I haven't done since before the divorce—and talk to a perky receptionist who tells me my sister is in a meeting. I don't have a number for the sitter Cassidy hired, and today is her day off anyhow. I try to reach Lydia, but she doesn't answer either. The tow truck arrives while I'm listening to her cheerful voicemail.

I hang up, watching Otto shake hands with the overall-wearing middle-aged man whose name patch reads *Wally*.

Wally is efficient, loading my car quickly. All I have to contribute is filling out a form and handing him the key. I also pull the booster seat out of the sedan's back seat since it's looking increasingly likely I'll have to pick Tommy up in an Uber.

Cassidy hasn't called me back by the time the tow truck pulls out of the parking lot. And Otto is still here.

"I can give you a ride," he says.

Immediate déjà vu.

There's a noticeable pause, during which I think Otto might be recalling our first meeting too. I should be flattered, I guess, that he remembers the details since he's undoubtedly met lots of women since.

"I'm fine. Thanks for offering."

Otto exhales, a muscle in his jaw protruding in an annoyed clench that's new. "Caldwell, do not be—"

"I have to pick up Tommy from preschool," I say in a rush, nodding toward the booster seat propped against my calf. "I'll take a—"

"I will drive you, Claire."

He's no longer asking. He's telling, *and* he used my first name. Then grabs the booster seat and strides away with a purpose that makes it obvious he expects me to follow.

Nerves prickle my skin as I open the passenger door. His car is brand-new, by the smell of it, with a screen taking up most of the console. He starts the engine by pressing a button.

"Landslide" is playing from the speakers. I glance at him, startled, but Otto's focused on reversing out of the parking spot.

He brakes at the Stop sign along the side of the lot, grabbing his phone out of the cupholder and passing it to me. "Put in the preschool address."

His screen background is green. No picture. Just solid color.

I stare at it, then state, "It's locked."

"Same passcode."

It doesn't occur to me until I tap the numbers and the screen unlocks that I remember his passcode. It's his birthday.

I open Maps, very tempted to snoop through his three hundred eighty-six unread messages, and enter Little Red Wagon's address.

Otto doesn't comment on the fact that I remembered his passcode.

Just like I pretend not to notice "Songbird" playing after "Landslide" ends. Or that the music is streaming from a playlist on his phone, not a random radio station.

I text Cassidy, letting her know that I found a ride, then stare out the window until we reach the preschool.

"You can just pull up…there," I say, pointing toward the curb that runs parallel to the sidewalk in front of the brick facade.

It's 3:02, according to the clock on the dash, so I'm only a couple of minutes late.

As soon as Otto stops, I'm out of the car, hurrying toward the front doors.

"Claire! Claire!"

I spin, tracking the shout to the playground. Tommy's waving at me from the top of the slide, the boy beside him giggling and waving too.

I wave back, walking toward the wood chips. A little girl with matching pigtails joins the two boys, all three talking animatedly.

Tommy glances this way again, his expression lighting up, and he rushes down the slide before running over. I smile at his excitement, until he reaches me.

"Otto's here?"

I spin toward the SUV. Rather than sitting in the driver's seat, where I assumed he'd stay, Otto has one of the rear doors open and appears to be installing Tommy's booster seat in the back.

He's taking charge again. Annoyance and appreciation coalesce in my chest.

"My car wasn't working," I say.

Tommy isn't listening to my explanation. He's headed toward the SUV, leaving me to snag his backpack from the pile by the bench, wave a hasty goodbye to Mrs. Combs, and follow behind.

None of the well-dressed moms I pass are staring at me. They're all focused on the eye candy that is Otto squatting down to talk to Tommy at eye level. His biceps flex as his elbows balance on muscular thighs, and the sight is practically pornographic.

They've only met once, but Otto appears perfectly at ease as he chats with my nephew.

"Time to go, Tommy boy," I announce cheerfully, setting his backpack in the footwell.

Tommy pouts. "I want to stay and play."

"Not today."

"Why?"

"Because you can't today."

"Why?"

"Because I'm telling you no," I say in my firmest *listen to me or else* tone.

Tommy sighs dramatically but climbs in the back seat.

"You should check his seat," Otto tells me quietly. "Make sure it is installed right."

I nod, ducking my head in to check the clips and ensure the straps are tight. While I do, Tommy perches on the console and admires Otto's car.

"This is nicer than Grandpa's," he comments as I tuck the seat belt under the arm of his booster seat.

I'm tempted to laugh. I settle on a noncommittal, "Mmhmm," before stepping back and shutting the door.

Otto's standing about a dozen feet away now, surrounded by one, two, *four* women.

One exclaims, "Oh, I *loved* Berlin!"

I round the trunk and climb in the front seat, feeling young and frumpy, tempted to sniff my shirt to assess how much I smell.

Tommy chats nonstop from the back seat, mostly about his upcoming birthday party, then abruptly asks, "Is Otto your boyfriend?"

I glance over my shoulder. "No. He's one of my coaches, remember? We're, uh, friends."

"I like him," Tommy continues, blessedly oblivious to how much his question unnerved me. At least he didn't ask it in front of Otto. "He's nice."

"He is," I agree, watching through the windshield as Otto's fan club grows to six sophisticated women. "Super friendly."

Luckily, Tommy has yet to discover sarcasm.

"Can I invite him to my birthday party?"

"No."

"Why not?"

I exhale. "He's too old."

"You're old, and you're coming."

I laugh despite the jealousy seething in my stomach. "I'm

your aunt. Otto isn't related to you."

"Josh is coming, and he's old and not related to me."

Otto's headed back this way.

"It's different, Tommy, okay?" I say quickly. "Are you hungry? I might have a granola bar in here..."

I'm happy to have an excuse to lean down and dig through my soccer bag as the door opens and Otto climbs inside. I locate a bar, avoiding eye contact as Otto starts the car.

"Here you go." I hold the snack out to Tommy.

"I don't like that kind," he informs me.

I sigh, tossing it back in my bag. "Okay. I'll make you something at home."

"Can we stop at Freeze Palace?"

Otto asks, "What is Freeze Palace?" before I can say, "No."

"It's the best ice cream in the whole world," Tommy announces dramatically.

Otto glances at me. "Do they have non-dairy?"

I'm too startled by the fact that he considered that to speak. I just nod.

"Sounds good to me," he says, shifting into drive.

Tommy cheers in the back seat.

I assumed the past six years of silence meant he never really cared. I blamed Otto for not fighting for us.

But the truth is, I gave up first.

And for the first time since I left Paris, I allow myself to wonder if that was the wrong choice.

Chapter 28

Otto

Teal and purple collide in midair, fighting for possession. The ball lands wide, left of the goal. The Portland player pivots, knocking her defender into the post. The huddle of players gathers, then parts as the referee's whistle sounds, stopping play. He beckons with one hand, calling the trainers on the field.

I'm already in motion, unaware of anything except shrinking the distance between me and that end of the field.

The Portland players have scattered outside the box, separating themselves from the teal Siege jerseys surrounding Claire.

"Back up," I bark, reaching the goal.

They do because I'm their coach. Because I'm supposed to be an authority figure with answers, not a panicked spectator. There's a reason family members aren't seated on the sidelines during matches. I try to recall that, to rein in my spiraling emotions. To keep them off my face at the very least.

Claire is conscious, sitting up with her elbows resting on her knees. The band around my chest loosens a little, panic receding as I scan her over and see no visible signs of injury.

"Caldwell?" I crouch on the turf beside her.

"I'm fine," she says, reaching up to gingerly touch her forehead. She winces.

"Let me look." I gently grip her chin, tilting her face so I can see where her head collided with the goalpost.

Red is blooming along her temple, and there's a small cut just above her eyebrow. Shallow and less than a half-inch long, but welling blood.

I drop my hand fast, aware of the eyes on us. "You are out."

She exhales, "I'm fine."

I hear the waver in her voice—the fear below the adrenaline. As it fades, the pain will appear.

"You will *be* fine. Right now, you are bleeding, and you need a concussion protocol."

"Did you lose consciousness, Caldwell?" Eliza kneels next to me.

I shift back a few inches, letting the head coach and the trainer who accompanied her—Michael—take precedence.

"No," she replies. "It just… It stunned me for a minute."

Michael asks her a few questions, then helps her up. The crowd immediately begins to clap as Claire is escorted off the field.

"Daley or Lewiston?" Eliza asks quietly as we walk back to the bench.

It takes me a minute to realize she's consulting me on who should replace Claire in the match. "Daley, I think."

Eliza nods. "I agree."

Daley subs in, and play resumes. We're in the sixty-third minute, and extra time will be added.

I stand, arms crossed and jaw clenched, as purple and teal jerseys mix again.

We're playing well, ahead by a goal, and I...don't care. I've never experienced this level of indifference on a football field. Not on the bench as backup. Not during the most grueling of matches. Not standing on the sidelines as an assistant coach.

It terrifies me. Not because I think my love of football is eroding away. Because it makes obvious what I already suspected—I'm not attached to the Siege.

I respect Eliza. I enjoy working with Meg and Nicole and the two keepers. I like coaching, appreciate being part of this organization and the purpose it provides while my shoulder heals.

But it's Claire. She's the reason I'm excited to go to practices, that I'm invested in games, that I look forward to traveling to other American cities.

It's incredibly obvious now that her presence has been stripped away. There's a hollowness that I suspect would have always existed if I'd been sent to work with any other team. A level of disconnect, as I'd have known that my role was secondary and temporary.

And I have absolutely no idea what to do about it. Go back to Kluvberg and try to forget? It's been six years, and I haven't forgotten. I have regrets about how things ended between us. Does she? Would it be better or worse if I knew she did?

It's not just my feelings for Claire that haven't changed. Nothing else has either. I play in Germany. She plays here. Unless one of us retires or changes leagues, we're looking at a relationship limited to the couple of months our offseasons overlap. Can I do that? Can I ask her to do that?

The match ends, Siege winning, and my mind is still spinning in answerless circles.

We have our usual locker-room debrief, and then Michael pulls Eliza aside to update her on Claire. Meg, Nicole, and I hover on the periphery, listening. The medical team doesn't think she has a concussion. She passed evaluation, not displaying any common symptoms, and was cleared to leave with her sister and rest.

Tomorrow is a day off, so I won't see her until the next practice. I'm hit with a mixture of relief and annoyance, realizing that.

I'm not sure what I'd say. My emotions feel raw and discombobulated, and it's for the best that I have time to rein them under control. But I know I'll lie awake tonight, replaying the moment she went down, and I wish I'd seen her before she left so I could verify she was okay.

After Michael finishes his update, I head back to the stadium office to grab my belongings.

Eliza calls my name, catching up with me as we head down the hallway. I brace myself for a chastisement—I should have talked to her before heading on the field, regardless of the referee's signal—but that's not what she wants to discuss.

"How is your shoulder?" she asks quietly. "Any updates on your recovery timeline?"

"I had an appointment on Tuesday. I am still working on different strengthening exercises. Another month, and they will evaluate the progress again. They think I will be able to start an adapted version of my usual training program in six to eight weeks."

"That's fantastic news, Otto."

I nod. “It is.”

They’re projecting a full recovery. It’s the best surgical outcome, no sign of nerve damage or scarring or chondrolysis. Every American doctor I’ve seen has praised the work of the surgeon who operated on me. There’s a very good chance I’ll be back in goal for the start of next season, that the best-case scenario is going to be reality. That I’ll be able to continue with my career like the injury never happened.

I’m thrilled about it, obviously. But it’s dulled. I’m nervous to trust any recovery until I’m standing in goal, testing the shoulder. I’ve never been out for this long before. Injuries carry psychological trauma, not just physical harm.

“I spoke to Laurie—Coach Willis—yesterday,” Eliza says. “She’s still planning to return in August, but she can come back sooner, if you need to depart earlier?”

The league schedule is structured around a summer break stretching from late June through all of July. When the details of my arrangement with the Siege were first worked out, it was expected I’d stay until the start of the break, and then Coach Willis would return from maternity leave and stay for the remainder of the season. Staying until June sounded like an eternity when I first arrived. Now, it sounds short.

“I will stay,” I say. “No need to change the plan.”

Kluvberg’s season ended a few days ago. And there’s nothing else for me to rush home for.

Eliza smiles. “I was hoping you’d say that. I hope it goes without saying, but I’ll say it anyway: you’ve been an enormous asset to the Siege this season. I know it’s been a challenging time for you personally, and the entire organization appreciates your contributions. I trusted her judgment, but Saylor undersold you, frankly.”

I laugh. “That sounds right.”

“I also wanted to mention, the Boston Sports Foundation is having their annual gala in a few weeks. Eloise Knight, the Siege’s general manager, personally asked that I invite you. It’s a charity event first and foremost, but it will also be a fun evening. I’ll be there, along with Meg and Nicole, and so will representatives from all of Boston’s professional sports leagues. Team owners and political figures tend to attend as well. I’m sure you’ve attended similar events before. Someone from the front office will email you all the details.”

I nod. “Sounds good.”

“Enjoy your day off.” Eliza grabs her bag, then departs.

Leaving me alone with all the thoughts I’m trying not to think about.

Chapter 29

Claire

"What are you doing?" Cassidy exclaims.

I glance up, my hand frozen mid-stroke. "Frosting?"

I say it as a question, but it's fairly obvious.

"You're supposed to be resting," she informs me, walking over to the fridge and pulling out an assortment of lemonades.

I sigh, resuming the process of icing Tommy's birthday cake. Today is his party. "I'm fine, Cassidy."

I woke up with a headache. Every time I woke up, which was every two hours, thanks to my concerned sister and her online research.

The Siege medical staff cleared me. I passed the concussion evaluation and haven't experienced any of the symptoms that indicate anything might be wrong. My hair is down, the curls mostly concealing the bruise by my hairline. Painkillers are managing the lingering ache from my collision with the post.

But Cassidy is still freaked out. She, Josh, and Tommy were all at the game last night. We literally carpooled since I'm without a car, which worked out well because I didn't have to drive home after leaving the game early.

My sister hasn't been to many soccer games. That wasn't the first time I'd left a game to be evaluated, after a messy tackle or a bad header or a collision with another teammate.

When I told Cassidy that, she frowned and said, "Maybe you should retire." She followed it up with a sly mention of how "romantic" it was that my coach ran onto the field to check on me.

Two topics I've avoided discussing with her—leaving soccer and Otto—and at least I could claim being tired and not feeling great as an excuse to dodge the subjects. Which was when Cassidy pulled out her phone to set a series of alarms throughout the night.

"Seriously, Claire," she says, walking over, "I have everything handled. Josh will be here soon to help. So will—so will Dad and Lindsey."

The soy milk I ate with my breakfast cereal curdles in my stomach at the reminder. "I want to do it," I reply stubbornly.

Mom would always stay up late the night before my or Cassidy's birthdays, making a homemade cake to celebrate. The last one she made was for my eighteenth birthday, nearly a decade ago. I offered to make Tommy's this year. Followed the same recipe, written out in Mom's messy scrawl. We'll visit her later this week, on Tommy's actual birthday, but we agreed that her attending today's party would be overwhelming and confusing for her.

"It looks just like hers," Cassidy says quietly.

I clear my throat. "Thanks."

My sister studies me for a few seconds as I continue to smear chocolate frosting on the cake. "If you're really fine—"

"I am," I interject.

"Then you're coming out for drinks with me and Josh tonight."

I groan. "What? No."

"We won't stay out late. But he wants to celebrate the anniversary of me becoming a mom, which is lame but also sweet, and I want you there."

"I don't drink during the season," I remind her.

"Paul Rebeer's has soda."

"Is this another double date?" I ask warily.

"No. Just the three of us, hanging out like old times."

"Okay."

"Speaking of double dates… Walker told Josh you guys, uh, fizzled out?"

I'm surprised, honestly, that it's taken her this long to ask. "Yeah. We weren't…compatible."

It was a massive relief, when Walker told me a colleague at work had asked him out. I assured him I was too busy with soccer anyway, and that was the end of the one-sentence texts we'd traded back and forth for a couple of weeks. My stomach never flipped, not once, when his name showed up on the screen. Let alone the fireworks display that used to go off in Paris when Otto sent me a new message.

The doorbell rings.

"That must be the caterers!" Cassidy exclaims, bustling around the island and heading toward the front door.

As soon as her back is turned, I make a face.

I kept my mouth shut about the party. I knew any negative input would upset Cassidy, and Tommy was obviously thrilled about the elaborate plans. My dad's gift—well, one of them, I'm assuming—was a bouncy house for the party. That was delivered and assembled first thing this morning. Tommy has been jumping in there ever since.

My phone begins buzzing on the counter. It's a number, not a name, on-screen, so I answer hesitantly. "Hello?"

"Hello? Is this Claire Caldwell?" a deep voice asks.

"Yes. This is she."

"This is Travis Malcom from 617 Towing. I'm calling to let you know your vehicle is ready to be picked up whenever you'd like."

I exhale a relieved sigh. "Great. Thank you. I'll be by tomorrow morning. What-what is the final total for the repairs?"

A pause.

"The bill has already been paid, ma'am."

"What? That must be a mistake. There's…" My voice trails as I realize there *is* someone who would have paid it on my behalf. The same person who had called the garage and arranged for my sedan to be towed.

"Thank you," I repeat, then hang up, carefully setting my phone on the counter.

I shouldn't have asked Otto how much the repair would cost. But it never occurred to me he'd cover the expense.

And I'm grateful. It was a thoughtful gesture. But I resent how inferior it makes me feel. Most people would describe me as efficient and organized. But around him—the person I most want to see me as capable? I'm constantly needing help. My phone dies, or I drink too much tequila, or my car quits.

Voices drift from the front hall. The distraction is a relief, until I recognize the deepest one.

My dad appears in the doorway a few seconds later. Lindsey

is right behind him, as impeccably dressed as every other time I've seen her. Hair highlighted and nails manicured.

It should be a consolation—that my father's second wife is about as opposite of my mom as could be. I can admit now that he and Lindsey are better-suited as a couple. A practical pair. But their ideal match came at the expense of what I considered a perfect family, and their happiness only serves as a reminder.

"Hello, Claire. Nice to see you." Lindsey speaks first, as unfailingly polite as ever.

She's never forced any relationship between us—easy when our lives barely overlap at all. I could count on both hands the number of times we've been in a room together.

"You too, Lindsey."

She smiles, then turns to Cassidy. "Did the bouncy house get delivered?"

"It sure did. Thank you again. Tommy is thrilled. I haven't been able to drag him out of there all morning."

"What about the extra tables?" Lindsey asks. "Did the layout I mapped out work?"

"I think so," Cassidy replies. "But I wanted you to look at whether some should be farther from the swing set."

Lindsey nods, heading for the sliding doors that lead onto the deck. "I thought about that. Maybe we should..." The rest of her sentence trails as Cassidy follows her outside and shuts the door.

Leaving me and my dad alone.

I fiddle with the knife I was using to spread the frosting. "Hi, Dad."

"Hello, Claire." He approaches the island slowly. He's dressed up, same as Lindsey, wearing slacks and a button-down.

My current attire—Siege T-shirt and ratty sweatpants—

isn't helping me feel any more mature. In my defense, I took a metal pole to the forehead last night. But I should probably sneak upstairs and put on a dress, before kids and their parents start to arrive.

I clear my throat, so we're not standing in silence, then bang the knife against the bowl for the same reason.

When I glance up, Dad is staring at the recipe card on the counter.

"Haven't had one of those cakes in a while," he comments quietly.

"Me neither." I use up the last of the frosting, setting the bowl and the knife in the sink.

"Could I talk to you out on the sunporch for a minute?"

I still, searching for an excuse. I have to change, I have to check on something, I have to… I deflate, deciding it's better to get this conversation over with. "Yeah. Sure."

Cassidy seems settled, with her job and with Josh. Tommy is making friends. He's playing T-ball now and talking about starting soccer in the fall. It would surprise me if they moved again soon. Maybe ever. There are going to be more birthday parties. More holidays. The sooner Dad and I find some way to coexist, the better, and having this conversation is one step closer to civility.

I follow him into the small room off the kitchen. Mom's desk remains tucked in one corner, but the surface is no longer covered with papers. They were all sorted months ago, either recycled or transported to Echo Glen with her.

Aside from the desk, two armchairs are the only furniture out here. I sit in the left one; my dad takes the right.

"Cassidy said you were injured during yesterday's game."

I nod. "It's not a big deal. I just bumped a goalpost. No concussion."

Dad's frowning, looking concerned. Looking like…a parent. He came to all of my games in high school after the divorce even though I refused to acknowledge him. Yet I never told him when I signed with the Siege. I'm not sure how he found out. Cassidy probably.

For the first time, I regret that. He should have heard it from me.

The awkwardness between us is stifling, expanding to fill the small room.

"Are you okay?" I finally blurt.

I really, really can't deal with a second sick parent.

My dad's face creases with confusion, then smooths with understanding. "I'm fine, Claire. Perfectly healthy, as far as I know."

I nod, relaxing deeper into the cushions. "Good."

Dad exhales. "Cassidy told me about your mother's diagnosis."

"I know."

"You should have told me, Claire."

"I know," I repeat. "I was going to…eventually."

I was. My parents' communication dwindled down to practically nothing after I turned eighteen. I got a full athletic scholarship to Lincoln, so Dad didn't even have to contribute to tuition. He came to my college graduation, and Mom and I saw him at the hospital when Tommy was born. I think that might have been the last time they saw each other in person. It was the last time I'd seen my dad in person, until Cassidy moved back.

Despite my many issues with how he'd handled the end of their marriage, my plan wasn't to keep Mom's illness from him.

"She didn't want you to know," I add. "She wanted time to accept it herself."

Dad glances at his lap, clasping and unclasping his hands. "I understand. She's at Echo Glen?"

"Yes."

"I looked it up. It's very nice." A pause. "Expensive."

With my dad, it almost always circles back to money. He didn't grow up with much, but makes a lot now. I'm sure he's thrilled to be paying for Tommy's preschool. I think he was almost disappointed he couldn't pay for my college.

"It's being handled."

"How?"

I bristle. "Mom's finances aren't any of your business."

"They are if they're impacting my daughter's."

Did Cassidy imply that? Or is he assuming on his own? I haven't had to pay for any of Mom's care yet. But there's a good chance her savings won't cover everything. The book she's working on is unlikely to ever release, and royalties tend to trend lower over time as new titles draw more attention and dominate sales.

I remain silent, neither confirming nor denying his statement.

"I've set up a trust to supplement your mother's care in any way necessary. Your mother's accountant has all the relevant details. You will never need to support her financially."

I stare at him. Dad offering money isn't a shock. For all his faults, my father has never been greedy. He gifted Mom this house. Paid her more than the allotted amount of child support, plus covered the costs of the travel teams and out-of-state camps I attended. Bought Cassidy a car when she turned sixteen and offered the same to me. But offering and doing are different actions. There's always been a choice, not a firm decision already made.

"You-you didn't need to do that. I'm not sure Mom would want—"

"I broke vows to your mother, Claire, and I'll be the first to admit that."

I still. Since it happened, we've never discussed the divorce.

"But *sickness and health* isn't one I'll renege on," Dad continues. "I'm not asking. I know she gave you power of attorney, that you could fight this if you choose to. But this is something I owe her. And I know, without a doubt, that it's the right thing to do."

Beneath the surprise and uncertainty, another emotion trickles in. Relief. The responsibility of possibly having to pay for Mom's care was…heavy. A separate weight from the emotional burden of witnessing her lose parts of herself. And it's…gone, just like that. Cassidy will agree with him. Mom might have, and it's one of many things I wish I could ask without confusing or upsetting her.

Dad seems to understand I need time to process. "If you want to discuss details or have any questions, you know how to reach me. This is Tommy's big day; I'm not trying to overshadow it with serious topics. But I wanted to talk to you in person, and that's… Well, I don't see much of you."

I swallow hard, guilt resurfacing.

"You can talk to me about anything else too. I hope you know that. Even if it's something you don't… I'd rather we discuss the hard things than not talk at all."

I nod, too overwhelmed to respond.

He smiles, stands, and heads for the doorway.

"Dad?" I manage.

I don't turn to see, but I hear his footsteps stop.

"Thank you."

Chapter 30

Otto

"You're a little boring as a coach."

I smile as soon as I hear her voice. It stays on my face as Claire takes the seat next to me.

"Am I?"

"We won, it's a Friday night, and you're not out partying?"

"You are here," I state.

"Yeah, but I've always been boring."

"You were never boring," I counter. "And I did not party in…Paris."

I throw it out there as a test. We're… I don't know what we are. Friends in some ways. Coach and player in others. But my relationship with Claire has always been unique. It's never been easily definable.

Sometimes, the past feels off-limits between us. Sometimes, it feels like the past just took place, and we're existing in the immediate aftermath.

"You partied after."

"We had just won a gold medal. If I tried to disappear, everyone would have had questions. And I did not want to talk about it."

She's silent for a few seconds. "I never congratulated you."

I exhale. "You did not need to congratulate me, Claire."

"I should have though. I'm sorry I didn't. I just..." She props her feet up on the chair in front of her, sinking down in the seat. "I was so wrapped up in my own disappointment. I felt like I'd let the whole team down. Blown my one big chance. By the time I was able to look past that, it felt like it'd been too long. And you never reached out, so..."

"I wanted to. But you told me to no*t show* up at that match. After you lost, I did not know what to say. Did not know if you blamed me or had any solution for us or know if you wanted to hear from me."

Claire says nothing.

We stare at the empty stadium.

"This might be my last season."

I glance at her, startled by the statement. "What? Why?"

"I signed a two-year contract."

"They will offer an extension, Claire."

"Probably," she agrees. "But I'm not sure if I should take it. Someone else could have my spot. Someone who...wants it more."

I frown. "You do not want it?"

"I don't know if I want it. I haven't loved playing in a long time. I love parts of it, and I hate parts of it, and I want to retire before I hate all of it. Before all I remember are the losses and the letdowns and the bruises. Does that make sense?"

"Of course it makes sense."

"So, you…agree? I should retire?"

I laugh. "Of course not."

"But you just said…"

"You think I have not had hard days? You think I have not let goals in? You think I have not lost games? You think I have not had days I wondered if I should have taken over my grandfather's construction company, that he was right all along about football being a mistake?"

She sighs. "It's different for you."

"It is the same."

"It's not. You've won a gold medal. You've won a World Cup. You've made millions. They'll retire your jersey when you decide you're done. You're so famous that Kluvberg flew you halfway around the world so you could recover away from scrutiny. I'm not saying you don't deserve any of that—you deserve all of it. But I-I don't have any of it. I don't feel like I've accomplished what I wanted to. And at some point… It feels like I should accept that and try something else."

"When we met in Paris, you said you wanted to play professionally. *Here*, in the US."

"I remember."

"What do *you* mean, you did not accomplish what you wanted to? You came back and did that."

Another exhale. "I was so excited when they announced Boston as the location of the next expansion team. When the Siege made an offer. It felt like a fresh start even though I was moving home. I got used to being a background player in Denver, and people paid more attention to me here. *I* was the hometown success story. I didn't deal with the pressure well to begin with, and then Mom got diagnosed, and things at home were more challenging… I told Coach Taylor, and she had me meet with a sports psychologist."

"Did that help?"

"Not really. Everything we worked on—pregame routines and bonding with my teammates and visualization—was helpful in certain moments. But then when I really needed them… nothing."

"Is your mom… What is the…" I can't figure out how to phrase the question, but Claire realizes what I'm trying to ask.

"Every case is different," she says quietly. "She has good days and bad days. She can't control it—I couldn't control it—and I let that affect everything. We went to visit yesterday for Tommy's birthday, and she was confused. It was easier to play along with her reality when it was just me and her. But her not recognizing Tommy? That's hard. Especially for Cassidy."

"Sorry."

"Don't apologize like it's your fault. I'm just telling you… because I want to tell you, I guess."

"How was the dinosaur party?" I ask.

Claire smiles. "It was good. Tommy had a blast, which was the important part. My, uh, my dad was there." She plays with the zipper of her Siege windbreaker. "We talked a little. It wasn't great, but it wasn't horrible either. So…progress? He'll be around more, it seems like. And it's been fourteen years. I've spent more than half my life acting like I don't have a dad, but I do, technically. I can hate what he did and not hate him… Maybe?"

I nod.

"I'll pay you back."

"For what?"

"You know for what."

"It was not a big deal."

"It was a huge deal, and I really appreciate it. But I can't accept it."

"Why not?" I challenge.

"Would you have paid for Savannah's car to get fixed if it had bro*ken d*own in the park*ing lot? Or Reyna's?"*

"Probably not."

"That's why, Otto. Right before it happened, you said you were going to treat me like every other player."

"I was frustrated when I said that."

She fiddles with the zipper again. "Because I stole your shirt?"

"Because you shut down every time Paris comes up."

"Living it once was hard enough. And we were talking about your fiancée, not Paris, which I really don't want to discuss."

"She is my ex-fiancée, Claire."

"Who called it off?"

"I did."

"Why?"

"There were lots of reasons. Lots of times it did not feel… right. But we went out to dinner for my birthday, a night she had planned, and it was a fancy restaurant. It was just us; none of my friends or teammates were there. I knew we were different. I thought that was…healthy? But I realized she did not know me that night, not just the footballer. We did not agree on enough important things, let alone the small things, like where to eat. I ended it that night. She left the next morning."

"Was it different when you first met?"

I sigh, leaning forward to rest my elbows on my knees. "No. It was never different."

"Then why did you propose?"

"I thought it would make our relationship better. Beck got

married and had a kid. So had a lot of my other teammates. I wanted that. I have never had a family really. I had only… We were the closest to a serious relationship. I thought that things felt different with Juliette because I was older. I did not realize I was comparing being in love to…not being in love." I glance over as I add that last part, wanting to gauge her reaction.

Claire bites her bottom lip, blinking rapidly as she stares at the empty field.

I turn my head, looking at it too. Maybe it doesn't change the past, but I don't regret saying it.

The clock above the scoreboard shows it's seven thirty.

"I have to go," I say reluctantly. "Beck is landing at eight. I am picking them up from the airport."

"Them?"

"Saylor and Gigi came too. They are only here for a couple of nights, and then they are going to visit Saylor's family."

"Oh. Okay. Have, uh, have fun."

"Thanks." I nod. Then stand.

"I'm going to pay you back."

"Fine." I start walking down the aisle.

"And, Otto?"

I glance back.

She's staring after me, a small smile tipping up the corners of her mouth. "I was in love too."

• • •

My grandfather calls while I'm driving to the airport. Anyone else, I wouldn't answer. I'm busy replaying my conversation with Claire in my head.

But it is Opa. And he rarely calls, let alone when it's the middle of the night for him.

So, I answer.

"Hallo, Otto."

"Opa. Hallo. Is…is everything okay?"

"Fine," he grumbles.

I was expecting a problem. An issue with the house or something concerning Mila.

"Has your hip been bothering you?" It's the only thing I can think to ask him about.

"No. They did a fine job, fixing me up."

"Good."

An awkward pause falls before I ask the most obvious question. "Is something wrong?"

"Papers are saying you'll be playing again soon."

"You read the Sports section?"

"It wasn't in the Sports section. Front page."

"Oh."

I didn't consider that, but it makes some sense. Kluvberg ended the season decidedly mediocre, and although Banks wasn't to blame, we had been first in the league when my injury happened.

"You'll be back before training starts?"

"Yes. I still have commitments here, but they'll wrap up by the end of June."

"You'll be back in July then?"

My forehead furrows in response to the unexpected question. "Yes?"

"Good. Goodbye, Otto."

"Bye," I say, and then the line goes dead.

Leaving me with the realization… I think my grandfather called me just to check in.

Chapter 31

Claire

PARIS: SIX YEARS EARLIER

I rest my head back against the cinder-block wall, closing my gritty eyes and attempting a few deep, grounding breaths. I barely slept last night, and that's not an exaggeration. Every time I got close to dozing off, I'd be jolted awake by a reminder of today's gold-medal match. Or I'd replay my breakup with Otto.

Breakup isn't really the right word. We were a fun fling, one I knew wouldn't last past the end of the Games. Well, logically, I knew that. I didn't realize how badly I'd wanted to be wrong until I realized how right I was.

It hurts, far worse than ending things with Nolan did. Worse than when I caught my senior prom date kissing a teammate at the after-party.

Heartbreak is aptly named because it does feel as though

something is fracturing inside of me. A piece is splitting off, the part that foolishly fantasized about him coming onto the field to congratulate me after we won.

If the ache in my chest wasn't so visceral, I'd laugh with relief. My whole life, my practicality has been pointed out to me. Pragmatism was a character flaw, according to my carefree sister and adventurous friends, and commendable, according to my creative mom.

Unfortunately, I discovered romanticism at the worst possible time—when I should be fully invested and focused on nothing outside the four boundary lines of a soccer field.

Football, my brain automatically corrects, the European terminology pulling my thoughts right back to Otto.

He texted me this morning—a simple, Good luck, Boston—and I stared at it for twenty minutes until my alarm went off, torn between relief and resentment. In many ways, it would have been easier to have a clean break. But Otto has been the center of my Olympic experience ever since the night we met. A source of advice and encouragement that built me to a certain level of confidence. Just because the foundation fell away doesn't mean I can't forge ahead.

"Caldwell?"

My eyes fly open, registering the matching jersey in front of me. Saylor Scott is appraising me with a speculative tilt of her head, her expression amused and also a touch concerned.

"Hey, Saylor." I straighten so I'm no longer supported by the cinder blocks.

Unlike me, our team captain looks energized and confident. Every other time we've interacted, I've been intimidated by Saylor's reputation and intensity. I'm too drained to summon the typical awe from being in the presence of a player who is already being heralded as one of the greatest of all time.

"Everything okay?" Saylor questions, reaching up to adjust her blue headband.

I nod. "I'm good. Just...needed a minute. Big day, you know."

Her expression softens with sympathy. "It's just another soccer game, Caldwell."

That's the crucial difference between athletes like Saylor and me. It is a soccer game. It's also a global event that will be watched by millions, dissected by commentators, and ultimately, crown a world champion.

But if Saylor, who's facing ten times the pressure as me—someone who isn't even starting and might not play at all—thinks so, then I can at least fake that mentality.

I smile and nod. "I know."

"See *you in there," Saylor says, then* continues down the hall to the locker room.

I can hear the ruckus from here, the combination of nerves and excitement evident in my teammates' loud voices as they suit up for the coming match. Sweat prickles on the back of my neck and on my palms as my heart knocks against my ribs.

I suck in a deep breath.

"It's just another soccer game."

One last deep inhale. I exhale as I turn the corner, headed for the locker room.

...

The first half of the game is a blur, right up until Sierra Sanders goes down and doesn't stand. Blood whooshes in my ears as I watch her limp off the field, avoiding placing any weight on her ankle, supported by two members of the Team USA staff.

The official holds the board up with her number, then mine displayed, and I'm su*dde*nly called to the pitch during a tied gold-medal match.

I run onto the field to thunderous applause. The cheering isn't for me. It's a rallying cry, an attempt to help buoy the entire team into a comeback.

The wall of sound is enormous. Above me. Around me. Suffocating me.

I've been ready during every game I've ever played in.

And this—the game—feels like the exception.

My muscles feel leaden. My steps are uncoordinated as I reach my position. My nod to Ali Lewis, the closest defender, is an awkward bob.

It's like a nightmare where everything feels wrong and detached. Except I'm wide awake. Onstage, under a spotlight, surrounded by towering stands, packed with tens of thousands of spectators.

I risk one last glance at the spectator box with reserved seats for athletes. It's full since this is a final, and I scan every face.

He's not here.

I told him not to come, so the crush of disappointment is ridiculous. Some part of me hoped he'd show up anyway.

Play resumes.

I focus on the game. Recall all the tournaments and travel teams and tryouts that got me here, a gold-medal match.

Saylor takes a shot that I think will make it past the Australian goalie. There's an audible exhale of disappointment when their keeper manages to knock it to the side, keeping the score tied.

Seconds tick higher, closer and closer to the ninety-minute mark. Every time the ball winds up on the opposite end of the field, I pray it'll end up in the net. Every time it travels this direction, I pray the score will remain the same.

And then, finally, there's a breakaway with five minutes left. We all sprint after Mackenzie, watching a yellow jersey rush to guard her.

I'm a runner. Distance, but I have speed too. If I hadn't wholly committed to soccer by the time high school rolled around, I would have participated in track and cross-country.

I also have fresh legs, having subbed in.

So, it's not a massive surprise I beat most of my teammates into the offensive zone.

It *is* a massive surprise when Mackenzie kicks the ball past the defender blocking her…straight at me.

Nothing's a blur. Nothing slows down. The biggest moment of my career—of my life—and time ticks along like everything's normal and nothing unusual is taking place.

I've got the shot. A clear view of the net. I track the trajectory with my eyes, the din of eighty thousand fans fading into white noise as I aim all my focus at the open stretch of net.

Australia's goalie is ready. She's been practically perfect tonight.

Is he watching on television? Does he care that much at least?

I grit my teeth, plant my left foot, and swing my right.

The ball hurtles toward the net. It's an accurate kick, but it's not flying as high or as fast as I know my foot is capable of.

My big moment—the shot that matters more than any other I've ever taken—and I know, even before her yellow glove connects with the ball, that it won't get past the goalie.

A collective loud groan echoes through the spectators sporting red, white, and blue. The disappointment is palpable in the air, an acrid taste coating my tongue.

I want to collapse on the turf right there. Dismay sinks down to my very marrow. My muscles, trained to perform for hours, quiver with the simple effort of staying upright.

But the game isn't over. Not officially at least.

I race back to our zone with a boulder of depression and disbelief strapped to my chest. That wasn't a miraculous save or an awkward angle. I should have made that shot. And if I had, we'd be winning.

Australia's pressing harder, energized by my failed attempt.

Thirty seconds later, the officials add three minutes to the clock.

Three minutes.

One hundred eighty seconds.

"Chin up, Caldwell," Saylor says, jogging past.

I nod an acknowledgment I'm not sure she sees, desperately fighting the sinking sensation in my chest.

It's not over yet, but it feels over. Or maybe I'm just projecting the helplessness I'm experiencing. The whole world is tinted gray by my melancholia.

A little over two minutes later, Australia scores.

Another forty-five seconds pass, followed by the blow of the final whistle. That high-pitched tweet sounds so final.

The end of this match.

The end of the Olympics.

The end of Paris.

The end of me and Otto.

The end.

Chapter 32

Otto

"What about this place?" Saylor says, nodding toward a wooden sign swaying ahead.

"Good with me," Beck replies. "Berger?"

"It's just a little farther," I say, continuing down the brick street.

At least, I think it is. I looked this location up months ago, when I first moved to Boston, but I've never been before. When Saylor suggested getting another drink after we finished dinner at an Italian restaurant, this seemed like a perfect opportunity to go.

"You've been saying that for ten minutes," Beck grouses, but he and Saylor continue after me.

I glance over my shoulder and grin at him. "Tired, *Kaiser*?"

"Yes," he replies grumpily.

Saylor and Beck—and Gigi—are only in Boston for one more

night. They stopped here specifically to see me rather than fly into Atlanta, like they normally do as part of their annual trip to Saylor's hometown. Will's brother, Tripp, offered to watch Gigi for the night so that Saylor and Beck could enjoy a parents' night out.

Weirdly, despite us seeing less of each other than ever before, I feel closer to Beck now than before I got injured. Most of our phone conversations have centered around topics other than football, which was rarely the case when we were playing together. I've always been closer to Beck than any other guy on the team. He mentored me, offered me advice and insight, as soon as I joined the team. At the time, it was widely considered that Stefan Herrmann would be in goal for the foreseeable future. Beck was one of the few who bet I'd be starting sooner. It's nice to know our friendship extends beyond being teammates, especially now that he has a family of his own.

"Paul Rebeer's?" Saylor laughs, spotting the sign ahead. "That's awesome."

I exhale, relieved to have found it.

The wood-paneled pub is loud and busy. A trivia game is taking place in one corner, and the tall stools along the length of the bar are all occupied.

Saylor and Beck head for a back booth while I split off to use the restroom. There's only one, with a line, so I lean against the wall to wait my turn, surveying the vintage sports pennants attached to the wall. The first team I look for is the Siege, finding a teal triangle tucked in the bottom right.

My phone keeps buzzing in my pocket—Will and Sophia responding to the photos Saylor sent during dinner, I'm guessing. I don't pull it out to check.

The last time we talked, Will mentioned plans for another

trip to Boston this summer. He also asked how much longer I'd be in Boston.

I made some vague response about needing to talk with the Siege coaching staff.

It's late May. I have three months before Kluvberg's preseason begins. By the time it does, I need to be the same player I was when my injury happened.

In a few weeks, my role on the Siege will officially end. Past that point, there's no requirement for me to stay in this city. I could book a flight home. Could have already been back in Kluvberg if I'd taken Eliza up on her offer last week.

The bathroom door opens. The brunette woman exiting holds the door for me, appraising me with a lingering look that I respond to with a polite smile before ducking inside the small restroom.

Back in the main section of the bar, I scan the crowd for Saylor and Beck. Before I find my friends, I spot a guy who looks vaguely familiar. I stare, trying to place him, until he leans back and reveals the woman seated next to him. I glance away, looking around the bar with renewed interest.

Claire's standing at one end of the bar, elbows leaning on the shiny wood as she chats with a dark-haired man with a white towel slung over one shoulder. His grin is familiar—and instantly pisses me off. I'm walking that way before the bartender turns toward the rows of bottles, pushing through the crowd of people who couldn't find seats or opted to stand.

I sidle up next to her, purposefully knocking my elbow into her arm.

She glances over, irritation, then confusion, and finally recognition spreading across her face. "What-what are you doing here?"

I rest an elbow on the counter, angling my body toward hers and using the bar's busyness as an excuse to lean closer. "If I buy you a drink, will you insist on paying me back?"

"Yes." She's fighting a smile though, tapping a credit card against the counter. "Technically, Josh is paying anyway. We were going to come here last weekend, after Tommy's party, but looking after twenty five-year-olds for four hours was kind of exhausting."

"So, Josh can buy you a drink, but I cannot?"

"Exactly." She purses her lips, glancing around the immediate vicinity. "Seriously, what are you doing here?"

"I am with Saylor and Beck. We went to dinner, and then Saylor suggested getting another drink. So, we came here."

"Oh." She relaxes some, and I wonder if she thought I was here on a date. "That's a…coincidence."

"Not really."

A furrow appears on her forehead. "What do you mean?"

"Well, you are the one who told me about this place. I did not know you would be here tonight, but it is why I chose it."

She stares at me.

"Claire? Claire Caldwell? Oh my God, it *is* you! Hi!"

I step back so Saylor can hug Claire. Beck, hovering behind her, gives me a long, searching look that tells me he's put together the identity of the woman I told him about.

I nod once, not sure what I'm trying to convey.

"How are you?" Claire asks Saylor.

"Right now?" Saylor beams. "Amazing. It's nice to be home. Well, *closer* to home. It's been a while since we visited. We were supposed to visit my friend Emma earlier this year, but plans fell through." She glances at me. "Beck and I decided to stop to visit Otto on the way to see my parents."

"Oh." Claire is looking at me, too, because when I glance her way, her gaze quickly flicks in another direction. "Fun!"

She's not a great actress. It's fairly obvious from her tone that Claire was not as surprised to see Saylor as Saylor was to see her.

"How do you two know each other?" Saylor asks.

I'm highly suspicious of her tone. It's a little too innocent.

"I play on the Siege now," Claire answers.

"Oh. Wow! That's awesome." Saylor's reaction seems genuine, and I reassess my assumption that Beck told his wife the real reason I was hesitant to come to Boston. Saylor focuses on me again, a mischievous smile pulling up the corners of her lips. "Must be rough, having Otto as a coach."

"Fuck off, Scott," I say.

Saylor just smiles wider.

"He's been really helpful to the team," Claire says, a trace of defensiveness in her tone.

I think Saylor might hear it, too, because she looks at Claire, not me, as she replies, "I'm just giving Berger shit. He knows I know he's the best Kluvberg player."

"Standing right the fuck here," Beck comments.

"Here's the lager and the whiskey sour." The bartender Claire was talking to is back, setting two glasses in front of her. "I'll bring the Coke over to your table. That way, you won't have to balance three glasses."

"I can balance three glasses, Blake," she tells the guy.

"I know." He grins at her. "But you're not working, and it gives me an excuse to come over to your table."

A muscle in my jaw pops, and I try to force it to relax.

"Uh, okay. Thanks." Claire's uncomfortable, but I can't tell if it's because of his flirting or because Saylor, Beck, and I are all witnessing it.

She turns toward us, one glass in each hand. “Enjoy your night, guys.”

“Come over to our booth before you head out,” Saylor says. “I’d love to catch up more.”

Claire nods. “Of course. Yeah, I’ll stop by. See you then.”

As soon as Claire walks away, Saylor turns toward Beck. “You know what I want. I’m going to the bathroom.”

Beck says nothing as we stand alone by the bar. Then, “Assume you’d prefer to order from a different bartender?”

I roll my eyes, then lead him down to the opposite end.

Chapter 33

Claire

I'm in Otto Berger's apartment. The place where he sleeps and showers and probably does other naked activities with women, like the ones who were swarming him at the bar earlier.

It's sparsely furnished, even after months of habitation. All of the furniture clearly came with the apartment. There's a Kluvberg T-shirt tossed over the back of one of the armchairs and a binder with the Siege logo set on the coffee table. There's a print from the Museum of Fine Art tacked up on one wall, slightly crooked.

No photos.

No bras lost between cushions—I checked before sitting on the couch.

"What about Mackenzie Howard?" Saylor asks. She's sprawled out on the plush rug, nursing a glass of wine as I catch her up on players she remembers from college. "Is she still with Dallas?"

I shake my head, reaching for my water and sneaking a glance at the kitchen in the process. "She retired at the end of last season. Something with her ACL, I think."

Otto and Beck are leaning against the counter, talking in rapid German.

I'm still not sure how I ended up here. Explaining to my sister why I hugged the blonde woman Otto was with evolved into Cassidy slyly insisting I go over to their booth. Which evolved into Saylor insisting I come back with her to Otto's apartment so we could talk "somewhere quieter."

If someone had told the twenty-one-year-old who showed up in Paris that she'd one day be hanging out with Adler Beck, Saylor Scott, and Otto Berger, she would have laughed in their face. All these years later, I'm still having a hard time comprehending it.

When I refocus on the living room, Saylor's expression is grim. "She was only a couple of years older than me. She should have rehabbed it."

I sip more water. I don't need to ask Saylor what her opinion on me retiring would be.

There are logical reasons why I should walk away at the end of this season. Money, job security, the unforgiving training required to keep up at the professional level. It's a decision I get to make for myself now that Dad's stepped up regarding Mom's care. Somehow, that makes it a more difficult decision, not an easier one.

"What about Samantha Cole?"

I think. "Still plays for Dallas."

"Good. I always liked her." Saylor sighs. "It's so hard to keep up with people. It'd have been hard if I hadn't moved to another country and had a kid, but since I did, it's practically impossible. Most days, I barely have the energy to collapse into bed after practice and taking care of Gigi."

"I'm sure," I say. I adjust my position on the couch. "My sister moved back to town recently, with my nephew. Helping take care of him is exhausting enough. I can't imagine doing it full-time."

"How old is he?" Saylor asks.

"He just turned five."

Saylor smiles. "That's a fun age." She sips more wine. Leans close, lowering her voice. "Is Otto dating anyone?"

I stare at her, taken aback by the question itself and the rapid conversation change. "I don't—I don't know. Why?"

"Just curious. I've been worried about him. Beck too. I thought maybe you'd noticed or heard something. I know how locker rooms are." She runs a finger around the rim of her glass. "Football is everything to Otto. Without it… Well, I was hoping he'd at least start dating again."

"He, uh, stopped?" I ask, knowing I shouldn't and unable to stop the question from coming out anyway.

"He got engaged a couple of years ago," Saylor tells me. "I never thought Juliette was right for him, but they seemed happy-ish. Then Otto showed up for dinner, alone, said they broke up, and never mentioned her again. As far as I know, there hasn't been anyone serious since."

"Oh," is all I can manage.

"I mean, I get it's hard to play and make a relationship work, but—"

"What are you guys whispering about?"

Saylor rolls away, glancing at her approaching husband with a smirk. "Oh, I was just telling Claire about that time I beat you in a shoot-out." She winks at me. "It's my trademark move."

"Barely beat me," Beck says, coming to stand behind her.

"Don't be a sore loser," Saylor says. "Otto's here to act as my witness that it happened."

I fight the urge to glance in Otto's direction. I didn't realize he had been there when Saylor and Beck met, but it makes sense. It's obvious he's close with both of them, and I'm glad. He might not have much family in the traditional sense, but he has people who care about him.

"I am not getting involved," Otto calls *f*rom the kitchen.

Saylor laughs. "One of my proudest accomplishments," she tells me.

I smile. "I'm sure. I doubt I could get a shot past him."

Saylor's eyes dance. "That too. But I was talking about beating Beck. Otto was just a baby goalie back then."

"You guys have a kid to check on, yes?" Otto asks.

"Nice hospitality, Berger," Beck drawls, then glances at Saylor. "But Tripp did text. Gigi woke up and keeps asking for you."

Saylor somersaults upright. "Shit. Okay."

She gives me a huge hug while Beck and Otto converse in German. I only manage *to transla*te a few words.

"It was so good to see you, Claire. I hope I'll see you in LA."

I hug her back. "Thanks, Saylor."

Even if I choose not to retire, it's very unlikely I'll make the roster for the next Olympics. I'll be nearly thirty by then, my only caps earned almost a decade ago.

But very unlikely isn't impossible. And I can't confidently say that I'd rather never know for sure than fail to get a national team invitation.

Saylor hugs Otto while I say goodbye to Beck. He's been friendly this entire impromptu evening, but I feel awkward around him. Not only because *he's* Adler Beck. He called or texted Otto countless times when we were together in Paris. I associate him with that tumultuous time in my life.

Saylor and Beck depart in a flurry of activity a couple of minutes later.

Without them, the apar*tment* feels smaller, not larger, tension expanding to fill all the empty space. Otto and I have barely spoken all night, allowing Saylor's easy chatter to fill any silence.

"Nice place," I comment, swallowing a large sip of my water. I'll finish this, mention how late it is, and hightail it out of here.

"Not really mine," he replies.

"Right." Right. Exactly what I needed—a reminder he's leaving soon. "Well, I should—"

"Are you dating Blake?"

In my frazzled state, it takes me a minute to remember who Blake is and answer. "No. I don't, um, I don't date coworkers."

"Are you dating anyone?"

I swallow hard. "No."

He nods once. Decisively. "I am finished pretending, Claire."

"What do you mean, you're—"

"I will not tell anyone about us. But I am not talking about Paris and everything that happened then. I am talking about pretending now. About how I still think about you."

I fight—fight *hard*—to prevent those words from sinking too deep, pulling in a long, unsteady breath.

"Are you pretending, Claire?"

"I'm..."

I'm in no way prepared to have this conversation, is what I am. Somehow, celebrating my nephew's birth spiraled into this discussion I never expected to happen. We—sort of—settled the past. We talked about it at least. But acknowledging former feelings is very different from *now*, a collision of past and present I wasn't anticipating.

I fell for Otto fast, hard, and uninhibited. It was thrilling. Exciting. Wonderful. Devastating when it ended. And it's normal for an experience like that to leave a lasting impression, right?

We've only been alone for a few minutes, and I'm struggling to remember anything else that happened today. These minutes easily eclipse the rest of my day, just like his presence in Paris diminished everything, even my nerves and fear, making me feel like I could conquer the world. Could become the athlete I had grown up admiring. Could win when it mattered most.

I fought tears the entire flight home from Paris, clutching the velvet case that contained my silver medal. Feeling like I didn't deserve it, that I hadn't earned it. Like I'd let everyone down, including Otto and his *Good luck, Boston* text.

Those feelings of sadness and failure are so tangled up with happy memories involving Otto that I'm not sure how to even approach unknotting them. I've never had to. I just tried to shove them away and move past it all.

"I don't know," I finally say. Hoarsely. Honestly.

I don't know if I still care or if I've started to care all over again.

And that uncertainty is suddenly unacceptable. Intolerable, like an itch I can't reach to scratch.

Otto frowns as my reply registers. Either because it's not what he wanted to hear or because he's remembering saying that phrase to me.

That's not why I said it. But I do recall the heavy echo of how those words felt, the sinking realization of how deep in *us* I was while he was in the shallows.

We've gravitated closer over the course of this conversation. Near enough that all it takes are two steps and rising on my tiptoes.

It takes about a millisecond of contact for me to confirm what I suspected, but I continue kissing him anyway. His mouth is warm and firm and familiar, the soft press sending sparks of awareness skittering everywhere, too many and too widespread to keep track of. So I don't bother. I relax into the sensation, well aware I'd rather regret doing this than let him leave with what-ifs echoing in his absence. Determined not to make the same mistake twice.

I allow my hands to wander into his hair, the strands just long enough for me to grip. Tug his lower lip between my teeth.

It takes Otto—*Otto Berger*, world-renowned for fast reflexes—about ten seconds to kiss me back.

Once he does, I lose control fast. He seizes it, scooping me up and walking us toward the couch.

He's the only athlete I've ever hooked up with, and I forgot how arousing it was to be manhandled by someone who did it so effortlessly. I can feel the contours of his muscles as they flex against me, the strength obvious as I run my hands up his arms to his shoulders—

His shoulder.

I yank my mouth away. "Your shoulder!" I say urgently, attempting to wiggle my way back to the ground.

Otto has the audacity to laugh. "Claire?"

"Yeah?" God, I sound *breathless*.

"I do not give a fuck about my shoulder right now."

He does. His injury, his recovery, his football career—they're all essential to who Otto is.

I know that—know him. And his willingness to prioritize me affects me more than I allow to show.

We reach the couch. He sets me gently on the cushions. I fist the front of his T-shirt to roughly tug him on top of me, too eager for slow and sweet. He presses me against the soft cushions, holding some of his weight over me but letting me feel most of it. All I can hear, aside from our breathing, is the steady hum of the air conditioner. The world around me is still and quiet, and I feel as though I'm standing in the center of a tornado. I'm sure I look like I am, based on the havoc Otto's hands are wreaking on my clothes and hair.

He's kissing me urgently, desperately, like this is the first time and he's only just discovering how good it can be.

I wrap my right leg around his waist, the nonexistent space between our bodies not close enough.

I want sex. Crave it with an intensity that's essential and scary and that I've only ever experienced with him. It's like I've already jumped and the outcome feels inevitable. No decision to be made.

I lift my hips as high as the weight of him will allow, trying to simulate the friction I need.

Otto chuckles against my mouth, like my impatience is amusing, the vibration only making the throbbing need more unbearable.

"How wet are you?" he asks, mouth ghosting along the column of my throat.

My head tilts back, offering him more access. My breasts feel heavy and hot, nipples rasping against the confines of my bra.

"You tell me," I challenge.

He laughs again before his mouth covers mine. My lips are swollen and sensitive, even the lightest glide of his tongue actively unraveling me.

"Please," I pant. "*Please*, Otto. Please."

My breathing is ragged, my voice nearly unrecognizable beneath the layers of lust.

I don't know why it's so different with him, and I'm done searching for a reason or pretending it's not. I just want to exist. Experience. Live. If I turn fifty-five and start thinking my family is stealing my glasses because I can't remember where I left them, like my mom and my grandmother, I don't want to discover I missed my life while it was happening.

His fingers find the button of my jeans, deftly flicking it and then yanking the zipper down. Some distant part of my brain is impressed by his dexterity. And aware that his experience isn't all athleticism. Rather than jealous, I feel possessive.

He's here, with *me*, right now. He wants *me*.

And he was right—this isn't about our past. It's about how aware of him I still am. How we feel like an active game, not a recorded match you watch, already knowing the outcome.

We both groan when his hand slides between my thighs.

The contact hits me like a jolt of electricity as I finally feel some pressure so close to where I really need it.

Otto mutters something in German, low and dark and far too fast for me to comprehend a single syllable. He rarely reverts to his first language, and it feels meaningful that he is now. Like he's as overwhelmed as I am.

The heel of his hand grinds against my clit, providing pressure, but not enough friction. His middle finger finds my entrance and presses inside. I clench around the intrusion, and he grunts more German. This time, I recognize the swear.

He pulls away. I don't have time to protest before he's tugging my jeans off my hips and down my thighs.

I spare a second to try and remember if I'm wearing matching underwear, then decide it doesn't matter. My underwear is gone a few seconds later anyway.

He holds my gaze for a few seconds before my eyes trail lower.

I swallow hard, then let my knees fall open. Shiver when a cool rush of air gusts against the wetness there.

Otto looks. Long enough that I feel impatient, not self-conscious.

His fingers trail up the inside of my thigh, and he watches the bumps rise behind. I bite my lower lip, fingers curling around handfuls of the couch's fabric.

He shifts farther away, knocking several pillows to the floor.

I know what's coming next. When I touch myself, my hand has a tendency to turn into his mouth.

It feels like I'm lost in a fever dream. Like I'm living in a fantasy world mere imagination would be unable to muster. My awareness of the world has narrowed to nothing except him.

He ruined more than sex for me.

I accept, as his mouth lowers between my parted thighs, that I'm very much still in love with Otto Berger.

Chapter 34

Otto

"*I don't know."*

My fingers press harder into her hip. I hate that I said that to her.

"I don't know."

I graze her clit with my teeth, then flick it with my tongue. I hate that she said it back to me.

"I don't know."

I push one finger inside her quivering cunt, then add a second.

Claire gasps. Moans. Begs me for more.

She's not pretending right now—I know that for sure. Just like I remember everything she loves most, and I am making sure to remind her how I acquired that information. I press a palm to her stomach, feeling her abdominal muscles bunch and flex as she squirms beneath me.

She's close. Her cheeks are flushed. Her breathing is choppy.

Her thighs are trembling.

I feel like a fucking god, registering her reaction to me. Claire has a hard time relinquishing control. That she's handing it over to me so willingly feels like a gift.

Attraction is one thing. Want involves action. Includes a level of trust I worried might have been permanently destroyed between us.

I stop teasing her. Eat her out in earnest, biting and sucking and swirling and consuming, until she flies over the edge. My erection passed the point of painful a while ago. It was fucking aching long before Claire started moaning like this, but the erotic soundtrack is really not helping.

She goes still, so I sit up and slump against the cushions. Adjusting myself doesn't help much. Not while Claire is naked from the waist down a foot away, her pussy pink and wet and puffy from my mouth.

Claire slowly sits up, breathing heavily. "That was..." Her voice trails. She's blushing, eyes on the bulge in my pants. Her gaze moves higher, over my chest, and lingers on my right shoulder.

Claire leans closer. I catch a whiff of the shampoo she uses in her hair, the one that was in her bathroom at the Village and also in her LA hotel room, mixed with the smell of sex as she flicks open a few buttons of the dress shirt I wore to dinner. She tugs it aside, staring at the two incisions on my shoulder. Neither's that long. The surgeon explained the entire process to me, but I was too stressed and scared, frankly, to pay close attention to the details of the procedure. They were as noninvasive as possible, wanting to minimize the scar tissue.

Will, who went to the appointment with me, said the surgeon was probably more nervous to operate on me than I was to be operated on, which wasn't super reassuring. Beck said he seemed like an FC Ludlin—Kluvberg's biggest rival—fan, so I'd be fine.

Her thumb slowly traces the lower line, then the higher one. The incisions are fully healed, but the knit skin is paler and more sensitive. I fight a shiver in response to the light brush.

"Do they hurt?" she whispers.

"Not anymore."

Claire's hand moves again, following the row of buttons down the center of my chest.

I'm barely breathing, silently praying this is headed where I hope it is.

"What about this?"

She palms me through the pants I'm wearing, and I swear I could come from this alone. I haven't hooked up with anyone since I got injured, and the fact that this is Claire touching me? I'm going to have to jerk off after she leaves at the very least.

"Does this hurt?"

I laugh, but it comes out as more of a pained gasp. "*Claire*."

"Yeah, I thought so." She sounds smug, sliding off the couch and kneeling in front of me. "I'm not a doctor, but I could try to help?" Her fingers trail back and forth, teasing, and I can't focus on anything else. "If you want me to?"

"*Ja*. Yes. Yes, Claire."

She smirks as she spreads my thighs with her hands, settling between them. She holds eye contact as she unbuttons and unzips and tugs.

Fuck me. This is actually happening.

My cock appears, fully hard and leaking pre-cum.

Claire looks down. Her tongue swipes across her lower lip, and I can't restrain the groan that spills out as she stares at my erection.

"You still wear the same brand of boxers." She seems amused by that as she pulls my pants the rest of the way down.

"They send me free ones," I croak.

Claire giggles—a light, happy laugh that causes a different sort of seizure in my chest—and then finally fists me.

I grunt, battling the urge to thrust in her hand.

"Not so fun, being teased, huh?"

"You loved it," I manage between heavy breaths.

"Yeah, I did." She circles the rim of the leaking tip with her tongue, then traces the pulsing vein that runs the length of my shaft.

And then, *finally*, she sucks me into her mouth.

I sit back and watch, letting her decide it all. The pace, the depth, to do this.

I'm well aware this resolves very little between us. That getting each other off doesn't decide anything about the future. It's a relief though to touch her. To have her touch me. To acknowledge that we want each other.

She licks a straight line along the length of my dick. I curse loudly, not caring if the whole building hears. I doubt any blood is reaching my hands—I'm clenching them so tight. Her mouth is perfect—slick and smooth and hot—tongue rubbing the underside as she sucks me deep. The tip is brushing against the back of her throat, and I can't think straight anymore. Can't think at all actually.

There's a distinctive tug in my groin that tells me I'm close to coming.

"Claire, I—I am close."

Rather than pull away, she sucks harder, her nails leaving crescent marks on my thighs.

"Make sure you swallow it all, Boston."

Claire moans, the vibration sending me over the edge. I come so hard that my vision blurs, heat streaking down my spine as my groin muscles contract, filling her mouth.

She does swallow it all, then reaches for her jeans like she didn't just destroy me. She avoids eye contact as she pulls them on slowly, stuttering a half step as she stands. If not for her flushed cheeks and swollen lips and tangled curls, I'd think what happened was a fantasy in my head.

I'm hit with another wave of déjà vu. "Claire..."

"Don't. Just...don't. I have to go. It's late, and I'm—you were right. I've been pretending. And I have to show up for practice tomorrow and keep pretending, so just...let me."

I nod, yanking my boxers back up.

I shouldn't have let it go that far. I want Claire to take my feelings for her seriously, more than I wanted that blow job, and I'm worried what happened gave her the opposite impression. Like I'm still that horny twenty-three-year-old who fucked her every chance he got. I mutter a chastisement to myself, then stand too.

"Don't do that."

I glance at Claire. "Stand?"

"Blame yourself. I wanted it too. I kissed you first. Don't say you messed up."

I blink at her, slow to comprehend. "You speak German?"

She flushes, tucking a piece of hair behind her ear. "Not really. I just know more than I used to."

"How much more?"

Claire bites her lip. "One of my mom's doctors... I asked if there was anything preventative I could be doing. Studies have shown that learning a new language can strengthen the brain's neural networks and prevent cognitive decline."

"So, you learned it with her?"

"I…I learned it for me. Mom wasn't able—it was already too late."

I frown. "What do you mean, you learned it for you?"

Based on Claire's expression, it's a question she wishes I hadn't asked.

"Dementia can have a hereditary component," she says quietly. "Certain genes can increase the risk. My grandmother was older, but she developed it too."

"Your genes?"

I'm stunned—paralyzed—by the possibility of her having to go through that. I got a call that my grandfather needed major surgery, and I was fine. Worried, but fine. Functioning.

Yet I suddenly can't breathe, imagining Claire being sick in any way. It's the awful moment of her hitting the ground, before knowing she was okay, all over again.

"I don't know all the details. There are certain tests they can do, but I decided I don't want to know. There's no cure. Nothing they can do either way. Figured another language would be a fun challenge." Her voice has changed, injected with fake cheerfulness.

She doesn't want to discuss this anymore, I can tell.

I'm still reeling.

I don't just care about Claire; I'm in love with her. I think I knew when she went down on the field, but it was washed away with the relief of her being fine. I didn't have to confront the possibility that she wouldn't be. Didn't have to consider what it would be like to live in a world where she didn't also exist.

Loss has a devastating way of putting things in perspective. I appreciated football all over again as soon as I found out I could be done. I discovered what being in love felt like by losing it.

And I'm about to lose it again.

Claire's finished fixing her appearance. She's grabbing her phone and bag, setting her water glass down by the sink. Heading for the door.

I trail after her like a lost puppy. "Why German?" I finally ask.

She stiffens, reaching for the door handle, so I know she heard me.

But all she says before leaving is, "Bye, Otto."

Chapter 35

Claire

Coach Taylor greets me in her usual no-nonsense manner, then tells me we're waiting on Eloise Knight, the Siege's general manager.

My stomach, already stuffed with wriggling nerves, performs a cartwheel. I rub the coin in my pocket, trying to calm my racing pulse.

Otto wasn't at practice today. Coach Taylor said he had a doctor's appointment, which I took as a stroke of luck that allowed me to avoid him a little longer. I'm now spiraling over the possibility that was a lie.

What if they *know*? What if I get traded to another team and it's impossible to visit Mom weekly? What if this is how my career ends—decades of literal blood, sweat, and tears diminished to a shitty kick in Paris and an illicit affair with an authority figure?

I've never blamed Otto for that failed attempt—not directly.

I've blamed myself for being distracted. And I'm distracted again.

"What's this about?" I ask tentatively.

Coach Taylor doesn't look up from the sheaf of papers she's rifling through as she answers, "Let's wait for Eloise. I know she wanted to deliver the news personally."

"Okay," I say weakly, relieved by Coach Taylor's distraction. I don't think I'm doing a good job of keeping the apprehension—the guilt—off my face.

I rub my damp palms against my practice shorts, wishing the mesh were more absorbent.

I'm staring at the framed diplomas on the wall, busy assembling excuses in my head. If someone took a photo of me leaving Otto's apartment, there's no proof anything scandalous happened. Was it bad judgment to go to a coach's home? Yes, but I can tell them I went to see Saylor. I don't want to involve her, but I will to save my job. She can explain why I was there.

The door to Coach Taylor's office opens.

I jump to my feet, propelled by nerves and grateful to have an excuse to move.

Eloise Knight steps inside, wearing a linen pantsuit and a serene expression. I've only met the Siege's general manager a handful of times before, and I'm as intimidated now as I was then. She's petite—even in heels—polished, and has the presence of someone important. If I wasn't seventy percent certain she was here to discipline me, I'd appreciate being part of an organization helmed by such badass women.

"Hello, Claire," she says, holding a manicured hand out for me to shake.

"Hi, Ms. Knight," I reply quickly, holding her hand a beat too long before I drop mine to discreetly wipe it on my shorts again.

"Eloise, please. Take a seat." She gestures toward the chair I just leaped out of as she gracefully perches on the matching one angled toward Coach Taylor's desk.

Eloise and Coach Taylor exchange pleasantries as I sit silently, saying, *It'll be okay,* on repeat in my head.

My current contract expires at the end of this season. I was considering retiring anyway.

"Have you heard of the EmpowerEd Foundation, Claire?"

I blink at Eloise. "Uh, no."

She nods. "They're an education initiative, partnering with local public schools to create scholarship opportunities for underserved youth in the Boston area."

"That's…great," I manage, feeling like I just jumped off a merry-go-round.

This meeting has nothing to do with my personal life, it seems, and I'm so relieved that it's taking effort to not slump out of this chair and exhale a massive sigh.

"EmpowerEd is being honored at the Boston Sports Foundation's annual gala, which serves as a fundraiser for some of the scholarships they offer. This year, they're announcing a new scholarship exclusively for female athletes. The foundation asked me to select a Siege player to make the announcement at the gala, and I immediately thought of you."

"Me?"

Eloise nods, smiling. "You're an integral part of this club, Claire. I hope you know that. Plus, with your connections to this city, I couldn't think of a better person to represent this organization publicly."

She *definitely* has no idea about me and Otto then. I don't feel like much of a role model at the moment.

I glance at Coach Taylor. She's smiling too—a rare sight.

"I-I'd love to," I tell their expectant expressions.

"Perfect." Eloise stands. "The gala is two weeks from this Saturday. I'll have my office send you the details, as well as the relevant talking points for your speech."

The mention of a speech stirs some anxiety. The last public speaking I did was presenting my senior thesis in college. But I'm still swimming in relief that this meeting wasn't Otto-related in any way, so the apprehension is easy to shove away for the time being.

"Sounds good. Thank you, Eloise."

"Thank *you*, Claire." One final firm handshake, and Eloise is gone.

"Something else you wanted to discuss, Caldwell?" Coach Taylor asks, grabbing a black binder off the shelf behind her desk.

I startle from stillness, shaking my head. "No, Coach. Thanks."

"See you tomorrow."

I nod, then head into the hallway. My teammates are all gone, so I walk to the parking lot solo. Toss my equipment bag into the trunk and sink into the driver's seat, tapping my fingers against the steering wheel.

I don't want to do this. But I need to. I took the easy way out the other night, and I need to grow up. Still, I second-guess this decision the entire drive to Otto's apartment. Right up until I knock on his door.

No answer.

I guess he's not home. Maybe he's still at his doctor's appointment?

I turn to leave, but only manage three steps down the hallway before the door opens.

When I glance back, Otto is standing in the doorway. The knuckles of his left hand are stark white against the dark wood frame. "Hey," he croaks, looking absolutely awful. Pale and exhausted.

I don't remember moving, but I'm in front of his door again. "You're—what's wrong?"

Otto rubs at his forehead with his free hand. "Migraine," he finally mutters.

I frown.

At Lincoln, I had a roommate, Ramona, who had episodic migraines. Once a month, sometimes more often, she'd lock herself in her dark room for hours. Days sometimes. She tried medication, diet changes, been to dozens of specialists. Nothing helped.

Is that something Otto's been dealing with? It feels like something I should know, even though I can't come up with a logical reason why I would. He never had one in Paris. Or if he did, he never told me.

"Do you get them often?"

"No," he answers. "It has only happened a few times before. I went to a doctor in Kluvberg, who suggested some lifestyle changes. None since."

"Did you go to a doctor here?" I ask, worried by how heavily he's leaning on the frame, like it's the main reason he's vertical.

"I did not want to drive," he tells me. "I was supposed to have an appointment for my shoulder. I had to cancel. And there is nothing the doctors can do. It will pass."

"How long has it lasted for?" I ask, like I have any medical knowledge to offer.

"I woke up with it."

I chew the inside of my cheek, remembering something Ramona griped about. "It's not because we…"

Mercifully, Otto understands my meaning without me spelling out specifics. "It has never triggered one for me before."

I nod, then step inside his apartment. The shades are drawn, only a thin strip of daylight sneaking in between the curtains. There's no evidence he's eaten in the kitchen, no indentation on the couch. I glance through the open doorway at his unmade bed.

He's alone here. Thousands of miles from home. From friends, from familiarity, from his usual doctors. Injured and now sick.

Otto always seems so capable, so assured. I assume he must miss his former life. I never considered how lonely being here might be.

Sympathy is the easy explanation for why I'm still here. But the full reason is more complicated. With Otto, it always is. After what happened between us last night, I can no longer hide behind the nonchalance I've used as a shield since he showed up in Boston. Not while we're alone.

"Have you eaten?" I ask, opening his fridge door.

He *has* food at least. More than is in mine since it was Cassidy's week to grocery shop. I'm convinced she and Tommy lived on takeout in Florida. I'm going to have to stop at the store after I pick him up from preschool.

"I'm not hungry." Otto's moved, leaning against a framed map of Boston. Maybe it's just the white wall, but he looks paler.

"What's helped before?" I question, feeling…helpless.

"Nothing," he says dully. "I wait for it to end."

I gnaw on the inside of my cheek, thinking.

A flash of inspiration appears. Who knows if it'll work? But it's better than nothing. I open the freezer, searching for a bag of frozen peas.

He has some.

I grab the bag, shut the freezer door, and head toward his bedroom. "Come on."

I don't wait to see if he's following. I'm also careful to keep my gaze as far from the messy sheets as possible as I pass the bed and continue into the bathroom. It smells like him in here, the scent of his shampoo and soap and aftershave distinctively masculine.

His bathroom's neater than I expected. The counter is completely clean. I've never lived with a guy, but my experiences with their spaces have mostly been traumatic. He even has the toilet paper on the roll.

I reach into the tub, pulling the stopper and then turning the hot tap.

"What are you doing?"

He did follow me.

"I had a roommate in college who got migraines," I say, watching the tub fill. Steam swirls, coating my face and coiling my curls tighter. "She said this helped."

Once there's about a foot of water in the tub, I shut off the water.

"Take a seat on the edge and stick your feet in the water."

Otto looks skeptical. But he listens, making the tub look tiny as he settles on the side and submerges his feet.

I hand him the peas. "Hold that against the back of your neck."

Our fingers brush as he grips the plastic bag, cold against hot. I shiver for no apparent reason.

I take a hasty step back, clearing my throat. "Well, I—"

"You came to talk?" Otto's head turns, intense gaze trapping me in place.

His color looks better than it did when I arrived, or maybe it's just wishful thinking that I actually helped.

I swallow hard. "You're not feeling well. Now's not the best time to—"

Otto interrupts. "I could use the distraction."

He's *my* distraction. And he has a bad habit of showing up during the moments when focus is most important. The Olympics. My final season maybe. He's muddling that decision too. Because I'm playing better than I did last year, and I can't tell how much is attributable to him.

"I, uh, yeah. I thought we should…talk."

"We should." He slouches against the tiled wall, settling in like he expects this to be a lengthy conversation.

I exhale. "You know it can't happen again. You're one of my coaches, and—"

"What if I was not?"

"You *are*."

"Only for a few more weeks."

I figured that would be the case, but my reaction to the confirmation he won't return after the summer break is unsettling. I shouldn't be so disappointed.

"Right. And then you're leaving."

He shifts on the side of the tub. "I am not officially cleared yet."

"That wasn't a question, Otto. You'll leave whether you get cleared or not. Why would you stay?"

It's meant to be rhetorical.

But Otto looks me straight in the eye and responds, "You."

The tiled floor tilts. My heart flops around in my chest like a dying fish.

Everything about this moment is absurd. Us in his small bathroom. Him in the tub with a bag of peas. Me hovering.

"Don't say that," I whisper.

He's still staring, unflinching in his focus. "You asked."

"You—you're just confused. You got injured and had to come here, and—"

He scoffs, eyes sparking with irritation. "I didn't *have* to do anything, Claire. I could have stayed in Kluvberg if I wanted to."

"Fine. But you had to stop playing. You're—"

He exhales. "I figured you would do this."

"Do what?"

"*It was a mistake.*" His imitation of my voice is annoyingly accurate. "That is what you came here to say, yes?"

"We had this exact conversation six years ago, and nothing has changed since then. No matter what I decide to do about playing next year, I'll still be in Boston. My life is here—my mom is here. And we both know you'll get cleared. Your shoulder seemed plenty sturdy when we…you know."

His "Ha" is half-hearted.

My smile doesn't last much longer. "You'll play next season, Otto. Your life will revert to normal. The fact that we're still… attracted to each other doesn't change any of that."

Otto studies me. Not agreeing. Not disagreeing.

My phone buzzes in my back pocket. I suck in a deep breath, like I just emerged from underwater, as I pull it out.

It's an email. Information about the gala I agreed to attend. The time above the notification serves as a more important reminder—I'm running late to pick up Tommy.

"You have to go?" He sounds resigned.

I swallow, shoving the phone back into my pocket. "Yeah, I… Yeah. I have to pick up Tommy. Can I do—do you need anything else?"

"No. Thank you." He gestures to the tub. "This is helping."

"Okay. Good. Bye."

I flee the steamy bathroom, wishing—just once—a conversation with Otto could end with some closure instead of more confusion.

Chapter 36

Otto

With a frustrated huff, I roll out of bed. It's only five a.m., but I'm sick of staring at the ceiling, and I have to be up in an hour anyway. We're flying back to Boston today, fresh off a victory against Phoenix last night.

My third-to-last game as part of the Siege. Only two matches remain before the summer break.

The team has won six of their past seven games. Assuming that streak continues when the season resumes in August, they'll dominate, not just make, the playoffs.

I won't be here to see it, no matter how much I want to witness the team win a much-deserved championship. I also want—*need*, according to my contract—to return to Kluvberg.

I'm fucking stuck.

I get dressed quickly, pulling on shorts and a Siege polo shirt. My shoulder doesn't twinge the entire time. My injury has become an afterthought, not my main focus whenever I need to move my arm, waiting for pain to appear. I will get cleared, I'm certain. Whether or not that translates when I'm in goal will be another story.

I gather my phone, wallet, and room key, shoving them all in my pockets as I head down the hallway. I'm back to running regularly—and early, thanks to the heat that has recently blanketed Boston and is even more oppressive in Arizona.

When I step out of the elevator, I start toward the automatic doors that lead outside. Glance around the lobby out of necessity, not interest, trying to remember the layout, until I spot a familiar head of hair buried in the hands of someone slumped in one of the couches.

I stride over, the flash of alarm unwelcome and unexpected. "Claire?"

She doesn't move.

"*Claire.*" I sit beside her, grabbing her knee and squeezing once. "What is wrong?"

It feels like my stomach is being folded inside out as I wait for her to reply. A knot cinches tight inside my chest.

"Is your mom…"

Claire lifts and shakes her head, but the knot doesn't loosen. "Nothing's wrong."

I raise a disbelieving eyebrow.

She blinks rapidly. Sniffs. "My sister's boyfriend called me last night. He's planning a trip for them this summer, and Josh wanted to make sure I could watch Tommy before he booked everything."

She smiles, but it's a sad one.

"He also asked… Josh is planning to propose on the trip. And I'm glad. He's great for Cassidy, and Tommy adores him, but...everything *just* changed with my mom moving out and Tommy and Cassidy moving in. Now I have to figure out what to do with the house and with—I woke up early and decided to go for a run, and I realized..." She looks down at the carpet. "I have this token—"

"The Detroit Zoo coin?"

"I can't believe you remember that." Claire swallows. "Actually, I can," she adds softly.

"What about your coin?" I ask.

"I-I can't find it. I know it's stupid—"

I cut her off again. "When did you last have it?"

"At the stadium before the game yesterday. It must have fallen out of my bag at some point. I searched my entire room this morning. It might be on the bus. Or..." She swallows hard. "Left at the stadium." She nods toward her phone, sitting on the coffee table. "I tried calling every number I could find online, but no one's answering this early. I'll try again later. If I can reach someone, maybe they'll search for me. Mail it."

Her voice holds no confidence.

I stand. "Or we can go look ourselves."

"The bus leaves at eight for—"

I'm already on my phone, ordering a car.

"Otto." She reaches for my wrist, halting my movements. "We can't—"

I hold her gaze. "Car will be here in three minutes. I will go alone if you want to stay here."

I mean it. I know what the coin means to Claire. She carries it during every game and not as some superstition. It represents happy memories with her dad, a way to keep him as a part of her career, even when she's shut him out in every other way.

I stride toward the doors, looking around for the silver SUV that's supposed to be arriving soon. Claire hurries after me. She spends the three minutes waiting for the car and the first ten minutes of the car ride attempting to talk me into returning to the hotel and forgetting what she diminishes to a "lump of metal."

I'll search the entire city of Phoenix for that lump of metal, if necessary.

Fifteen minutes later, the driver drops us off at the main entrance of the stadium. It's a flash of color amid a whole lot of beige and gray, surrounded on all sides by asphalt parking and sprawling desert. It's also gated.

I head left, attempting to find the side entrance the team used yesterday. Reaching it requires circling half the stadium in rising heat.

One of Claire's arguments against this trip was correct—we might miss our plane. I texted Eliza in the car, letting her know Claire had forgotten something important at the stadium and I was accompanying her to look for it. She responded, saying she'd try to contact the Phoenix coach and see about having someone here assist. But I have no idea if that was successful. It's a commercial flight. They wouldn't delay the departure for the entire Siege team, let alone two people.

I'm preoccupied by a more pressing problem when we reach the side entrance—it's gated too. But this opening is smaller, meaning the gate is lower. There are no spikes across the top either.

Claire sighs. "Otto, I really appreciate this. But we should go."

"I will give you a boost, Boston."

Her wide eyes wheel between me and the gate. "Otto…"

I raise an arm, comparing my height to the gate. "It is eight feet, at most."

"Which is *high*."

"I will catch you."

"How?"

I wave a hand, gesturing her toward me. "Come here."

When she does, I spin her to face the stadium, then rest my hands on her hips. Claire inhales sharply when I touch her, and I have to remind my cock that this is a rescue mission with a ticking clock.

"Reach for the top when I lift you," I instruct. "Pull yourself up and try to sit on the top. Wait for me there."

Suddenly, Claire starts to struggle. "Your shoulder. You can't—this is—"

"*Reach*, Claire." I heave her upward.

My shoulder doesn't hurt, but I'm well aware this isn't a movement any doctor or physical therapist would endorse. Just like I'm aware I'd do it if even my shoulder was bothering me.

Claire grips the bar across the top of the gate, balancing on her stomach like a gymnast.

I gauge the distance for a few more seconds, then hoist myself up too. My muscles protest, but it's not the searing pain in my shoulder, just general discomfort. I don't stop at the top, like Claire. I propel myself over, utilizing the momentum to land on the other side. The impact ricochets up to my knees, but that's the worst of it.

Claire's staring down at me. "I can't believe you just did that."

Her tone is chastising. But there's some awe, too, underneath the disapproval.

And impressing Claire Caldwell is one of my favorite pastimes, so I flash her a smug smile before lifting my arms. "Spin around so your legs are facing me, then start to slide down.

I will catch you."

She grimaces before complying, inching to the side until she's facing the opposite direction. Her legs drop as she scooches backward, ass up.

Now's not the time to ogle the curve, but I have a perfect shot up the hem of her shorts, pulled tight by the movement.

"Okay. Let go."

I'm expecting her to need some encouragement. Claire instantly dropping is a surprise, but I'm prepared. I catch her, holding her to my body, back to front, feeling her heart pound wildly against my biceps.

"Shit," she breathes. "That was higher than I thought."

She feels so fucking good, pressed against me. Warmth, unrelated to the rising sun, trickles through my veins.

Proximity is underrated. I've missed talking to Claire. Touching her. Fucking her. But this, being near enough to hear her breathing and smell her shampoo? I missed this the most. Simply being near her.

Essentially, I'm screwed. Entirely and utterly fucked.

Because there are about to be roughly four thousand miles between us.

"Otto?"

"Sorry." I let Claire go so fast that she stumbles before turning around. "Locker room is this way," I say, heading in that direction.

"Is your shoulder hurting?" she asks, hurrying after me. "Because if you—"

"I am fine," I call over my shoulder as I continue down the hallway. One, two… Five seconds later, I hear her footsteps following me.

We reach the locker room a few minutes later. The *locked*

locker room.

I swear under my breath. Couldn't one part of this be easy?

I'm debating the best approach to tackle this obstacle when a strange voice calls, "Hey! What are you doing?"

Claire explains the situation to the bearded security guard.

He nods. "I got a call about you. Went out front to let you in, but no one was there."

I avoid looking at Claire. If I did damage my shoulder, that's my problem to deal with.

"Can you let us in?" I ask, nodding toward the locked door.

"Oh. Sure." The guard tears his eyes away from Claire's bare legs, reaching for the jangling ring of keys hanging from his belt.

It takes him long enough to find the correct one and fit it in the lock that I contemplate breaking the door down anyway.

"You need any help looking?" he asks as Claire hurries inside, gaze on her ass now.

"We are good," I reply sharply, stepping to block his view of her.

When I enter the locker room, Claire's on her hands and knees, peering under a bench.

She underplayed how much this meant to her, which I already knew.

"I'll take the left side," I say, starting to search each cubby systematically. I go slowly, making sure to look in every possible nook and cranny.

When we meet in the middle, Claire looks defeated.

"Thanks for trying," she says, sincerity mixing with disappointment.

I do one final scan of the room, trying to think of any other spot the coin could be. There aren't many options. Not only is it clear of equipment, but the floor is spotless. The artificial smell of cleaner hangs in the air, and there are vacuum lines on the carpet.

Claire pulls her phone out and checks the time. "It's seven," she tells me. "If we hurry, we should make it back to the hotel on time."

"One second," I say, returning to the hallway.

The security guard is leaning against a wall, whistling between bites of a glazed doughnut.

"Who cleans on this floor?"

The security guard scrambles to straighten, nearly dropping his doughnut. "Uh… I dunno. They have a closet on each floor and rotate between—"

"Show me the closet."

Claire's caught up to me. "Otto, it's fine."

I ignore her, following the guard a few doors down the hall. He unlocks this door and opens it, revealing a large closet. Shelves are stacked with bottles of cleaner and other supplies, with a plastic cart parked between them. And set on a roll of paper towels, next to a mop handle, is a coin from the Detroit Zoo.

Relief rushes through me as I grab it, turning to hand it to Claire. "Here."

Her mouth gapes as she stares at the silver coin in my palm.

"*Now*, we need to go," I say, hustling toward the nearest exit.

Chapter 37

Claire

"What are you watch—oh. Reliving your greatest hits?" Cassidy plops on the couch beside me and pulls a pillow to her chest, staring at the television.

I tap a pen against the notepad in my lap, studying my ten-year-old self on-screen. "Searching for inspiration."

"What does that mean?"

"I have to give a speech on Saturday at this fancy gala to announce a new scholarship focused on female athletes."

Cassidy yawns. "What are you wearing?"

"I don't know."

"Will *Otto* be there?"

I doodle in the margins. Endless loops that lead nowhere. "Possibly."

Probably. As far as I know, the Siege's entire coaching staff will be attending the event.

"How's that going?"

The loops continue. "Fine."

"Really?"

I glance up. "Why wouldn't it be?"

"Well, it must be a little weird, being around an ex. Especially, like, working with him." Cassidy reaches for the remote, tapping it against her thigh. "We should watch *Bend It Like Beckham*, if you're searching for inspiration. Remember how much you used to love that movie?"

I nod, chewing my lower lip. Ironically, a film with a player-coach storyline. At the time, I just loved that it was a sports movie with a female athlete.

"I kissed him," I admit.

My sister whips her head in my direction, eyes searching my face for signs of seriousness. "You *did*?"

"Mmhmm." It's entertaining, watching the shock play across Cassidy's face.

Growing up, she was always the one with scandalous stories to share. Now, her life is stable. Job, soon-to-be fiancé, kid.

My career is uncertain. I'm in love with a guy I can't have. It feels like our former roles have flipped.

"Traffic was bad, huh?" she teases.

I roll my eyes. That's what I told Cassidy when she commented on how late I'd come home that night.

"And?"

"It was...illuminating." I roll the pen between my fingers. "I'm worried... I'm worried I'm still in love with him."

"Would that be so bad?" Her tone is soft. Maternal.

"Yes! Because it took me years to get over it, and then he showed up here, and I have to start all over again." I mutter a German swear.

I've been practicing more since he found out I've been learning, even though I know it's pointless. Probably the same reason I kept texting him in Paris, knowing I was sinking deeper and deeper.

"Why do you have to get over it?"

"Because nothing has changed. We tried, and it didn't work, and trying again would…would hurt."

"Well, it seems like you have three options," Cassidy tells me.

"I do?"

"Yep." She lifts a finger. "One, you keep acting like a coward."

"That's—"

Cassidy continues, ignoring me and lifting another finger, "Two, you stop stressing about what could go wrong and go after what you want. At least get some good sex out of it."

I huff.

She flashes me three fingers. "Or, option three, you could be honest. You could tell him how you feel and why you're scared to try again. Figure out a solution to be *together*, together."

I'm silent.

Cassidy is, too, letting me think.

"There's no solution," I finally say. "That's why—how—things went wrong the first time. He lives thousands of miles away. That's not a distance that works."

"They have these things called planes, Claire."

"What sort of relationship would that be? Especially when we're already traveling for work?"

"Ask him to move here then."

"I-I can't do that."

"Why not?"

"Because he couldn't. Because he wouldn't. He's a huge deal

there. And his whole life outside of football is there too. Asking him to give all that up… It'd be pointless. Not to mention embarrassing. And selfish. He's here on a forced hiatus—that's all."

"Did he know you were in Boston?"

"I'm not sure."

When Otto apologized for not giving me a heads-up about his arrival, I assumed he'd found out I was on the Siege recently. Once he was already in the city possibly.

"Then how do you know he didn't come here for you?"

I snort. "Because I know he didn't stage an injury that could end his career just to spend some time with me. He wouldn't even ”

"Wouldn't even what?"

I sigh. "He suggested I move to Germany when we tried to figure things out…before. He *laughed*, talking about playing here. He's… Kluvberg set up this whole arrangement for him. They're one of the top clubs in Europe, and he's one of their top players. He can't just decide to play somewhere else, even if he wanted to. Which he doesn't."

"You could still ask," Cassidy says quietly.

I nod.

I'm not sure I can though. I think it would hurt Otto to tell me no. No matter what he's said about wanting me, he's never once implied, much less said, he could or would consider leaving Germany.

And I can't picture moving overseas. Starting over in a new league, on a new team, with a new coach. And that's assuming a German club is interested, which isn't a guarantee. It would be the end of my career, and I'm not sure I'm ready for that. I'm still in a position on the Siege, where I could win a league championship. There's a slim possibility that Saylor was right, and I could be selected for the national team again. Soccer aside, moving would mean leaving Mom. Losing out on the time we have left. Missing Tommy getting older, missing planning Cassidy's wedding, missing any opportunity to improve my relationship with my dad.

No matter how many times I turn it over in my head, nothing shifts. Nothing changes.

Cassidy unmutes the TV, seeming to sense I'm finished discussing the subject.

"There you go, Claire! Great job, honey!"

I keep my gaze on the screen, watching and listening to Dad cheer for me, but I feel Cassidy's eyes on me.

"Dad asked about coming to your last home game with us. I told him I'd ask you."

"Dad can do whatever he wants."

"He wants to know if you want him there, Claire."

On-screen, my dad cheers as I score another goal. I jump around, celebrating, my pigtails bouncing everywhere, as Cassidy swings in the background.

I reach for the remote, shutting off the television. This isn't doing anything to inspire my speech, just depressing me. I can feel the outline of the oval coin pressed against my hip from its spot in my pocket. Since Otto recovered it for me, I haven't let it out of my sight.

My dad has spent years—over a decade—attempting to make amends. When Cassidy was gone and Mom was here, it was easier to brush those attempts away. Mom and I were an unshakable unit, even when I lived in Denver part-time. Brief replies to birthday texts or the occasional check-in were much simpler then.

I'm tired. So tired of the energy that hating and avoiding my father requires. I just don't know how to let go of the resentment. I'm so accustomed to carrying it around.

I glance at my sister. "How did you forgive him?"

I've asked her, "How *could* you forgive him?" before. There's an important distinction between the two questions, one I hope Cassidy hears.

She exhales. "I didn't forgive him. I haven't. But…you and Mom were always so in sync. When I got busted for skipping class or scratched the car or took a pregnancy test, I knew what Mom's reaction would be when she found out. She'd ask me why I couldn't be more like *you*. I resented her for it. And I resented you for it. Dad always listened, especially after the divorce. Out of guilt maybe because he was stuck on the outside of our family too. I…took advantage. And then I had Tommy, and Marcus took off, and things got really hard. Mom would have told me to move home, back here with her. Dad sent me money and flew down to Florida to help me set up the nursery. I know that he's been a shitty dad. But he's been an awesome one, too, to me, and I know he wants to be one to you. You've just…never let him."

"He visited you in Florida?"

"Yeah. Once a year. Sometimes twice."

"You—I didn't know that."

"We barely talked as it was. I wasn't going to bring up Dad."

I tug at a stray thread on the seam of my sweatpants. Cassidy's not wrong. Starting with her decision to attend his second wedding, our different relationships with Dad post-divorce have always been a point of contention between us. I feel guilty all over again, realizing new ways my distance from Dad impacted my relationship with my sister.

"You remember him leaving," Cassidy continues. "Do you remember how much he and Mom fought? Because I used to sit at the top of the stairs and listen. They weren't happy together, Claire. He fell in love with someone else. It was messy, but it wasn't malicious."

I nod slowly. The thread tugs free, falling to the fluffy rug.

"You're a lot like him. Steady and responsible. Smart and driven."

"So are—"

"I'm more like Mom, Claire. Organized chaos. She always said she loved writing because it allowed her to try on different lives, and I'm like that too. But I kept trying new things, not writing books about them. You've stuck with soccer since you were five. You commit. Same with Dad, except when..."

Neither of us finishes her trailing thought.

"You never needed him, Claire. You never needed help. You took care of yourself. And you took care of Mom. I don't think Dad knows how to be part of your life. He doesn't want to get in the way or cause problems or embarrass you... Whenever he hasn't shown up, it wasn't because he didn't want to be there."

I'm silent.

"Good luck with your speech." Cassidy stands and stretches. Yawns. "I'm headed to bed."

Right before she reaches the stairs, I call out her name.

"Yeah?" she replies, pausing.

"Tell Dad he's welcome to come to the game."

I catch her nod before I drop my eyes back to the pad of paper, pick up the pen, and start to write.

Chapter 38

Otto

PARIS: SIX YEARS EARLIER

I stare at the final score.

It feels like a leaden weight is sitting on my chest.

Australia won, 3–2. Their third goal was in the last few minutes. It was a close match, which is never reassuring to the losing side and irrelevant to the winning team.

I hang my head, scrubbing the palm not holding my phone across my face. *Fuck*.

She never responded to my text from this morning, wishing her luck.

Beck hasn't returned from the game yet. He's probably waiting to talk to Saylor. She wanted this win as badly as Claire did.

The rest of my teammates are busy preparing for the final tomorrow.

And I was banking on the US winning. I thought it'd be easy to revisit the topic of us during the high of a victory. That plan was just shot to hell.

I don't even know when she's leaving. I never asked.

I lean my head back against the wall, surveying the empty locker room surrounding me.

One thing I simultaneously love and hate about being a goalie: it's isolating. Every other position on the pitch has duplicates. Standing in goal, it's just me. Maybe that's why, off the field, I've always surrounded myself with lots of people—to counteract that on-the-field seclusion.

This—right now—is the most alone I've ever felt. I don't want to talk to anyone about Claire. I want to talk to Claire.

But I doubt she wants to talk to me. I don't know what I'd say if we did talk. No magical solution appeared as I lay awake in bed last night, listening to Leroy Wirtz snore.

Losing sucks. There's no way to sugarcoat that. You sit with it, let the sting wear off some, learn what you can from it, and pick up and prepare for the next match. But with the Olympics, that isn't for four fucking years. It's a mountain ahead, of training and selection, just to get back to this point, and then the rounds of wins required to make it back to a final.

"Berger." Wagner walks into the locker room with one of the trainers, studying me with visible concern.

I don't normally hang out in here, alone. And there's definitely not a smile on my face.

Wagner says something to the trainer, dismissing him, then walks over to me. "Is something wrong?" he asks.

I could tell Kluvberg's head coach—Germany's head coach—that it feels like someone is carving a cavity in my chest. That it feels like something important is slipping through my fingers, and I don't know how to stop it from happening.

"I'm fine, Coach."

He studies me for a few seconds. "It's normal to have nerves before a big match."

"I'm not nervous."

I'm not. I'm devastated and conflicted, but I'm not nervous about tomorrow. My focus on the pitch has always been an immovable object. It's lonely, blocking everything else out, but I'm fucking good at it. It's just me and the goal out there. Everything is within my control.

He nods. "Good."

When he's halfway to the door, I call after him, "Are you married, Coach?"

Wagner pauses, and I prepare for him to tell me to mind my own business.

Instead, he sighs. "I was."

"What happened?"

"I had to choose between being a good husband and a good coach."

"Do you—do you regret it?"

"Depends on the day. Rest up, Berger."

He leaves, and I resume staring at the text she never responded to.

Chapter 39

Otto

There's a tiny balcony off the living room of my apartment. I head out there with my laptop and a glass of water, still sweating from what's become a daily run along the Charles River. I haven't seen Claire there since the frigid morning we ran into each other. I've kept my distance as much as possible since the afternoon she came over here.

Only two games remain on the Siege calendar before the summer break—one home this weekend, one away next weekend—and then my commitment to the team will have officially ended.

I still haven't booked a return ticket, but that's not what I'm doing now. I swallow a large sip of water, nearly draining the glass, and then navigate to my Bookmarks. Lean back in the small chair that matches the small table, both barely fitting out here, and watch as the video begins to play.

My unease mounts as the minutes tick up, same as always. My hands clench into fists as I hear, "And what a moment for Claire Caldwell, who's subbing in for Sierra Sanders. Caldwell, out of Boston, has had very little playing time during these Games. She's one of the youngest players on the team. Only one cap earned in her entire career."

The coverage continues, listing off some of her stats from Lincoln University.

Claire runs onto the field, nodding to a teammate as she takes her position.

And then…she glances to the side of the field. My heart spasms painfully when the camera zooms in that direction, the spectator section reserved for athletes to watch events they aren't participating in. Where I would have sat if I'd shown up to the game. I spot Beck and a few other familiar faces.

The camera refocuses on the center of the field as play resumes, following an Australian forward who's a streak of yellow on-screen. My knee bounces as I watch the US goalie make a stellar save.

Time ticks higher. My knee bounces faster as I sense what's coming at any second. During the eighty-fifth minute, an American player has a breakaway.

I watch her approach Australia's goal, watch the wild ponytail that I know belongs to Claire as she sprints up the field after her. Even from farther behind, she passes other blue uniforms. There's a brief, undeserved surge of pride as I watch her trap the pass from her teammate.

It's not a bad kick. It flies fast off her foot, straight on target.

But she gave away too much with her positioning. The yellow-clad goalie guesses the correct corner, diving for the ball that's slowed too much and making the save.

I watch Claire's face fall. Watch her fight to keep her composure, jogging back to the opposite end of the field.

Regulation ends with a tied score.

Three minutes of extra time are added.

I'm nervous, watching the match, even knowing how it ended. I can't imagine how the spectators and players felt. A game doesn't get much more high-stakes than this.

Australia scores.

The final whistle blows.

I close my laptop, uninterested in watching Australia's celebration.

And think, *I should have been there.*

Chapter 40

Claire

I'm standing in line, waiting to order a club soda from the open bar, when a throat clears behind me.

I spin toward the sound, relaxing my face into a friendly smile as disappointment sinks through my diaphragm. I wasn't positive Otto would be here, but I assumed—hoped—that he would be.

Instead, Boston's star quarterback, Brady Simmons, stands before me. I've never met him before, and I don't consider myself much of a football—American football—fan, but it's practically impossible to live in New England and not know who he is.

"It's Claire, right?"

Shockingly, he also appears to know who I am.

"Right," I confirm, grasping his offered palm.

He holds my hand for a few seconds longer than necessary, lightly grazing my knuckles with his thumb.

"I was hoping you'd wind up playing in my stadium," Brady comments.

When Boston first announced the Siege as the latest expansion team, it was rumored we'd play our games at Liberty Stadium. Thanks to private donations and investors willing to bet big on women's sports, we wound up with a brand-new facility. This season at least, we've made it worthwhile. We won our final home game before the summer break, 3–1, in front of a sold-out crowd earlier.

I shrug a shoulder. "It was too small."

Brady laughs. It's a nice sound, low and deep. The expression on his face has changed, morphing from arrogance to admiration. "I guess I'll have to stop by yours sometime. Check it out."

"You should," I say, not to encourage his flirting, but because I know it'll be excellent publicity if he follows through and shows up at a Siege game.

"Can I buy you a drink, Claire?"

"From an open bar?"

His smile grows. "Unless you're ready to leave with me and go to a bar that accepts my card?"

He'd have trouble finding one, is my guess. I'm sure he drinks for free wherever he goes; the allure of being able to say, *Brady Simmons was here*, is better than any marketing campaign.

"I can't leave," I inform him. "I have to give a speech."

"What for?" Brady asks, looking intrigued.

"EmpowerEd is establishing a scholarship for female athletes. My coach asked me to announce it."

"Miss? What would you like?"

I turn to face the bartender. "Club soda with lime, please."

The man nods, then turns to the fridge to pull out a can.

"You're not drinking?" Brady questions, sounding surprised.

"I'm giving a speech," I say. "So, no. Public speaking and I don't pair well together under sober circumstances, so I'm trying not to make a fool of myself in front of the entire city by talking into a microphone while tipsy."

Brady laughs again as the bartender delivers my drink, ordering a whiskey for himself. "If you're nervous, just picture everyone in their underwear."

I shake my head. "Has that line ever worked for you?"

He grins. "One, it's not a line; it's commonly shared advice. Two, you tell me. I've never used it before. I'm not exactly in the habit of asking my dates to give speeches when we go out."

Brady's whiskey gets delivered. We move aside so that the next person can order.

I'm expecting for him to move on to talk to someone else, but he sticks by my side, heading toward one of the raised tables that's been set up around the periphery of the ballroom.

"Have you worked with EmpowerEd before?" Brady asks.

I take a sip of my soda and then set it on the crisp tablecloth, shaking my head. "I hadn't heard of them before," I admit. "You?"

He nods. "I'm on their board of directors."

"Oh. Wow. That's great."

I pegged Brady as being boastful and superior and now feel guilty about that presumption of a swaggery quarterback stereotype. I don't know anything about him really, aside from his profession.

"Guess I should have led with that." He winks. "Historically speaking, mentioning my house on Nantucket or—"

"Caldwell."

That's all he says—my last name—and the rest of the room blurs around me. I spin, staring at Otto.

He's with Nicole—Coach Green—but I barely register her presence. He's wearing a tux, the stark black fabric contrasting his tan skin and golden hair. I saw him a few hours ago in the Siege locker room. I've seen him hundreds of times in the past few months. Yet I'm still not immune. Some part of me has always been aware that our time together is limited, that his presence is finite, and so I'm still greedy. Still soaking the sight of him in, even though I have his features memorized, to the extent that I could draw them in the dark, blindfolded.

"Hi, Coach Berger." I glance at Nicole. "Hey, Coach Green."

She smiles. "I think you can get away with calling me Nicole here. Eliza mentioned you'd been selected to announce the scholarship. That's a huge honor. Congratulations, Claire."

"Thanks." I smile back, battling the urge to look at Otto.

I reach for my glass, swallowing a large sip.

"You're...Brady Simmons," Nicole says, glancing past me at the man I was talking to.

Brady grins. "Guilty as charged. Nice to meet you..."

"Nicole," she supplies. "Nicole Green. I'm a coach for the Siege."

"Nice." Brady looks at Otto next. I tense as he holds out a hand, not sure why. "Hey. I'm Brady."

"Otto Berger," Otto says, reaching past me to take Brady's extended hand. His fingers graze my arm—unintentionally, I think—and the brief brush sends shivers dancing along the surface of my skin.

"I thought so," Brady comments. "The soccer player, right?"

"And you're the football player."

I seem to be the only one who catches Otto's slight emphasis on *foot*. I know, from the many times he corrected me in Paris, how ridiculous Otto finds the American nomenclature. But he's polite—or indifferent—enough not to make a big deal about it now.

"Sure am." Brady grins. "You work with the Siege too?"

"Only for one more game," Nicole says, glancing at Otto and turning her lips down playfully. "Then we lose him back to the big time."

I focus on my glass, running a finger down the rim. Unhappy about the reminder of Otto's upcoming departure and also resentful of Nicole voicing my own insecurities. It's exactly what I told Otto—our careers aren't on comparable planes. And while that might be the reality, I don't enjoy hearing others acknowledging it. Especially a member of the Siege organization. We may be a new women's team, but we're still professional athletes.

"The Siege is the big time," Otto says quietly.

"Oh. Of course we are," Nicole says quickly. "I just meant… comparatively…" She clears her throat, voice trailing awkwardly.

"Is your final game home?" Brady asks.

"Away." I speak up, worried how much my silence might be saying.

"Too bad." He gives me a lingering look. "I'm free next weekend. When is your next home game?"

"Not until August. You'll probably be on Nantucket."

Brady laughs. "Not if you're not. Looking forward to seeing your massive stadium, Claire." He nods at Otto and Nicole, grabs his whiskey, and walks off.

Total silence remains after his departure. I'm dimly aware of the overlapping conversations and classical music in the background, but I'm not really registering any of the sound.

Nicole speaks first. "Brady Simmons is coming to a Siege game?"

I reach for my glass again. "I doubt he'll actually show up."

"He will show up."

I glance at Otto, our gazes colliding with an intensity that knocks all the air out of my lungs.

"I agree," Nicole says, nudging my arm with her elbow. "He seemed really into you."

I clear my throat, opting to swallow more soda rather than reply. I view Nicole the way I should see Otto—as an authority figure. I'm not in the habit of gossiping with her, no matter how friendly she is. Also, I have some one-sided beef, territorial over her interest in Otto.

"We should head to our table," Otto says. "Eliza sent us over to grab you, Caldwell."

I nod.

Otto heads toward a table toward the center front. I see Coach Taylor and Coach Jackson already seated, both with men who I assume are their husbands. I knew Coach Taylor was married; I didn't know Coach Jackson was.

"I tried to keep him from interrupting," Nicole whispers to me as we walk. "Sorry."

"Don't worry about it," I reply.

We reach the table, prompting a flurry of introductions. Coach Taylor's husband is named Matt. He works in real estate, he tells me. Coach Jackson's husband, Louis, is a journalist. He's also written some short stories for the *New Yorker*, Coach Jackson brags, obviously proud of her partner. I wind up seated on Louis's other side, so I mention that my mom is a writer. He's heard of her books, he tells me, then asks a series of questions about her work.

Answers come easily, until he asks when her next novel is releasing.

"Did you see the review of *Bridge Through London* in the *New Yorker*, Louis?" Otto asks, interrupting.

Louis brightens. "I did! I thought…"

I tune the rest of Louis's reply out, glancing down at the dinner that the waiters delivered. I've barely eaten, nerves about my speech occupying most of the space in my stomach, but I take a small bite now as an excuse to opt out of the conversation for a moment.

It's going to be harder to say goodbye to Otto this time, I realize. I didn't think that would be possible. I was so resolved when he arrived to keep the armor around my heart impenetrable, and he drilled through the safe anyway.

It's not just the physical awareness or the draw to be close to him. It's him being defensive about my career. Him knowing that my mom's next book would be a difficult topic for me to discuss. All of those add up to him knowing me in a way few people—maybe *no* people—do. And I can't write the past few months off as young love or Olympic excitement or naivete, the way I attempted to forget Paris.

After the dinner plates are cleared away, the speeches begin. I play with the napkin on my lap as a variety of important people I've never heard of speak about the importance of education and athletics, about Boston's sports legacy and always striving to achieve more. Brady's speech is brief and charming, highlighting the work done by EmpowerEd. Photos of him tossing a football with little kids scroll on the screen behind him, but I am barely paying attention.

Finally, Eloise Knight steps onstage. She introduces herself, sharing the short history of the Siege organization and mapping out all that she hopes to see ahead. She ends with, "And here tonight to make an exciting announcement about EmpowerEd and Boston

Sports' partnership to support and advance girls and women in sports is Siege player and Boston native…Claire Caldwell!"

Polite applause scatters throughout the room as I stand, taking small steps away from the table so that I don't step on the hem of my dress. Cassidy was thrilled when I asked her to help me pick out an outfit for this event. I love the dress I wound up wearing, green and Grecian-inspired, but I'm not used to wearing a gown or heels. Falling on my face isn't the first impression I'm aiming for.

I weave around the table in front of ours, then take the steps that lead to the platform that's been set up with a lectern.

Eloise gives me a hug when I reach her, whispering, "You'll be great," before heading off the stage.

I know she meant to be reassuring, but it only mounts my anxiety. I hate letting people down. Hate feeling like I didn't do my part.

I adjust the microphone, tilting it up to accommodate for being taller than Eloise is. She's reached our table, but I don't watch her sit down. My gaze slides left, focusing on one face in this ballroom full of strangers.

He's already looking at me.

"Good evening, everyone. I fell in love with soccer when I was five years old. I scored twice in my first game—once in the wrong goal—and it was the highlight of my week. I couldn't wait until the following Saturday, so I could do it all over again. My parents had to buy a second jersey because I wore the original so often that holes started forming in the fabric. As I got older, everything else in my life changed. Relationships with family, friends, and school evolved, but soccer always remained a constant. It shaped me and challenged me. Gave me purpose and gave me confidence and became such a central piece of me that it really wasn't until I sat down to try to write what I wanted to say tonight that I realized the full extent of its influence."

I suck in a deep breath, releasing some of the nerves with my exhale. Some confidence seeps in. So far, so good. The audience is attentive, listening raptly.

"It's an honor to be here tonight, to announce EmpowerEd's new scholarship, Game Changers, aimed at expanding access and encouraging a new generation of women in sports. I've been lucky enough to have access to incredible opportunities over the years—coaches who believed in me, teammates who lifted me up, family who cheered me on. Their encouragement was essential, and so were the role models I looked up to.

"This scholarship will not only inspire female athletes with the drive and the potential to take their athleticism to the next level; it will ensure they have the financial means to get there. It won't only support individuals; it will forge an important path. It will provide opportunities where they may not have existed before, empower girls and women to believe in themselves, to chase their dreams, and to know that their potential is limitless. I am so proud to see these organizations, to see this city, take steps toward supporting that mission.

"Thank you to all of you for your generosity, for your belief in women's sports, and for your commitment to making a difference. Together, we can inspire future champions."

I smile as the crowd applauds, relief streaming through me as I carefully retrace my steps off the stage.

My whole table is standing and clapping when I return. My cheeks feel as though they're radiating heat, and the sweat from my palms has dampened the note cards I wrote my speech on.

I meet his gaze again as I reach my chair.

Otto nods.

This time, I nod back.

Chapter 41

Otto

"I could come out of retirement if you want to practice some shots."

I glance over my shoulder at Nicole, who has a stack of cones tucked under one arm. Practice—my final practice with the Siege—ended a little while ago. We leave tomorrow for Miami. When we return, I won't be part of the Siege any longer.

I shift my foot off the ball, nudging it a few inches away.

"Making shots is not what I need to practice," I tell Nicole as she stops beside me. I look back at the empty field. Exhale. I'm restless, anxious to test my shoulder. Just because it doesn't hurt and can perform normal functions, that doesn't mean I'm recovered. "This is the longest stretch I have gone without playing since I was six."

"A few months off isn't going to matter then. Sounds like you were due for a vacation."

I muster a smile, appreciating her attempt to cheer me up. "Probably."

"There's talk of a Siege trip to see you play," Nicole tells me. "The team wants a chance to critique you from the sidelines for once."

I smile. A real one this time. "You should come. That would be fun."

A pause.

"Are you going to tell her before you leave?"

"Tell who what?"

"Tell Claire how you feel about her."

I still, head twisting slowly to stare at Nicole. Clear my throat before asking, "Am I that obvious?"

She shakes her head. "No. You're not obvious at all. It was a guess. Most times I look at you, you're staring at her."

I scratch my jaw. "I did not mean—"

"Don't, Otto. You don't owe me any explanations. It's none of my business."

"We have history," I say awkwardly. "It is not…recent."

I'm straddling an awkward line, trying not to break my promise to Claire by disclosing details, but wanting Nicole to understand this was nothing new.

"You mean, I never had a shot." A wry smile curves her lips.

"I do not think anyone has since I met her," I admit for the first time, realizing I've known that for a lot longer.

"Does Claire know that?"

"She has an idea. It is…complicated. I—my life has looked very different these past months than it does normally."

Nicole nods. "Well, I hope it works out."

"Thanks, Nicole."

"See you tomorrow," she tells me, then heads for the path

that leads up to the practice facility.

I take a seat on one of the metal benches, pulling my phone out of my pocket, pressing a name, and listening to it ring.

"*Hallo*?" My grandfather's gruff voice answers a few seconds later.

"It's me, Otto."

I don't think his phone has caller ID, and I'm not sure he can recognize my voice from two words. It's not like we talk very often.

"Is everything okay?"

"Everything is fine. I just—I wanted to let you know that I booked my flight back. I'll be in Kluvberg on Tuesday. I'll have a couple of meetings and doctor's appointments, but I was thinking I'd visit Tannfeld once I do."

"No surprise visit this time?"

His voice is too dry to tell for certain, but I think he's joking.

"No. And I don't have to come at all if you're...busy."

A pause, and then he says, "I don't have anything going on next week."

"Okay. I'll see you then."

"See you then."

Chapter 42

Claire

I break through the surface, sucking in a deep breath of air. Swipe a hand across my eyes, clearing the chlorinated water away.

He's there, lounging in one of the cheap plastic chairs that surround the pool.

My heartbeat, already accelerated from the exercise, kicks into a higher gear.

He says nothing. I say nothing. We appraise each other, me standing in the shallow end and him seated, rolling an unlit cigarette between two fingers.

"You smoke?" I ask, surprised.

It's the antithesis of everything I associate with Otto. He sorts his priorities around what will make him a better athlete, and smoking only detracts.

"Used to, when I was younger. Thought it looked cool."

"Why'd you stop?"

He flicks the cigarette on the table, next to the opened pack. "Got distracted by a girl, and it did not seem like her thing."

My fingers swish through the cool water. "Seems like most Europeans must be accustomed to smoking."

It was one of the first things I noticed in Paris—how prevalent the habit was.

"She was not European." Otto leans back, spreading his thighs and smirking. "In fact, she did not even know the French word for taxi was *taxi*."

Realization slams into me. Warmth spreads through my trembling muscles.

"Not my finest moment."

The smirk blooms into a full smile. "I would disagree."

I walk over to the steps, climbing out of the pool and grabbing the towel I left on one of the loungers. I wrap it around my torso, shoving my feet into the pair of flip-flops I packed.

Humidity hangs heavy and damp in the air, nearly as thick as the awareness between us. Our match earlier ended with an announcement from Coach Taylor that Coach Willis would be returning from maternity leave in August. I watched a line of my teammates say goodbye to Coach Berger, and then the majority of them went out to celebrate today's win, which leaves us ranked third in the league standings, headed into the second part of the season.

I begged off from celebrating, sensing the approaching melancholia, knowing I'd spend the evening faking smiles while secretly miserable.

I'll be spending the next five weeks training, spending time with Mom, and—once Josh proposes—helping Cassidy plan her wedding. I'll probably pick up a few shifts at Paul Rebeer's, too, although I don't need to supplement my income now that Mom's care is covered, which is a relief.

I'm feeling restless. Reckless. I've spent so long treading water; I forgot how freeing it felt to swim with purpose instead.

I always pack a bathing suit for away games since most hotels we stay at have a pool, but I rarely use it. Swimming is another thing I associate with my dad—from sun-drenched summers at Michigan lakes to lessons at the YMCA down the road.

Otto stands, the scrape of the chair's plastic legs against the concrete floor fracturing the silence between us. "You headed up?"

"Yeah." I tighten the towel under my armpits, reaching for my phone and the room key I left on the cushion. "You?"

"Yes."

We walk in silence to the door that leads inside the hotel. Otto swipes his card against the reader, pulling the door open and holding it for me.

My "Thanks" is so low that I'm not certain he hears it.

The elevator is right inside, tucked in the far corner across from the main lobby. I jab the Up button with my thumb, water streaking down my calves and dripping on the carpet.

The restlessness is multiplying, expanding, spreading to every crevice of my body. Swimming didn't subdue it the way I hoped. Maybe it would have if Otto hadn't been there when I emerged, like my tortured thoughts had summoned him somehow.

Finally, the doors *ding*, then part.

He waits for me to enter first again. A memory tugs at my mind, snippets of Paris appearing, like his mention of our first meeting opened the vault I'd welded shut. Driving past the Eiffel Tower, exploring the Louvre, dancing in the street. The memories have the same shimmering dreamscape of *Les Murmures de l'Aube*, hazy yet lingering. Unmarred by our ending. Maybe because it doesn't feel like we did end.

"When do you fly home?" I ask, hitting four.

Otto taps six, then answers, "Tuesday."

The elevator doors glide closed, shutting us in more silence.

It takes twenty-six seconds to reach the fourth floor. I know because I count each one, flipping between the three options Cassidy laid out. Debating which form of regret will hurt the least.

The doors open, and I glance at Otto. He's already looking at me, hands in pockets. A proud stance that's also patient. I'm not. Tuesday is…soon.

I reach out, pressing the button to close the doors without breaking eye contact. I memorized its position during our ascent.

"You sure you want to do that, Boston?"

I don't have to think about my response. "Yes."

I'm sure I *want* to do this. I'm just not sure if I should. If I'm prepared for the inevitable heartbreak that's going to accompany losing him again to include this extra torment. It's the final line that hasn't been crossed.

Knowing pain is coming never makes it hurt any less. Losing him will hurt—hurt a lot—no matter what. I can feel the ripple of it already, another crack forming in my heart. Might as well take what pleasure I can, while I can.

My entire being is pulsing with anticipation, the awareness pounding an unrelenting rhythm. Now that I've decided, any delay feels excruciating.

I don't know how long it takes to reach the sixth floor. I'm too distracted to count seconds.

My steps are cautious as I follow him out of the elevator and down the hallway. I'm sure there are other Siege players or staff staying on this floor. And while Otto might not technically be affiliated with the team, as of about four hours ago, I don't really want to explain to anyone why I'm sneaking into his room, wearing only a towel. They're still my colleagues.

Thankfully, we don't encounter anyone. Otto flips on the lights while I set my phone and room key on the round table in one corner of the room. It smells like him in here, even though we've only stayed at this hotel for one night.

I face him, letting all the air out of my lungs in a lengthy gust. "I'm glad you came to Boston."

He grins, walking toward me. "We are in Miami."

My fist twists the soft cotton of his shirt as soon as it's in reach. I can feel the heat emanating from him, the solid support of the latent strength in his muscles.

"That's not what I meant."

His eyes soften. "I know what you meant. And I am really"—his fingers skim up my arm—"really"—his hand unknots the towel with one deft tug—"glad I did too."

"I told you that you'd be back next season."

"You did," he agrees, toying with the strap of my bathing suit.

We won't have a chance to talk, starting tomorrow. I don't want to draw this goodbye out unnecessarily, and I doubt he does either. That was one small mercy in Paris. We didn't go through cycles or phases of being together and apart. It was a clean break that should have healed.

"I'm glad," I tell him. "I-I wish some things were different, but I'm really glad you'll be back next season. I don't want you to think I don't—I want you to know that."

"I know that, Claire."

I nod. "You don't *need* football, Otto. It's just…lucky to have you." I sniff, then laugh. "Sorry. I'm killing the mood."

His fingers trace a line across my collarbone and curve up my throat. He tips my chin up, forcing me to meet his gaze. "What did I say about apologizing to me?"

"Not to." I basically breathe the words—because his thumb is ghosting across my lower lip and I can barely focus on anything else.

His expression turns serious. Severe, the planes and angles sharpening. "Take what you want, Claire."

"I will. I mean, I'm going to. I'm planning—I'm going to play next season. I'm not done."

I already decided. But I sort of want to make the decision all over again, just so I can say it another time and watch the pride break across his face. Otto undoubtedly realized that counseling me to continue playing would tie me tighter to Boston. Would make even visiting him next to impossible.

He told me to play anyway, and I love him even more for it.

"We shouldn't do this," I state, my hands already under the hem of his shirt, exploring all that hot, taut skin.

This feels different and the same. Familiar yet new.

"Probably not."

I graze my fingers lower, tracing the waistband of his shorts. He's changed, too, since the game earlier.

"Glad we agree," I say. Then rise up on my tiptoes and kiss him.

It's supremely satisfying. Toppling the first domino. A cleat colliding with a ball in a perfect kick.

His shirt falls first, joining the terry-cloth towel, followed by my bathing suit a few seconds later. The zipper of his shorts snags, and I release an impatient growl as I tug at it.

"Patience, Caldwell," Otto tells me in his Coach Berger voice.

I scowl, tugging on the metal teeth again. "You told me to

take what I want."

He laughs. "Fuck yeah, I did."

His zipper finally cooperates, and he's gloriously naked a few seconds later. I've only glimpsed him in parts, until now. Shirtless in LA. Pantless in his living room.

Otto partially naked is distracting. Otto fully naked is one of those sights you stare at, blinking, not believing it's real.

Even more unbelievably, he's looking at me with the same awed disbelief.

"Do you think about *this* when you think of me?" I ask. Half teasing, half really wanting to know.

"All the time," he replies seriously. "You?"

"All the time," I whisper.

Air-conditioning hums in the background.

I kiss his shoulder before tracing my tongue along the ridge of his collarbone. My mouth lands on the base of his neck. I suck, long enough to leave a mark. It's a childish instinct, a base urge to preserve this moment with something tangible. I kiss the scars on his shoulder next, my breasts brushing against his firm chest.

Otto groans; I moan.

We're moving closer to the bed. I'm relaxed, not paying close attention to anything except staying close to him, letting him lead. Not thinking or worrying about what's about to happen. It's a sensation of safety. A unique sort of anticipation. Knowing what will happen, but also not.

I straddle him, setting my left knee outside of his right thigh, then my right knee outside of his left leg.

His hands flex, curl, fighting the urge to touch me.

"*Gut gemacht*," I murmur. I'm playing with fire, I know, and as soon as I drop the match, the flames will consume everything else.

Otto's eyes heat at the praise. It's a minor miracle I'm able to recall any German right now because most of my brain is busy processing that this is truly about to happen.

"*Du bist schön*," he tells me.

I scoff. "My hair's frizzy, and I smell like chlorine."

A shower would have made sense. But tonight, I'm aiming for impulsivity, not practicality.

"You are always beautiful, Claire."

Unexpectedly, those five words make my nose sting. I stamp a smile below it, desperate to remain in the moment. To stay in the present and ignore the future.

Otto grunts as I grip his erection, the cords of his neck growing taut. His thighs tense beneath me like malleable marble, strong yet flexible.

I swipe my thumb across the flared tip, smearing the moisture beaded there before sliding my fist down the many inches it takes to reach the base. It's overwhelming, seeing him like this. I want to rememorize everything, but I'm fighting my own impatience.

Otto is looking down, watching my hand stroke his substantial length. My inner muscles clench as I recall what it felt like to have him inside. The stretch, the build, the relief.

"Claire." His hand lands on my thigh, the touch searing my overheated skin.

"You're breaking the rules," I inform him.

Otto's smile is brief. "I did not bring a condom."

"Oh." I'm embarrassed I forgot that important detail.

"I did not think—there was not—" He blows out a breath, tilting his head back to study the ceiling briefly.

I study his palm on my leg. Trace the map of veins that begin between his knuckles, traveling up his forearm.

"GLOVES OF GLORY: HOW OTTO BERGER IS REDEFINING

REACTION TIME" was the title of the first article I saw about his Olympics performance after leaving Paris. I was proud for a second, like his success was something I could claim partial credit for, before bitterness descended. I never thought then that his talented hands would touch me again.

"We can do...other stuff?" I suggest, sounding like a teenager.

His hand slides higher up my thigh, nearly to the crease of my hip bone. My next inhale gets caught in my throat.

"I was not suggesting we stop. They ran every test before my surgery, and I have not been with anyone since. But we—"

"You haven't?" I blurt. "What about—" I can't bring myself to say her name. Not during such an intimate moment.

Maybe Otto feels the same way. Because all he says is, "I have not wanted to. With anyone else."

I suck my lower lip into my mouth, replaying his words in my head. They settle around me like a cozy blanket, cocooning me in the special sensation of the one person you want picking you back.

"I've never not used a condom with anyone else," I tell him. "But I want to. With you."

The tendons of his throat appear as I guide him inside me, sinking down. It's a slow, delicious, devastating spread.

I want to savor it. I want to rush it.

Either way, it will end.

Chapter 43

Claire

I wake up just before four a.m. The bathroom light was left on, its glow muted by the mostly closed door. Otto is fast asleep, sprawled out on his back beside me.

I roll over, tucking my hands under the pillow. For a few minutes, I stare, trying to imprint this memory in my mind. We've never slept in the same bed overnight before. It's bittersweet, a step ahead that's about to predate a lot of backtracking.

That was it.

We're done. Over before we ever started again.

I dress silently, relieved my dry suit requires minimal shimmying.

There's a pad of paper and a pen on the table next to where I left my phone and room key. After a minute of indecisive hovering, I scribble a short message. I'll see him on the shuttle to the airport and on the flight back to Boston, obviously, but this feels like my last chance to say anything private. Or meaningful.

I wrap the chlorine-scented towel around my midsection, grab my belongings, and slip into the hallway. It's quiet and empty—unsurprising at this hour, but still a relief—and beeline for the elevator. While I wait, I check my phone. I have a few notifications, but I fixate on one from a few hours ago, when I was asleep and thought he was too.

otto_berger has requested to follow you

There's a blue check mark next to his name. It's his official account, not one of the fan pages I used to follow.

I accept the request and click on his account. They're all soccer photos. His last post was in January, just before he was injured. No personal photos. No reference to his recovery in Boston. If he hadn't requested to follow me, I would've assumed this page was run by someone on his team.

He has 9.4 million followers.

Following? Two.

I swallow hard as I tap on the number. FC Kluvberg…and me.

The elevator arrives. As soon as I'm inside, with the doors closed, I release a long exhale, letting my phone drop back to my side.

I'm exhausted, in a good way, physically spent and satisfied.

Empty, too, like I just left a concert put on by my favorite band. There's residual excitement and happiness, but it's mixed with plenty of disappointment as well. That *what do I have to look forward to now* sensation that inevitably follows the end of anything special.

The doors ding open on floor four. I huff out another shorter exhale, chastising myself for already overthinking. For looking back when I should be focused forward.

"Claire?"

I really should be focused forward. Because I failed to notice, until now, that the hallway on my floor isn't unoccupied.

"Reyna. Hey." I pair the greeting with a lackluster wave as I step out of the elevator, like that will normalize running into a teammate in the middle of the night.

"What are you doing up?" Her eyes are on the towel wrapped around my torso, which I momentarily forgot I was wearing and isn't going to make this explanation any simpler.

I blurt the first word that comes to mind. "Sleepwalking."

Reyna's forehead furrows. She's wearing a set of matching pajamas, patterned with tiny soccer balls, which I would tease her about under other circumstances. "What?"

"I sleepwalk sometimes. I take medication for it, but I forgot. Tonight. It's a minor case, but when I wake up, I'm disoriented. I decided to go swimming to wake up."

"But you're not…wet?"

"Pool was closed," I say, smacking my forehead. "Duh."

Thank God there's no way for her to tell I was coming down, not up. At least, I don't think there is.

"Oh-kay," Reyna replies carefully. "Are you sure you're okay? You were acting weird earlier too."

"Just bummed about the break," I tell her.

Most of the worry clears from her expression. "You should have come out with us earlier. We missed you."

"I'm sure you had more fun without me. I know I can be a downer."

Reyna frowns. "Claire, you're not a downer. You're literally the center of this team. Coach Taylor knows it. We all know it. We all want you around. You hold things together."

More tears threaten to appear. I swallow hard, managing a,

"Thanks, Rey."

"You missed Sav singing karaoke. And we were talking about trying to go to a Kluvberg game this fall, after our season ends. You've never been to Germany, right?"

"Right," I reply right as we reach my room. Fake a yawn, which isn't hard, considering I'm running on a few hours of sleep. "I'm going to head back to bed."

"Do you want me to stay with you?" Reyna asks.

I give her a confused look.

"In case you sleepwalk again," she explains.

Oh.

"I'm fine," I tell her. "I never sleepwalk twice in the same night."

I really hope Reyna never researches sleepwalking because my guess is, I'm spouting a lot of inaccurate facts about the disorder.

I pull her into an impulsive hug, squeezing her tight. "Thanks."

Her forehead creases when we separate. "For what?"

"I'm just lucky to have you as a teammate."

She smiles. "Back at ya, Caldwell."

Something occurs to me. "Wait. What were *you* doing up?"

Reyna blushes. "Uh, I was going to see Daniela."

My eyes widen. "What about Paige?"

"We broke up back in March."

"Why didn't you tell me?"

"You had a lot going on with Cassidy. The season was just starting. I didn't want to talk about it. It's new, with Daniela. If you could not..."

"I won't say a word," I promise.

Reyna exhales. "Thanks. Night, Caldy."

I flip her off before swiping my room key, her throaty laugh the last sound I register before the door shuts and my smile instantly disappears.

Chapter 44

Otto

Landing in Germany is bittersweet. Everything I brought to Boston is with me this time, but I can't shake the sensation of leaving something behind.

I disembark behind the other passengers, tugging the brim of the ball cap I'm wearing lower as I enter the airport, where the number of looks I'm getting multiplies. The line for customs is long. I sign autographs for two teenage boys while I wait to show my passport, prompting excited exclamations of my name throughout the waiting area. When I travel with Kluvberg, we fly in and out of the private terminal. Until I signed the autographs, most people likely assumed it couldn't possibly be me.

Finally, I make it outside. The late June air is balmy. It was hot when I left Boston, so it shouldn't be a surprise, but the contrast from my last trip here is stark. A reminder of how long I was away—the longest stretch I've ever left home for. It feels like more than four months have passed. This isn't how I anticipated my triumphant return—with what's been deemed a healthy shoulder by a dozen American doctors—would feel like.

I climb into the waiting car, not missing how the driver's eyes light up when he sees me. I wasn't forgotten during the second half of last season, like I'd feared. Wasn't replaced entirely.

Again, it leaves me feeling hollow, not vindicated.

I pull my phone out as the driver heads toward Kluvberg's training facility. I have a meeting with Leon Wagner, Kluvberg's head coach, then an appointment with the team doctor for him to assess my shoulder.

Unsurprisingly, there are a lot of messages. From Beck and Aster and Banks and the rest of my teammates. One from Saylor, inviting me over for dinner next week. A few from numbers I don't have saved, but the contents make it clear they are from female senders. I block the numbers rather than just delete the texts, send one quick message, then drop my phone on the seat and reach into my pocket.

Despite careful folding, the creased paper is more crumpled than it was before my flight. I should have stored it somewhere else, flat and impenetrable, but I wanted to keep it on me.

I have the message memorized, but I scan the short note just to see her handwriting.

The best is yet to come, Otto. I know Kluvberg knows how lucky they are to have you, and I feel lucky to have had you too. No regrets.

I'll be cheering you on.

Love,
Claire

There's a gap between the *O* and *V* in *love*, like she second-guessed the word halfway through before finishing it.

She snuck out of my hotel room while I was still sleeping. A move that was not entirely unexpected, although it sucked, waking up alone.

Then, at least I knew she was in the same building. The same city. The same country.

Now, we're on separate continents.

Twenty minutes later, I'm standing directly outside Leon Wagner's office.

I'm sure about this. I sat in the studio apartment that never really felt like a home for two days after returning from Miami, wrestling with why I was so conflicted about leaving Boston. Thinking and planning and worrying until my brain felt like one of those toy tops, spinning around.

I've decided. But it's still strange as I stare at the Kluvberg crest on the wall, knowing what I'm about to tell the man who's one of the primary reasons I have any career, let alone an incredibly successful one. Kluvberg bet big on me as a scrappy teenager with no backup plan. The fact that I've repaid that investment several times over doesn't make this any easier.

"Come in," Wagner's deep voice rumbles after I knock.

When I appear, he flashes a rare smile. "Otto. It's good to see you."

"You too, sir."

We shake hands, and I notice the approving glance he gives my shoulder as I grip his palm tightly.

We met briefly when I flew home for Opa's surgery. And I know Wagner has been receiving regular updates from my rehab team in Boston. But we rehash the basics anyway, then go over my training plan for the summer—assuming nothing comes up during today's assessment—until I can't hold the announcement in any longer.

"This will be my last season, sir."

I've never witnessed Wagner struck speechless before. He's a stoic man who takes his job seriously, rarely effusive with praise and pointed with criticism. He's been my coach for over a decade, and I've never witnessed him look so stunned.

He taps the folder that contains my medical records. "There's no indication that—"

"This has nothing to do with my injury. And I'm not retiring. I've decided to play…elsewhere."

Confusion edges into anger. "This organization has made you one of the top-paid players in Europe, Berger. I'm aware your contract ends next year, and I can assure you that last season won't affect any salary negotiations—"

"I'm not worried you won't resign me. Or about the money."

Both arrogant statements. Both true.

Wagner glowers, waiting for me to continue.

This is actually going better than I anticipated. I figured he'd have started yelling by now.

"I've decided to move to the States. Play for an American team."

For a few seconds, he stares at me. Then Wagner barks, "Why the fuck would you do that?"

I shift in my seat. I'm not accustomed to discussing my feelings with anyone, especially with my coach. But I owe him the full truth.

"There's something—someone—there. I love… I love her. And I chose this club over her once before. I won't—can't—do it again."

Wagner steeples his fingers under his chin, studying me.

I fight the urge to fidget as the silence between us stretches longer and longer. I hold his gaze, waiting for him to respond.

After what feels like hours, he sighs. "This the same woman who had you so moody in Paris?"

I wasn't expecting him to recall that conversation, let alone bring it up now.

Hesitantly, I nod. "Yes, sir."

He leans back in his chair, appraising me. I hold his gaze, waiting.

Finally, he sighs. "You're completely certain about this, Berger?"

"I am."

Another heavy exhale. "Not the news I was hoping for."

"I know."

"But I will respect your decision. I'm aware your life outside this organization hasn't been the easiest, and you've always prioritized this club. I understand you might need to shift those priorities now."

I nod. Wagner is one of the few people who knows most of the truth about my childhood. Who's aware my support system outside of football has been nonexistent for most of my life. But he's never mentioned it to me directly, and his acknowledgment means a lot.

"It wasn't an easy choice, sir. I appreciate—"

Wagner holds a hand up, silencing me. "You're under contract for another season, Berger. We can save the sentimentality for next spring. Especially since this really should have been done by your agent, informing the club management."

I nod. "I'm aware. But I wanted you to hear it from me, before any announcements are made or the news leaks some other way."

"How many people know?"

"Just, uh, you."

Wagner's graying eyebrows rise. "You haven't told…"

"Claire," I supply.

"You haven't told Claire what you're planning?"

I shake my head. "When I got injured, I realized…I realized how much of my identity had become playing for Kluvberg. I love this city and this club. Playing for FC Kluvberg was always my dream. But I need to see who I am, as a footballer and as a man, outside of this club. I'll be a better player and a better person for pushing myself to transition to somewhere I feel less comfortable. And, uh, I'm pretty sure she'll be happy about it."

I'm *pretty sure* Claire will be happy about it. But I'm aware it will be a big surprise. I didn't so much as hint this was something I was considering before I left Boston. I didn't want to disappoint Claire if I decided it was something I couldn't follow through on. I also assumed she'd try to talk me out of it. Tell me to prioritize my career.

Wagner stuns me by laughing. "You've got balls, Berger—I'll give you that much."

I grin. "Thank you, sir."

He points a finger at me. "But if anyone asks, I knew *nothing* about this plan of yours. I'll do what I can to mitigate the fallout, but a media firestorm will hit once the news is out. This entire city—the entire country—has been waiting impatiently for you to return. Return for *years*. They expect you to retire with the Kluvberg crest on your jersey."

"I know, sir."

Wagner gestures toward his office door. "Yves is waiting for you. Go get checked out so you can get officially cleared and we can figure out a plan for summer training."

I nod and stand, heading for the door.

"Berger?"

"Yes?" I pause, glancing back.

"You're hoping to wind up in Boston?"

"Yes, sir."

Wagner nods. "I know a trainer on Beacon. They'd be fools not to make an offer anyway, but I'll put in a good word."

"Thank you," I say thickly.

He nods again. "Get going, Berger."

I take the stairs down one flight and wind up in the medical and training wing. The staff is all here for me, so there's no wait. I'm ushered into one of the exam rooms as soon as I arrive.

Yves Durand, the club's head doctor, asks me a few preliminary questions, noting my responses on my chart before launching into more specific inquiries about my shoulder. "Any clicking, catching, or sensations of subluxation or looseness?"

"None. Just fatigue after longer sessions."

"That's normal. How's the strength compared to your nondominant side?"

"Pretty even now."

Yves does a clinical assessment next, checking my range of motion, scapular control, strength, and stability.

"Range is full, no impingement, strength is symmetrical, and I'm not seeing any instability or apprehension." He grabs my chart again, signing the bottom with a flourish. "Based on today's evaluation, I'm officially clearing you for unrestricted return to match play."

Thank fuck. The tension saps from my muscles.

"Make sure you continue with your shoulder maintenance protocol. Rotator cuff and scapular stabilization work shouldn't drop off just because you're back in full competition. We'll monitor the load carefully when you're back in goal. If you experience any change in shoulder stability or function, report it to a trainer immediately."

I nod, sliding off the table and pulling my T-shirt back on. "I will. Thanks."

"Berger?"

I glance back, halfway to the door. "Yeah?"

Yves smiles. "It's good to have you back in goal."

I grin back, attempting to ignore the squirming sensation in my chest. Wagner was right. Everyone's expecting me back—to stay.

"No one's happier than I am."

Coming off an injury isn't the smartest time to be shopping around for a new club. I'll have a short window to prove I'm able to perform at the same level, that my track record pre-surgery wasn't impacted by time away.

Before leaving, I stop by the locker room. I hover in the doorway for a few minutes, staring down at the FC Kluvberg emblem painted on the floor before walking over to my locker.

A banner has been hung above it, reading *Willkommen zurück!*

"I would have written *Claire Caldwell's Coach*," a deep voice says.

I grin, turning to watch Beck enter the locker room. "You're *still* annoyed about the *Saylor Scott's Inspiration* sign?"

"Nah, I just missed giving you shit."

We share a brief hug, and then he claps me on the back, nodding to my shoulder. "How'd it go?"

"They'll keep an eye on it, obviously, but I'm cleared. Starting training tomorrow, and I'll be in goal for the charity match against Ludlin."

Beck exhales, "Great."

"Yeah. I was pretty sure, based on what the American doctors said, but injuries are unpredictable."

"You headed out then?"

I nod. "What are you doing here?"

"Came to check on you." His answer makes it sound like an unnecessary question. "Want to go grab a pint to celebrate? Saylor took Gigi with her to look at wedding dresses with my mom and Sophia, so I've got the afternoon free."

"Yeah, that sounds great. But first, uh, first, I need to tell you something."

This news might land better over beers, but I don't want to risk anyone else overhearing if we're out in public.

"Now?"

I nod. "Now."

"All right." He props a hip against Banks's locker, crossing his arms. "Go ahead."

I rub the back of my neck, gathering my thoughts.

This is harder than telling Wagner was.

Beck isn't just my captain. He's been my mentor. An older brother. Not to mention one hell of a teammate. You can't win a football game by stopping every shot that comes your way. Any legacy I leave in this sport will be largely thanks to the number of Beck's kicks other keepers couldn't save.

I thought we had longer than one year left to play together. I'm sure he did too.

"Next season is my last," I state.

Beck connects the dots faster than Wagner did. "You're going to play in the US?"

"Yes."

He releases a long sigh, shaking his head once. "I owe Saylor fifty euros."

I roll my eyes, miffed but mostly relieved. "You told her?"

"She told *me.* Why do you think she invited Claire back to your apartment? Saylor wanted to hang out with her more, but she was convinced something was going on between you guys. You weren't exactly subtle, staring at her in the bar all night."

I scowl. "Fuck off."

Beck just chuckles. "I'm happy for you. Banks was solid this spring. He's not you—no one is—but the club will be fine. I'd rather you be there and happy than here and miserable. If Saylor hadn't decided to play here, I would have done the same damn thing."

My throat feels thick, but I choke out a, "Thanks, Beck."

As we walk out of the locker room, he asks, "What'd she say?"

"Claire?"

He nods.

"She, uh, doesn't—I haven't told her."

This time, his reaction is identical to Wagner's. Once he's finished laughing, Beck tells me, "Usually, that's the sort of thing you discuss."

"She'd try to talk me out of it. I don't want her to know yet. It's my decision. No matter what she says, when she finds out, it's been made."

Chapter 45

Claire

I freeze in Mom's entryway, seconds from shouting my usual, *Hi, Mom*, listening to the low timbre of my father's voice in one of the places I never expected to hear it.

We haven't spoken since he came to my final home match pre-break. That was a brief exchange—him congratulating me on the win—Cassidy, Josh, and Tommy's presence easing most of the awkwardness. Dad didn't mention then, or anytime else, that he'd ever visited Echo Glen before. But his voice is unmistakable, low and calm, followed by my mom's quiet laugh.

I slip out of my other sandal, rounding the corner barefoot.

They're seated at the dining room table, surface littered with its usual piles of Mom's notes, looking through a photo album.

"No, she was a fairy that year," my dad says, then glances up and sees me.

"That's right," Mom replies. "Was it—" She notices Dad's

attention has drifted, then follows his gaze to me. "Claire!"

"Hi, Mom." I shift my weight awkwardly, foot to foot. "It's such a nice day. I was thinking you might want to go on a walk. But I—" I look at Dad, not sure what to say about his presence here.

"I have to finish this chapter." She pats her laptop, set right next to the photo album. "Why don't you two go without me?"

I'm not sure who's more startled by the suggestion—me or my dad.

"Oh, no—" I start.

"That's not—" Dad says at the same time.

We talk simultaneously, then stop in sync as well. I'm uncomfortably reminded of Cassidy's comment—that Dad and I are awfully similar.

Mom is undeterred. "Go on. Like Claire said, it's a beautiful day." She gives me an encouraging nod.

She appears aware of the awkwardness between us. Like she's living in the present or somewhere close to it today, which makes this even stranger. She hasn't seemed to have forgotten that Dad and I don't go on walks. We don't do anything together.

We used to though. My right hand slips into the pocket of my shorts, fingering the coin. Cassidy was a fairy for several years during my zookeeper phase. I'm sure the old album he and Mom were just looking at is filled with photos of the two of us together. Probably some at the Detroit Zoo.

I clear my throat. "I… Sure. I have some time."

My dad's face lights up. "Me too."

His obvious excitement makes me feel about two inches tall. Worse than my dad's choices all those years ago is the growing realization that I played a huge role in our estrangement too. That I've never tried to forgive him, merely accepted our relationship was ruined beyond repair.

"Great." Mom opens her laptop and begins typing, disappearing into a fictional world I've always been envious of.

I'm too practical to have the same imagination. Cassidy inherited that romanticism and wanderlust, but not me.

Dad and I don't say much, trading simple comments like, "Left here," and "After you," as we walk Echo Glen's winding hallways toward a set of doors that lead to the gardens. There's a pond out here, too, where a family of ducks lives.

We walk along one of the paths, surrounded by the chirps of birds and errant pieces of conversation as we pass other visitors. The loudest sound is the crunch of gravel beneath our feet.

"Does Lindsey know you come here?" I finally ask.

"She does."

"That doesn't bother her?"

"She knows your mother and I have a...complicated relationship."

I suppress a snort. What a concise way of framing cheating.

But I don't say so because I know it will ruin this moment.

"How often do you come?"

"I try to get here once a week. Bring her some new books and just...check in." He tucks his hands in his pockets. "I should have mentioned it to you."

"It's fine."

We continue walking, gravel continuing to crunch underfoot as we traverse the peaceful path. It is peaceful, walking with my dad, which isn't an adjective I've used to describe our relationship in a long time.

"I'm watching Tommy this weekend, during Cassidy and Josh's trip," I finally say. "I was thinking about bringing him to Southwick's Zoo on Saturday, if you want to join us?"

There's a pause, and I'm not brave enough to look over to check the expression on his face.

"I would love to." He clears his throat. "Lindsey has an event this weekend, so she won't be able to make it, but all I had on the agenda was some golf. I can easily reschedule."

I nod, privately relieved Lindsey's busy. She's always acted perfectly pleasant toward me, but I can't picture us ever being more than civil. I have no reason to forgive her. At least, with my dad, there's something to salvage. She was a stranger when she and my dad got married, and she's barely not one now.

But I am trying—or trying to try—so I say, "I went to a gala a few weeks ago—I was invited by the Siege. It was put on by the Boston Sports Foundation. I saw some—it seemed like Lindsey's company had planned it."

Dad nods. "She did. They're one of her regular clients." After a pause, he adds, "She filmed your speech. Sent it to me. I hope that was...okay."

"What did you think?"

He seems surprised by the question. "You were incredible, Claire. You always—you've always excelled at anything you put your mind to."

"Thanks, Dad."

"I hope—I hope you know how proud of you I am. How proud I've been."

I glance down, letting my hair fall forward to partially cover my face as I blink rapidly. "Thanks, Dad," I repeat.

During the most important, meaningful moments, I have the hardest time expressing my thoughts. I can't find the right words to convey how I'm feeling to my dad—that I'm happy and sad and confused and guilty and angry—when I'm around him or when I think about the state of our relationship or when I recall the many years we hardly spoke.

"Josh mentioned he told you about his special plans for the trip."

"He did."

I'm not surprised Josh asked Dad for permission before proposing. He's traditional like that. Stable and somewhat predictable. The kind of guy I assumed I'd end up with, not Cassidy.

But she and Josh fit.

The same way, weirdly, that Otto and I fit. I feel more myself with him than anyone else.

"It's exciting," Dad comments.

"It is."

There's a natural lull where I could say more, offer information about my own love life, which I think my dad is wondering about, but I stay silent. I don't know where to begin discussing Otto with anyone, let alone my father. His absence is a noticeable ache, prompting a slew of second-guessing of what I should have said before he left. I should have told him I loved him. It might not have changed anything, but at least the words would be expelled, not contained. Instead, I impulsively scribbled the four-letter word in the middle of the night.

"What?" I ask, belatedly realizing my dad's been talking while I was adrift in a sea of my own thoughts.

Curiosity lingers on his face as he repeats, "Are you missing playing?"

Not a question I get often. Most people assume the break midseason or between seasons is a relief. But even in the moments I've hated soccer, when I've cursed my foot for not making that fateful shot and my reflexes for not reacting faster, allowing a striker to slip past, I've never wanted to do anything else.

"I was considering quitting actually."

Dad stops walking.

It takes me a few steps to realize, and then I circle back, meeting his startled eyes.

"Why?"

I lift a shoulder, then let it drop, debating how honest to be. "With everything happening with Mom, I thought it made the most sense. Not just the money–it was before you set up the trust–but spending more time with her. A normal job would have typical hours. It's a sacrifice, training and traveling, and it's always been worth it to me. But at some point...I made it. I played professionally. Played in Boston even. I wasn't sure what else was left." I shrug again, letting the uncertain motion bookend my explanation.

Dad frowns. "Considering? So, you've decided to continue playing?"

I nod. "Assuming the Siege offers an extension. I signed a two-year contract that expires at the end of this season."

"What changed your mind?"

"I fell back in love with it, I guess. I decided to prioritize what I want and worry less about what is practical or what other people would tell me to do."

A pause, and then Dad says, "If you meet someone who doesn't support your career, Claire, he's not the right person."

I think of Nolan for the first time in years, who acted like soccer was an inconvenient hobby. My most recent ex, Steve, who was on the partner track at a major law firm and would joke that my job kept me busier than his did. Even Walker seemed unsure what questions to ask during our brief period of exchanging texts, as if a woman being a professional athlete was a foreign concept to him.

Otto told me to play.

"It's not that."

Dad nods, appearing relieved. "Good."

The path veers right, curving back toward Echo Glen. A fountain trickles water, some of the spray misting my arm as we pass it.

"There's an ice cream place down the street. We could see if your mom has finished her chapter, then take a quick trip there? They have sorbet."

I study my dad, two important details striking me at once. One, the way he's accepted Mom's insistence that she continue working when we both know it's unlikely she'll ever finish another book. Two, that he noticed they had a nondairy option.

"Sorbet sounds great," I say.

Dad smiles, and we head back toward the building together.

Chapter 46

Otto

Opa's sitting outside in one of the chairs that matches his kitchen table when I pull into the driveway.

I climb out of my car, spinning my keys around one finger as I approach the trimmed section of the front yard, where he's reading. "*Hallo*, Opa."

He glances up, saying nothing. But he smiles, the corners of his eyes wrinkling, and that expression alone makes it a warmer reunion than we've had in a long time.

"What are you reading?" I ask.

He flashes me the cover. "I read it last year," I tell him.

He nods. Approving almost. Reading is one of the only interests we share. When I returned from the academy on breaks, I'd work my way through most of his extensive collection.

Opa closes the book and stands, setting the novel carefully on the chair. "Should we take a walk?"

"Sure." I smother my shock.

It's a reasonable suggestion. Today is a beautiful day, sunny and warm. But my grandfather has never, not once, suggested we walk together when I've visited Tannfeld.

I watch carefully as we head down the street, but my grandfather doesn't appear to be having any trouble walking. He's carrying a cane, but isn't putting weight on it. Holding it seems more habit than anything else.

I speak first. "I was cleared by the club's medical team. I'll resume normal training next week, so I'll be ready for a charity match we have in a couple of weeks."

"That's good."

"It is," I agree.

"Who are you playing?"

"Ludlin," I answer, taken aback again.

Our conversations about football usually consist of me talking and Opa—maybe—listening, with the animosity of our previous disagreements on the topic of me and football a rocky current running beneath any exchange.

"You expect to win?"

I smile. "I always expect to win."

"They must be happy to have you back."

I nod. "I'm happy to be back."

We continue walking in a silence that's surprisingly relaxed. Sections of Tannfeld have cobblestone streets, including the original area near where Opa lives. And we're headed toward the oldest portion of the village, the spire of the slate-roofed church visible past whitewashed houses. I typically take the longer route into town to avoid driving past that church. My one and only memory of it is attending my mother's funeral there.

But that seems to be our destination now. My grandfather

attends services here every Sunday.

It's a beautiful church, despite my negative association with it, painted white with yellow accents. It glows in the afternoon sunshine, the cemetery sloping behind it a stretch of immaculately manicured grass.

We pause by the black iron fence that separates the church from the street.

"Should we head back?" I ask, preferring that to lingering.

"I'm ill, Otto."

I stare at my grandfather. I don't see him often enough to catalog daily changes, but he looks the same as I recall from my last trip here. Improved, I thought when I first arrived, more color on his face and better balance.

"What-what do you mean?"

The solid stone I'm standing on seems to be sloping all of a sudden. I'm five years old again, watching my grandfather stare into space with an empty glass in one hand.

"I've been wanting—needing—to tell you. Mila has been badgering..." Opa sighs, glancing at the graves. "I should have told you a while ago. I kept putting it off. We don't see each other often. And when we do, it's..." He looks at me, then away again. "I owe you an apology. Lots of them really. After Lina died... I didn't handle it well. I know that, and I know you know it too. And I've spent all these years too embarrassed to—"

"Opa," I interrupt, "you don't have to—"

"I do." He turns his head, fixing his steely gaze on me. "I've been stubborn and prideful and allowed it to interfere with the only meaningful relationship I have left. I didn't agree with your decision to play football professionally. But I never should have allowed that to become a reason you wouldn't come home."

I exhale. "I could have done more too. I got swept up in being on Kluvberg and what being part of the club meant, let it become everything to me. I realized, when I got injured and lost it for a little while, just how much I'd relied on it."

"That wasn't your responsibility. No matter what you chose to do with your life, I should have supported it. Your-your mother would have been ashamed of my behavior."

I hardly remember my mom. I have no sense whether she would have wanted me to play football or not. But she and Opa were close. I'm not certain she would have told me to choose football over him, which is essentially what I did.

"What do you mean, you're ill?" The question comes out slowly. I'm dreading the answer.

Opa isn't one for dramatics. Him telling me means it's serious.

His grip on the cane tightens. "They found the tumor a few months before I fell. It's part of why I resisted the hip surgery—it seemed pointless. But Mila said she would tell you herself if I didn't have the operation, and I wanted to tell you. And then you came for the surgery, and I still hadn't decided what to say."

"You're getting treatment?" I ask, hating the hope in my voice.

Opa wouldn't be saying all this, bringing up my mom, if he thought he'd be around on the day I did retire to ask what I planned to do with the rest of my life.

"There's nothing they can do."

I was worried it was coming, but it still knocks the wind out of me. Burns in my chest and behind my eyes. I assumed my moving to the States would involve seeing him as often as I do now. Maybe more, depending on the length of my trips home. I even thought the change might improve our relationship, jolting us out of a routine we were too accustomed to.

And now, I'm not even sure I *can* leave. There might have

been no point in telling Wagner or Beck a thing if leaving Kluvberg next year will also mean abandoning my grandfather when he needs me most.

"How long?"

"Six months."

I glance down, blinking rapidly, absorbing the impact of another hit. My grandfather just told me he'll be dead in less than a year, and I can't even look him in the eye. I'm so swamped in regret and anger and uncertainty that it feels like drowning. I can't breathe. Can't move.

"Otto." Opa grips my shoulder, his hold surprisingly strong.

I sniff, rubbing a palm across my face. There's hardly anyone around. The nearby vineyard that attracts tourists is on the opposite end of town, and it's not a Sunday that draws locals to this location. But I feel on display anyway. Out in the open, during one of the moments I feel most vulnerable and most alone.

I lift my head, finally meeting his gaze. "And you decided to tell me this at a *cemetery*?"

Opa nods. "I wanted to show you where I'm moving."

I stare at him.

One corner of my grandfather's mouth lifts. Mila often comments how funny Opa is, and I've rarely seen any evidence of it. We're not comfortable enough around each other to joke around. But I guess I inherited the playful part of my personality somewhere after all.

"You'll get everything, of course. It's not much, but—"

"Stop it," I say. "Just…stop."

"We need to discuss it."

While there's still time, he means. Before there's no time left. Because, in some contexts, six months is a long while. But in others, like our relationship, it's an average amount of time for us not to see each other.

"I know. I'll come back soon, and we can talk about it. Not… now."

I expect him to argue—he normally does—but today, he nods.

"Okay." His hand drops from my shoulder as he turns back toward the street, appearing ready to head back to his house.

Suddenly, I'm scared to. I don't want to revert to the heaviness that house contains. None of the memories there are particularly happy ones.

"I'm moving too," I blurt.

My grandfather turns back to face me, a quizzical frown on his face as he says, "Where?"

"Boston, hopefully. The details are still—I'm under contract with Kluvberg for another season. It won't be…before."

"Can I meet her?"

When I aim a questioning look his way, Opa has the temerity to roll his eyes at me.

"I know how you feel about that club. Only a woman could have prompted such a major change." He glances at the graveyard. "I was the same way about my Ella."

Opa mentions his late wife even less often than my mom. She died during a rare complication following childbirth, and it occurred to me, years after she passed away, that my mom's death must have felt like losing all he had left of his wife. And also like history repeating itself, leaving him with a child and a whole lot of grief for the second time in his life.

"I'd love for you to meet her," I say.

Opa nods like the matter is settled. I don't mention, as we walk the blocks back toward his neighborhood, that my future is far less firm than I made it sound. Not only have I not told Claire that I intend to swap leagues, but I have nothing certain to tell her. I can't guarantee I'll wind up in Boston or anywhere close to Massachusetts—only that I'll be closer than Germany.

My grandfather has enough on his mind without me burdening him with the details.

When I first started playing professionally, retirement was the furthest thing from my mind. Now, I've realized that day will come, and I might not be able to pick it. If believing I have something—someone—in my life aside from football will offer him some peace, then I fully intend to give that to him.

Halfway back to Opa's, a young boy—probably about ten—runs out of his front yard with my jersey in hand. I talk with him for a few minutes before signing the shirt with the marker he shyly offered.

Opa leans on his cane and watches, an inscrutable expression on his face. He's seen me interact with some fans before, but not many. I haven't invited him to a match since I called him with the news that I'd been named the starting keeper for Germany's team at the Paris Olympics. When I offered tickets, he said he'd rather watch from home, but I'm not sure he ever did.

I've resented his indifference toward football plenty of times, but I don't hate it. It protected this escape, provided one place—one person—I was simply Otto to. I've had teammates who were berated by family members for poor performances or constantly asked for money. I was never treated as anything more than ordinary, and it was a pocket of normalcy I should have appreciated more.

The boy runs back into his yard, his mom calling a thank-you that I respond to with a wave, and we continue down the street.

"I remember when that was you," Opa says quietly.

Chapter 47

Claire

Low buzzing wakes me. I reach for the spot where I keep my phone, brushing soft nylon instead of hard wood. That contrast is enough to wake me fully, blinking and disoriented.

Cassidy and Josh left on their—unbeknownst to Cassidy—engagement trip this morning. Tommy wanted to camp out in the backyard tonight. I agreed, thinking we'd wind up inside after the novelty of the tent wore off, but he fell asleep an hour ago. I dozed off at some point too, apparently.

My phone's still buzzing. I locate the device, flipping it over so I can see the screen. Instantly, my stomach somersaults with a mix of nerves and excitement.

I accept the call, whispering, "One sec," before tucking the phone in the waistband of my sweatpants and crawling past a snoring Tommy. I unzip the tent as quietly as possible, then tumble out onto cool grass.

I walk past the row of blooming dahlias, taking deep breaths as I approach the swing set that was my tenth birthday gift. After the wedding, I hope Josh winds up joining Cassidy and Tommy here. It's a house meant for a family to live in. And I want to not live here, surrounded by ghosts of Mom in every nook, cranny, and flower.

"You still there?" I ask, raising the phone to my ear as I sink onto one of the swings.

"Yes," Otto replies. "And I just realized how late it is there. Sorry."

He sounds more tired than I do, but I don't say so.

"I was up."

"Liar."

Rather than deny it, I laugh. "How could you tell?"

"I just can. Your voice gets higher."

"I wasn't expecting to fall asleep. I'm camping in the backyard with Tommy. Cassidy and Josh are gone for the weekend."

"The proposal trip?"

I shouldn't be surprised. He's proven multiple times that he listens to me. That he remembers. But I'm so used to expecting people won't, I guess, that it still catches me off guard.

"Exactly." I tip my head back, staring at the starry sky overhead. The same one he looks at, even halfway around the world, and the thought is oddly comforting. Like he's not that far away, even though I know, logically, there are a lot of miles between us right now. "How is…being back?"

"Good—mostly. Busy. Kluvberg's doctors officially cleared me. My first day training in goal is tomorrow. We have got a charity match coming up next week."

"You're starting in it?"

"Yes." I can hear the smile—the relief—in his voice.

"That's incredible, Otto. Congratulations."

"You were the first person I wanted to tell when they cleared me."

I open my mouth, then close it again. I'm not sure how to reply to that. So, I start swinging, the whoosh of summer air combing through my loose curls.

"I was not sure if I should call," he continues. "We did not really talk about…boundaries."

"That wouldn't have been as fun as sex."

He chuckles. I feel it low in my stomach. With my eyes closed, I can almost pretend he's on the swing next to me.

"You can always call, Otto," I add.

I'm torn between the desire to stay close to him and the impulse to push him away. Both hurt, in different ways. Neither seems sustainable. Talking to him makes me miss him more. Not talking to him makes me miss him more.

We're both silent for a minute. And I wish it were awkward, for the week since I saw him to have grown into an obstacle of uncomfortable pauses as we struggle to come up with things to say to each other. Instead, I'm more relaxed than I've been in days, swinging under the stars, listening to him breathe.

"I saw my grandfather last week," he tells me.

"How did it go?" I can't tell, based on his tone.

"Good. And awful. He is sick. The illness is terminal."

My feet hit the ground with a thud, nearly pulling me off the swing. "*Otto*, I'm—"

"I do not want to talk about it. I-I am not ready to talk about it. I just wanted you to know. You were the person I needed to tell."

He's never said he loves me. Again, it's a tug-of-war in my chest—I want to hear the words but know they'd only hurt in the long run. But needing someone and loving someone sound very similar.

"This might not make sense, but it was the best visit we had in a long time," Otto continues. "We talked about some things we had needed to for many years."

"That makes perfect sense," I reply. "You appreciate everything more when you know time is limited."

"I knew you would understand," he says quietly.

Otto probably thinks I'm talking about my mom, and I am. But I'm talking about us too. Honesty is easier under a ticking clock. It's the only reason I was brave enough to add *love* to the note I left him.

"How long does he have?"

"Six months. They found the tumor before his hip surgery. It had already spread. Even if he did treatment, which he has decided against, it would not…" I hear him exhale before he asks, "Do you think Cassidy will say yes?"

"I do," I answer. "She's more…unconventional than I am, but she loves Josh. And she's always wanted to get married. When we were younger, she'd have me officiate. Gabe, our dog, was the groom."

"Are there photos?"

"No," I say quickly, although there probably are. Maybe in the album my parents were looking at together.

He laughs, likely hearing the lie, then asks, "What about you?"

"What about me?" I stall, unsure if I'm misunderstanding.

"Have you always wanted to get married?"

"No. I…I think that stability scares me."

He waits, so I continue, "Before my dad left, we were whole. After, we weren't. It happened so fast, and I never saw it coming.

Trusting that things will stay the same feels...foolish now that I know how easily they can change." I chew the inside of my cheek until I taste copper, forcing myself to add, "You saying, 'I don't know,' in Paris—well, it hurt at the time, but I appreciated your honesty. That you told me the truth instead of what I wanted to hear."

Silence follows, and I start to panic a little. That was too honest, and I said too much and—

"My answer would be different now, Claire. I was scared to—my parents were never together. I never met my dad. I had no example of what a healthy relationship looked like. I was scared for you to rely on something I was not certain I could give you."

I press a hand to my mouth, stifling any sound that might escape. My nose is doing that tingling thing that happens before I start crying.

I search my brain for anything that might resemble a neutral topic, blurting the first thought that occurs to me. "My dad and I are taking Tommy to the zoo tomorrow."

There's a pause before Otto asks, "Do they have tokens?"

I cover my sniffle with a short laugh. "Not sure. We'll find out. I'm...nervous about it. We haven't spent much—any—quality time together since the divorce. I ran into him, visiting my mom, and it went better than I thought it would, so hopefully, this is the same."

Movement catches my eye. Tommy's emerging from the tent, rubbing his eyes, looking around for me.

"I've got to go," I say. "Tommy just woke up. Fingers crossed he's ready to head inside and sleep on an actual mattress."

I could call him back, but I don't offer, and Otto doesn't ask. He saved my number, I'm realizing, and I'm terrified by how much that matters to me. More evidence that I was wrong—that he didn't forget about me as fast as I'd feared. Maybe he never forgot about me at all.

He replies, "Okay," acknowledging that he heard me.

"I—bye, Otto."

"Bye, Claire."

I'm glad Tommy is waiting for me. Otherwise, I know I would sit there, staring at the sky, for a while.

Chapter 48

Otto

The sun beams down on Sieg Stadium, bright and relentless. My palms are damp inside the gloves, my jersey wet with sweat. I clench and unclench my fists, waiting for the first kick as I study the line of my teammates. They're not all on the field, but they're all here. On the sidelines, sprawled in the shade of the bench. Watching. Waiting. Wondering.

The stakes are highest for me. But they exist for the entire team. If I'm not up to the task, my speeches to Wagner and Beck won't matter. Kluvberg won't want me anyway.

"Go, Pires!" Wagner calls out.

Olivier nods. Plants a cleat and kicks.

I read left correctly. I dive low, extending my arm, punching the ball clear from the open net. My left shoulder slams to the ground, but there's no sharp stab after. There's no twinge in my healed right either as I push upright and stand, rotating my arms.

I glance at Beck first. He's grinning.

Wagner right after. He nods, the relief clear on his face.

"Attaboy, Berger," Aster calls out.

I don't allow any emotions to soak in. One save is nothing impressive for me. I still have more shots to block. Including attempts by Beck and Will, who are considered to be two of the best players in the world.

Friedrich Schneider is up next, his usual cocky smirk in place. Some of his bluster is earned. He's not always accurate, but he's fast. He also opts for a stutter step before taking his shot to the right. I hesitate for a split second longer than I did with Olivier, and it almost costs me. My fingertips barely graze the edge of the ball, but it's enough to send it spinning harmlessly to the side.

"Aster!" Wagner shouts.

Will walks toward the ball, no sign of teasing on his face now. He won't take it easy on me. He's still trying to prove himself to the club, and the entire point of this exercise is testing what shape my shoulder is in.

Sure enough, Aster fakes high, then kicks low. I guess left, and he aims right, but my foot reaches the ball in time.

Applause starts on the sidelines, quickly silenced by a sharp glare from Wagner.

I want to smile, but I don't. Assurance is spreading through me, steady and slow and sure. I'm fine. I'm better than fine.

It's still too soon to celebrate though.

Beck is stepping up last, and I know he'll be the toughest opponent. Not only because of who he is, but because we know each other so well. We've played together for the past eleven years. He used to pull me out on this field, under the guise of practicing his penalty kicks so he could coach me on improving. It's the only reason I witnessed the moment he met his future wife. And it feels like all that history is stuffed in this stadium now as we stare at each other, facing off.

He wants this triumphant return for me, knows that temporarily losing football was as devastating for me as it would have been for him.

But he wants a goal more. His ability to focus on his own performance first is what makes him such a dominant athlete.

I'm drenched with sweat and flooded with adrenaline.

There is nothing—*nothing*—like facing down a penalty kick. There's no distraction of other players. Just me, the net, and an incoming shot. No clues in the form of angles or approach to guess which direction the ball will go in. No defenders running interference.

I dance back and forth, waiting for Beck to move. Inside my gloves, my palms are slick, but that won't matter when I reach for the ball.

Beck strikes.

Right, which I predict correctly based on nothing except my gut. He usually goes left first, and he's trying to test me. He also knows which shoulder I injured, that I'll possibly be more protective of this side. I pick the correct direction, but it's a beautiful shot—high and fast and accurate—blasting through the air so fast that I swear I can hear it whistle. I launch toward it, unsure I'll reach it in time, until it collides with my fist and boomerangs in the opposite direction. There would be a prime rebound opportunity if this were a game, but it's not.

I twist just in time to hit the ground, the impact with the turf uncomfortable, but no more painful than normal. I didn't injure—or reinjure—anything.

Then I roll flat on my back, beaming up at the blue sky.

Fuck, that felt good.

Hoots and hollers fill the stadium.

This time, Wagner doesn't silence my teammates' cheers.

• • •

A dozen people are waiting in the hallway. A mixture of my team and Kluvberg employees. My hair is still damp from the shower I took after practice, the cold air blasting from the vents ruffling the wet strands. I'm run through approved talking points as we make the short trip to the media room. I nod along, not really listening. I've never stuck to a script in interviews before, which is probably why I'm the player reporters always want to talk to. Today, the first time I've talked to the press since my injury, right before my first match back, is especially juicy.

This year's charity match was already hotly anticipated since we're competing against Ludlin. Add in that my medical clearance was leaked already and that I'm participating in a press conference, and it means there's more attention on this match than most regular season games.

It's just me, here, even though the entire team assembled for practice earlier.

I can hear the noise inside from down the hallway. It grows exponentially louder as a staff member opens the doors.

I make my way down the side aisle to the front of the room, smiling for the cameras flashing in time with each step. There's a rush of commotion when I take a seat, and everyone else with one hurries to do the same. It's standing room only, and even that space has been taken up, people lining the walls of the room.

I twist open the cap of the water bottle set next to the microphone and take a sip from it.

"Too bad more of you couldn't make it."

Laughter fills the large room.

"Thank you for being here," I continue into the microphone. "As some of you might have already heard, I've been officially cleared for match play."

No surprise shows on the faces of the first row of reporters.

"I'll be back in goal for our upcoming match against Ludlin and for the start of this upcoming season. Any further questions?"

What looks like every hand in the room flies up.

I take another sip of water while a guy wearing a Kluvberg polo calls on a journalist.

He stands eagerly a second later. "I know I speak for the entire city—the entire country really—when I say, welcome home, Otto."

I smile. "Thanks."

"Do you anticipate that your active status will be reassessed on a regular basis, or are you certain your shoulder is fully healed?"

"I doubt there's a doctor in Germany who *hasn't* looked at my shoulder," I answer, which prompts more laughter. "Not a single one has suggested I won't be able to perform at the same level. The consistent verdict is, everything healed perfectly. I'd like to take this opportunity to thank the surgical staff at Sankt Marien Krankenhaus for taking such excellent care of me, along with the physical therapists at Mass General and, of course, Kluvberg's medical team. Injury is a risk for any athlete. But I have no reason to believe my performance moving forward will be affected. In fact, if you ask any of the teammates whose shots I just blocked, they'd probably tell you my shoulder's better than it was before."

The journalist who asked the question smiles, jotting something on his notepad.

I answer a series of more questions—inquiring about the rehab process, how I've had to adjust my training, what it was like, returning to Sieg Stadium—before a woman with a neat bun stands. She's one of the few female reporters in here, probably only a few years older than me.

"There were reports you spent time during your recovery assistant-coaching an American women's team. The Boston Siege. Is coaching something you're considering after retirement? Was that a test run?"

I swallow some water before answering, "I did some coaching, yes. And I would consider it again in the future. But I'm not planning to retire anytime soon, so I can't give you a more definitive answer than that."

"Did coaching help with your recovery?"

"Only one question per—"

"It's fine," I tell the staffer. "It did, yes. It was motivating to be around the game when I couldn't play myself."

"It's unusual for a contracted athlete to coach for another team. What role did—"

"We really need to move on," the moderator states, gesturing to another reporter.

"I have a related question actually," the next reporter says. "Would you say coaching was the most inspiring part of your recovery?"

"It was motivating, as I said. But"—fuck it, I decide—"no, it was not the most inspiring part. What helped me most, through the uncertainty, was…love."

The reporter frowns, clearly taken aback by the answer. "Love…of football?"

"I love football. I always will. It's been the biggest part of my life for as long as I can remember. But in Boston, I fell in love—fell *back* in love—with someone. She was certain I would make a full recovery, when I was worried my career was over, even though she has no medical training whatsoever." I smile. "When my injury first happened, I was not sure what my life would look like without football. Thanks to her, I know exactly what it would—will—look like."

There's a beat of pure silence, comical in the crowded room.

I clear my throat. I wasn't planning on saying any of that. But having it out is a relief.

"Since I am sharing personal updates, I guess I'll also announce that the upcoming season will be my final with FC Kluvberg. I'm..."

The rest of what I was intending to say gets lost in the din of the dozens of questions shouted my way.

Chapter 49

Claire

Coach Taylor looks up when I knock on her door.

"Do you have a minute?" I question tentatively.

"I do." She reclines in her chair, elbows on the arms, as I take a seat. "I thought you might stop by."

"You did?"

I spent the entire drive to the Siege's practice facility deliberating how to word this. Debating how to broach the topic.

"I read the news, Caldwell, especially articles that mention former members of this organization. Otto Berger is a well-known name. He also spent most of his time in Boston traveling and working with this team. Not a giant leap to think he might have been referring to a member of it during his press conference. You were in Paris, with Saylor, and Berger played in those Games as well, so you could have met there." She raises one eyebrow. "I've been reading some of your mother's novels. How are my deductive skills?"

I manage a weak smile before launching into an apology. "I'm so sorry, Coach. I should have told you we had a preexisting relationship at the start of the season. I hadn't seen him since Paris, I didn't know he was coming, and when he showed up, I—I didn't think it would matter."

"And now?"

"I'd like to talk to him in person. I can't believe that he would…" I let my voice trail. "But there's a good chance, if I go, I'd—we'd be seen together. He's famous there, obviously. I don't want to cause any problems for this club. Any more problems, that is."

Coach Taylor points at the phone on her desk. "That has been ringing nonstop this morning. I finally had to disconnect the damn thing. Marc Meadows"—the head coach of Beacon FC—"is giddy. He wanted my opinion on how best to approach Berger's agent. I understand wanting to keep your personal life private, and you're entitled to now that he is no longer part of this organization, but I would have appreciated a heads-up on—"

"I didn't know," I blurt, interrupting my head coach for the first time ever. "I had *no idea* he was going to do that press conference. That he'd decided to leave Kluvberg. That club is his home. His dream. I never thought he would even consider playing anywhere else."

She studies me for a few seconds. Her sudden smile catches me off guard. "Well, that's rather romantic."

I scoff. "Or idiotic."

Coach Taylor's expression becomes even more amused. "You don't feel the same way about him?"

"I-I do," I say awkwardly. I've discussed personal matters with Coach Taylor before, when I've had to pick up Tommy or was running late because of Mom's doctor appointments, but never my love life.

She nods like she already knew the answer. "It didn't sound like an impulsive decision, Caldwell. Do what you need to do, and we'll have a conversation when you get back."

• • •

Cassidy drives me to the airport with a wide smile on her face. July sunshine reflects off the diamond ring nestled on her left hand, nearly blinding me as she navigates the Boston traffic.

My sister came home from work to me hauling a packed suitcase down the stairs, and didn't hesitate to offer to drop me off at the airport. Josh has been coming over most nights after work to cook dinner and to see Cassidy and Tommy and was happy to watch his future stepson.

"Dreams" is playing on the radio, Cassidy singing along loudly, and it feels like a sign.

I'm angry with Otto. Furious he told the world that he was leaving FC Kluvberg and that he loved me before bothering to inform me.

I also know exactly why he did. Because he knew what I would have said if he had told me first. It's what I'm flying to Germany to tell him anyway.

"What about Nantucket?" Cassidy asks me as she takes the airport exit.

"You hate boats," I remind her.

"Your quarterback beau probably has a helicopter he'd let you use."

I roll my eyes. I made the mistake of mentioning my conversation with Brady Simmons to Cassidy, and now she's trying to rope him into wedding plans.

"He's not my beau. If you want to get married on Nantucket, you'll have to wait five years for a venue and take a ferry over."

Cassidy sighs, then brightens. "Does Otto have a helicopter?"

"Terminal E," I say, pointing at the sign.

Cassidy flicks on her blinker, navigating over a lane. She pulls up alongside the curb, outside the terminal, a few minutes later.

"You know what Mom would say if she were here."

I glance at my sister. "What?"

"It only has to make sense to you."

That's what my mom told me whenever I worried if a career as a professional athlete was a foolish choice. And I know Cassidy is right; it's what she'd say to me now. She'd say not to worry about all the outside noise and focus on what I wanted.

I give Cassidy a quick hug. "Thank you," I whisper. "I'm glad you're here."

Her arms tighten briefly before she lets go. "Me too."

For the first time ever, I walk into the airport under the three-hour window recommended for international travel. The security line is ridiculously long, and my flight is already boarding by the time I make it to the gate. I white-knuckle the armrest during takeoff. And then it hits me, as the flight attendants are passing out headphones, that I have no clue where in Kluvberg Otto lives.

The absurdity of that—I'm flying halfway around the world to see a guy whose address is a mystery—makes me giggle. Once I start laughing, it's hard to stop. I'm still in shock, I think, from watching his press conference. From having the extraordinary become reality. I'd accepted that Otto and I were an impossibility.

The woman seated next to me raises her silk eye mask to aim a disapproving look in my direction.

"Sorry," I whisper, swallowing my nervous giggles, settling in my seat, and staring at the digital map that tracks our progress. We're already over the Atlantic, the tiny plane on-screen moving deceptively slow since we're hurtling through the sky.

I doze on and off, nerves giving way to sheer exhaustion, only waking when breakfast is served before the plane starts its descent. I nibble on a biscuit between sips of coffee, searching for glimpses of land beneath the cloud cover.

By the time we land, I have a partial plan. I could just call Otto, obviously, but that feels like cheating. He hasn't reached out since the press conference. He's giving me space to react, or he's assuming I haven't seen the news yet. I want to surprise him, to follow this impulsivity through. Match his gesture.

He put love on the line, and I want to do the same.

Once I'm in a car headed toward the city, I search Saylor's name in my Contacts. I have her old number saved from years ago, and she shared her new one when she was in Boston.

I tap my fingers against my thigh as I listen to it ring, unsure what I'll do if she doesn't pick up. Impulsivity doesn't allow for a plan B. I've barely come up with a plan A at this point.

Finally, Saylor answers. The first thing she says is, "Did you see it?"

"Uh, it's Claire," I say, not sure if she's expecting a call from someone else.

Saylor laughs. "I know, Caldwell. Did you see the press conference?"

Oh. My jet-lagged brain manages to put the pieces together. "Yeah, I did."

"Thank God. I was going to send you the link, but Beck said I should mind my own business and stay out of it."

It's strange, realizing Beck knows. I'm so accustomed to Otto and me being private and separate and secret.

"I can't—I can't believe he said that," I tell Saylor.

"I can." She sounds smug. "I bet Beck fifty euros he would." Her response is the last one I expected.

I straighten in the back of the taxi. "What? Why?"

"I was pretty sure something happened between you guys in Paris. I was certain when he was acting weird about working with the Siege and I saw your name on the roster. And then I saw how he looked at you in Boston, and I knew he'd end up staying there."

"I didn't ask him to—"

"You didn't have to, Claire. And you shouldn't have needed to. Beck didn't ask me to move to Germany. Your priorities change when you fall in love. Mine did. So did Otto's."

"I can't let him do it," I whisper.

I doubt the driver cares about my love life, but it feels strange to be having such a personal conversation in front of a stranger. And if he's a Kluvberg fan, he might actually care about my love life.

"I don't think Otto is asking for permission," Saylor tells me, sounding amused. "And my guess is, his agent is having a really busy week."

I tap my fingers against the door. "Can you send me his address?"

"Sure. He's not home though. Kluvberg has a charity match against Ludlin this afternoon. Beck left an hour ago."

I sigh. If I'd stopped to think, I would have realized that on my own. Otto mentioned the charity match when he called. But I haven't stopped to think. And now that I'm here, I wanted to talk to Otto immediately, not camp out on his doorstep until he got home.

"Is it—"

"It's sold out," Saylor tells me. "But you called the right person. I've got connections. Let me make some calls, and I'll get you a ticket. Do you have somewhere to stay until the game? I'm with Beck's parents, dropping off Gigi, but I can—"

"I have a hotel," I say swiftly. Technically a lie, but she's doing enough. I don't want to impose any more than I already am.

Kluvberg is smaller than Boston, but it's still a major city. I shouldn't have any trouble finding a hotel at the last minute.

"Okay. I'll be in touch soon!"

I hang up with Saylor, then start searching hotels on my phone. I was wrong; I will have trouble. It occurs to me, as I reach the second page of results with no vacancy, that it's likely because of Otto's match.

I finally find an available hotel, relay the address to the driver, and then relax against the seat, staring out the window at the passing scenery.

Chapter 50

Otto

I'm halfway back to the goal when I hear my name called. It's a miracle I hear it, considering the noise level in Sieg Stadium. Every seat is occupied, and every occupant is cheering as we return for the second half of the match.

I turn to watch Beck jog toward me.

"What's up?" I ask when he reaches me.

"One hundred twenty-four," he tells me.

"What?"

He shrugs a shoulder. "Saylor texted me. Said to tell you one hundred twenty-four. That's all I know."

"What is that? Some sort of code?"

Beck shrugs again, then jogs back to his position.

I continue my trek toward the goal, puzzling over the three numbers until I reach the box and snap into match mode. We're winning by one goal, a bullet by Beck, and I haven't allowed any attempts in. A shutout is the exact statement I'm hoping to make to mark my return, and it will only happen if I remain focused. Ludlin is our main rival for a reason, and Nübel will be hard to get another ball by.

Play resumes for the second half. Ludlin is aggressive from the start, angry about Beck's goal and anxious to even the tally. I block shot after shot, including a header off the corner kick that nearly slips past me. It's not until I'm sipping some water, waiting for Ludlin's trainers to finish talking with one of their players who was tripped during a battle for the ball, that my gaze drifts off the field and into the stands.

I wasn't sure what to expect of my return after my announcement. Had I not shared that I was only playing in Kluvberg for one more season, I would have known what to expect. I was surprised—humbled—by the standing ovation fans greeted me with, even knowing my time on this field was limited. I want to repay that unwavering support with a win.

But I'm not paying attention to the crowd right now. I'm staring at the *101* visible at the top of the section to my immediate right, visible now that most of the spectators are seated.

I whirl to the left when the Ludlin player stands and the crowd applauds politely. And there it is—section *124*.

I start systematically scanning faces, aware I have seconds until play resumes and my attention needs to be elsewhere.

I hear the whistle and have to glance away before I make it through more than a couple of rows.

I'm tested right away—by the same striker who was lying on the turf. I hold the save, since another Ludlin player is too close for a rebound opportunity. Pass the ball to a teammate. The urge to look left is a persistent itch I can't scratch. The ball barely makes it to midfield before Ludlin is attacking again, a hasty steal ending with another accurate shot I save. This time, I can't hold the rebound, and it bounces off my left glove into the danger zone.

It's a rush.

The screaming crowd—our charity matches are typically well attended, but this is the first time one has sold out.

The short stretch of turf that separates me and the Ludlin player—Günter—who's dribbling around, looking for an opening.

The mounting pressure—knowing I'm the one who will determine if they gain a goal.

Günter is focused on my right side. He knows about my shoulder and that today is the first test in a full match. He's waiting—hoping—I'll falter.

Günter glances at a fellow midfield. It's Konstantin Auer, an Austrian midfielder who just joined the league and is being hailed as the next Adler Beck.

"I'm still fucking playing," Beck snapped when that comparison was mentioned in our locker room earlier.

Günter's focused; Auer is arrogant. He traps the pass from his teammate easily, then approaches me with the inflated confidence of a player who's accustomed to being the best on the field.

I know that confidence. I had that confidence when I signed with FC Kluvberg. A near decade ago, which feels far more recent. Now, I have that confidence and the experience to back it up.

Auer fakes left, then shoots right.

I make the save, then watch my teammates carry it up the field. One attempt, which Nübel keeps out, and then it's coming back to me. I think it enters offsides, but the linesman doesn't raise his flag, so I refocus on the approaching ball, waiting for the kick. It comes sooner than I expected, Günter not waiting to pass this time. I physically can't get to the far end of the goal in time. My right shoulder collides with the goalpost, my momentum too fast, and I hold my breath, waiting for pain to hit. When nothing except a slight throb appears, I exhale, straightening. Glance at the Kluvberg bench, where Wagner is already talking to a referee. He's challenging the goal.

I roll my shoulder, stretch, and rub the spot on my arm that collided with the post, which will likely bruise, as I wait for the verdict after the review. Resume searching the stands, glancing over each face.

Sieg Stadium seats seventy thousand. There must be a few hundred people in that section.

She's halfway up, seated in the center of an aisle, wearing a Kluvberg jersey.

I stare, blinking rapidly, not sure if I'm hallucinating or not. There's no way that Claire could be here, right? I don't know what coverage yesterday's press conference got in the States, but the Siege coming up probably means Boston will cover it some.

Claire isn't looking this way. She's focused on the officials, along with the rest of the stadium, waiting for the final call. Only eleven minutes remain in regulation time. And if this goal stands, we're no longer winning.

Offsides is the verdict. No goal.

I bounce on the balls of my feet, my focus sharpening to a razor's edge. I wanted to win before I realized she was here. Now that I know she is, losing isn't an option.

Four minutes later, Will scores off a pass from a throw-in.

Regulation ends, 2–0. Only two minutes of extra time get added. For a match against Ludlin, the game has been fairly clean, with few fouls or stoppages.

As soon as the final whistle blows, I'm swarmed by teammates. They, too, surprised me with their reaction to the news. There were good-natured grumblings about my upcoming departure, but everyone, including a nervous-looking Banks, said they were excited for me. Once our preliminary celebration ends, we line up to shake hands. As soon as I've dropped Nübel's palm, I jog toward the sidelines rather than the tunnel.

A few confused shouts follow me, which spawn into many more as I vault over the barrier that displays advertisements, followed by the barricade separating the closest seats from the photographers and press. Everyone I pass wears a startled, confused expression. Just like during my press conference, no one is sure what the protocol is. Athletes don't cross the boundary. Security is focused on keeping fans off the field, not keeping players on it.

I hustle up the aisle, taking advantage of the surprise that doesn't last long.

A few rows up, spectators start reaching for me, grabbing my jersey and shouting congratulations. Autograph requests are shoved in my face. Security is rushing over from multiple directions, trying to achieve some semblance of order—or more likely, telling me to get out of the stands.

I could. I could return to the field, walk down the tunnel, and find my phone. Text her where to meet me.

But I'm too impatient. Too ebullient. She flew four thousand miles to see me. The least I can do is jog up a few flights of stairs.

So, I keep moving forward. And the crowd has either realized this isn't a meet-and-greet opportunity or figured out where—who—I'm headed toward because people start to part. Helping, not hindering my progress.

Claire's realized it too. When I reach the start of her section, she's moving down the row, blushing at the dozens—hundreds—of eyes on her.

I hear her murmur a polite, "*Entschuldigung*," as she passes the last person in her row.

We reach the same step at the same time, like this was coordinated rather than impulsive.

I pull her against my chest without hesitating, needing her in my arms to believe this is all real. Claire presses her face against my neck, her long exhale brushing against the hollow of my throat.

"Fancy running into you here," I say against her ear, and her laugh vibrates against my shoulder.

There's a lot we need to talk about, but none of it needs to be said here. Except for one thing.

"I love you."

Claire pulls away enough to see my face, hers adorably stunned. "You-you do?"

"I do." I tuck a loose curl behind her ear. "I have for a long time. I think since you told me you had a goalie kink."

She laughs. Blushes. And I also brush a stray tear away before it can travel down her cheek.

I kiss her before she can say a word, slow and languid. For the first time, it doesn't occur to me that it could be the last time. It feels like a beginning.

I can't stay in the stands, even though I want to. I'm causing chaos, and a frazzled security guard is hovering nearby, talking into a hidden microphone. I kiss Claire once more, instruct the guard on where to bring her, and then jog back down to the field.

Chapter 51

Claire

The closer we get to the front door, the more nervous Otto seems to become. His house is gorgeous, unsurprisingly, and not at all what I expected. The yard is huge, the distant view of the mountains breathtaking. It's quiet and peaceful and idyllic. Big for one person.

We reach the door, and Otto spins his key chain around one finger. His other hand is carrying my suitcase, and his equipment bag is slung over one shoulder. I offered to carry my luggage, but he didn't reply. Just laughed.

"I have a hotel room," I remind him.

That's where I thought we'd head after leaving the stadium. But Otto insisted we grab my belongings and continue here instead. I was curious to see his house, so I agreed. But now I'm wondering if that was a mistake. We still have a lot to discuss, and I did ambush him by showing up here.

He makes a face. "You are not staying at a hotel, Claire. I just… I did not know you were coming."

I manage a small smile, still nervous. "Yeah, that was the point. It was a surprise."

"It was a *great* surprise. Just—" He rubs the back of his neck. "I do not want to freak you out."

I squeak out an "Oh" as he unlocks the door—because of course *that* freaks me out.

Coming here was impulsive, and I don't have a lot of experience with impulsivity...or the flux that follows. I'm still registering that I'm in Germany. Still processing everything Otto said during his press conference and during that surreal moment in the stands after the game.

The front door swings open, and Otto flips on the interior lights.

At first, I'm in awe. The inside of the house is as beautiful as the exterior. Wide wooden floorboards and creamy white walls. Matching furnishings. I wonder if he hired a professional decorator to—

Oh.

I make a small, startled sound as soon as I see it.

Otto glances at me, a muscle in his jaw jumping as he shuts the door and drops the bags. "I would have moved it if I had known you were coming."

I'm frozen, staring at the wall that's becoming increasingly blurry. "How—when did you get that?"

"I went back to the Louvre after the final. I wanted—they sell the prints in the gift shop. Bought one and had it framed."

I taste salt and realize the tears have streamed down to my lips.

Otto swears and reaches toward the print.

I grab his wrist. "Don't."

I was sure—so, so sure—that Otto had moved on easily from us. Two days later, he became a gold medalist. Two years later, he won another World Cup. Professionally, he was thriving. He was dating, then engaged to someone else.

Since he showed up in Boston, there have been plenty of moments I second-guessed that assumption. But I'm staring at evidence he didn't. A print of *Les Murmures de l'Aube* hangs on the wall directly across from the front door. It's prominently displayed. Impossible to miss.

Otto shakes off my hold on his wrist, using his thumbs to wipe away my tears. "Come on." He takes my hand, leading me into a huge kitchen that overlooks the sprawling yard.

"This isn't where I pictured you living," I tell him, glancing around the pristine space.

The counters are a dark marble, the appliances all shiny and seemingly brand-new.

"You have spent time picturing my house?" He rests a hip against the counter, smirking. It doesn't reach his eyes though. He's still worried about my reaction to the print.

"Yes." I perch on one of the stools that line the counter, spinning slowly. "It's...big."

From the exterior, it looked large. But it extends back even farther than I realized.

"You say that to me a lot."

I roll my eyes, but his cocky comment dissipates more of the tension. "Why'd you buy this one?"

He rests his elbows on the counter, leaning closer to me. "I have a flat in Kluvberg too. I liked being closer to the city and the stadium when I first signed with the club. But as I got older, had more attention on me, I wanted some privacy. Land around, where I could go outside and relax. Did not need the big house, but it came with the property, and I had the money, so…"

I pause spinning, resting my elbows on the counter too. "I saw your press conference."

He nods, appearing uncertain. "I figured you had not suddenly decided you could not go another day without seeing an FC Kluvberg match."

"I had no idea the charity game was today," I admit. "I got on the first flight I could." I blow out a long breath. "You can't do it, Otto."

He holds my gaze. "Of course I can. My contract ends—"

"You *shouldn't* do it."

A muscle in his jaw tics. "It is done."

"Then undo it and—"

"No."

I sniff, tucking a piece of hair behind my ear. "Don't do this for me. I know what Kluvberg means to you. Everything in the past few months has been about getting back here. You should be celebrating being cleared, not—"

"Claire"—he reaches out, tucking my hands between his—"there is a reason I did not talk to you about this before I left Boston. I did not mean for you to find out during a press conference—it just sort of came out—but I did want you to find out after it was already decided. For you to know it was real and happening and something you could rely on. Yes, Kluvberg means a lot to me. Too much. I built my entire life around that club. And I do not regret it because it got me to where I am, but there will be a day when I cannot play for them. I will be replaced, or get injured again, or retire. It will end, someway, someday, and I want to decide when and how. And I do not want to live four thousand miles away from you. It is done. We can talk about what it means, but do not try to talk me out of it."

"You're going to resent me," I whisper.

His grip on my hands tightens. "I am not expecting anything, Claire. I want to figure things out, but if you do not want me to try to end up in Boston—"

"Of course I want you to end up in Boston. What I want isn't the problem. It's what you want that—"

"This *is* what I want. I want to prove myself on a new team. I want to stop coming home to an empty house. One of us has to move. I am in a position to; you are not. It is simple."

"It's not simple at all, Otto."

"I was not ready for us in Paris, Claire. I wanted to be, but I was not. I am now."

"What about your grandfather?"

Otto exhales. "I still have some time left with him. We can discuss… Talk about things we should have talked about years ago. My staying here after he is gone will not change anything." A small smile appears. "He knows I am moving. He wants to meet you."

"He does?" I ask, startled and pleased.

"He does."

We study each other. Him patient and me struggling.

I want so badly to believe him, to accept this. But it's surreal. I've never allowed myself to believe it might happen. Me and Otto, real and permanent, never felt like anything approaching a possibility. I can't think of a way to match the immensity of this gesture. To convey what him giving this up for me means.

"I will take the print down," he tells me.

I blink at him, confused. "What? Why?"

He smiles sadly. "I know you regret parts of Paris. It is a reminder—"

I interrupt him this time. "I don't regret parts of Paris. I wish that final had ended differently. I wish we had ended differently. But you were right—that one missed shot doesn't define my whole career. Not the years of work to get to the Olympics or all the practices and games and trainings since. And us... I wasn't ready either. I hadn't finished college. Hadn't started my professional career. I would have wondered if every offer or opportunity I got was a way to get to you. If I'd signed with a German team, I wouldn't have been in Boston to take care of my mom or gotten to play for the Siege. Is it all happy memories? No. But I don't regret any of it. And I love that you bought the print. It—I—" Emotions threaten to overwhelm me again. "It makes me feel less weird about wearing your T-shirt for the past six years."

Otto smiles and straightens, using our clasped hands to pull me off the stool toward the living room.

"Where are we going?" I ask, uncertain.

He didn't give me a chance to reply to what he said when we were in the stands, and he hasn't brought it up since. That was the only thing I came here certain I'd tell him, and I was close to summoning the nerve. They're only three words—I just managed four—but I've been waiting a long time to say them to him. The perfect moment feels paramount.

"I am showing you my favorite part of the house," he answers.

"Let me change first," I say.

I showered and napped at the hotel before the game, but my hair is undoubtedly a mess from the humidity and chaos during the game. I can't do anything about the photos that were likely taken when Otto ran off the field, but I can at least brush my teeth and tame my curls now. Confirm I wasn't too bleary-eyed to select matching lingerie.

Otto laughs. "Not that. Yet."

Yet stirs warmth deep in my pelvis. I don't know how to be around Otto and not want him, and it's slowly hitting me that I might not have to. That we might end up in the same place and stay in the same place. Based on what Coach Taylor said, there's an excellent chance Beacon FC will make him an offer.

Otto leads me through a side door I didn't notice, out onto a deck with stairs that lead down to his backyard. It's much cooler out now than it was earlier. Once we reach the grass, I discover his yard extends even farther than I realized. It's tranquil, like he said. After seeing the commotion around him earlier, I understand even more why he'd need that escape.

He turns left, and that's when I see the soccer field tucked behind the garage I'm assuming houses his car collection. It has lines, two goals, flags.

I gape at it. "You have a soccer field in your backyard?"

Logically, I know he's rich. But I didn't realize he was private-field rich.

"*Football*, Caldwell."

I roll my eyes. "You're going to have to call it soccer when you play in the States, you know."

He scoffs, but there's a smile on his face. "When?"

I glance at the ball by the field, blushing. "Can I try to score on you?"

It's one thing I never got to attempt when we trained together in Boston. His shoulder wasn't fully cleared yet. And I got to see him in goal earlier, but that felt very different. This is just us.

"You can *try*."

I grin, sprinting toward the ball.

"My last name looks good on you," he calls after me before jogging toward the goal.

I smile before turning around, appraising the goal like I

would during penalty kicks. There's a lot of net to aim at. But I've never faced Otto before. He's the best in the world. Players far more famous than me have tried and failed to get a shot past him. He shrinks the space around him, somehow, in full command of his surroundings as he watches me. Waiting.

I dribble up the field slowly since I have no defenders to worry about, deliberating about my approach. Pause outside the penalty arc.

"I cannot save it if you do not shoot it," Otto comments dryly. His voice is casual, but his body is tense, position identical to during the match earlier.

He's teasing me, but he's also treating me like a worthy opponent. He pushes me and supports me, and it suddenly becomes impossible to contain what I came all this way to say.

I call out, "I love you!" then plant my left foot and swing my right. It's a decent shot—moving hard and fast—but I've seen Otto make many more challenging stops.

I watch him rather than the ball.

I've never been less invested in whether or not a shot lands in the net.

Either way, it'll feel like winning.

Chapter 52

Otto

"This is Tannfeld?"

My fingers clench around the steering wheel, and then I force my grip to relax. "This is Tannfeld," I confirm.

Claire watches the white church pass by, then glances at me. "We can do this another time," she says softly.

I shake my head. "No. Now is the right time."

We've spent the past three days in our own private bubble, removed from the rest of the world. No football. No responsibilities. No distractions. We were standing in the stillness, was how Claire described it, cooking dinner in the kitchen last night.

But reality is becoming inescapable. I have a training session tomorrow morning. Claire's Siege teammates have been blowing up her phone, and she told me Eliza wants to meet with her as soon as she's back in Boston. Plus, Cassidy wants her help with wedding planning. She'll have to leave soon, and I'm not sure when we'll see each other next. We haven't discussed the logistics of the upcoming year.

That doesn't scare me. I have full confidence we'll figure it out.

What I am apprehensive about? Introducing Claire to my grandfather. He's a separate, unpredictable section of my life I've never included anyone in before.

The fact that Opa and I are on better terms than we've been in over a decade should make this easier. But it's the opposite. I don't want to upset the recent balance between us. I have no precedent for how my grandfather will act around a girlfriend. I'm embarrassed how detached we are, embarrassed Claire will see how detached we are. It took him months to tell me he was *dying*. That summarizes the state of our disconnect pretty succinctly.

I can't go back and change any of the past. All I can do is stop avoiding, and that starts with showing up. Time is never a guarantee—Claire's as aware of that as I am. I want to ensure this meeting takes place, and I want it to go perfectly when it does.

A few minutes later, I park in the empty driveway, staring at the white cladding and the pitched, red-tiled roof. The closest I have to a childhood home and also the host of my most painful memories. Hazy visits to see Opa with my mom. Endless arguments with my grandfather.

"Is he home?" Claire asks, studying the house too.

I nod. "He stopped driving a few years ago."

Claire reaches into the back seat, grabbing a wrapped rectangle. She wanted to bring Opa a gift, so we stopped at a bookstore on the drive here. I suggested she get one of her mom's novels. Mystery isn't Opa's usual genre, but I think he'll appreciate the personal connection. And if he doesn't, then he'd better pull out some of the manners that are normally nonexistent during my visits rather than say so.

We walk toward the front door, hand in hand. Claire swings our clasped palms back and forth playfully, and my mouth curves up in a reluctant smile. She can tell I'm nervous, and I love her for attempting to alleviate my anxiety.

I knock using my left hand so I don't have to drop hers.

Only a couple of seconds pass before the door opens, which surprises me. Opa usually takes a minute or two to lumber over to the door, even on the occasions he knew I was coming.

"Good morning," he greets.

I blink at his appearance. I was braced for his illness to be more visible—prepared for gaunt cheeks and baggy clothes. But he's clean-shaven, his hair neatly combed. Dressed like he's headed to Sunday church, although today is a Wednesday. No cane in sight.

"You must be Claire," Opa continues, not waiting for me to make any introductions.

"I am," she confirms, tucking the book under one arm and reaching for his offered hand. "It's very nice to meet you, Mr. Berger."

"Call me Karl, please."

He likes her. I sense it immediately, from the second they shake hands, the certainty expanding when we enter the living room and Claire compliments Opa's overflowing bookshelves. After unwrapping her gift, he listens raptly to Claire's summary of her mom's book. I think he'll actually read it, despite the fact that he prefers nonfiction. And he's prepared tea—an herbal blend he says Mila brings him.

When I duck down the front hall to use the bathroom, I check the liquor cabinet. It's empty, causing a contrary spasm of comfort and fury in my chest. Why couldn't all of this have happened sooner? I should have driven him to doctor's appointments myself rather than trusting that he was looking after his health. Should have dumped this cabinet as many times as it took, shipped him to rehab until it stuck.

I was worried, if I did, that would be the end of any goodwill between us. Opa is proud, and he values his independence. All the assistance I offered, I never forced him to take any of it. I left the decisions up to him, same as I wished he'd allowed me to do. He didn't let me choose football; he had no other choice but to accept I'd signed a contract.

Claire and Opa are bent over a book I've never seen before as I return to the living room. It's twice the size of his normal novels.

I don't quite understand the look on my grandfather's face when he glances up and sees me in the doorway. It's part strain, part peace.

"I'm going to grab a glass of water," Claire says, standing. "Can I get you anything, Karl?"

"All set," he replies. "Thank you."

Claire passes by, giving my arm a quick squeeze before she continues toward the kitchen.

I take her spot on the couch, peering over the open page. They're newspaper clippings. Old newspaper clippings, the trimmed edges yellowed with age. And they're all about me. Signing with Kluvberg, my first match, World Cups, championships, London Olympics. I flip through a few pages slowly, scanning each bolded headline.

Opa reads the paper every morning. But I've never seen him

so much as skim the Sports section, let alone take the time to cut out every article that mentioned me. It must have taken him hours—dozens of hours—to do all this.

"I was planning to give this to you when you retired, but..." He clears his throat, both of us uncomfortably aware of why he can't wait. "I thought Claire could take it over for me."

I nod. Sniff, swiping one palm across my eyes while my other hand continues flipping.

"Football won't last forever." Something he's told me many times before, and I always took it as an insult. Maybe it was always a well-intentioned warning. Cautionary advice.

My career could have concluded with that dive, and I was wholly unprepared for that to take place. Arrogantly assuming I'd be the one to decide when my athletic career ended.

"This will," he adds, nodding to the book.

I nod again. I don't know what to say—my emotions are too chaotic. Even if the perfect words appeared, there's a massive lump in my throat blocking them from exiting. I *can't* say anything.

"Your mother trusted me to take care of you, Otto, and I felt like I kept failing her. I didn't know anything about football. I had no idea how to help, how to advise you. I wanted you to follow a path I knew I could guide you along. By the time I accepted you were doing just fine—more than fine—on your own, it was too late. You weren't coming back on breaks anymore, and I knew you resented how I'd reacted. The company folded, and I lost my purpose all over again. By the time I got to a better place, you were farther away than ever."

"I'm sorry," I say thickly.

"Don't be." He taps an article titled "Gloves of Glory: How Otto Berger is Redefining Reaction Time" from the Paris

Olympics. "I wish you'd had my support, but you should be proud you never needed it. Your mother would be proud too. I wanted you to have all of these to look back on one day, to see everything you accomplished. To show my great-grandkids, if you and Claire have any."

My laugh is watery. "We haven't talked about kids. Marriage hasn't even come up yet."

Technically, we've been together less than a week, though that really doesn't encapsulate our history. I'm expecting those conversations will come up soon.

"Well, when you're ready." Opa opens the cigar box that's always sat on the table next to his favorite chair. He used to smoke regularly, before I moved in with him. The cloves scent still clings to some of the furniture.

When his hand reappears, there's a small velvet box inside. I know what it is, even before he casts a furtive look at the doorway. Claire's been gone for a lot longer than the time it takes to pour a glass of water, and I'm certain it's on purpose. That she's gifting us this time alone, lending silent support.

"It was Ella's," he tells me, passing the box. "I know your grandmother would have wanted you to have it. To give it to Claire, if you'd like."

I flip the lid open, studying the diamond ring. My grandparents got married young. They grew up together, in this town, a neighbor once told me. Opa rarely talks about his late wife. Even now, nearly fifty years after her death, I can see the sadness in his expression. A football field is where I've spent most Sundays, but that doesn't prevent me from hoping there's some reunion ahead for them. That death isn't a final parting.

I shut the box and stand, words still hard to summon.

Opa stands, too, without needing any assistance. I can't decide if it makes it better or worse—that he appears perfectly healthy. It makes what's coming harder to accept. But I'm glad that he's still well enough to move around with assistance. That his grip is firm as we shake hands and as we share a quick embrace. It's not as awkward as I expected, considering we haven't hugged since I was a kid.

"I'm proud of you, boy," he tells me.

• • •

I swear under my breath, spotting the crowd gathered ahead. I'm guessing Saylor, Beck, Sophia, and Will have already arrived. We're running late since traffic heading into the city was especially slow. Claire and I spent twice as long in Tannfeld as I had expected to. We walked to the white church, stopping under the oak tree, where my mom and grandmother were buried. Went to a *gasthaus* in town for lunch and stayed at his house until Mila stopped by in the afternoon with groceries for Opa.

It was a good day. A great day. And I refuse to let a horde of press and fans detract from it, even though I'm more irritated by the paparazzi than I've ever been before. I went from basking in the attention as a teenager to adjusting to it as an adult, and I also became accustomed to a certain absence of it in Boston. In Kluvberg, interest in me is at an all-time high. It would have been anyway, probably, coming back from my injury. The press conference and the scene I made in the stands only fanned the flames. And it's not just me under scrutiny anymore.

I glance at Claire, who's already spotted the clamoring in front of our destination. She's smiling, which is a relief. After everything we've been through, I didn't think some nosy reporters would scare her off. But I know it's an adjustment.

I pull up to the valet stand, climbing out and tossing the keys to a wide-eyed guy who looks to be in his early twenties.

Having Sophia choose the restaurant tonight was probably a mistake. She has a tendency to select trendy, popular places that attract attention. And patrons who follow football and care about three FC Kluvberg players appearing.

I round the front of the car, pulling open Claire's door and offering her a hand. The flashes come even faster once she's out of the car.

"Holy shit," she murmurs as I shut the door and pull her tight to my side.

A pathway has been cleared to the entrance of the restaurant, but it's lined with people snapping photos on their phones. White spots dance across my vision as we walk into the building.

I glance at Claire. "You okay?"

She nods, taking my hand as we follow a hostess over to a corner table.

Saylor jumps up first, flinging her arms around Claire, forcing me to drop her hand, and essentially ignoring me. I roll my eyes as I greet Beck and Will, then hug Sophia.

When Saylor finally releases my girlfriend, I hug her too. I also whisper, "Thank you."

I assumed—and Beck confirmed—that Saylor was the one who had gotten Claire into the stadium for the charity match.

"You're welcome," she tells me, smirking. Then her smile fades, expression shifting to serious. "I'm really glad I got to be a part of your love story, like you got to be a part of mine and Beck's."

I manage a nod, words slippery again. My emotions are still raw from my conversation with Opa earlier, especially now that I'm in the midst of people who have served as my family on the days it felt like I had none.

Everyone takes their seats, and a waiter comes over to take our orders. I've had a lot of dinners with these four people, but this one feels entirely different.

We don't discuss football as we eat, drink, and talk, even though it's what the five of us have in common. We talk about Gigi, who's starting to show an interest in football, to her parents' delight. About Will and Sophia's upcoming wedding.

And my friends pelt Claire with questions. She and Will bond over Boston.

Midway through the meal, it occurs to me that I'm no longer unsure of what my life post-retirement will look like.

Whether I play in Boston—my agent assured me Beacon FC is *very* interested in signing me—for one year or ten, whether it's a conscious choice or because of an injury I can't rehab, it won't be the sinkhole that swallowed me after my shoulder tore.

It will be hard. Will be an ending.

But it'll be a beginning, too, the same way right now feels like one.

Epilogue

Claire

"And we are mere minutes away from the final whistle in this gold-medal match between the United States and Canada. If you're just joining us, it's been a grueling tactical battle between these two teams. The stakes of this game aren't lost on either side. They're leaving everything on the field. After two stellar first-half goals—Scott for the US and Buchanan for Canada—the score remains tied at 1–1.

"Here comes the US, pushing up the right flank—that's Robbe leading the charge—but Canada's holding strong. McGill steals it back. What a resilient back line the Canadians have maintained this entire tournament. Their keeper has only—

"Wait a minute—the Americans regain possession at midfield. It's cleared out to—hold on—here comes Claire Berger! Berger pushing forward… She takes a touch—what a kick! From that distance, I don't think she can—it's still airborne—IT'S IN!

IT'S IN! That's a good goal by Claire Berger! From THIRTY yards out! The goalkeeper didn't even move!

"You can hear the cheers from the American fans. It's absolute chaos on the US bench, celebrating that goal. It should seal the gold medal for Team USA. Berger is being mobbed by her teammates! WHAT A GOAL!"

• • •

"Caldy," Mackenzie shouts, nudging my arm with her elbow.

Legally, my last name might have changed, but my Siege teammates have stuck with the same moniker. Everyone on the national team—at least everyone who was on the national team with me in Paris—has followed suit.

"Caldy," she repeats, elbowing me harder.

I drag my eyes away from the pandemonium surrounding us to glance at her. Odds are, I'll never win another Olympic match, let alone score a goal during one. I'm determined to be fully present for this moment.

When my gaze meets Mackenzie's, she smiles and nods toward the sideline. I whirl right, searching faces and running once I find a certain one. My exhausted muscles protest the extra exertion, but my shaky legs carry me to my destination.

Field access is extremely limited, but I'm unsurprised they made an exception for Otto Berger.

He catches me as I literally collapse against his chest, my hamstrings quivering. My head nestles perfectly in the hollow of his throat while his arms band around my back, over the sweaty jersey plastered to my skin. I register the insistent *click, click, click* of the cameras around us, capturing the moment, but I'm too tired and thrilled to care about the invasiveness. Or that I must look a red-faced mess.

I just won a gold medal. And my favorite person was here to witness it.

My favorite people, I should say. My dad and Cassidy and Josh and Tommy and Quinn—my new niece—are all here somewhere. Lydia texted me last night, saying she was planning to spend the day at Echo Glen with Mom, watching the match on TV.

Otto is the one who trained with me though. Who was my first call when I found out I'd made the final roster again. Who understands what this moment truly means to me.

I'd like to say I always knew we'd be back here. That I always had faith in a second shot.

But I didn't. I didn't think I'd make it back here. I didn't think he'd be here to witness it.

I appreciate it more because of that uncertainty. The doubt makes this moment feel especially significant. Exceptionally precious.

I'm not sure how long we stand like that. It's easy, around Otto, to let the rest of the world fade to white noise. There must be thousands of spectators staring at us, dozens of cameras aimed in this direction, and I'm only distantly aware we're not entirely alone.

"I can't believe we won," I murmur.

He kisses the top of my head, then pulls back far enough to see my face. The corners of his eyes crinkle as a wide grin stretches the sides of his mouth. "I can."

"I'm so—" My throat constricts suddenly, making more words a challenge to get out. "I'm so glad you're here."

Otto's hands run up and down my back, creasing the *5* and the letters spelling out his last name. "It took me six years to watch the last final you played in," he confesses quietly. "Because

I knew that I should have already seen it. That I should have been there, in person, to watch it live. If you had decided to retire, I would have supported you. But I am so—" His voice cracks. "So glad I am here too."

I rise up on my tiptoes—my trembling calves protesting—and kiss him. The clicking around us picks up in frequency. Our house in Cohasset sits on several secluded acres, and most of our time is spent at Echo Glen, the Siege or Beacon practice facilities, or my parents'—now Cassidy, Josh, Tommy, and Quinn's—house. All private properties, meaning paparazzi shots of us are rare.

I was already breathing heavily from ninety-six minutes of play. But I'm a little smug about how rapid Otto's inhales are when our mouths separate.

"I would have been here even without working with the Siege, Claire," he tells me, voice low and earnest as he brushes a wayward strand of hair off my forehead. "Maybe not the making-out-with-my-wife bit, but I would have come to see you play."

I believe him.

Otto doesn't let many people in, but once he does? I saw it when he moved to Tannfeld during his grandfather's final months since Karl didn't want to leave his home, adding an extra hour to his commute to Sieg Stadium. When he read my mom's entire backlist so he could talk to her about her novels during our visits, laughing when he got to the title featuring Otto Serger. When he flew back to Kluvberg to watch his former team win their first championship without him. Somehow, during those few weeks in Paris, I had become one of those people he showed up for. He's proven it over and over again.

"And"—his tone turns teasing, as he's likely noticed the suspicious sheen I blink rapidly to remove—"I would have at least asked you out to dinner after talking my way onto the field."

I smile. “How original.”

“It worked in Paris.”

I roll my eyes. “Of course it did. I had a massive crush on you from the minute we met. You could have suggested we inflate balls together, and I would have said yes.”

“Is *inflating balls* part of your goalie kink?”

I blush. Hopefully, my face is too red for him to tell, but the knowing gleam in his eyes suggests otherwise. He knows me too well.

“I can cancel the party I planned if you want to *inflate balls* instead?”

“You planned a party?”

He nods. “Lindsey helped a little. I hope that was okay.”

I’m not on close terms with my stepmother, and I doubt I ever will be. But we spent a fair amount of time together while planning Cassidy’s wedding. I no longer dread seeing her, which is definite progress. And I appreciate that she wanted to play a role in today.

“What if we’d lost?”

“Then we would have celebrated anyway.”

“CALDY!” Mackenzie calls out. “We need you for a photo!”

“Go,” Otto urges, dropping his hands from my waist.

I rise up for one final kiss, whispering, “We can inflate balls after the party.”

I feel his lips curve against mine before he kisses me back. “Love you, Boston.”

“*Ich liebe dich*,” I reply.

My German is steadily improving, according to Otto, but I’ll have to ask Beck for a second opinion next time we’re visiting Kluvberg. Otto is not exactly an unbiased instructor.

I face the field again, my steps slow this time. Not only

because of my weary legs, but so I can savor walking onto the pitch as a gold medalist. So I can appreciate the view from the top of a mountain I started climbing when I was five years old and answered an emphatic, "Yes," when Mom asked if I had fun at soccer practice. I reached the top.

I thought I'd lost Otto. Lost my shot at this moment.

I've never been happier to be wrong.

Acknowledgments

A few years ago, a scene got stuck in my head. In it, a driven female soccer player critiques a world-famous superstar on his home field. I wrote that chapter of *First Flight, Final Fall* first, then built the rest of the book around that dynamic between two elite athletes. It feels so fitting to end this series with the story of the third person on the field in that chapter—Otto. Especially since *Love on the Line* would not exist if readers had not embraced Saylor and Beck so enthusiastically. Whether this is the first, second, or twenty-seventh of my books you've read—thank you for doing so. Like Otto and Claire, I'm living my dream.

Jovana, editor extraordinaire. Thank you for treating every manuscript I send you with such careful attention to detail and for improving every sentence. You push me to be a better writer. I can't wait to work on many more books with you.

Sophie, I am so grateful *First Flight, Final Fall* brought us together. Thank you for being such a bright light in the book community and for your unwavering support through many releases. Manifesting that 2026 is the year we finally get to hug!

Megan, this book is much better for having received your brilliant feedback. You have a gift for understanding and elevating plotlines along with enhancing specific details, and I feel so lucky you shared that expertise with this story.

Sahara, you were the first person to read this book. That's always a scary handoff, and this novel couldn't have landed in safer hands. Thank you for your time and suggestions and for cheering me on through multiple versions of this story. I feel so fortunate to call you a friend.

Sierra, your insight is always spot-on. I am so grateful this book got to benefit from all your knowledge. You played a pivotal role in edits, so it felt fitting to include a Sierra in that high-stakes game.

Lauren, my incredible agent, thank you for the many ways you've enhanced my career. Having five books in stores feels like a fever dream, and I will never forget receiving that call from you. I'm so excited for all that's ahead.

The entire team at Entangled: especially Jessica, Sarah, and Bree—I couldn't imagine a better publishing partner. Thank you for all of your hard work. Writing this book, knowing I'll be seeing it on shelves in May, was so surreal, and wouldn't be possible without your support.

And to my family, who show up to signings and send me photos of my books on shelves—I feel so incredibly lucky to have you all in my life. This journey has been wild and wonderful and stressful, and the way you've remained so loudly proud throughout the highs and the lows truly means the world. I love you. Thank you.